Forbidden

alharam الحرام

by F. Stone

Published by

Romance Under Fire

http://www.featherstoneauthor.com

Edited by

Leigh Carter

Consultant and Translations

Dr. Sahar Albakkal

Book Cover by

Extended Imagery

"When the tyrant gods are overthrown, when individuals walk out from under the shadow of Saturn, when they reject collective expectations and seek their own path, then justice returns."

Under Saturn's Shadow: The Wounding and Healing Of Men, Jungian psychologist, James Hollis

Copyright

The characters are fictitious. Any similarity to real persons, living or dead, is coincidental and not intended by the author. The setting is the author's vision of the Middle East's future, year 2047.

Library and Archives Canada

Forbidden ISBN

Hardcover: 978-0-9951509-2-8
eBook: 978-0-9951509-1-1
Paperback: 978-0-9951509-0-4
PDF: 978-0-9951509-3-5

Cover Design:

Extended Imagery http://extendedimagery.com/

Images:

iStock and Shutterstock

NOTE: *The author does not claim to be an authority on Islam. Great effort was made to obtain advice from people in Canadian Muslim communities. The author followed the advice of imam Khattab - to portray an unbiased view of the culture of moderate Muslims, "the middle path." Forbidden is her vision of a possible future – a stormy transition from war to peace in the Middle Eastern regions.*

This book contains violence and some vulgar language. It is, therefore, not suitable for readers who are immature or under the age of eighteen.

Dedication

Forbidden is dedicated to my dear husband, Ralph Weir. Throughout our nearly fifty years of marriage, he has been my most loyal friend. A fierce critic of art and prose, he has encouraged me to not settle for mediocrity.

Ralph grew up in a generation that believed women should be content with standing in the shadow of their men. Not Ralph. From the time when I decided to be a paramedic, he has nurtured that part of me that reaches for higher ambitions. When we bought our first snowmobiles, he invited me to be an equal with him on snowmobile trips climbing the mountain ranges in Canada and United States of America. He's been the most incredible mate and companion.

I have been so blessed. I owe my success to my wild man of the mountains, to this man with a heart of a poet, and courage of a decorated soldier.

Table of Content

PROLOGUE

May 28, 2013, City of Rumi in war-torn Iraq

The woman glared at her husband. She clung to her son's hand as if he was about to fall into an abyss. She straightened her back, shoring up her defenses. "Hashim is only five. He still needs his mother."

"My dear wife, I told you the day he was born, I'd send him away if the war reached Rumi. Baghdad has fallen. It is time." His gruff voice ensured she would know there was no room for debate. "Pack his bags now. His escorts will be here in half an hour."

Hashim yanked his hand away from his mother's grasp. "Papa, please. I want to stay. I have proven I'm a most worthy son. I do my chores without complaint." He pointed to his mother's vegetable garden in the back yard. "See, I've hoed and weeded all morning. And my bedroom is clean and tidy. And, if you wish, I'll help in the clinic today."

His father knew that was a desperate offer. Hashim hated needles. "Have you completed your English lessons?"

Hashim nodded, reluctantly. "Please don't send me away, papa. You will be glad I'm here to help." The boy's smile wavered. "I'll do anything you ask, papa." Tears filled his eyes. "Please?"

"Give him more time," his mother begged. "We are safe."

"Enough!" roared Dr. Sharif. Standing in the kitchen of the family's ancestral home, his gut twisted into a painful knot. The terrorist vermin were banging on Rumi's gates. Suspicious strangers had been stopped at the mountain pass, the only road into Rumi. Extra police guarded the airport. They'd heard of the devastation beyond their borders.

"You are going, Hashim. That's final. Go pack. Pack only warm clothes. Wear your work boots. Be ready for a rough hike. Understood?" He hid the trembling in his voice by shouting. Yes, his son was young to be travelling over the mountains. But if he fell into the hands of the terrorists, he'd be taught to kill. And hate.

He grabbed his son's arm and dragged him into the boy's bedroom. "Pack quickly." Sharif grabbed the backpack from under the bed and threw it onto the quilt. "In ten minutes stand in front of me on the front steps." Sharif turned away before his cherished son could see the pain on his face.

Hashim's mother, devoted Muslim and wife, sat in their modern kitchen. Her husband sat down beside her. Tentatively, he placed his hand on her shoulder. She jerked away. "Who are the escorts?" she asked, looking out across the meadow to their orange orchard.

"Three climbers. I paid them well. They will get our son across the border and into France. From there, he will be handed over to people who will ensure he gets to England. Once he is with our daughter and her family, Hashim will be safe."

"There's no better way?" she whispered, unable to speak any louder.

Sharif watched as his wife fell apart. She doted on Hashim. The rest of their children, five daughters, had married and left by the time Hashim was born. Her surprise baby arrived when she turned forty, a gift from Allah.

Dr. Sharif and Hashim stood on the front steps as an SUV pulled up the driveway. No words were spoken. No glances or nudges.

One of the three men got out of the vehicle and strode up to Sharif. "This is the kid we're taking to France?" The man had a short beard and crooked teeth. Sunglasses hid his eyes. His clothes, made for hard work, were ripped and repaired. He held a toothpick in his teeth, and waggled it about with his tongue. "Kind of scrawny."

"Yes, this is my son, Hashim Sharif. How soon will he be handed over to the French connection?"

The Iraqi man chuckled. "Depends on how many times I have to carry the little goat. Maybe a week, maybe two. Should be in England by the end of the month."

Sharif noted Hashim's scowl. The boy was thin, but he was tough from climbing trees and working the garden. "Once I hear from his sister, you'll get the rest of the payment."

"Sure. Get your ass in the truck, kid."

Dr. Sharif kneeled down to hug his boy and say goodbye. Before he could reach his son's shoulders, Hashim darted past him, got into the SUV and slammed the door shut.

Ω

June 26, 2020: City of Samarra, Iraq, on the east bank of the Tigris in the Saladin Governorate, 78 miles north of Baghdad.

The bomb blast catapulted Abdul Zydan across the street. His mangled body fell among the rubble of The Guardian's Mosque's south wall. His adrenalin surged. Using the butt of his AK-74 as leverage, he crawled a few yards further, putting a mound of bricks between him and the rebel forces. He had not yet realized his legs were nothing more than shredded flesh and bone fragments below his knees.

Abdul gasped when he saw his bloody clothing. "My legs. Where the fuck are my legs?" Shock had dulled the pain. He called to Aamir, the soldier who had charged with him through the mosque's doors. "Aamir, where are you? Answer me." His heart thundered in his chest. His lungs burned for more air. "No, no. Allah, most merciful, please no." He tried to sit up but he fell back, dazed. "Aamir, I'm hit." His desperate cries became barely a whisper. He gasped for more air. The battle sounded distant, muffled as if he was under water

Sergeant Aamir and Captain Najeeb ran to his side, wild-eyed and out of breath. Rasheed rushed in, skidding to a halt beside Najeeb. Their eyes burned from the swirling smoke and gunfire. A spray of bullets smacked the wall beside them. They dove, creating a barrier between their fallen soldier and the terrorist's attack. When

3

there was a break in the gunfire, Rasheed and Aamir grabbed Abdul by his wrists and dragged him as if he was merely a bag of rice. More bullets chased their feet. Blasts from Najeeb's weapon forced the enemy down. While they settled Abdul behind a wall, Najeeb reloaded his weapon. "Die, you bastards. Burn in hell!" he hollered.

Aamir knelt down beside Abdul. "My brother, you are most brave. You pushed them back when they stormed into the mosque." Najeeb touched what was left of Abdul's legs. A look of shock flickered in his eyes. "I'll get you to the medic station. Hang on."

When Najeeb turned to give orders to his men, Abdul clenched onto his arm.

"No. Too late." The desperate soldier panted, grasping at the clothing of Aamir. "Those bastards have taken the north side of Samarra. My wife, my daughters - ." He wept grievously. "My dear wife, my family, they will have been taken prisoner." He gasped for air. "Aamir, you know what they'll do to them." Abdul looked frantic. He grabbed Najeeb's shirt and pulled him down low. "You know it's true. It's unthinkable. I cannot bear their suffering." Abdul wailed. "Najeeb, Aamir, Rasheed, you must go there. Put an end to their suffering." Even as Abdul's energy bled, his face remained transfixed as if witnessing the horror. "Quickly, Najeeb. They must not suffer."

Najeeb swallowed hard. A look of revulsion froze on his face. "No, no, no. Abdul, you cannot ask this of me." The soldier pulled away from Abdul. "No, I cannot. Allah forbids killing of innocents."

Abdul's eyes glazed, starring into space. "You must, Najeeb. I already hear their screams." His lips quivered. "Mercy. Najeeb, Allah will forgive. Allah …"

Najeeb wept. He embraced Abdul, shedding tears into the man's hair. Angry that such a monstrous request had been made, angry that the truth was that the women would be savagely treated and die after suffering wicked humiliation. He gritted his teeth and swore, "I will end this brutality, the injustices, the insanity. I promise you, my dear friend, I will cleanse this land of the evil."

Under the dark cloak of a starless sky, the three men found the camp where women prisoners suffered degradation and torture at the hands of their vile captors. Aamir wept as he readied his rifle and pulled the trigger. Rasheed shouldered his and cursed as he fired.

A curse fell onto one of them.

It would take another ten years before Najeeb could make good on his vow. When he did, world governments watched, suspicious, as he amalgamated all the region's Arabic nations into one super nation – The Republic of Islamic Provinces and Territories (RIPT). All tribes, all Islamic sects, all peoples, now represented equally in a democratic authority.

Islam returned to its original foundation - focused on obedience to Allah's word. Prayer, modesty, and compassion again became the hallmarks of a faithful Muslim. All variations of Islam joined into one mission. Peace.

Not all agreed to the vision of Najeeb and his cabinet ministers. One powerful businessman undertook a mission to destroy President Najeeb; and to murder a police captain by the name of Hashim Sharif.

Chapter 1

October 13, 2047

Eliza stepped up to the window overlooking the airport's tarmac. The tower's search beacon sliced through the ebony sky like a knife's sharp blade. She shuddered. Her cold hands fidgeted with her head scarf. Deep in her solar plexus something twisted into a painful knot. It whispered,

Get out of RIPT

She turned to watch the last passenger hoist his carryon luggage strap over his shoulder and proceed to the boarding ramp. His aircraft, a massive 888, dwarfed the departing fuel trucks. She spotted the pilot inside his cockpit, gesturing with his hands in some kind of signal to the ground crew. He appeared eager to get the last flight out of Republic of Islamic Provinces & Territories (RIPT) airborne.

Get out of RIPT

Eliza Ramsay had felt excited this morning when the Habitat office called her. They apologized for the short notice, but requested she replace their paramedic for the RIPT mission. She had been chosen, having become fluent in Arabic. "No problem," she had said doing her happy chicken dance, relieved they couldn't see her child-like enthusiasm. "I'll meet up with your team at Samarra's International Airport tonight."

She packed fast and light. Work clothes, some casual outfits in the required modest style, one down-filled parka, and one paramedic uniform. Her medical backpack contained supplies to treat everything from minor complaints to dealing with catastrophic injuries. She was thrilled to finally put her Arabic and Islamic studies to use. She picked up a flight in Dubai and landed in Samarra well in advance of the American team's arrival.

Her bravado had all but evaporated while waiting at the crowded airport. *The American's flight is two hours late. They must have cancelled the mission.* Impatience morphed into anger at having not been notified of the change. She checked her cellphone. No missed calls. Her gut repeatedly sent her a message. *Get out of RIPT.* Her intuition seldom misfired.

She called the Habitat office on her cellphone. No answer. She heard the beep inviting her to leave a message. She stammered, "Ah, no message. Um, call later."

Get out of RIPT.

Airport staff was still tidying up the boarding kiosk. *Perhaps there's still time. Beg, no, never beg. Can't appear desperate. Ask, yes, just ask if there's room for a last minute passenger on the 888. Explain that your Habitat team failed to arrive. They'll understand.*

The foreboding eased. She liked taking action, having control over her destiny. As Eliza rushed to gather her luggage and backpack, she heard the unmistakable sound of a door slamming shut. She spun around.

Breathlessly, Eliza stood transfixed as Air Arabia 267 began to taxi away, and then pause before racing down the runway. She heard its jet engines roar as it reached takeoff speed. In seconds, the 888 disappeared into Samarra's night sky like a homesick angel.

Get out of RIPT.

I can't get out. I'm trapped. She trembled. The feeling of being ensnared pushed her mind to brink of a freefall. *No, no, stay in control.* Tapping the back of her hand the way her psychologist showed her, Eliza fought to maintain her sanity.

Exterior lights flashed onto her window. She saw flames. She jumped back. A shoulder harness pressed into her flesh. Blood splattered her steering wheel. Somewhere a child was crying. "Nathan? Noah?" she shrieked.

Eliza's most terrifying adversary had surfaced - post-traumatic stress disorder, the punishment for having survived while her children and family members died.

Wide eyed and gasping for air, she darted through the crowd.

"Stop," shouted a security guard. He grabbed her arm and yanked her aside. His painful grip and spicy cologne instantly cleared her mind. A second guard pushed her forward. "Move," he commanded in Arabic.

The officers collected her luggage and escorted her through a maze of hallways. They shoved her into an office where a heavy-set man sat behind a desk. His tan-colored military uniform barely fit his broad shoulders. A sign on his desk read 'Sergeant Muntazar'. He merely glanced in her direction while thrusting his sidearm into his shoulder holster.

Oh God. She swallowed the last of her saliva. *No one knows I'm in Samarra.* Eliza struggled to take a deep breath. *What if – stop it. You're a MacKay. My dad wouldn't crumble like this.* She wrestled her panic into submission.

"Sergeant, why have I been treated like a criminal?" Her Arabic was fluent, albeit with a Canadian accent.

"You've been here five hours. Nervous. Explain, please, miss..." His voice sounded casual, almost sultry. But his eyes said, 'Don't fuck with me.

"Ramsay, Eliza Ramsay." She pulled out her Canadian passport from her purse and handed it to the sergeant. "I've been worried about a group I'm supposed to meet. Their plane is late."

He gave the passport a cursory glance and tossed it back to her. Sergeant Muntazar sat back in his chair, casually observing her, perhaps to make her feel small and vulnerable. She recognized the ploy. As a supervisor in charge of a platoon of paramedics, she found a silent glower an effective tool in eliciting the truth from a cocky staff member who had ignored protocol.

Five hours ago, her loose-fitting, navy blue linen pants and top would have passed the cultural need for modesty. Now creased and coffee-stained, her credibility as an intelligent, professional woman might lay on shaky ground.

Her long blonde hair, tamed into a French braid, threatened to escape into a knotted mess. Eliza tucked a wayward strand of hair under her royal blue head scarf. Her heartbeat escalated. She resisted shifting her posture or fidgeting, all red flags in the world of security officers. *I've done nothing to deserve this crap. Do something. Now.*

She managed to present herself as a woman in control. Even dared to make eye contact. She pulled a chair up and sat down in front of the sergeant's desk. She had worked with men for fifteen years and learned that once men got over the shock that she wasn't going to play the role of the weaker sex, they appreciated her forthright manner.

"I arrived early from Dubai. Supposed to meet up with a group of Americans, a Habitat for Humanity group. United Air 719 should have arrived two hours ago."

"Ah, you didn't hear the announcement. A problem with the aircraft. They had to detour and attempt to land in Damascus."

She gasped and reached for the edge of Muntazar's desk. "They crashed?"

"No, the aircraft landed safely." The sergeant checked information on his computer. "Ah, I see your friends have had good fortune. They are on another flight and should arrive in two hours, at ten-forty-five. I'll ensure their progress through customs is quick. No unnecessary delays."

"Wonderful. They will appreciate your thoughtfulness, sergeant. We are expecting a police escort. Should someone tell them of the delay?"

"Captain Sharif has arranged for your escort. I know him." Muntazar released a sly grin. "Many of the criminals in Samarra have had the misfortune of knowing him." With a wave of his hand, he said, "One hundred percent reliable." Muntazar keyed in numbers on his desk phone and punched the hands-free button.

"Central Police Station. Captain Sharif here. Stand by." He continued growling at someone. "Fine, but do not let that bastard out of your sight." He paused a moment, then barked, "Hello. Who's calling?"

"Captain Sharif, this is Sergeant Muntazar at the Samarra International Airport. I have an update about the Americans."

"Yes, my men assigned to escort the Americans reported they are overdue. Problem in customs?"

"No. The pilot had to make an unscheduled landing at Damascus. The Americans have been fortunate in connecting with another aircraft. Should be here at ten-forty-five."

"Fine. Get them processed through customs quickly. Sharif, out."

Muntazar disconnected the call and dismissed his guards. "What is your role with Habitat?"

"I'm a paramedic. My role with Habitat is medical support and interpreter. But if there is no need for a medic, I do help out with the manual labor. We'll be here for two weeks."

"Your husband and children must miss you."

Eliza's body seized, instantly encased in ice. She had to say the words but her mouth refused to open. The sergeant's eyes trapped her, waiting for an answer she must provide. Her mind, like a wild wind, scurried to avoid the memory. *Dead, all dead. I survived, but they died. Horribly. It was my fault. I killed them.* Tears threatened to spill down her cheeks.

She heard a ping, perhaps from his computer shutting down. *No, my cell phone's warning of a low battery. It needs charging. If Nathan or Noah call and I don't answer, they'll panic. I must recharge my phone, quickly. Where?*

Sergeant Muntazar stood near. His voice, deep and gravelly. "Perhaps you should call them now?" A door opened. "You can use my phone, Mrs. Ramsay."

A rush of cold air made Eliza shiver and eased her out of her prison. "Thank you, sergeant. She straightened her back, lifted her chin and managed to stand. She rehearsed the reply once in her mind before uttering the painful words. It should be easier by now, after four years. "I'm a widow, sergeant. No husband, no children." She picked up her purse and backpack and slipped past him, still gathering elements of stability, of sanity. "No one to phone." She swallowed hard, took a deep breath and headed to the door. "I've got time for a coffee. If you could point me in the right direction, sergeant?"

"Come with me Mrs. Ramsay," he said, grabbing her luggage. "I will escort you to a café."

On their route to the café, Eliza inquired about the best way to not cause further trouble.

The sergeant shrugged. "If you're having a problem, ask for help. Otherwise you'll look suspicious. Tell the truth. Absolutely, one hundred percent. If the guards or police think you're hiding something, you could get roughed up." As the sergeant relaxed, he showed his pride in his relatively new country, the Republic of Islamic Provinces and Territories. "We are beginning to see progress. President Najeeb is proving to be a wise and resourceful leader. We still have a high crime rate. The old ways die hard. Best you not go anywhere alone."

By the time Muntazar had left Eliza, she had regained a marginal hold on her trademark tenacity. She hadn't realized how much she needed a meal and coffee. Her confidence bolstered, she transferred her passport into her backpack's hidden compartment. Risking the sting of regret, she retrieved the last photograph taken of her family.

She lovingly smoothed out the folds and tears. She smiled at the two little boys, suspended in an eternal moment of joy. She ignored her husband's bored expression. Nathan and Noah sat grinning, posed on the lawn of their backyard - four years ago.

The highway of hell destroyed everything she had lived for – her entire family, killed by the sweep of an out-of-control tanker. Miraculously, she recovered, physically.

Eliza yearned to once again be the happy mother in the photograph. She ached for it. She pressed the photo to her chest, and tucked it back into the secret pocket. *You had it once.* Her chin trembled. *Hell will freeze over before I let another cheating man touch me.*

When she looked for the breath mints in her purse, she pulled out her travel brochure. Workmates had admonished her for trusting the propaganda. She had reminded them that fifteen years had passed since the dark terror in the Middle East with civil war, Iran's nuclear 'accident', and terrorists' insanity. "This is 2047," she said, defending her plans. "Women don't wear the burqa now. They even hold government positions." Her colleagues continued to point out every news report of vicious government oppositions, high crime rate stemming from poverty, and many citizens' distrust of the western influences.

Eliza admired the pamphlet's colorful images depicting exotic hotels and exciting markets. City of Samarra, capital of RIPT, promised a delight for the senses. A photo of several shoes at the entrance to a mosque had a caption, *"Experience reverence and sacred contemplation during prayer at The Guardian Mosque."*

Music, excursions, shopping, quiet reflection – all guaranteed to be a *memorable and unique cultural experience.*

Much of RIPT's technology remained in the early 2000's. Civil war had prevented RIPT from keeping pace with modern advances in transportation and communication. Vehicles still relied upon fossil fuel. A visitor's experience would be a time warp in reverse, going back 40 years.

Even so, Eliza knew there was risk. Consulates warned of zero tolerance to cultural insults, intoxication and immorality. A traveler needed to be aware of acceptable dress code - modest for men and women. Sharia law was now moderate, but the midnight curfew maintained strict order. Punishments were known to be final and harsh. She shivered. *Perhaps I should have told someone that I would be here for a few weeks.*

She shrugged. *I'll be fine. There hardly seemed time to let anyone know I was making the trip. My PTSD triggers have withered since working with Habitat.* She smiled, recalling her work with Habitat leader, Charlie, in El Salvador.

She chastised herself for so easily falling under the PTSD's grip earlier. *You're a paramedic superintendent. You got a friggin' medal.* Memories surfaced of responding to murder scenes, working with the police SWAT teams, ordering a biker to 'Get the fuck out of my way'. The tough, slightly tomboy, farm girl was back in charge. At least until the next trigger.

At ten-thirty, she headed to the customs' doors. A rush of relief washed over her as she saw the Habitat leader, Charlie, come through the doors. His wavering smile betrayed utter fatigue.

"Ah, Mrs. Ramsay, I got word you would be joining our group."

Like a border collie corrals sheep, Charlie gathered the group around their luggage. He nodded at their police escort - three sour-looking men wearing black uniforms, flak jackets, and helmets. They each carried an automatic weapon slung over their shoulder. "We're here at last." His voice sounded hoarse.

He continued to address his fourteen American volunteers and Eliza. "Do you have all of your luggage?" Charlie fidgeted with his coat's zipper, pulling it up and down, again and again.

Everyone nodded. Hunched shoulders and pale faces reflected their exhaustion. Their impatience to leave the airport showed. Their gaze focused on the exit doors. Red flashing lights of the parked police vehicles bled through the glass doors. Eliza shuddered.

Airport baggage handlers began transferring their luggage into a one-ton truck with a canvas canopy. The weary Americans piled into a small bus leading the convoy. Two police officers on motorcycles followed at the rear behind the supply truck.

They expected a two-hour drive from the airport to the farm work site. Less than a half hour into the trip, the convoy stopped at a gas station. The group took the opportunity to use the bathrooms, buy some water, and stretch their legs.

Eliza walked past the officers and on to the back of the supply truck. Out of the men's view, she jumped up and through the canvas opening. She switched on her pocket size flashlight and located her suitcase. Quietly, she pulled out her dark blue down-filled parka and put it on.

The moon cast long shadows in front of the gas station. Eliza noticed the lights of RIPT's capital city, Samarra, a few miles to the east. Murmurs of conversation drifted from a huddle of men. They argued. Apparently, this was an unscheduled stop.

She heard someone grunt, then sounds of men wrestling. *Roughhousing like school boys. Probably bored with extra duty.* As she sat on the luggage, her intuition begged her to remain silent. She should have felt safe, but her unease refused to be coerced into indifference.

Chapter 2

The Habitat group trudged back to the bus. Eliza caught the eye of a woman she had been sitting beside and told her she would be staying in the supply truck. The woman nodded and shuffled on. The police on their motorcycles took their positions behind the supply truck. Eliza decided to sit low and out of their visual range.

Within twenty minutes, she noted they were arriving in a city's suburbs. It worried her. Their worksite was supposed to be on the perimeter of a distant rural town. She saw the outline of houses, a mosque, market stalls, then a hotel, then more service stations. She wondered if Habitat's information package had been inaccurate. Places of business, banks, and coffee shops flashed by. The streets were almost empty, barren of traffic and pedestrians.

This is Samarra. We're not supposed to be going through the city.

An armored truck with a mounted machine gun roared up behind the two police motorcyclists. *Something is terribly wrong.* She ducked deeper behind the luggage and stared into the darkness. She desperately searched for a rational explanation. A cold knife pierced her core.

After speeding through intersections and red traffic lights, the vehicles came to a sudden halt. Gate hinges squealed in protest. The impulse to leap from the back of the truck fought with her intense need to remain hidden. If it were not for the armed vehicle at the rear, she would have jumped and disappeared into the night. In another moment, the opportunity vanished.

The vehicles lurched forward. Through the flap's opening, she saw a massive iron gate. High walls extended on either side. The vehicles stopped.

The motorcyclists drove to either side of the truck. The armored vehicle surged forward, nearly crashing into the back of the supply truck. Eliza scrambled to put more of the luggage between her and the mounted gun. It bore down on her as if it had spied her. She gasped.

Eliza strained to hear a pleasant greeting, an apology for the change of plans, anything that would tell her heart to stop its thundering in her chest.

Someone shouted, "*Ikhrog men al Araba*," then in English, "Get out of the bus!"

"Stay together," Charlie called out. At first the volunteers sounded merely annoyed, but their mood rapidly deteriorated.

"Charlie, there's a mounted automatic weapon on that truck. Something's not right here." The man's alarm ricocheted through his companions. Quick footsteps reminded Eliza of nervous horses in a corral – wild-eyed, snorting and circling as they searched for an escape.

Charlie attempted to calm his group. "I'm sure this will all make sense. I'll see why there's been a change. Who's in charge here?" he called.

Scattered thoughts fed her fear. The unmistakable sound of large guns being maneuvered sucked the air from Eliza's lungs. Near the supply truck, she heard the ping, ping of a cell phone, then the trembling voice of a woman crying, "Ralph, pick up the phone. Please. Oh God ...." The woman screamed. With a blast of gunfire, her cries stopped. Bullets pierced the canvas and shattered a suitcase in front of Eliza.

Her body trembled violently. In minutes she would be killed. The luggage offered no protection. Terrified to make any sound, yet frantic to hide, she pressed her backpack to her chest. She gasped as if starved for oxygen. Tears ran down her cheeks as she heard the terrified people and Charlie beg for their lives.

This is only one of my nightmares. I'll wake up and everything will be fine.

The truck with the mounted machine gun swerved around the supply truck. Deafening sounds of machine gun blasts and screams tore through her chest. She plunged down among the luggage.

A man came into her view as he lunged toward the gate. A police officer ran after him and fired several shots into the man's back. The American dropped, bloody and lifeless.

Suddenly, an armed man dashed to the rear of the supply truck and saw her. She gasped. *Oh my God, he's going to kill me. I've got once chance. Get his gun.* Her martial arts training kicked in. She lunged forward. As they grappled, both fell.

Falling on top of him Eliza punched his groin. He cried out in agony. She crab-crawled on all fours toward his weapon several feet away. Too late she saw a boot aimed at her head.

She ducked for cover under the supply truck. Too late. The cop stomped on her head, ramming her forehead into the pavement hard. Her momentum pushed her under the truck's back end.

Dazed, she checked to see if he followed her. He was struggling to free his boot, snared in her scarf. A gun's muzzle appeared, aimed in her direction. Bullets ripped through her coat's shoulder. Puffs of down feathers stuck to the sweat and blood on her face. *I'm hit. Get out. Run.* Eliza kicked and crawled out from under the truck on the far side of the killers. The deafening gunfire and screams surrounded her. Her mind froze. She pressed her body into the truck's solid frame.

More bullets smacked the ground near her. More vehicles arrived. Bright headlights blinded her. She turned away to shield her eyes. Desperate, she ran an erratic, aimless course. Silhouettes of shapes, helmets, guns and bloody bodies flashed in front of her. *Keep running. Dodge. Find cover.* She ran like a wild animal, blind to the teeth that would tear her apart.

When the thunder from the machine gun stopped she glanced back. The man at the machine gun tumbled head first off the truck. His companions continued to fire their weapons, but now toward the gate. More shots came from behind the blinding lights. The men ran toward the front of the supply truck. Riddled with bullets, their bodies twisted and fell.

Silence.

Eliza gazed in bewilderment at the tall form appearing in the light. He raced forward past the open gate, his weapon raised in her direction. More men followed behind him. She ran, searching for cover.

He shouted, "*Tawakaf and am, la tatharak Kiff.*" Then in English, "Stop where you are. Don't move! Stop."

A short burst of gunfire. Bullets struck the ground a few yards in front of her. She skidded to a stop. Breathless, she turned toward the gunman. She could not make out his face below the dark helmet. He wore a police uniform like the killers had - black from head to toe. If not for his vehicle's headlights, he would have been invisible. He raced toward her, his weapon held steadfast in her direction.

Gasping for air, she looked around her. To her horror, all her companions appeared to be dead. Flesh ripped, vacant open eyes, clothes soaked in blood. She saw a person writhing in pain and ran to her.

Eliza knelt down beside her. The woman's skin was cold and clammy, and her lips were blue. A chest wound bled freely. She struggled to breathe and grabbed Eliza's arm.

"You'll be okay," Eliza reassured the woman. "Let me see where you're hurt."

Eliza believed the woman had a collapsed lung. She needed to set up a valve to release the air trapped in the pleural sac. "I'm a paramedic. I'll get my kit and you'll be okay." Eliza's hands were trembling as she struggled to release the woman's grip. As she ran back to the supply truck, someone attempted to block her path.

"Stop!" demanded the officer who spoke English.

She noted the stripes on his coat's sleeve. He held the rank of captain. Her adrenalin surged like an angry river. "That woman is still alive. Get out of my way!" She dodged him and jumped into the supply truck. She grabbed her backpack and ran to her patient.

The captain continued to follow but gave her enough space. In seconds she set up her equipment to start an intravenous line. Eliza managed to calm her shaking hands enough to insert a large-bore needle into the side of the woman's chest. Trapped air escaped. She continued to stop the bleeding and to get an intravenous line running. The woman continued to gasp for air.

Eliza knew she required surgery. The injuries were far beyond her training. She held the woman's hand and pleaded with her to not give up, but her pulse faded and then stopped.

The captain walked away with one of his officers. Sounds of men and machines surrounded her. She stumbled back and slumped down against a wall. She stared at the grisly scene. Numb with disbelief, her body felt weightless. A breeze lifted torn pieces of paper and carried them in a ghostly fashion toward her. The passage of time ceased, held frozen in the cold horror.

She let her head fall back against the wall. As she gazed up into the black void, a flash caught her attention. A distant falling star, a meteor hurtled through the Earth's atmosphere – silent and fatal. An ominous sign.

One of the cops grabbed her arm and forced her to stand. She struggled to get her mind into gear. Someone forced her to move forward. A surge of hatred erupted with such velocity that she escaped the man's grip as if he had the strength of a mere child. More hands grabbed her and bullied her forward to a building, down a hallway and into an office.

The men appeared still pumped by the battle. Their hands trembled and their voices were edged with urgency. They tried to force her into a chair near a desk. Her determination to survive blinded her to the fact that these men were different.

They cursed in Arabic. "Damn stupid woman. Where's Captain Sharif?"

She tried to fight off two short wiry men as they pulled off her bulky coat and tossed it into a corner. They twisted her arms behind her while another attempted a body search. She managed a sharp kick to his shin. He stepped back and threatened her with a fist aimed toward her jaw. With her hands held near the thigh of the man behind her, she clawed at his groin. He shifted his body but his grip never wavered.

Someone pushed a chair behind her knees. She fell hard onto the seat.

The men grunted and cursed as they fought to keep her in the chair. She could smell their strong odor. She gagged as beads of their sweat fell onto her face. Handcuffs came into her view. She became desperate and cried out, "Let me go!" in Arabic.

A large muscular man came into the room. "Stop. Leave her alone," he ordered his men in Arabic.

Her wrists were released. She flew across the large wood desk.

"I'm Sergeant Abdul-Muqtadir. Sit in the chair." Assuming she didn't understand Arabic, he motioned with his hands toward the chair.

"*La*," she hollered in Arabic. "*Daany athhab*, No, let me out of here." She glared at the four constables. "*La talmasny*, Don't touch me."

The men glanced at each other, surprised that the woman spoke in their language.

The captain bolted into the room. "Stop," he said to her in clear English. "You will not be harmed."

"Bullshit!" she replied in English. Eliza trembled, overwhelmed with rage and shock.

The captain turned to his sergeant and hollered, "*Zabet I gal almokeh aamin*. Set up for ID and disposal," The sergeant gave a series of orders to his men. They rushed out though the sergeant remained at the door.

Unable to switch off her frantic efforts to escape, Eliza scanned the room for a way out.

"Sit down." The captain's voice sounded harsh.

Eliza noted his commanding posture. His eyes fixed on her, the expression on his face fierce and tense. He wouldn't hesitate to put her down hard and without mercy. She glanced at the doorway. The big man stood there.

"*Sharif, Takalmet Arabia.* Sharif, she spoke Arabic," said the sergeant.

The captain's eyebrows twitched. "*Takalmet Arabia?*"

"*Naam.* Yes."

The captain moved to stand behind his desk. It forced her to return to the front of the desk. "Please sit down, miss."

She moved toward the chair. At the last second before reaching the chair, she lunged toward the door. The sergeant standing in her path hadn't been prepared for her kick to the groin. He went down hard. She leaped to the exit door, jumped down the stairs, missing all six steps.

She ran to the gate and tugged on the bars. The gate held fast to the locks. The bars, spaced horizontally and vertically five inches apart, rose about fifteen feet high. At the top, the wire mesh spanned the length of the wall. Seeing no barbed wire Eliza figured it would be simple enough to climb over. She leaped up onto the gate, climbing up several feet at a time. The captain and his men gathered beneath her.

The captain shouted orders. "*Ighlogh al Tayar. Ighlogh alaan*" Shut off the current now!"

Eliza only heard her own racing heart.

As she got closer to the wire, she realized it surged with a deadly charge. She could feel the hum in her hair whipping around her face. Beyond the wall she viewed a dark empty street - no friend or place of refuge in that street or for thousands of miles. Below her stood men who, she believed, had killed her companions.

She heard someone yelling at her to not touch the wire. Oh, she wanted to. *I could end it all right now*, she thought. *Maybe this time it would work. How many times have I failed? At least three,* she remembered. She reached for the wire.

"Stop. Do not touch that wire," someone hollered in clear English below her.

Eliza looked down. The captain stood beneath her. Eliza's hand stopped in mid-motion, her fingers just an inch away from curling around the current that would stop her heart. Her limbs trembled. She gasped as she fell like a bird with a broken wing. Pain punctuated her joints from the jolt of shoulders and arms bracing to break her fall.

Chapter 3

She hit the ground hard. As the last dregs of energy burned, she struggled to sit up.

"Get up and stand still." The captain enunciated each word in English. "You will remain here until after my investigation. Get up!"

Testing for injuries, she did a mental body scan. She hurt everywhere. Her head pounded. Her blood-saturated hair stuck to the back of her neck and side of her face. Tentatively she touched the gash on the back of her head. The swollen wound had stopped bleeding.

The dirt and blood stains on her simple clothes reminded her of the "bag women" in her home city. She tucked strands of hair behind her ears.

She looked up at the officer. There appeared to be no concern in his dark eyes. She was transfixed by his gaze. In an odd sort of way, she gained strength from his calm-but-in-command demeanor. Eliza stiffened as her emotions began to descend into self-pity. She believed tears would be viewed as weakness. Men hated weakness. And tears.

As she attempted to stand, he grabbed her arm and roughly guided her to lean against a vehicle. Her sweat-soaked clothes did nothing to protect her from the cold air. She crossed her arms across her chest. "I need my coat."

"Later." The captain removed his flak jacket and coat, and then handed his coat to her. Returning to the ugly business before them, he barked orders to his sergeant. "Sergeant, I want photos of the scene and each body. Make sure the men wear gloves. Get the ID from the victims and the killers. Fingerprint all the deceased. Get as much information off the killers as you can."

The sergeant directed his squad to complete the tasks. "Bag all the bodies and load them into the half-ton trucks." The sergeant called to another man. "Get all the information from that armored vehicle. I want everything from the tires to the engine to the gun."

The captain watched as the men followed their sergeant's orders. "Sergeant, how many are there?"

The large man that Eliza had kicked turned to the captain. "Fifteen victims – ten men and five women." He handed a document to the captain. "This looks like a Habitat list."

The captain read it. "Yes, this identifies the fifteen Americans. See if you can find their passports. Bag their valuables, rings and wallets, anything of value that we'll need to send back to Habitat. How many killers?"

Six killers, sir. Definitely not our people. No ID, no documents, nothing."

"We need to find out what happened to the four police officers assigned to escort these people. Find the bus. I'm hoping this woman can explain what happened after these people were picked up at the airport." The captain lowered his voice. "Omar, be ready for the chief's arrival. This is going to get ugly."

"Agreed. Be careful, Hashim. The mayor has reason to get rid of you. This may be the opportunity he's been waiting for. I'm sorry to say, but he will accuse you of criminal neglect, mishandling the protection of the Americans."

"That would require an arrest and a trial." Sharif shrugged. "For the past year I've accumulated dirt on that bastard. Not enough to satisfy his superiors, but enough that he won't risk exposure." Sharif grimaced. He wasn't sure if President Najeeb was in league with the payoffs. "Don't worry about the mayor. You've got enough to deal with here. Warn your men there is to be absolutely no discussion of this with anyone. Understood?"

"Yes, one hundred percent." The sergeant nodded. "As usual."

"I'll collect the woman's belongings and turn them over to you for inspection. *Inshallah*, by morning we'll know who's responsible for this. Normally, terrorists are eager to take credit."

More lights illuminated the compound. Men scrambled about, moving bodies and vehicles. Eliza remembered her trauma kit still at the side of the woman. As she put her body into motion, every joint complained. Every muscle trembled with fatigue. Her energy had hit rock bottom. Gathering up some residual anger, she mustered the strength to walk through the bloody hell. The captain stepped in her path. "Stay here."

"I must get my kit," she said through clenched teeth.

He adjusted his assault rifle and kept pace with her. His men focused on collecting evidence and placing the bodies into bags. Others picked up spent bullet casings. Signs of the massacre disappeared. The foul odor of blood persisted.

When she tried to pick up her trauma backpack, her hand failed to grip and hold the thirty-five pound weight. The captain lifted it and asked, "Is there anything else you need tonight?"

She grabbed it away from him and shifted it onto her back. Her body swayed with the weight and she struggled to think coherently. *Come on*, she chastised herself. *Don't let them think you can't handle this.* She straightened her posture and took a deep breath. *Center! Pull yourself together, woman. Get your stuff!*

Eliza glanced at the captain. He appeared distracted, watching the activity of his men. He pulled out his cell phone, but hesitated to make a call. *Thinking of calling his superiors*, she figured. His boss would be in bed. Since she had been a paramedic superintendent with the ambulance service, she knew the repercussions of calling a boss at his home in the middle of the night. Trouble, big trouble. Investigations, confrontations, reprimands, accusations, protocol breach reviews, interviews, and the bothersome media.

He turned toward her. "Miss, there is something I must tell you right now. Are you listening?"

She noted his expression - so like the restrained rage and disbelief she'd seen on the faces of police officers she worked with. When they arrived at the scene of child abuse, or some other horror in progress, lips tight, voice harsh, hands trembled, breathing shallow, eyes narrowed, and they swallowed with every breath. She nodded. "Yes, I'm listening."

"I am Hashim Sharif, the captain of the police in this section of Samarra. What happened here, the death of your companions was not, I repeat, was not by the police force. Is that clear?"

A buzz from his two-way radio interrupted him. "Dispatch to Captain Sharif."

"Sharif here."

"Sir, we've received a report that there are three bodies about thirty miles east of the airport. The army patrol found them." The dispatcher paused. "Sir, they're ...."

"Say again, dispatch."

"I'm sorry, sir. They are three of the police officers you assigned to escort the Habitat people. Their throats were slashed."

Eliza detected a trembling in the dispatcher's voice.

"What are your orders, sir?"

Captain Sharif barely hesitated. If Eliza hadn't been standing beside him, she would not have heard the groan he uttered or have seen the slight slouch of his shoulders. "Send Captain Ahmed's crew out to investigate. Ask the army patrol to remain on scene and keep the public out. Who's in charge on scene?"

Captain Sharif received the information he needed, and then called to his sergeant. "Sergeant, the three police officers who were escorting these people have been found murdered."

The sergeant's mouth hung open and he shook his head. "But there were four assigned as escorts."

"I'll need you to investigate that scene. Call the army base to get the coordinates. Take a man with you and meet up with Captain Ahmed's crew and army patrol on scene. Report back to me when you arrive." The sergeant spun around on his heels, grabbed an officer and ran to his sedan, still parked outside the gate.

Captain Sharif turned back to her. "Someone has executed a very daring attack on your people and mine. I need your full cooperation, miss."

She hesitated, still eyeing him suspiciously. "I don't mean any disrespect but I'm not ready to believe this is not the doing of your people." Eliza glanced at officers placing a woman's corpse into a body bag. "This is insanity."

"Whether you believe me or not is immaterial. Right now, I need you to complete a witness report. Come back to my office. Do you have all you need for the night?" His tone had softened.

Eliza asked for her handbag, and suitcase in the supply truck. "The American government will need to be notified. Who will make those calls?" she asked as he led her to the supply truck.

"The police chief will handle that."

At the back of the supply truck she identified her belongings. He grabbed them and led her back to his office. "You'll be remaining here for the night."

Eliza stood frozen in disbelief. "Captain, am I under arrest?"

"No. The police chief may want to talk to you."

She had no strength left to put up an argument. He had said 'for the night' so perhaps, if she hung on to hope, she might be sent home tomorrow.

Chapter 4

In his office he motioned for her to sit. She removed his coat and went to retrieve her navy blue, down coat from where it had been thrown into a corner. Captain Sharif grabbed it, sending puffs of downy feathers into the air as they escaped from the bullet holes. He noted the holes and looked at her shoulder. The down continued to swirl about him like miniature angels.

"Do you need a doctor?"

"Not right now. Later, I'll need stitches and some antibiotic."

"Fine, after my superiors arrive." He returned to check the contents of the coat pockets. He found a few coins and tossed them onto his desk.

He tossed the coat to her. "Sit down." He checked the denomination of the money. "Canadian coins," he remarked. "You're not American?"

"No. I'm from Alberta, Canada." She slumped into the chair and released a chuckle.

"Something amusing, miss?"

She looked down at her hands and sighed. Pulling her shoulders back, she looked into the captain's face. "I wasn't assigned to this group until this morning. Said they needed a relief paramedic, but, for my safety, I should meet the group at the airport. Lucky me, eh?" She closed her eyes and shook her head. "Sorry."

Shock had begun to wear off. The full magnitude of what just happened became clearer. Massacre. Fifteen - no eighteen - innocent people just lost their lives. She tried to process the madness, the devastation and suffering of so many families. In the next few hours, governments around the world would be clamoring to blame, maybe incite revenge.

He picked up her luggage, purse and backpack. "Come with me to the evidence room."

Eliza slipped into her coat and followed Sharif to a large room. Cabinets and shelves lined the walls behind a fenced barricade. He set her stuff on a long table and dumped out the contents of her purse.

She looked on, stunned with the overt invasion of her privacy. Her mind whirled, attempting to understand his actions. "I'm a victim, not a damn criminal! Captain, why …."

He interrupted. "What's your name, miss?" His attention remained on her personal items.

"Eliza MacKay."

He glanced at her left hand and must have seen her gold wedding band. "Mrs. MacKay?"

She thrust her hands into the coat pockets. "No. Miss MacKay will do." Her level of irritation increased. "Why are you going through my things?"

"Procedure." He continued to paw through the contents of her purse - airline boarding stubs, baggage claim tickets, used Kleenex, breath mints, lip balm, and her sunglasses. He set aside her international cell phone, wallet and iPad. He unzipped the purse compartments and pulled out the remaining contents: small packet of Tylenol, lipstick, and a package of Kleenex. "Where's your passport, Miss MacKay?"

She hesitated as if trying to recall where she had put it. "I moved it from my coat pocket at the airport into my suitcase, I think. Anyway, I went through all this at the airport's customs department." She resisted reaching for her backpack.

He glared at her. She managed to restrain the signals of her lies. Her self-discipline faded when she crossed her arms across her chest. *Damn!*

"Open your luggage, miss."

Eliza decided to attempt a distraction. "Where's the bathroom, captain?"

Again, he ignored her. He opened her wallet and studied the cards in each compartment. "This birth certificate confirms your name is Elizabeth Leigh MacKay. However, you're not going anywhere until I see your passport."

Eliza stepped to within arm's reach of Sharif. "If you don't want a puddle on your floor, direct me to the bathroom now."

He appeared repulsed by her statement and stepped back. He motioned upward with his hand. "Only men's bathrooms on this floor. The office staff locks up theirs at night. You'll have to use the one in my apartment upstairs." He motioned for her to head toward the hallway.

She grabbed her backpack and followed him up the wide metal steps. Open doors on either side of the hallway revealed discarded office furniture strewn about. He moved ahead of her and used a key to unlock the door. "The bathroom is here," he said, indicating a door just inside.

Inside the tiny bathroom she breathed a sigh of relief. It had the standard western style toilet, shower and pedestal sink. It had been kept clean and tidy. A hint of a spicy cologne from his toiletries helped to calm her. Her dad's Old Spice aftershave had had a similar fragrance.

She hoped the captain might get distracted with some other task and forget about the passport. She believed that once he got his hands on it, she wouldn't get it back. Besides, he would also discover her true identity. Whenever people knew her legal name, they soon discovered reports of her madness. Her life became unbearable.

When she returned to the captain, he was pacing in his kitchen while making a phone call – that call he hadn't made earlier to his superiors, she assumed. She could hear a loud angry voice coming from his phone. The captain held his tongue. She knew what it was like to be on the receiving end of a boss's accusation of a screw-up, accused of negligence of security protocol, and responsibility for a national crisis.

It shook her a bit to realize she had some sympathy for Sharif. She had, in the past, experienced the wrath of a paramedic service manager on a rampage hoping to deflect his responsibility for an incident onto the alleged incompetence of those under his command.

The captain slammed the phone shut and shoved into it his coat's inside pocket.

"Do you have some ice, captain? It'll help the swelling go down and close the wound," she said, gently patting the back of her head."

He grimaced as if bothered by the inconvenience. He went to his refrigerator and pulled out a small tray of ice cubes. Eliza wrapped the ice into a tea towel. It appeared clean. She applied the cold compress to her head. "Feels better already. Thank you."

He motioned for her to sit at a small kitchen table. Before he sat down he called on his radio to one of his officers. "Bring a pot of coffee to my apartment."

He sat down across from her and brought out a pen and notepad. For a few minutes he made some notes in Arabic. His pen nearly cut through the page. He glanced at her. "If your passport has been lost, I'll get the records from the airport. You can then notify your Canadian consulate in Dubai for a replacement." A knock at the door made Eliza jump.

"Come in," Sharif barked. The coffee arrived. He got two cups from his cupboard and poured the coffee. "It's quite strong," he said placing her cup on the table. "You take milk or sugar?"

"A little milk, please. Thank you, captain," she said, wrapping her cold fingers around the chipped blue porcelain cup. He set a carton of milk on the table and sat down. She added some milk, took a sip and settled for a momentary truce. "It's nice and hot." She managed to fabricate a smile.

"Miss MacKay, the police chief and probably more officials will be here soon. I need to have a report ready. Tell me exactly what happened from the moment you arrived at the airport."

Eliza told him everything.

"Did you hear anyone called by name or anything else that would identify the killers?"

She had to think. "They said very little. When we arrived here, one of the killers ordered everyone off the bus. He had a British accent, like yours." But then she did recall something odd. "Captain, when we stopped at the gas station I went into the supply truck. The escorts didn't notice as they stood at the front of the bus. A short while later, I overheard something, like men wrestling with each other. Then I saw a van racing back onto the road. It must have been there before we arrived."

"The drivers should not have stopped. That was a breach of protocol. Whose idea was it to stop at the gas station?"

"Our bus driver said he was stopping so we could stock up on water, use the bathroom."

"Why were you in the supply truck?"

Eliza hesitated. *How much does he need to know?* "The bus was crowded. And I prefer to be outside. No one seemed to notice or care."

"Anything else happen at the gas station?"

"No, sir."

The captain's radio buzzed. "Police Chief Ganem and Mayor Aamir are here."

Eliza caught a grimace on the captain's face.

"Stay here. Stay out of sight," he commanded. "Understood?"

"Yes, captain. I'll just get my stuff."

He headed to the door. "Later." The door shut with a thud.

Eliza viewed the scene below from the apartment window. A man in a police uniform walked with a hunched and choppy gait. Another large, well-dressed man stood with dignity and walked as though he owned the ground beneath his feet. They greeted the captain with a menacing air, stabbing their fingers at his chest. Captain Sharif maintained his solid stance, feet firmly on the ground, slightly apart.

The compound appeared devoid of battle signs. She watched as the captain pointed and gestured, probably describing what had occurred. The truck with the bagged bodies headed to the gate. She heard Captain Sharif holler to the driver, "Drive back here."

The officer drove back to the front of the station. The men inspected the rear of the truck's covered box. Captain Sharif continued his report. He glanced up at her window. She jumped out of view.

Seeing the men enter the building, Eliza cracked the apartment door open and eavesdropped on their conversation. She needed information. Her future rested in the hands of agitated men. As the captain and his superiors entered the building, she heard panic in their voices. They spoke Arabic so quickly Eliza had difficulty understanding them. She crept down the stairs but stopped just short of the hallway.

"Sharif," one of the men shouted, "this incident will have a disastrous effect on our country's future."

Chapter 5

Captain Hashim Sharif used everything in his personal arsenal to remain calm. As Police Chief Ganem ranted on, Sharif knew he had to present a moderate and rational response. Over the past five years Ganem had proven to be a competent leader though the mayor's influence had led him to be occasionally unscrupulous. And, anything that threatened his wealth or position of power drove the man to a venomous response.

When it appeared Ganem's rant had lost its steam, Sharif dove in. "Gentlemen, we are going to be the focus of American scrutiny. It is imperative that our facts stand up. If we are forthcoming with the details about this massacre, and demonstrate positive action to find who is responsible -."

The police chief grabbed Sharif's wrist. "You will say nothing." Spit flew out of his mouth. "Understood? Aamir and I discussed this on our way here." Ganem let go of Sharif and lowered his voice. "The fact that the killings took place in a locked police compound will make us appear complicit. We could be charged as accomplices to the murders. President Najeeb will make sure we are held accountable, Sharif. At least for the sake of his public image and retaining his seat in the UN. You, me, and Aamir, we'll not just lose our positions. We'll be imprisoned with people we put there. None of us will survive that."

Sharif resisted falling into Ganem's bleak prediction. "President Najeeb is an intelligent man. Yes, he will view this as a national crisis, but to put his officers in prison would be paramount to conceding to the possibility of corruption." In truth, Sharif couldn't predict the president's reaction. Sharif never moved among the ministers' chambers or circle of advisors.

Sharif watched Mayor Aamir wander around his office as if bored. It annoyed Sharif that one man appeared to be on the verge of a meltdown while the other seemed indifferent. Since his promotion to captain three years ago, both Aamir and Ganem had proven to be devious.

Damn, they're heading in the direction of a cover-up. He eyed the camera on his desk. Abdul-Muqtadir had trained his elite force to take pictures of everything. Perhaps they hadn't had enough time. Dispatch had called for more support. Gangs had been causing an uprising throughout the city.

Mayor Aamir sat down at Sharif's desk. He picked up the camera and looked up at Sharif. "Got photos of the shooting?" His voice sounded mildly curious. His eyes revealed a measure of excitement.

"Just photos of the bodies, the vehicles and weapons used by the killers." Being evasive or deceitful to his superiors proved to be too difficult for Sharif. In spite of his superiors' nefarious deeds, he still had the inclination to demonstrate loyalty. His level of devotion to his country and government dictated a high level of blind faith that their actions were for the good of the people and Islam.

"Connect your camera to the PC." Aamir sat back as if looking forward to watching a video of a family gathering. "Download the SUV's video here, too."

"It is quite graphic." Sharif winced at his foolish statement. There had been whispers of an occasional disappearance of a disloyal staff member found dead in the desert. Some suggested that Aamir carried out the hit himself.

Aamir smiled. "Do it." The smile never wavered.

While Sharif downloaded the flash drives, Mayor Aamir took Ganem to the hallway and spoke softly. "Terrorists are not going to come forward."

Sharif heard what sounded like an admission that Mayor Aamir had suspicions about who was behind the massacre. He carried on as though he hadn't heard a word. *Play his game for the time being.*

"We've got to get rid of those bodies," muttered Mayor Aamir to the police chief. "Make sure there's no evidence of the killing, written or otherwise. Understood?"

"Ready," called out Sharif. Aamir took Sharif's office chair while Ganem stood behind the mayor. Sharif hit the 'play' prompt and watched the reactions of both men. Ganem and Aamir raced through the photos. In a flash, Sharif realized his life was going to get dangerously complicated.

Miss MacKay – a witness.

He turned his back to them. His thoughts raced. So focused on the crisis, he had said nothing about there being a survivor. *They'll have the woman executed before daylight.* A cold sweat enveloped his body. He lifted his helmet off his head and slapped it back down again.

Damn. If I attempt to defend her, Aamir will question my loyalty. He clenched his fists, gritted his teeth. I'll be brought to his personal execution grounds. If I do kill her, Allah will condemn my soul. A wave of nausea hit his gut and his knees nearly buckled.

Sharif lived according to the word of Allah and with the guidance of his imam at the Guardian mosque. He could not execute the woman.

And yet, he could not put himself at risk. If he died, his children would suffer a terrible life. They would be sent to live with their mother in England. The thought made him shiver. His son and daughter would be twisted to adore money, bow to a god of self-interests and greed.

He turned and watched his superiors lean in closer to the monitor. The video disc whirred inside the computer like a cat purring after a successful hunt. His heartbeat thundered in his ears. The tension inside him grew as if waiting for a bomb to explode. When Aamir frowned and turned to Sharif, the burning fuse detonated the bomb.

Aamir bolted out of the chair. "There is a survivor?" He pointed to the monitor. "Where is that woman?"

Sharif stepped forward, shoulders square with his straight back. "She's upstairs. She was injured. Instead of taking her to a hospital I allowed her to attend to her head wound in my apartment."

Aamir's eyes narrowed as he stepped close to Sharif. His shoulders hitched up and leaned in toward the captain. "Who is she?"

Before Sharif could respond, Aamir waved his hands. "Never mind. It doesn't matter who she is. Will she die without medical treatment?"

"No. Just a …."

"Fuck!" Aamir turned to the police chief. "We have to get rid of the woman."

"Execute the woman?" Ganem blanched. "Aamir, so far we don't have blood on our hands. Why put ourselves at risk? Sharif, until we can make other arrangements, you must keep the woman out of sight, in your apartment."

Sharif gasped. "Absolutely not. Never. I will never allow …."

Aamir stepped up to Sharif. "The future of the Republic of Islamic Provinces and Territories is in our hands. We must protect RIPT." He placed a hand on Sharif's shoulder. Did the mayor know Sharif's single-mindedness to protect? "I'm counting on you, captain. Protect our nation's honor. We failed in protecting those people. How will our government ever be trusted again if it becomes known that Americans died in our capital's police compound?"

Sharif winced at the mention of his failure. The weight of blame threatened his resolve to remain professional. Even so, the knowledge of being deficient reminded him of his father's rejection. He lost the fight to counter the mayor's devious plan. Almost mute, he conveyed his compliance with a nod.

"I know I can count on you, captain. It is unfortunate, but that woman is a threat to everything our president has achieved."

"Surely, Najeeb will -."

"Minister Rasheed and I will handle communication." Aamir's approach resembled more of a benevolent father figure than a man contemplating a cover-up. "Since your men have seen her, we'll have to make her disappear in a way that puts no blame on our administration." Aamir smiled maliciously. "Be forewarned. If you or your men screw up, that woman won't be the only one that disappears." His eyes were cold. "Is that clear?" The mayor calmly enunciated each word.

"Understood." Sharif grimaced as if tasting something sour.

As the mayor collected the digital files, his instructions continued. "Send the sergeant and a team to search for the missing Americans within our jurisdiction. Report only that the escorts were found murdered and it is presumed the Americans are being held for ransom. Your log should only report that you have duly informed your superiors of the crisis and that an intensive investigation is underway. Our military will initiate a search. This afternoon you will meet with Ganem for your orders. Until then, do nothing. Return to your normal routine. End your shift like any other."

As he headed for the exit, Aamir turned back to Sharif. "Captain, what time did the Americans arrive at the airport?"

"Roughly two hours ago. Should have been much earlier."

"Ah, yes. How fortunate for you. You would have here alone during the attack. Allah protects the protector."

Sharif grabbed his police radio and updated his sergeant. "Our orders are to start looking for the missing Americans." He stressed the word 'missing.' "Get a team. Search only the city's jurisdiction. The army will cover the remainder of RIPT. Understood?"

Chapter 6

Eliza slipped back to the apartment careful to not alert the angry men. She collapsed onto a sofa, dazed with disbelief. *It'll be okay. They're just panicking. By daylight, they'll realize what is sensible. Once the dust settles, the cop will throw me onto a plane and I'll be home in a day. Maybe two, tops.*

Goosebumps popped up on her arms. As she burrowed under her down coat and laid down, she uttered a mocking chuckle. *Man, am I going to get a blast from Mike.* Two hours later, she woke to the sound of someone entering the apartment.

In the dim light she recognized the tall form. Sharif. She feigned a sleeping pose. His footsteps approached the sofa and paused. He muttered under his breath in his foreign tongue, "Cursed woman." He bumped into a chair she'd moved and uttered a profanity in clear English, "Fuck!"

She breathed a sigh of relief when he retreated to his bedroom. She heard the thud when his bed slammed against the wall upon suddenly receiving his full one hundred and eighty pounds of bone and muscle.

Her head pounded as she sat up. So far, she'd had about two hours of sleep. Her mind replayed the massacre. *Shut up. Get busy.* She got up to take a closer look at her surroundings. She shuffled to the kitchen. She winced with every movement, as if she had been run over and dragged for miles. Every step became more clumsy until she had to brace herself against the bathroom door.

Her reflection mirrored a pathetic creature - face swollen, filthy. Dried blood covered much of her tangled hair and the side of her face and neck. Thirty-six years old, her friends had considered her lovely; 'a natural beauty' they'd said. *God, if they saw me now.*

Eliza managed the shower, a tepid sluggish flow of water. She used his toiletries. Too late she realized she hadn't brought clean clothes with her into the bathroom. The water had revived her enough that she sprinted to the sofa and slipped into her coat.

She dressed in fresh cream-colored cotton pants and top. The gash in her skull shrieked and bled with the slightest tug. She applied several sterile 4x4 bandages from her medical kits and applied pressure for a few minutes. The angry wound settled down to a slow leak and clotted again.

She had enough energy left to snoop in Sharif's kitchen cupboards and fridge. On the counter she discovered a note under a bottle of water.

'DO NOT LEAVE THE APARTMENT.

FOOD IN FRIDGE.

CAPTAIN SHARIF.'

As she drank the water, she surveyed the fridge's contents. Milk, flatbread, some kind of sauce or spread, a jar of olives, figs, cheese, all grab and run stuff. On the bottom shelf she found a plate of food covered with clear plastic wrap.

She set it on the table and sat down, staring at the banquet of food. *Perhaps the captain will get good news today. Perhaps the terrorists have publicly bragged about the attack. I'll be home by tomorrow morning.*

Eliza devoured the grapes, cheddar cheese slices, flatbread, and orange juice in minutes. She decided to save the crispy fried chicken, potato salad and bottled ice tea for later in the day.

He actually picked up food that I might like? Perhaps there's a heart behind the scowl, a small one, like the Grinch. Her boys loved the Grinch and watched it for days after Christmas. Her vision blurred.

Overwhelmed with fatigue again, she lay down on the sofa and fell asleep. At noon, a trembling of the sofa woke her. Sharif, dressed in a long beige thobe, had kicked the sofa to wake her.

"Go wait in the hallway while I perform my noon prayers."

She muttered a curse and shuffled to the hall in her bare feet. He followed and watched her lean against the wall and slide down to sit on her butt. Wrapping her arms around her knees, Eliza glanced up at Sharif. He appeared to be assessing if he could trust her to remain just outside his door. He turned back to his apartment and shut the door.

While she waited outside his apartment, she could hear him perform ablutions, the required ritual cleansing of the body prior to prayer. She shivered. Sounds of the day shift officers drifted up the stairs. They laughed at crude jokes.

She looked down at her cold bare feet, turning blue and leaving traces of her footprints in the linoleum's dust. The prayer stopped. When he let her back into his apartment, Captain Sharif had showered and dressed in his black uniform.

"Sit down," he said without eye contact. His gravelly voice and haggard expression betrayed his fatigue. As he continued to prepare for his night shift, his swift movements indicated that any attempt at conversation would be met with hostility.

The four gold bars on his shoulder boards and a gold badge on his black shirt's breast pocket confirmed his rank. The police crest on both shoulders depicted the Republic's flag – a royal blue background, with a circle of several small red diamonds representing each of the Republic's provinces and territories; a gold phoenix in the center of the circle spoke of the region's ancient culture. RIPT's citizens had adopted the motto, 'The phoenix never sleeps.'

Without turning toward her, he said, "I'll update you on your status after my meeting with the police chief. Until then, remain in this apartment. If you try to leave, several officers downstairs will toss you back here." His eyes flashed in her direction. "And they won't be nice. Is that clear?"

Eliza nodded. She considered offering an olive branch. "How are you?"

"Never mind." He turned away.

In his kitchen he strapped on his flak jacket and holstered his Glock handgun. She heard the thunk of metal plunging into the leather pouch. He tugged on his heavy army boots. Eliza heard the leather laces whip as he cinched his boots tight. Tension cut through the small space. She picked up one of his engineering magazines and flipped through pages of bridges being constructed.

He sounds really infuriated. Her heart kicked up its pace. In her mind, Eliza heard the ticking of a clock. Its alarm pinged as if time had run out. She swallowed what remained of the saliva in her mouth. Her gut clenched. *Perhaps the mayor decided to not wait for the terrorists' claim.*

Eliza gasped as his MP5 flew into her field of vision. She had noted that particular weapon behaved as an obedient dog, always within its master's reach. Captain Sharif gave it a final check. She heard levers smack and click. Her hands trembled.

Without a glance in her direction, he marched to the door and slammed it shut as he left.

She considered Sharif handsome. However, his permanent scowl had dampened any hope her feminine charms could entice him to disobey the mayor. He would not commit treason. *Anyway, it appears he's a devout Muslim. Intimacy with her - forbidden. Just my presence in his apartment gives Allah enough reason to damn his soul.*

Two hours later, a constable escorted her to Captain Sharif's office. Sharif's glum expression dashed her hope for freedom. She sat on the edge of the guest chair in front of his meticulously organized desk.

Bloody smudges on the wall reminded her of the woman she tried to save. Downy feathers from the bullet holes in her coat still fluttered on the floor. Some were trapped in the corners.

He sat in his old, wooden, swivel office chair taking a moment to observe her. He pulled off his dark aviator glasses and set them down. She noted his posture - dominant and rigid. And yet, his demeanor lacked arrogance.

The wooden chair Eliza sat in creaked as she leaned forward. Impatient and anxious, she trapped his eyes with a direct stare. He remained unaffected by her boldness. "Bad news? Give it to me straight."

She spoke in English. If the captain's men were in earshot, she would have spoken Arabic. At this moment, she needed to hear and speak in the language that would ensure no misunderstanding. The captain's English, even with his highbrow British accent, was a blessing.

His scowl deepened. "My government has confirmed you are to remain here until the organization responsible for the massacre has been identified and apprehended." The gruff tone of his deep voice echoed the frustration written on his face. "It is for your protection."

God, he thinks I'm stupid. "You expect me to believe that? I heard your boss. He's cooked up a goddamn cover-up. If you think ..."

His hand flew up to silence her outburst. He continued in a dispassionate tone. "Don't interrupt. You will continue to follow my rules. You must remain inside my apartment. Brief periods for walking within my compound is allowed but only after receiving permission from me or the day shift captain, Captain Khizar. You must wear a police uniform so that it appears you belong here. And the walk is only on condition a police officer is available to watch you."

"Captain, haven't the terrorists - ."

"You must be dressed modestly at all times. If you're taken outside these station walls, do not draw attention to yourself. And, do not speak to anyone regarding what happened to your companions. Is that clear, Miss MacKay?"

Eliza narrowed her eyes. "Quite clear. Surely I have the right to call a Canadian consulate or a lawyer?"

"No, not at this time. My government --" he paused and inhaled as if attempting to remain calm. "Chief Ganem's orders are absolute. It's for your safety."

"Right," she sneered. "I know your gutless boss is worried about protecting his ass," she said through clenched teeth. She regretted the disrespect. *I have to get along with this disagreeable man. My fate rests on his shoulders, and his conscience, if indeed he has a conscience. If I piss him off, he'll give me up to his boss.* Her fingers gripped the seat of her chair.

She decided to present a more cooperative demeanor and softened her face. "My apologies for my impatience, captain." Her voice sounded calm, confident. "Evidence will be forthcoming soon and this will be over. I mean, given the magnitude of the assault. Wouldn't you agree?"

"Not soon enough," he muttered and grabbed his pen.

The remark stung. She gasped. "Look, I'm trying my best. If your government had more integrity, you wouldn't have to share - ."

Captain Sharif tossed his pen at his keyboard. It ricocheted and fell at Eliza's feet. She picked it up and tossed it back toward him - more forcefully than intended. He grabbed it as it landed in his lap.

He placed the pen on his desk with great care, as though it might break. "Miss MacKay, your situation is dire. Do you understand that?" A distinctly ominous tone in his voice made her catch her breath.

Eliza stood, shoulders back and chin raised an inch. With firm, deliberate speech she said, "Yes, captain. I know your superiors want me dead." She glared at him. "They just don't want to get bloody. At least, not today." She turned, marched out of his office and returned to his apartment.

Chapter 7

She stood at the kitchen's window overlooking the park that thrived beyond the police compound walls. The beautiful scene of river, trees, and happy people became blurred by tears welling in her eyes. *Yes, it is becoming clear. I'm going to die in this miserable land.* Eliza winced at the memory of gunfire and screams. *Perhaps it would have been better if I had died with the others.*

Her vision blurred, seeing herself as a rose planted in a desert, thirsting for the caring touch of someone's hand.

She had been allowed to keep her MP3 player. Captain Sharif had locked up her international phone and iPad in his safe. The only person who might become alarmed with her absence was Mike, co-worker and best friend. But he wouldn't miss her for another three months. Too long.

She studied his apartment furnishings, hoping to get more clues to the character of her jailer. His furniture was sparse, old, functional and clean. The cream-colored plaster walls bore no pictures or photos, and the two windows had no curtains. Plain industrial greyish-blue linoleum covered the floor. A threadbare blue and gold paisley print sofa faced the south window. Sharif either had not enough money to purchase comfort, or preferred a modest lifestyle. Perhaps both.

A couple of officers came into the apartment and placed a cot in the sitting room. They set it down against the far wall, farthest away from Sharif's bedroom. It had a thin mattress and the grey pillow had lost much of the feather stuffing. The sofa served as a divider between her cot and the dinette. The intent, it appeared, was to give her a small measure of privacy.

45

Before leaving, they stopped to gawk at her. Their prying eyes made her shiver and turn away. They were Khizar's men, far different from Sharif's. His men hustled and paid no attention to her.

Before Sharif left to begin his night patrol with his men, he escorted her to a large metal shed. She had to trot to keep up with him as they traversed the dark compound. Inside were several vehicles and the operation's supply room. "Pick out three black shirts. I doubt we have pants to fit you."

She studied the untidy shelves. "It's going to take some time to find a shirt to fit me in this mess."

Sharif pulled an armful of unfolded shirts from the top shelf and placed them on a table. "See what you can find here. These should be the smaller sizes." He appeared nervous and avoided eye contact with her.

"I don't need small. My arms are long. And my shoulders' muscles ..." She shut up. He turned his back to her and paused, perhaps uncomfortable with the description of her personal form. "I mean, from lifting patients all day long." She pawed through the pile of shirts.

He went to another shelf. "You work only the day shift in your job?"

"No, four on four off, two days, two nights." She avoided mentioning that she hadn't been allowed to return to full duty. Not since the accident and her suicide attempts. "I've got dark blue pants in my luggage, and work boots."

"Fine. I'll get you one of our caps. Keep your hair concealed under the cap when you're outside. You need to appear like another police officer in case this compound is being monitored by satellite. My government doesn't allow drones in the city so no one is going to be looking at you close up." Sharif again found his captain's voice, harsh and abrupt.

Eliza pulled out three shirts that would fit. "These will do." Eliza pulled out three black police shirts. As she turned toward Captain Sharif, a black cap was clamped down on her head. Her head wound stung. "Ouch," she screamed and batted his hand away.

Sharif flinched. He reached to her, and then his arms recoiled. "I'm sorry. I forgot. Can I, er, fix …." The gruff voice transformed to gentle, caring concern.

"I know you meant no harm." She inhaled and gritted her teeth. It hurt like a bugger. His face showed a hint of regret. "Actually, having a cap to wear will help keep the gash clean. I better go put some ice on it." A slight trickle of blood appeared behind her ear.

Sharif pulled out a shirt still in its package. "This is clean. He unfolded it and began to place it over the wound. He stopped and handed the garment to Eliza. "Here, you better put pressure on it. I'll make it worse."

Her gift as a seer conflicted with her training in medical science. Except for looking for someone's lost dog, she'd brushed off the images, the momentary leap to another time or place. But in this moment, his tender compassion, she couldn't deny the shift into heightened awareness. The essence of the captain emerged – Hashim. She saw a man of wisdom and zest for life. His life story came to her in the span of a breath. She would remember only a fraction, but as the bond merged into her soul, her knees buckled.

"Perhaps you should sit," he said grasping her arm.

"No, I'm fine." His shoulders lingered just above her chin. The room's walls faded. Other barriers faltered. His eyes softened. A rush of something old surfaced in her – desire. Desire to be held, maybe more. *You can't let your guard down. You're his prisoner. Remember where you're at. His boss wants you dead.* She stiffened.

He patted her shoulder. "You don't deserve any of this. Thankfully, you're a strong woman." Grabbing a coat from a shelf and wrapping it around her shoulders, he said, "I pray Allah will help me find a way to return you safely to your family."

A faint tremor in his voice shook her. His body's warmth beckoned surrender. She caught a whiff of soap on his hands and his aftershave's spicy fragrance. Eliza stepped back. "There's ice in the kitchen." Her voice had softened more than intended. "Have a safe night, captain." She trotted back to the station. As she rushed into the apartment, she slammed the door shut and leaned against it. *What the hell just happened? This can't be. It'll just complicate this mess.*

Eliza cleaned her head wound, placed a sterile 4x4 on it and gingerly placed the cap on to hold the dressing in place. She shut off the apartment lights and stood at the window facing the compound's gate. Sharif had driven his SUV to the gate, waiting for it to open fully. An officer ran up to Sharif, then after a few minutes, he sprinted back to the station.

The overhead light illuminated his form behind the steering wheel. His face turned toward her window. She watched, wondering what kept him from passing through.

He remained parked at the gate for another minute. She watched him lean over his steering wheel, embrace it. He flipped his hat off his head and smacked it back down again. The SUV wheels kicked up grit as he sped through the gate.

Even as the gate closed behind the SUV, Eliza stood at the window. She realized that a part of her sat in his passenger seat.

The tremor in her chest, a warm fluttering of delicate wings, signaled a resurgence of feelings Eliza had entombed. Something unexpected rose from the ashes of her defeated heart. Eliza admonished her foolishness. *Don't be ridiculous. I'm just needing a friend, a hug. That's all. He's a cop. Loyal to his corrupt boss, so get your head back on straight. Stupid woman.*

The next day, after Sharif's meeting with the police chief, he gruffly herded her into his office. He slammed the door shut. "Sit." Sharif's fury surged on as he shoved his chair aside.

She remained near the door. Unable to move, her fear went into overdrive. *I've got to get out of here.* She heard men rushing past. *A firing squad? Now? Oh my God.* She gasped and swallowed the bitter taste in her mouth. *Can't run.* Feeling trapped, her PTSD asserted its torture. *No, no. Not going there. Stop. Please stop.* Flames rushed to engulf her two boys. She cried as their screams faded with the roar of the fire. Frantically, she searched for the release from the shoulder harness. There was no escape from behind the wheel of her destroyed van. *Oh God, please no. No, No!*

"Sit down." A hand gripped her shoulder. Shoved her into a chair.

Pain and shock overwhelmed the trigger. She wondered if she had given away her secret. *Did I scream? Did I* - she shuddered. If he witnessed her in the throes of her mental illness, he'd abandon her, like almost everyone else had done.

"You don't need to push, captain." She massaged her shoulder. "Next time say 'please'." His demeanor didn't indicate that he'd seen her behave strangely. *Perhaps he hid his feelings well. Or, maybe the vision had ended before the ranting and running could begin.* She breathed a sigh of relief.

Sharif sat down and stared at her for a moment. "Miss MacKay, normally I don't discuss investigations or my findings. In your case today, I'm making an exception. But only so you understand how vital it is that you obey my rules. Understood?" His eyes narrowed.

Eliza nodded.

"The United States president's security agent has arrived and met with our president. President Najeeb has sold them on the prevailing theory that the Americans are being held for ransom."

Eliza groaned. "Captain, those poor people at home, the families are going through torture. Not knowing anything, if their loved ones are suffering, nothing. This cover-up must stop. It's inhuman."

"I'll handle this, Miss MacKay. If I do my job right, I'll find a way to restore my government's honor and get you out of RIPT. You just do as you're told."

"You can't do this on your own, captain." She stood and moved away from his desk. For the first time, Eliza realized the true depth of her predicament – hopeless. Feeling lightheaded, she had to grab the back of her chair. Her heart raced. "This is beyond you, even your city's entire police force."

She sat down again, trembling. "I've been naive. I thought the terrorists would claim the killing, then the focus would be on them and I could go home." She looked away toward a blank wall. "It's hopeless," she said, sounding breathless.

"Not yet. You have no experience in a country that has had to endure the worst treachery. My sergeant and his men are a special force, trained to deal with hard-core criminals. Whatever it takes, those responsible for the massacre will pay."

Eliza shivered. She couldn't bear the thought of more people dying because of her. Not again.

"Captain, I witnessed the skill of you and your men. I know you personally have been threatened by the mayor. Please promise me you and your men won't risk your life because of me." Sharif frowned. Before he could respond, she said, "I have no family, no one waiting for me to come home." A lump in her throat nearly choked the sound of her voice. She fought the tears welling in her eyes.

Emotions flickered on the captain's face. Eliza's paramedic career made her adept at reading people's state of mind. She noted Sharif's moment of annoyance morph into shock followed by a hint of sympathy.

He took a deep breath, turned to his computer and seemed to be focused on completing a task.

"Are you listening to me, captain? Promise you won't get heroic or do something stupid." She tried to sound firm. Even so, the tremor in her voice betrayed her fears.

Sharif moved the keyboard aside and looked at her. A grin had edged its way onto his face. His eyes shone with merriment.

"Me, do something stupid? Why, my dear Miss MacKay, I do believe you've just insulted my good character." He lifted his eyebrows, inviting her to challenge his dry humor.

Eliza greedily clung to his cheery expression. The warmth in his dark eyes wrapped a soft blanket around her shoulders. She opened her mouth to speak but knew words would have sullied the moment.

For a several heartbeats, they looked at each other as if seeing the other for the first time. The late afternoon sun streamed through his open window, casting a warm glow on the space between Eliza and her keeper. Sharif's computer hummed. The small fan on a side table whirred. The leather of Sharif's gun shoulder holster squeaked when he leaned forward, resting his elbows on the desk. Eliza's chair creaked as she relaxed into its warm wood.

I have to stop this, this, whatever this is. It will get both of us killed. Especially him. If he's killed, I don't have a chance alone against the mayor.

The sound of heavy boots with an uneven gait heading toward the office door interrupted Eliza's intent to steer the conversation back to the cover-up.

"Captain Khizar has returned from his day shift. Go," Sharif demanded, waving his hand at her as if she were a disobedient dog. The scowl returned, and brought with it lines around his mouth that marred his handsome face.

Chapter 8

Day three, Sharif met with Sergeant Muntazar at the airport. Within five minutes he discovered Eliza's true identity. Sharif held his breath as he gazed at the monitor. Half the screen displayed her photo, the other half displayed her passport information – the vital details confirming her citizenship and birth date, July 8, 2011. He stared at the name, Elizabeth Leigh Ramsay.

Sharif frowned, his jaw clenched. *I've been deceived by that woman.*

"Print a copy of that document for me."

Back at his office, Sharif Googled 'Elizabeth Ramsay.' He expected to see the usual Facebook account. In a flash, pages of news reports dating back four years appeared.

The first entry, dated December 22, 2043, caught his eye. It read, 'Spectacular Crash on Jasper Highway. RCMP closed the Yellowhead Highway near Jasper for twenty-four hours investigating the tragic head-on traffic accident.'

In seconds the full report came up. A black and white photo revealed the shocking devastation. A fierce inferno raged, consuming several mangled vehicles strewn in chaos across a two-lane highway. Thick black smoke threatened to smother fleeing bystanders. The caption read, 'Tanker crashed head-on, killing eighteen and injuring six.'

Sharif's curiosity surged. He clicked on a link. A photo popped up. Eliza MacKay sat with two small boys and a handsome man. The caption read, 'Elizabeth Ramsay is the sole survivor of her family. Her husband, two sons, parents, and siblings died in the fiery crash on the Yellowhead Highway December 21st near the town of Jasper. She remains in critical condition at the University Hospital.'

He stared at the image and soon realized he had been holding his breath. Taking a deep breath, he cleared his throat and resumed his investigation. The report continued, including a link to a passerby's video of the scene. A line of caution read, 'Viewing is not recommended for children or those who are sensitive to graphic images.'

He hesitated. *I don't give a damn about her past.* The callous thought recharged his sense of guilt at who he became at times. His sergeant, Abdul-Muqtadir, had recently barked out, "You're getting to be just as big a prick as Mayor Aamir." Aside from the overt insubordination, the worst part was being compared to the mayor. If the sergeant hadn't also been his best friend, he'd have fired him, right after knocking him flat on his ass. *Perhaps she's got secrets I should know about. I'd rather be armed and ready. Liars can't be trusted.* He clicked the play button.

In a few seconds, the video began, erratically panning a portion of a two-lane highway, snow banks flanking the road. Rugged snow-covered mountains bordered the background. A jagged line of vehicles appeared to have slid off the road in a desperate attempt to avoid collision. Ice on the road reflected the horror ahead of them.

Sharif viewed the remainder of the video. He saw Eliza, her face bloody, appearing trapped in the driver's seat. He listened to her gut-wrenching screams as she watched her two boys die in an inferno. The horror shocked him. He replayed the sound of her screams. Saw her desperate struggle, grasping the steering wheel for leverage, ramming her shoulder into the door. And then, her entire being seemed to explode. Wild with rage, she clawed her face and neck and quickly became unconscious. The segment lasted eight seconds.

Without thinking, he returned to the family photo. He noted her smile, her eyes, bright and open. He found himself smiling back at her image, and then gave his unprofessional diversion a kick. *Perhaps that accident destroyed more than her family. Maybe that's why she's been able to cope with the massacre. She's turned off any sense of loss. What if she's unstable?* For a minute he digested the risk he was taking by protecting her from the mayor. *She could be too much trouble. Maybe even put my family at risk.*

He continued reading more media reports detailed the ongoing lawsuits and the fuel company's culpability. Billions of dollars in settlements were anticipated. The last article reported the first anniversary date of the 'Jasper Mile of Hell', the adopted name of the accident. Elizabeth Ramsay was noted as being 'absent due to illness.' Sharif groaned.

Ω

Feigning sleep, Eliza listened to the sound of Sharif making coffee in his kitchen at the end of his shift. A breeze from the open window carried the scent of his clothes toward her. The distinct smell of gun-fired residue and blood made her gag. She decided not to wait for him to kick the bed to wake her. She got up and dressed in the bathroom. Without saying a word, Eliza zipped out to the hallway.

She listened as the ancient city of Samarra woke up to harmonic sounds. The city came to life each morning at six o'clock with the first call to prayer: *Fajr*, the prayer before sunrise. The haunting musical sound of the Muezzin called the devoted. Dogs, roused by the earnest supplication, barked. Even Eliza, who had no religious convictions, sat in quiet contemplation, deeply moved. She stilled her mind's chatter and waited.

Waited for a thread of wisdom to be shared by The One Most High. Waited for merciful revelation of why she had survived and her little boys had suffered and died. Waited alone in the heavy silence.

With each of the four daily prayers, Eliza had watched in awe as the city's ambiance shifted during prayer. Even within the compound walls, the Muslim faithful halted their activities for prayers. An air of tranquility was palpable. Even those who appeared less devout and ignored the religious practice slowed their pace. The

Muezzin's melodious voice reminded the devout of their connection with Allah, of the teachings of Islam's prophet, Muhammad.

She had learned that everyone - regardless of rank, wealth, sins, or honor - stood shoulder to shoulder and intoned their praises to Allah, the forgiver of sins, the lord of peace and harmony. Women were segregated to the rear of the prayer hall, the *musallah* – for sake of modesty, Eliza had been told.

She eavesdropped on Sharif's prayers. The change in his demeanor struck her. He became like a child singing songs of praise to an adoring father. His devotion to Islam and the teachings of the prophet Muhammad appeared to be based on genuine love, rather than fear of Allah's punishment.

When Sharif had gone to bed, she listened and watched as the city's soul burst forth. From her high vantage point, she could see the insane rush of traffic, businessmen competing for a cab, and women ushering their children to school. The vibrancy of the scene reminded Eliza of the excitement of Cairo. Old men bravely pushed carts of vegetables and fruit, others skillfully herded their goats among the passing vehicles. An air of expectancy, anticipation, even urgency in the way the citizens walked and talked spoke of their eagerness to get on with day.

She opened the kitchen window which offered a view of the city. A few blocks away, a wide river rushed toward the Persian Gulf, a few thousand miles to the south. A treed park bordered its banks. She spotted a soccer field, possibly a school, and a two-story mall. Tall office buildings and luxury hotels in the distance dotted the downtown section. The four minarets of the city's ancient Guardian Mosque reached high into the morning's tangerine sky.

In so many ways, Samarra appeared like every other urban center stuck in the 1990's, with a strong agricultural element. Adapting over thousands of years, the city had endured countless invasions and survived as a phoenix rising from the ashes time and time again. The land possessed a soul. It emanated an energy of an untouchable guru – indifferent and yet passionate, unconquerable and yet benevolent.

Eliza felt a connection to the land, its history, and its people. It was more than the exotic culture's sensory seduction of spices, architecture, and mystical landscape. As the human race migrated out of Africa thousands of years ago, tribes had settled in the Middle East. Perhaps the ancient bones of her ancestors lay in unmarked graves beneath her feet. She sent a prayer to the old ones, just in case they were open to favor her with a miracle.

Eliza began making breakfast. She placed the frying pan on the little stove, careful to not wake her keeper. She made scrambled eggs with peppers and onions mixed in. Aromatic coffee infused a feeling of home.

Sharif had bought her a jar of blueberry jam. "For good behavior," he had said as he set the glass jar onto the old wooden table with a smack, and left.

A white cloth covered the small worn table. Well, it used to be white. It looked as though it had been used for multiple tasks, perhaps wiping up spills from the floor and soaking up blood from a wound. It appeared clean.

The aromas of street food vendors blended with the car exhaust, her eggs, and the blueberry jam on her bread. Eliza settled in for another long day keeping her distance from Sharif, and dodging her PTSD triggers.

She glanced around the room. It was getting smaller. Her heart pounded. She forced her shoulders to relax. *I've got to get out of here*, she thought as she forced down a mouthful of her breakfast. Yesterday she had pressed Sharif for time outside. His reply remained steadfast, "Not today." When she had continued to push for more freedom, he threatened to put her in a regular cell and build a cement wall to keep her out of sight.

Over the past four days, she had developed a routine to pass the time. Yoga, meditation, snack, repeat. However, today she had reached the outer limits of controlling the PTSD, triggered by the walls closing in.

While Sharif slept, she planned to *inform* the day shift officer, Captain Khizar, she was going for a walk. She shivered.

When Sharif had introduced him to her, Khizar barely acknowledged her. She had detected the smirk on the senior officer's thin face. Her intuition emphasized the need to tread carefully around the officer who walked with a limp.

Eliza wore the required black uniform, put on her polished work boots, and pushed her hair up under the black cap. At the bottom of the stairs she listened for sounds of the men. She approached Khizar's office and sighed with relief to find he had left. Going down a short hallway, Eliza turned right towards the crew quarters' door. She hesitated, listening for sounds that indicated the mood of the cops.

Belly laughter and smacks against the wall made the door shudder. The men were absorbed in their amusement and might not be interested in challenging her request.

Eliza knocked on the door, careful to sound neither cowardly, nor aggressive. The door was swung open by a constable.

She held her breath. Skilled at hiding her emotions, Eliza looked into the officer's eyes. The officer relaxed a little. An intimidating smirk grew on his face. Three other men in the room gathered behind him.

The day sergeant, a heavy-set man, came forward and said in a trivializing manner, "The whore is mine. Leave her to me."

The sergeant sauntered up to her. His eyes lit up like those of a child about to open a birthday gift. He lowered his gaze to her dark boots, and then raised his focus to her mid-section, then to her chest. Finally, he looked at her eyes.

Eliza did not change her expression from that of bland indifference to his suggestive piercing stare. He had called her a whore, but she repressed the impulse to admonish him. She resisted the urge to put her hands on her hips. That would be sexually suggestive and body language might defeat her faster than the wrong choice of words.

"My apologies for the interruption," she said in Arabic, her voice trembling despite her resolve. "I'm going for a walk." She swung around toward the exit door.

The officers chuckled as the sergeant stepped forward and blocked her. His face came uncomfortably close to hers. He spoke with a grin, accompanied by the rhythmic flexing and gyrating of his hips.

"Welcome. Come in." The three men cheered as the sergeant grabbed her shirt and pulled her into the room.

Eliza froze. The four men closed in around her. She gasped as they taunted her, touching her shoulders, her hips. She shuddered as one of the men grabbed her hat and flung it to the side.

"No," she cried out in Arabic. "Captain Sharif will -." The sergeant slapped her face hard, sending her spinning against a muscular man. His hand pulled on her long hair and grabbed her belt, trapping her against his body.

Eliza shrieked as the sergeant took her shirt into his fist and in one swift move, ripped it away from her and flung it to the floor. Her white cotton tank top clung to her body like a second skin. The men gawked at the curves of her breasts.

She dug her elbow into the cop's midsection. His grip on her hair released enough for her to leap for the door. "Let me go!"

More hands clamped onto her body.

"No!" Eliza shouted in Arabic. She reached to grasp someone's throat. Her legs trembled, barely holding her body upright.

The sergeant gave the belt a firm yank and slipped it out of the belt loops. The men cheered. He pulled on the waist band. It held fast but scraped her skin. She shrieked in pain as she fell to the floor. Eliza screamed as he pinned her to the floor with his knee.

"Quiet," he growled. A large sweaty hand covered her mouth.

The rest of the men pounced on her, grabbing her arms and legs. Before they got a firm grip on her, she twisted and squirmed enough that someone lost his hold over her mouth. Eliza let out another ear-piercing scream. Her self-defense training evaporated.

"That's enough," one said. "Let her go, sergeant. Sharif will hear her and kill us." Two men let go of their grip on her legs.

"Fuck Sharif. Besides, Captain Khizar has plans to take Sharif's head," said the sergeant. "Shut her up!"

Kicking and biting, she escaped their grip, and once more bounded to the door. Just as she flung the door open, a man grabbed her by the hair, and she screamed again. "If Sharif can have her, so can we!"

Strong hands threw her to the floor again. She screamed until her lungs burned. A hand clamped down over her mouth, pushing her lips hard against her teeth. She tasted blood on her tongue. She kicked and twisted. Her muffled cries and tears seemed to excite the men. Their hostility escalated.

"Hold the bitch still," someone hollered. A hand groped her chest, squeezing her breast. She gasped at the crushing weight of a man on her legs attempting to pull her pants down. The band around her waist ripped. A knife flashed over her mid-section.

In one last effort, Eliza opened her mouth wide. The hand slipped between her teeth. Like a vice, she clamped down on the fingers and bit hard. He hollered a curse and yanked his hand from her teeth. She took a deep breath and screamed till her throat hurt. A rag was shoved into her mouth.

The men paused as the sound of footsteps thundered down the stairs.

The men gasped. Their hands remained clenched onto her as if welded to her skin. The door flung open. It crashed against the wall. Captain Sharif rushed through the doorway, wearing only his boxers. His face twisted in rage as his raised his handgun toward the men. They threw themselves onto the floor and begged for mercy.

Eliza pulled the rag out of her mouth and scrambled on all fours to a far corner. She tried to stand but crumpled to the floor. Panting and crying, she crossed her arms across her chest.

"What are you idiots doing? Get up," Sharif roared. "Up against the wall before I kill the lot of you swine!"

They scrambled to form a line in front of the captain. Each one got a dose of the disgust on the captain's face. The men stood rigid, gasping for air. Sweat rolled down their faces. Sharif paced in front of the sergeant and his three men. He glanced back at her.

"Get your shirt on!"

Eliza reached for the torn shirt and put it on. Rage fought for dominance over her shaky legs.

"Get out, MacKay!" Sharif's deep voice echoed his loathing.

She raced to the exit door, flung it open, and fell down the six steps.

Reeling with shock, she used the exterior wall of the building to guide her away from the front door. She ran, blinded by tears, and staggered around a corner.

The blood-stained compound wall loomed fifty feet in front of her. In an instant, ghostly screams and unrelenting gunfire pulled her back into the horror.

Traces of bullet holes and dark red splatter stains on the walls retold the story in gruesome detail. Eliza slumped against the station's wall, slid to the ground and squeezed her eyes shut. She clenched her fists as her mind catapulted to the night she arrived four days ago in the captain's compound.

She huddled against the cement wall. Her body ached. Bruises and scratches were on her arms and legs, golden tangles hung in her face. She clenched her fists and fought back the need to release a scream of anger and frustration.

Out of the corner of her eye, she noticed the captain's hurried approach. He had dressed in casual clothes, khaki pants and white short-sleeved shirt left untucked, only partially buttoned. Eliza had difficulty reading the man, his eyes hidden behind the dark aviator sunglasses. He stood in front of her and motioned for her to stand.

"Get up," he said, glancing in her direction.

She braced for a stern reprimand and punishment. *Get up and bow to the friggin' iceman*, she thought. *I haven't had a good night's sleep. I've been ordered about, shut up in a small apartment, sneered at, and treated like I've got the plague. Then, being treated like a whore this morning? Unforgivable. Damn!* She stood.

Her torn shirt fell open, revealing more than the captain, or any decent Muslim man should see. *Too damn bad!* His gaze appeared in the vicinity of her chest.

Once Sharif was thoroughly tormented, she tied the shirt tails at her midriff, closing off her cleavage.

Sharif turned away. "Come with me," he ordered and headed toward the arch-ribbed building.

"Come with me, *please*," she snapped, remaining steadfast.

He turned and looked at her for a moment. Briefly, she saw a glimmer of a smile. Just a hint of his white teeth and the softening of his face.

The captain stood a good three inches taller than her five foot nine inches. His cropped, curly dark brown hair and stubble style beard defined his strong facial bones. His eyes were obsidian. During the night, when he did not wear the aviator sunglasses, she had discovered the black depths were as soft as velvet.

"Okay, Canadian, come with me, please," he said, nodding his head.

Standing within the massive overhead doorway, she saw the purpose of the building. The domed steel building was two stories high. It served as the city's storage of police operation and administration supplies. The captain led her into a cavernous garage. Vehicles were parked on each side along the length of the walls. She saw five half-ton trucks, a compact excavator, a tow truck and a trailer with two motorcycles, a white van, and two quads. Storage rooms, as well as a staircase to the second level, were at the rear.

Sharif grabbed a couple of grey, metal folding chairs and set them up within the shade a few feet inside the building. He took his sunglasses off, slipped them into his shirt pocket and waited near his chair. "Sit down. Please." He face remained impassive.

After moving her chair a little farther away, she sat rigid, arms crossed.

His shoulders sagged as he sat and leaned forward. "Let me begin by saying that the attack on you this morning is unacceptable."

Her eyes narrowed. "Unacceptable? Bloody hell, those men should be behind bars by now, captain!"

"They regret their actions."

"Damn them," she growled. Frustration exploded. Eliza jumped up and flung her chair through the air. It smashed into the wall and collapsed to the cement floor. The crash sent echoes of the collision throughout the high ceiling. A couple of officers ran to the open overhead door.

Sharif stood up, waved them off and turned back to her. "Calm down, MacKay," he ordered.

She glared at him. "How dare you! After all I've had to endure since I arrived in this god-forsaken country?" Her hands tightened into fists. "I don't accept their regrets." Her rage soared. She kicked his chair and sent it tumbling across the cement floor. "Friggin' hell!"

The captain ran his fingers through his hair. "I'm sorry for any harm done to you. Were you injured?"

"Bruises and loss of respect for your officers." She thrust a fist toward him. "I'm a dog that's been kicked hard and nearly killed. I'm at the end of my leash and about to turn mean if my situation doesn't improve right now," she said, stabbing a finger toward the floor.

"First, those are Captain Khizar's men. Sergeant Abdul-Muqtadir and his men will never attack you. Secondly, I'd rather you remain the calm, intelligent, and rational woman I have observed."

"I'm long past being calm! Trust for you or anyone else here is gone," Eliza shouted, thrusting her hand in the air as if to swat a fly away. She kicked a stone on the floor. "It's just a matter of time, isn't it? Till I'm killed." Tears blurred her vision. She turned away. She hated shedding tears in public.

"Not while I breathe." Sharif retrieved the chairs and set them up again. "Miss MacKay, sit." He shrugged. "Please."

Defeated, she wiped her face. She hesitated to look into the dark eyes. She had no energy left to confront his scowl. Even so, she could not resist searching for a glimmer of hope. Eliza lifted her face and looked at him. "What does it matter anyway?"

Hashim Sharif hesitated. "It matters because you're better than those men."

His hands lightly rested on her shoulders. She clung to the warmth. Was his intention to offer brief, non-committal comfort, or was it to remind her of his control over her? She hesitated, eyebrows knitted, and then jerked away from his touch and sat down.

Sharif shifted in his chair, pausing as if searching for words. "Captain Khizar's men had assumed that we are intimate. I've set them straight on that matter. It won't happen again." He stood, reasserting his authority. "I cannot arrest them. Mayor Aamir will not allow the case to be heard in court. It would require revealing your presence in this compound and that would lead to the cover-up."

She stood up to him. "A damn goat has more rights than I have."

He shook his head and gave her a hesitant smile. "Never was good at herding goats."

Sharif's smile disarmed her anger. *Friggin' hell, why I can't stay mad at this man for more than ten minutes? Damn infuriating beast.* No other eyes had ever made her lose track of her argument. Not even William's.

"I have an idea. Follow me. Please," he added. He led her to the rear of the apparatus floor and into the uniform storage room. It looked more chaotic than on her first visit. Clothing lay everywhere, in heaps on the floor, or stuffed into a shelf.

Sharif pulled out an armful of shirts. "Replace your torn shirt. And, you need a helmet and a flak jacket. Over there," he said, pointing to a smaller box, "Get a knit skull cap for yourself. It'll keep you warmer at night, if I need to put you somewhere else."

Eliza's eyebrows shot up. "Put me where?"

Sharif waved his hand in a dismissive manner. "Just a precaution in case this station is no longer safe."

"And you think I need a flak jacket?" She frowned. "You're expecting trouble?"

Sharif grinned. "I always expect trouble. That's why I'm still alive." He grabbed a helmet off a shelf and gingerly placed it on her head. It tilted and slipped off. He chuckled as he caught it and handed it to her. "Maybe your head is crooked."

She lifted her chin, reclaiming her composure. "And where do I get my weapons?"

Sharif laughed. "In your dreams, Canadian. I don't trust you that far." He headed to the door. "I'm going to try to get some sleep before my night shift. You can take your time here. If you're bored, you can organize this room. Khizar's men won't bother you again."

"Wait. There's something you should know. Those men, they said something. Said Khizar has plans to take your head."

Sharif shook his head. "Him and a few others, miss. Just keep out of his way."

Alone, Eliza slumped to the floor. She hugged her knees close to her chest and closed her eyes. *I have to trust him. He's my only hope.*

She rummaged through the boxes. She found a flak jacket that fit her. One box appeared to have multiple used uniforms tossed into it. While examining the contents her hand struck a small object. The shape and texture was familiar. "Oh my God, it can't be." She pulled the object out so fast it flew high above her and back into her clawing hands. Someone had dropped their cell phone into the box.

Her hands shook as she hit the power button. It buzzed to life. *Will it make international calls?* She opened the supply room door and listened. No sounds other than a couple of men working outside the building.

As she keyed in her boss's phone number, pangs of guilt stung. She hit 'send.' She might trust Captain Sharif. He had been the epitome of a professional and a gentleman. She liked him. *Ringing.* She held her breath. . *Ringing. Damn!* She realized how much she needed him to trust her.

If he discovered she had made a phone call, all trust would be sacrificed. *He'll abandon me.* Ringing. *Without the captain I won't survive a week. And Captain Sharif will pay a heavy price if I escape. Perhaps his children....* With a slam she closed the phone before her boss answered. *I can't risk harm to his children.* He had briefly mentioned his children a day ago.

She tucked the phone under her shirt. *The dragon doesn't need to know I have an insurance option.*

Chapter 9

Sharif's sergeant interviewed the police officer originally scheduled to drive the bus. He had been brought in to study photos of known criminals but failed to identify the man who took over his duty. Either the killer-driver was not local, or the scheduled officer's silence had been bought.

Sergeant Omar Abdul-Muqtadir searched their police fingerprint database, photographs, and profiles. Nothing provided a hint of who organized the assault on the Americans.

Captain Sharif's efforts to connect with at least one informant had failed. His men had grabbed known kill-for-hire vermin, threw them into the station's interrogation room, and drilled them for hours. All they got were bruised knuckles, spit in their faces, and a bloodied floor.

When asked if they had information about the disappearance of the Americans, their eyes widened. "Don't know nothing," they muttered, then shouted, "Don't know nothing what you're talking about."

Sharif changed his tactics with the last detainee, Prince. He grabbed Prince by his dirty coat. "I'll spread the word you talked." He threw him across the room. "I'm done with you. Get the fuck out of my station. Next stop, the fucking morgue."

Sharif headed to the door. "Got no time for liars." He opened the door and hollered as if talking to another officer. "Get the police chief. We've got an informant. Prince is talking his head off." Sharif stepped back into the room, chuckling. "Word is going out you snitched. The man I'm looking for will take your head off. Shouldn't be too long. Maybe by morning?"

The frightened man sneered at Sharif. "You fucking prick." Prince spat a wad of yellow saliva at Sharif but missed. "That's against the law."

"You assholes know I don't play by the rules." Sharif shrugged, letting the man know it was of no consequence to him if a drug dealer was murdered. "Maybe we can stop the killers before they cut down to your jugular." Sharif released the handcuffs. "You can run, but my men will know where you go. You'll make perfect bait." Sharif taunted the man. "The dirt out there watches who gets pulled into my station."

Instead of running to the exit, the man paced. His eyes darted about as if watching a ping pong game. He gritted his teeth and sneered at Sharif. "You fucking bastard. Someday ..." he muttered, with his lips curled in hatred and his fist raised. He rammed the side of his fist into the cement wall. "Look, I know two things." His voice trembled. "The Americans are dead. The killers are not from RIPT. That's all I know." Prince retreated to a corner, squatted down to the floor and wrapped his arms around his knees. "Don't know nothing else."

Sharif pulled him up and threw him into a chair. "Now tell me something I don't already know."

His prisoner sprung out of the chair, "First, you stop that shit from getting out to the streets."

"I keep my sources confidential. Otherwise -." He motioned again to the chair.

The man sat and shifted away from Sharif's stare. "Sheikh drove the bus. There was a screw up. The bus arrived here too late."

"Too late for what?"

The man looked back at Sharif and snorted. "Too late to kill you."

"Where is this man, Sheikh?" Sharif suppressed his shock.

"Dead, I think."

"Were you part of the plan to attack the Americans?"

The prisoner shifted and edged away from Sharif. "No. We were told to draw the attention of your cops away from this compound. Keep the patrol busy with minor stuff. We didn't know what for, but we were paid well enough to make it worth risking arrest. And the bus was to get here before you left for patrol. Before eight. You're always here until eight."

"Who gave those orders?"

The man crossed his arms. "The lawyer, Drummer."

Sharif eyes widened. *Drummer, my most reliable informant - party to the massacre?* He wondered if his informant had been killed. Since the day after the massacre, Sharif had hunted him. Tonight, he had to find him. He locked up his prisoner and rushed to his SUV.

A few miles outside his district, Sharif pulled up to a service station. A red neon sign blinked 'Closed.' He rolled on quietly to the back alley. Blue shadows snaked across his dash. He paused, checking his rear view and side mirrors.

"Dispatch, this is Sharif."

"Go ahead, sir."

He gave them his coordinates. "If I don't report back by midnight, send in back-up. Sharif, out." If Drummer failed to show up this time within two hours, either the man was dead or had dared to renege on their agreement.

He rolled further down the alley, stopped, and lowered his window. The cold air carried the sound of an argument coming from a back yard. Tall grass and a broken wood fence concealed the gang arguing over payment for crack. He moved on and stopped again. He held his breath, listening for footsteps. The oily smell of his SUV's engine mixed in with the foul smell of garbage decomposing in the alley. His heart kicked up its pace.

His two-way radio crackled. He turned it off and continued to roll down to the next intersection, across the street, and passed a vacant lot. Tall weeds whispered against his SUV's black paint.

Sharif shut off his headlights. Dilapidated houses and apartment buildings on either side of the alley appeared sullen, indifferent to the lost souls that slept on their rat-infested floors.

He turned right, then parked tight up against an old cement blast wall on the left and waited. His eyes darted to his mirrors, scanning for the slightest hint of motion. A single story house on the right belonged to Drummer – one of his satellite offices.

Drummer was his street name. For ten years he had been the undisputed boss of the city's black market. His wealth allowed him to live alongside Mayor Aamir's luxury estate. Sharif shivered at the thought of Drummer's close relationship with his devious boss.

Sharif pulled his sidearm from his chest holster. His MP5 submachine gun rested in its bracket between the seats. As minutes dragged on, the night swallowed Sharif into its belly. An hour later, he caught himself nodding off.

He bolted up straight. Someone had tried to open the passenger door. A sliver of light passed across the rear view mirror. A boot crunched on the grit behind his SUV. Expensive aftershave wafted through his open driver's window.

Sharif grabbed his pistol. He held his breath, waited for a whisper of a sound. His cellphone buzzed. "Shit." The display illuminated, '*Caller Unknown.*' He gambled on the distraction and accepted the call.

Text came up. 'Open the fucking door. D'

Sharif glanced to his mirrors and texted his reply, 'Say please, asshole. S.'

'FY ... please. D.'

Sharif snickered and texted his reply, 'Not in this lifetime.' He adjusted the interior lighting so it wouldn't come on when the door opened. He hit his door unlock button and squeezed his gun's trigger, just in case Drummer had had a change of allegiance.

The passenger door swung open. A well-dressed man in his fifties faced Sharif and then checked the back of the SUV's interior. He climbed into the front passenger seat and eased the door shut.

"This better be worth my trouble. Saw you parked here on my monitor at home. Drove half way across town." Drummer presented the image of a professional businessman, clean shaven and trimmed greying hair, but his haggard look and blood shot eyes gave away his criminal lifestyle. "What you want?" His words slurred.

Sharif eased his grip on his gun. "Been looking for you." He pasted a worried look on his face, gestured with his hand to his heart. "Thought maybe you had suffered some misfortune."

The man in the tailored steel-blue business suit chuckled. "I'm touched. When did you start with the good manners?" He tugged at the cuffs of his white shirt and loosened his gold tie.

"Canadian woman is teaching me how to be polite."

Drummer snorted. "Boring Canadians. Can't you do any better?"

"Actually, she's nice. However, she doesn't like me."

Drummer laughed. "Maybe she's got some smarts. But teach you to be nice? Ha!" He rubbed a jagged scar on his right cheek. "Still can't talk right. Therapist says that nerve will never heal. Bastard! I'd still be a lawyer if you hadn't shot me."

"What you mean is you'd still be a lawyer for the local mafia if I hadn't caught you killing my prisoner. Still got your fingerprints on that knife. Just because you killed the snake I was after, doesn't make it legal. Murder file stays open. Ready to talk?"

"What do you want to know?"

"Simple. Who killed the Americans?"

"Don't know."

Sharif grabbed a handful of his fancy suit. "If I hear 'don't know' one more time tonight, I'll hand over that file and knife to the chief. Talk. I know you told the local criminals to draw the police away from my compound. Who gave you that order?"

"Look, a stranger came to my home, put an envelope full of money into my hand, and walked back to his rented car. Never said a word, never saw him again. A note gave instructions what to do and when. Like you said, I was to create some heat away from your compound."

"I want that note."

"You think I'd keep evidence around? I didn't know what was going down. Got equivalent to what I used to make as a lawyer in five years. Just knew it was from someone with deep pockets."

"And you didn't send me a warning."

"We never talked about fringe benefits." His voice had a menacing tone.

"You bastard, you hoped I'd be killed." Sharif harnessed his rage. "One more time. Who wanted the Americans dead?"

Drummer rubbed his fist across his lips. He exhaled and shook his head. "What I do know is that the orders did not originate in RIPT. I suspect Egypt. Writing on note had Egyptian style of writing. Did some snooping of my own. Don't like doing business with ghosts."

"And?"

"Look, anyone who even asks questions about this ends up dead. I stopped asking."

Sharif nodded. "Dead, I understand. Fifteen innocent Americans were murdered. Right now there are thirty-five American children who have lost one parent, three lost both parents, thirty parents who lost a child. Three of my officers were murdered. Combined, thirteen local children have lost their father. Shall I go on?"

Drummer fidgeted with his tie.

Sharif pressed harder. "How many grandchildren do you have?"

Drummer pulled out a flask from inside his coat and popped the top. Vapors of liquor escaped. After a couple of swallows, Drummer went on. "An associate told me something. He said, 'Watch out for Black Ice.'"

"Where do I find this Black Ice?"

"Not local." Drummer opened the door and stepped out. "See you in hell."

Sharif returned to his station. He burst through the front doors and discovered Sergeant Muqtadir and two of his men back early from their patrol. At one in the morning they should be checking out the hot spots between responding to calls. Instead, they were in the staff lounge with a fellow officer sitting in a chair, everyone's eyes on Eliza. The pale officer grimaced, and his sweaty brow indicated a high level of pain. "What's going on here," Sharif called out.

The two standing men bolted to attention. Eliza continued to inspect the injured officer's bare arm and chest. Sergeant Omar Abdul-Muqtadir marched up to Sharif.

"Corporal here fell down into a deep cellar. Miss MacKay says she thinks his shoulder is dislocated."

Sharif moved closer to observe MacKay. She pulled out a vial and syringe from her medical kit. When he saw the needle, he retreated back a half step. "What are you doing, miss?"

She answered in Arabic, focused only on drawing medication from the vial. "Sergeant Omar asked for my help. I'm going to give your officer something for pain. Then I'll reduce his dislocated shoulder." She took a moment to look at Sharif. "He'll not be able to perform his usual police duties for a few days." She turned to her patient.

Sharif momentarily became mute. Miss MacKay had usurped his authority. "At ease," he said to his men. "Miss MacKay, do you require assistance from these officers?"

The men again gathered around their injured colleague. She turned to the captain. "I might need their help. Not sure if I can reduce this dislocation myself or if he needs transport to the hospital." She held the needle up.

Sharif eyed the business end of the needle. He swallowed what remained of scant saliva in his mouth. "Fine." He turned away and headed to his office. Sounds of chuckling followed him to his chair. It had become common knowledge the courageous Captain Sharif paled at the sight of needles.

Curiosity got the better of him. When he figured the injection part was over, he returned to the lounge. The officer still appeared pale but in much less pain. Eliza had begun to maneuver his right arm. Sergeant Muqtadir supported the patient's wrist.

She shifted the elbow away from his side. Carefully, she rotated his hand behind his head. Once the arm was over the level of the shoulder, she eased his hand behind his head.

With the affected arm in place, Eliza instructed her patient. "Reach for your left shoulder."

Everyone heard the pop.

Eliza received cheers and expressions of gratitude from the men. She briefly accepted their praise and returned to help her patient. After she made a sling for him and gave instructions, she slipped past Sharif and hustled back to the apartment.

Sharif called to his sergeant. "Got a minute, Omar?" They had forged a close working relationship. Omar had twelve years' seniority over Sharif in age and experience. As police officers, they agreed on hard work and fearlessness. As men, the two men were worlds apart.

Omar Abdul-Muqtadir, forty-six, with a dozen children, openly adored his wife, and stood on principles of fairness and obedience to Allah. In spite of his large, muscular frame, he moved with swift agility, and had a reputation as a first rate marksman. He laughed easily.

Hashim Sharif, thirty-three, two troubled children, divorced. Since his wife's betrayal of their arranged marriage contract, and the subsequent war between them, Hashim claimed to have no interest in going down that path again. His relationship with his parents continued to border on resentment.

Distant from his parents geographically and emotionally since childhood, his detached upbringing by his sister had set the ground rules for all of his relationships. The need to please, to be worthy of his superiors, to constantly prove he could be trusted haunted his every move. He found little reason to smile.

Muqtadir sat down in Sharif's office. "Problem, Hashim?"

"Perhaps." Sharif updated his sergeant on the massacre investigation. "Somebody wants me dead, Omar."

Abdul-Muqtadir laughed. "We know that. They line up for a shot at you every night."

Sharif shrugged. "Amateurs. Somebody went to a lot of trouble October 13th. Whoever wanted the Americans dead also has a grudge with me. Any ideas who that might be?"

Abdul-Muqtadir stood up. "Captain, you've made a lot of enemies. Not all of them are criminals. Got to get back on patrol."

Chapter 10

After morning prayer, Sharif went to bed. After three hours of restless sleep, he lay awake listening to Miss MacKay's efforts to clean the spotless apartment. Apparently, the windows needed washing today. He could hear the squeak, squeak as she scrubbed. Then she moved on to washing something else and he tried to identify the object of her ministrations. He gave up on the guessing game and with getting back to sleep.

He got up and put on his civvies – a pair of khaki cotton pants, black golf shirt, and sandals. He tore off his bedding, dumped his soiled clothes into the pile, and then went into the bathroom for the towels.

While busy picking out the fresh linen in his hall closet, he ignored Eliza's trotting around the apartment, doing whatever. *Not important*, he thought. *Just ignore the mouse.* He snickered to himself at the sudden analogy of the woman to a mouse – hard to capture and just as hard to ignore its brazen invasion of personal space. And she loved cheese. He turned to discover his pile of laundry had disappeared. He glanced back toward Eliza to see that his sheets were disappearing with her through the doorway.

He raced after her. "Miss MacKay, what do you think you're doing?" he barked at her as she trotted down the stairs. "You must not; I mean I don't want you to …."

She paused on the stairs. "Never mind, captain. I'm quite familiar with washing men's clothes." She continued to the exit door.

He followed her to the building equipped with laundry facilities, a vehicle wash bay and utility tub. She sorted through the whites and colored items, including her own laundry.

He stood with his mouth wide open. "Are you intending to wash your clothes with mine?" He tore his gaze away from a black lace bra among his dark clothing. First, the invasion of his privacy, now a woman handling his underwear. In a matter of six days, his life had shifted out of his control. Nothing in the Koran had prepared him for such an impetuous woman.

She glanced at him and smiled. "Relax, captain. Is it not true that Allah, the Most Generous, blesses those who respect the environment? I'm just trying to use less water and electricity." She stuffed the light colored clothing and sheets into the mouth of the washing machine.

Sharif retreated to his office without another word. His mind hovered over the laundry room. A woman was pawing through his underwear. He Googled the local airlines for the schedule of departing flights. He eagerly flipped through the websites and noted a few possibilities. There was a nonstop flight out of the country to England at noon. However, by then she would have his underwear washed, dried, folded and laid out on his bed. In any case, mayor Aamir had instructed the airport security and immigration staff to arrest her if she showed up at the airport. A cold sweat erupted on his forehead.

An hour later, he returned to the laundry room. She glanced up at him as she pushed an armful of wet clothes into the dryer.

"I'm going to pick up some supplies. Is there anything you need?" he asked.

"Just milk, two percent please. Brown bread, free-range chicken eggs, cheese, not goat cheese, maybe some veggies. Fruit would be nice. Oh, and coffee." She slammed the dryer door shut and turned to him. "Can I pay for my share of the groceries, captain?"

Sharif winced at the bruising of his pride. "Of course not. What are you doing this afternoon?"

"Follow me, please." She led him to the police operation's storage room. When she flipped on the lights, he stood speechless. The room for the police uniforms appeared spotless, the shelves labeled and all the items folded and placed in the shelving unit according to category and size. In the adjacent room, the flashlights, handcuffs, flak jackets, and helmets were arranged on shelves for easy identification and retrieval.

"Sergeant Omar and his squad helped me with the writing on the labels. All I need to do now is to organize the weapons room." She wore a mischievous grin.

He put on his best scowl. "You're on a first name basis with my sergeant?"

She shrugged. "My next project is to clean the vehicles. There's an inch of dust on most of them."

"You sure you want to do all that? I don't expect you to work hard. Just keep yourself occupied to help pass the time."

"I like to keep busy, captain. Have a nice afternoon."

He watched as she headed to the area of parked vehicles. She swiped her fingers into the grime of an old white van, Sharif's personal vehicle. He drove it on trips home, once every six or eight weeks. Grit had dulled the paint. He walked up and kicked the new tires. They provided enough safety for travel through the hazardous mountain pass.

He watched her peer through the coating of dust on the back window. If she opened the back door, she'd discover the big teddy bear his daughter Farah used as a pillow for long trips. She walked on to inspect the cab. The windshield had a long crack along its length. Captain Sharif turned to leave.

He took a couple of steps and hesitated. On impulse he turned back. A shaft of light caught the halo of dust swirling above her head. Though she kept her long hair tucked under the police cap, loose strands had escaped. She had smudges of grime on her black uniform and on her nose.

"Miss MacKay, how long would it take you to clean up?"

She swung around, wide-eyed. "Clean up?"

He hesitated to answer. He shuffled his feet and shrugged his shoulders. "Shower, change your clothes. It would be easier if you selected your food at the market."

She took a few steps toward him. Her delight shone in her eyes and a smile escaped on her lips. She pointed in the direction beyond the compound walls. "Out there?"

He cleared his throat. "That's where the market is. How long?" he asked again, his voice tinged with impatience. This was nothing more than expediency, he told himself. The last thing he wanted was for her to think he was giving her special treatment. *I'm going to regret this. I regret it already.*

"Fifteen minutes." She tucked her loose hair behind her ears. "Maybe twenty. Will you wait?"

Sharif hitched his shoulders, searched for an excuse to back out of the deal. Nothing clever came to mind. "Fine. You'll blend in with the civilian women better if you wear your personal clothes. Just remember to dress modestly."

Sharif decided to change into his police uniform. When Eliza presented herself in the kitchen for inspection he nodded his approval. In fact, he liked the lilac linen wrap-around skirt. A soft ruffle at the hem revealed only her delicate ankles. The modest coordinated top, with sleeves rolled and buttoned at her elbows, hugged her hips. She could be on a date with girlfriends for an afternoon lunch. A long lilac scarf draped loosely over her head and around her shoulders. She wore white slip-on canvas shoes.

She grabbed her trauma kit and started to head for the door.

"No need to bring that, miss."

She ignored him and began to pass through the door. "You never know, captain."

"Come back, Miss MacKay."

She swung around, sighed, and placed it on the breakfast table. "Captain, I couldn't live with myself if someone needed medical attention and I didn't have my kit with me."

"I don't think you need all of it. Surely you can downsize this."

"Yes, I suppose you're right." She unzipped the lower portion of the backpack, removing the heavier and more advanced medical supplies. With the compartments zipped closed, Eliza hugged the reduced backpack to her chest.

A sly grin replaced his eternal scowl. "Still don't recall what happened to your passport, miss?"

Eliza tried to appear concerned. "I wish I could, captain." She glanced away from him, pretending to check the trauma kit's zippers.

He restrained the impulse to laugh. She was such a terrible liar. For now, he decided to not mention he knew of her past and legal name.

He moved in close to her. "Miss Eliza MacKay, you appear to guard this kit as fiercely as I hang onto my weapons." He swung the large gun up into his hands and noted her silence.

He made a show of adjusting his handgun in its shoulder holster. "The rules, Miss MacKay, are that you remain at my side within arm's reach. You speak to no one. And you make no effort to draw attention to yourself. Is that clear?"

She nodded. "Absolutely. Easy."

Sharif first headed toward Prophet Park, a detour from the route to the grocery store. Along the route he often glanced at Eliza. She appeared vibrant and excited to see the expanse of the city and its people. He wanted to watch her instead of the road. She glowed.

He drove over a bridge that spanned the wide Rumi River and turned onto a street that followed the river. Large poplar trees stood as sentinels along the two-lane street. Larch trees and willows were scattered nearer the river bank. Their bright gold and red leaves marked the arrival of fall.

"Oh, those trees, Captain," she exclaimed, pointing to the deciduous trees. "They're just like the trees in Alberta. I'm so surprised to see them growing here."

Her radiant smile made him catch his breath. "They're experimental. Our government looked for trees that grow quickly and large in our semi-arid environment. It's not as hot here in the northern provinces. We're pleased they've flourished." He smiled. "Under protection of Islamic law, a bit of composted manure, and nearness to water, it has led the way to more possibilities."

"Yes, I know. Last year I bought perfume, Middle East Peace, which is made from RIPT's orange blossoms."

He glanced at her. A lovely feminine woman had begun to emerge like a butterfly from its cocoon. Her delicate features and creamy complexion emphasized her English heritage.

The wide river sparkled in the late morning sun. The water raced over boulders as if it thirsted for the distant Persian Gulf.

"Perhaps you'd like to walk along the river?" He looked out his driver's window and squeezed his eyes shut. *Have I lost control over my damn brain?*

Her eyes opened wide with surprise. "That would be wonderful. Does Sharia Law allow me to be with you?"

"Being that I am a police officer and you're under my supervision, it is acceptable."

At the parking lot, Sharif stowed his MP5 in the locked and alarmed SUV. "Remember the rules." Sharif's heart kicked up its pace. He wondered if he'd pay for this risk. "Miss MacKay, the police chief would not approve of this, so it's vital you obey my rules."

Eliza nodded and hoisted her trauma kit onto her back. He pointed out the footpath that hugged the river bank. As they strode down the narrow paved path, Sharif remained on the alert, checking behind himself every few steps.

After ten minutes, his pace slowed to a relaxed stroll. Sharif and Eliza passed a soccer field. Children chased each other in a nearby playground.

Trees formed a bower on both sides of the path. The sun searched through the deciduous canopy and spilled its warmth sporadically onto the people enjoying the walk. A peaceful aura touched the old and young, some walking, some riding their bicycles. A few ambitious youths jogged.

"It must be difficult being away from your children, captain?" She appeared to have regretted the inquiry as soon as she'd made it. Her smile wavered and her arms protectively crossed her chest. She turned away from his gaze. She grabbed a long blade of grass and began to tie it into knots. She waved her hand as if to erase the last few seconds. "Never mind, captain, I shouldn't have asked that."

Her sudden nervousness surprised him. "They're adjusting. It's been two years since their mother returned to England." He noted her reaction. She looked toward the river and moved a few steps away from him. "That was a bad time for them. After she attempted to kidnap them, I moved them to live with my parents in our ancestral home near Rumi, on the west side of those mountains."

He pointed to the distant rugged range of mountains high along the country's spine. They were still capped with snow in the higher elevations. "Safer there since I work such long hours." His conscience berated him. He had committed the same abandonment as his father had.

Sharif watched as her hand moved to cover her heart. Her mouth opened but she appeared unable to speak.

She took a deep breath. "Surely the children still have contact with their mother."

He noted a definite quiver in her voice. "Yes, but only phone calls." He lifted his hat off his head and slapped it back down again. He pointed to a path heading down a bank to the river. "Mind your step over the boulders."

Once a row of trees concealed their location, he unbuttoned his police blazer and swung it over his shoulder. She had shredded the blade of grass, tossed it aside and grabbed another long stem.

An awkward silence fell between them. Sharif tossed a few stones into the river. Her grass stem suffered the same abuse as the first. As they entered a shaded section, he removed his sunglasses and tucked them into his shirt's pocket. Eyeing her from the corner of his eyes, he noted she appeared to be wrestling with an internal storm. Her eyebrows knitted across her forehead. Her mouth turned down with lips pressed into a hard line.

He wanted her to come clean with him about her past. He blurted out, "You had children."

Eliza stumbled as she swung to face him. Her eyes opened wide with shock. "What?"

"I know you were once married and had children."

Tears welled in her eyes. She appeared dazed, unable to move, eyes searching the landscape. He took her elbow, guided her to a boulder, and eased her onto its surface. She hunched over her knees, arms tucked close to her chest. When she squeezed her eyes closed, tears escaped.

Sharif grabbed a few small, flat stones and handed them to her. "Here, give these a good pitch. Helps me, especially when I feel like punching someone's lights out." He winced at reverting to English slang. He gave her a tentative smile.

She glanced at him and wiped her face, damp with tears. Her wet fingers wrapped around the stones. Half-heartedly, she tossed a stone to the river's edge.

"Eliza, you can do better than that," he bellowed. "Fling that sucker across the river."

She stood up and eyed him for a moment.

He watched her straighten and pull her shoulders back. Head up, she took a deep breath and hurled the stone, making it skip twice across the river's surface.

His right eyebrow twitched. "Better."

She prepared to toss another stone. "I taught my boys how." She threw another stone. It skipped three times. "Nathan and Noah. They loved being outside, rock picking." She turned to Sharif. "They're dead. Husband, too." Her chin quivered.

"I'm sorry for your loss, miss. What happened?"

"Traffic accident. Anyway, that's why I got upset over your wife's loss of her children. It's really none of my business. I'm sure you're doing the best possible for your children."

Sharif hung back. They were silent for a while, watching birds, and the river's desperate escape to the faraway sea, a reckless journey. Eliza had lifted her face to the sun, eyes closed. *Damn, she's the most odd and unpredictable person.* "What are you doing, miss?" His cop voice overrode any hint of concern.

She looked at him. "I'm fine, captain. Just meditating. Since the death of my boys, I've had to learn a few coping skills." She took a deep breath and let it out slow. "Close your eyes. Empty your mind of thoughts. Listen."

"Not closing my eyes, miss." After a couple of minutes he asked, "What am I supposed to hear?"

"Allah, the Most Compassionate." She smiled at him.

He knew she meditated but he had never given that endeavor much credit. The daily prayers provided Sharif all his spiritual needs. "You hear Allah?" He studied her face. A trace of sadness remained. But now she appeared to be cloaked with an aura of calm. He couldn't see it with his eyes – only the hint of change in her energy. The intimacy made him shiver – with pleasure.

"Oddly enough, when God took away my family, I received something that I can't quite explain. And, yes, I hear a voice. Maybe not Allah, God. Maybe just my higher self." She smiled. "And, no, I'm not crazy. Exactly."

Sharif motioned for her to return to the trail. "Let's go. My shift begins soon. We'd better get the groceries now."

They returned to his SUV and drove to the grocery store. He parked in the shade and turned to her. "There's something I need to discuss with you. The truth is I know about your past, about the accident. I know your name is Elizabeth Ramsay."

Her eyes grew wide, fearful.

"I'm a cop, Eliza. I needed to have all the facts."

He attempted to guess her thoughts by the tightness of her lips, the way she twisted the end of her scarf, the level of her chin. She had turned away from his gaze, to watch the people strolling into the local market and grocery store. He opened his door to allow a breeze into the cab.

"Miss MacKay?" He waited for her to acknowledge him.

Her face paled. She looked down at her hands. "When people find out about the accident, they are so horrified they either leave, or shower me with pity. That's why I do everything possible to keep it secret. Which are you going to do?" Her voice had a blend of both fear and anger. She eyed him critically.

"Nothing has changed. I will still protect you and find a way to send you home."

She refocused on the activity outside the SUV. "Is that all you know about my past?" Her voice quivered.

"I've been advised that you sometimes scream at night."

Eliza frowned. "Who said that?"

"Since the massacre I've assigned an officer to watch the gate, and you. He says that when you screamed, there was no indication you were in trouble and so he left you alone. You have nightmares because of the death of the Americans?"

"No." After a moment's hesitation, she sighed. "It's called post-traumatic stress disorder. Since four years ago. Started when my family died in that accident. I survived. Sometimes … I get flashbacks in the daytime, and nightmares." She looked back at him. "It's very hard to talk about. I'd rather not, if you don't mind."

Sharif nodded. He noted the straightening of her back, lifting of her chin, and the determined look on her face. Her armor resurfaced, burying her softer side under its cold metal shield. He understood. "Let's go. Are you ready?"

Eliza nodded. They jumped out and continued into the store. Eliza grabbed a cart as the captain trailed on her heels. He selected the food they had agreed upon – fragrant freshly baked flat, glistening black and green olives, rice, dates, grapes, coffee, jam, and dried figs cooked with cinnamon. They also got labnah, a thick cream cheese made by draining yogurt through cheesecloth, and then drizzled with olive oil, ful madamis, and pine nuts. The flat bread would be used to make sandwiches with the labnah, along with olives, tomato and mint. And finally, they chose laham bi 'ajin, a sort of pizza made with halal minced meat, tomatoes, and onions, and sprinkled with spices, parsley, and pine nuts.

On the way back to Sharif's station, Eliza said, "Pull over. Captain, there's something I should tell you."

"No time. Got to get ready for my shift."

Eliza reached into her backpack and pulled out the cellphone. "This is what I need to talk about."

Sharif swerved onto a side street and slammed on the brakes.

Chapter 11

Sharif's eyes narrowed. "Where did you get that?"

"I found it in a box of used uniforms." She handed it over to him.

He rushed through the record of phone calls made and discovered she had made a phone call five days after the massacre. "You called someone." He gritted his teeth. "Who did you call?"

"My boss."

He sat silent for a moment, barely breathing, just staring at her. "What did you tell him?" he growled.

"Well, you can see that call lasted a full seven seconds. I got the guilts and terminated the call before he answered."

He blew out his breath and sat back in his seat. "You didn't speak to anyone?"

"No. No conversations, no messages, no texting, nothing."

"Why not?"

"If I escaped, you and your family would suffer for my actions. Enough people have died because of me. My family died because of my selfishness." She looked down to her empty hands. Her chin trembled. She looked up and gazed at the people walking by. "I decided to trust you."

When she looked back into his face, he saw her fear, perhaps wondering if she had been a fool. Her eyes darted from his face, to the phone, and back to his face.

"Thank you." His voice, husky and low, betrayed his relief. "Here, you keep it." He handed it back to her.

"Are you sure?" Her mouth hung open. "You want me to keep it?"

"Yes, but the rule is you don't call anyone except me. I'm letting you keep it so that if you're in trouble, you can call me. I'll key in my cell number so all you need to do is hit this panic button." He completed the memory operation.

He gave her the phone and watched her place it in her backpack. For a moment he regretted his decision. Life had become complicated, almost spinning out of his control. When she looked back at him, he felt stunned. Her sweet character appeared from behind those lovely eyes. It was as if a veil had been lifted. She held him prisoner.

"You're a good man, Hashim Sharif." She gave his hand a squeeze.

He shifted in his seat, shocked by her declaration. She sounded sincere. No one had called him a good man. Certainly not his ex-wife. Ruthless cop, stubborn and callous, devoted Muslim, obedient son, yes; but he doubted he qualified as a good man.

He swallowed hard to free the restriction in his throat. She had no way of knowing how deeply those four words, *you're a good man*, touched him. He studied her for a moment. He had the distinct impression a barrier had been crossed. He wasn't sure if he liked it, or wanted it.

Ω

Ten days after the massacre, Captain Khizar charged up to Sharif's apartment and banged on his bedroom door. "Sharif, get up. Chief Ganem called. Wants you in his office now."

Arriving at the federal building, Sharif pulled his SUV into a staff parking space near the front steps. Within the walls of the building, President Najeeb and his ministers, military chiefs, Mayor Aamir and councilors, Police Chief Ganem, and the government administration conducted the affairs of the country, the provinces, and the capital city of Samarra.

The brick exterior still bore traces of its previous military fortification, having only narrow windows on the ground floor. The high wrought iron wall surrounding the property had replaced the bullet-riddled cement barrier. Spread over three city blocks, its three stories bowed to the grandeur of the Guardian Mosque's dome and higher minarets across the street.

Sharif climbed the expansive cement steps and glanced to the south. The mid afternoon sun showered its radiance upon the domed roof of his mosque. The surfaces of the nearby brick buildings illuminated the terrain with shades of terracotta, mocha and cream.

Everything merged into a symphony of sunlight and warm shadows, softening angles and blurring edges. The clean streets, birds singing in the trees, parks and fountains radiated a sense of calm. A river of harmony touched the space surrounding the mosque.

Sharif uttered a silent prayer. "اللّهُمّ ربّي إجعلْ ما يَصدُر ما منّي من أقوال "مِنْكَ متَقبّلَة وأفعال.Praise Allah, almighty. May my words and deeds be honorable."

He wondered if Allah had turned away from his prayers. For some time now, pleas for forgiveness had consumed his holy devotions. Abuse of prisoners, for whatever reason, and living with a woman – perhaps his soul was damned.

Sharif approached the federal building's massive wood doors. The architectural design had been restored to its original arabesque with patterns of scrolling and interlacing foliage and tendrils. In the arch above the entrance sat a brass name plate المبنى الاسلاميه والمقاطعات للمحافظات الرئيسي الحكومي 'Headquarters of Islamic Provinces and Territories,' glowed in contrast to the obsidian stone surface.

Sharif entered the enormous central foyer, open to the two floors above and the skylight. The sound of his army boots marching across the lapis lazuli marble floor resonated throughout the large hallway leading to the rear entrance. The floor's deep blue, laced with metallic gold-colored pyrite, appeared as a sunlit river.

Ornately-carved columns of Mexican Sand Aztec marble marched its breadth and width, marking entrances to hallways and stairways.

Warm wood banisters and dark walnut fixtures added an earthy feel. Hues of red, orange, gold, and brown in the Turkish hallway carpets provided a welcoming atmosphere. The aroma of baked bread and freshly-brewed coffee rose from the basement cafeteria.

In the center of the main hall, a fountain's hypnotic sound softened the marble's hard edge and men's heated discussions. Around the base of the fountain an inscription in Arabic read, "المبنى الاسلاميه والمقاطعات للمحافظات الرسمي " Lead in wisdom and faith in Allah, the most glorified, the most high.

Most of the Middle East countries had joined to form the inclusive Republic of Islamic Provinces and Territories. Ten years of democracy edged closer to a prosperous nation, though it was well understood that the Brotherhood in Egypt continued to chip away at the foundation laid by President Najeeb. Some doubt remained whether Najeeb had enough clout to repel the Islamic fundamentalists. Success rested on RIPT's seat in the UN, a trade contract with Europe and USA, and most of all, demonstration of stability within RIPT's borders.

Sharif cleared security and headed to the police chief's office. Chief Ganem met Sharif in the hall and ushered him into his office. Sharif and Ganem had only one thing in common. Both were divorced.

Sharif's six-foot frame towered over his boss's moderate but robust build. Grey peppered Ganem's short beard. His chiseled face wore the etchings of long hours and heavy burdens. To Captain Sharif's recollection, his boss had never smiled.

Ganem could be recognized at a distance due to his signature gait, always just short of a trot. His shoulders hunched and a half step ahead of his feet, the chief presented himself as a man not interested in small talk. His eyes darted about as though watching a dozen irons in the fire.

Ganem wore his black police dress uniform rather than a business suit. It bore the five gold stripes of his rank on its shoulders and sleeves. His office walls displayed framed awards of recognition as well as a medal testifying to his courage under fire during his military service.

"Sit down, Sharif," the chief snapped.

Sharif took off his hat and slid his sunglasses into his shirt pocket. He sat uneasy, as though the chair might collapse. "Bad news, chief?"

"Perhaps." Ganem stood behind his desk. He fidgeted with his pen, clicking it. "It's been ten days since the massacre. Is there no further information coming forth among your snitches?"

"They know more than they're saying. More scared than I've seen them before. Like I said before, Drummer mentioned a name, 'Black Ice. Our intelligence service may have some information about that."

"No. Can't get more people involved. Bad enough your squad ..."

"Sir, they never talk, never will." Sharif hoped Ganem trusted his word.

Ganem shook his head. "It's odd no terrorist has spoken up. Anyway, it's getting too difficult to keep this under wraps. If it wasn't for that damn woman, this whole mess could be handled diplomatically."

Sharif clenched his hat's brim. "You mean easier to cover up the fact we failed to protect the Americans." Sharif's temper breached his control. "What lowlife do you know has the money and balls to carry out this massacre?" Sharif reined in his anger. "Sir, it is possible that someone in our government is behind the assault?" He lowered his voice. "Perhaps President Najeeb?"

Ganem's eyes narrowed. "How dare you insult our most esteemed leader?"

"He's been pushing for the UN's approval of sending up our own spy satellite. If we had the ability to do high-resolution scanning of our vast regions, we could more readily spot active terrorist camps. This is evidence that he could have prevented the massacre if we had our own satellite."

"You're crazy, Sharif. He's shrewd, but -." Ganem hesitated, then bolted out of his chair. "Then he'd know we're covering up the killing. And ..." he muttered as he paced. "No, no, we must find out who else knows about the attack."

"If there's anyone in the city with information about who was behind the attack, I'll find him. You know I will, whatever it takes, sir. If only the mayor would approve of calling on our federal government security forces."

"No, not until we know more. Concentrate on preparing for inspection. A Habitat official and some forensic inspectors will be arriving in three days. President Najeeb has accepted the assistance of a CIA special agent. We have forty-eight hours to prepare." The chief passed a handwritten directive to Sharif. "Read this."

As Sharif read, his posture stiffened. A cold sweat enveloped his body. His eyebrows shot up, then frowned. He glanced at the chief and then continued to read. He tossed it back to Ganem. "Surely there's a more civilized way to handle this, sir."

"Mayor Aamir has ordered she be terminated."

"You mean executed. This is an order to commit cold-blooded murder." Sharif's lungs refused to take in air. He flexed his shoulders to regain his composure.

"Sharif, I don't want blood on my hands any more than you do. Just dispose of the woman any way that will keep Aamir at least half-satisfied." Ganem took out his lighter, set the directive on fire.

"One more thing. Mayor Aamir has been very explicit in his instruction to me. Just so you understand the severity of this situation, if we fail in this directive, or if the truth of the incident becomes known, the consequences will be fatal – for all of us! Including family."

Sharif fought off the urge to wrap his hands around the man's throat. Years of controlling his emotions gave him the skill to let the threat pass. "Understood, sir."

Sharif turned and walked away. When he got into his vehicle, he dialed his father's phone. "Papa, do you and the rest of the family have current passports?"

"Why, no. There seemed to be no need. Why do you ask?"

"Oh, no particular reason. I just thought perhaps that we should take the kids on a holiday. Soon. Perhaps within a week. Can you get everyone's documents updated?"

His father agreed.

Chapter 12

Captain Sharif's five sergeants gathered in his debriefing room. The setting sun's five o'clock glow cast warm shadows through the windows. Each man managed a district station and a squad. As they prepared for the night's pre-shift updates, the ceiling fan whirled and merged the late afternoon heat with the evening chill. The room echoed the men's banter, the clanking of coffee cups, spoons stirring, and the scrape of chairs pulled across the granite tile floor. The wood table bore the scars of men's abuse, shuddered with each pound of a fist, groaned under the weight of a hip.

Sharif waited in his office for the men to settle into the routine of duty. A sandwich remained untouched on his desk. Eliza had made it for him. She'd been doing special things since the trip to the market. She prepared his meals, ensured his sacred corner in the apartment was clear of her stuff, and stopped grilling him about the investigation.

Yesterday, as he crawled into bed, he listened to her hum while making her breakfast. The soothing sound washed over him. In seconds, he forgot about muscle aches and bruised knuckles. Later, shortly before noon prayer, he watched as she rescued a bee in the kitchen. She had gently caught it in a tea towel and released it outside.

He'd stood mesmerized. It wasn't the selfless act that caught him off guard, but that even the smallest of creatures received her protection.

Sharif now believed that Eliza might be as vulnerable as she was strong - a flak jacket worn in too many gun battles. She kept the best part of who she was concealed. Her gentle soul was carefully camouflaged from predators.

Sharif picked up the sandwich. Though it contained his favorite foods -- cheese, pickles, olives and a spicy spread -- his appetite had vanished. In two days, Eliza would suffer his dark side.

Sergeant Omar Abdul-Muqtadir entered his office. "The men are ready, sir."

"Fine. Here, you eat this." He handed the sandwich to Omar and headed to the squad room.

Once the sergeants received updates and duties for the night shift, he prepared them for the upcoming investigation. He hesitated briefly, shoring up his military posture. "You know about the Americans who have been missing for ten days." Muttering rippled around the room. "In spite of intense intelligence work, there have been no leads concerning their fate." He managed to submerge any hint of deceit. "Naturally, the United States is pressing for answers. President Najeeb has invited their assistance."

Sharif paused, studied their facial expressions. "If any of you have information regarding this crime, it's not too late speak up." The room fell silent. Sharif searched for signs of subterfuge, twitches indicating a guilty conscience, odor of fear. He walked around the room behind the chairs of the men. "Be forewarned -- if I discover vital information has been withheld, the consequences will be severe."

"Captain," growled the most senior sergeant, "Omar briefed us ten days ago." He frowned as if insulted at the accusation of withholding information. "He made it clear it is forbidden to discuss that event with anyone but you. We do know you are looking for information about who drove the Americans' bus. My squad has heard nothing." The men at the table nodded in agreement.

Sharif returned to the head of the table. "Fine. Several American officials are scheduled to arrive in two days. If you're approached by an American government representative, you are to comply with their investigation requests one hundred percent, without reservation. Any questions?"

After grumbling about foreign interference, the sergeants left – all except Omar Abdul-Muqtadir. Sharif instructed Abdul-Muqtadir to gather his men into the board room for a special meeting. Once everyone had sat down, Sharif shut and locked the door. The cops glanced nervously at each other.

Sharif stood in front of Abdul-Muqtadir and his twenty-five constables. "CIA and American government reps are scheduled to arrive on Saturday, shortly after midnight." In deliberate slow motion, he laid his pen on the table. "Does anyone here have knowledge that information has been leaked?"

Murmurs traveled around the table. Corporal Ahmed spoke up. "Captain, not one of us has breathed a word about the shooting. Your orders were clear. No one has uttered a single word, sir. We don't even speak of it amongst ourselves. We value our jobs and, and -."

Sharif interrupted. "Good. We have two days to prepare for a thorough inspection. Najeeb has given the US reps authority to go anywhere, talk to anyone. It's anyone's guess how much the CIA already knows. No doubt this city has been under surveillance. Since I am responsible for visitor escorts and safety protocol, I anticipate an inspection at this station. It is likely each of you will be interviewed." It worried him that his staff had no experience being on the other side of an investigation.

"Double check the ID kit for any residual evidence like blood stains. Destroy the cameras used to take photos of the scene. Make sure there is no trace evidence in the compound." His cold demeanor spoke volumes on the need for absolute compliance. "Set up your teams and get started." The men bolted out the door.

Sergeant Abdul-Muqtadir came forward. "What about the Canadian? What are we to do with her?"

Sharif gritted his teeth. "Mayor Aamir has ordered her execution." Sharif rubbed his forehead. A headache had started an hour ago and threatened to punish him all night long. "Omar, the mayor has threatened my family if the cover-up fails."

The sergeant stood still, speechless.

Sharif looked into the face of his trusted colleague. "She's a risk to the success of the cover-up. She knows too much." A band cinched around his chest, strangling his attempts to breathe.

Sergeant Muqtadir glared at Sharif. "Allah forbids murder."

Sharif headed to his office with Omar on his heels. He sat down and yanked open a drawer. "I've got a lot to do, Omar. Be sure your men are thorough with the cleanup." He proceeded to unlock his desk drawers and retrieve files and flash drives.

"Captain," said Omar reverting to their formal relationship, "do not do something you'll regret for the rest of your life. Allah will not forgive murder."

"Sergeant." Sharif bolted up from his chair. "Dismissed." The sergeant turned and stomped out of Sharif's office.

Sharif's most immediate task - destroy digital files, his computer's hard drive and the evidence in his safe. And, he had to find a safe place for his copy of the files on the massacre. His operations written ledger reported only the investigation into the 'missing' Americans.

By late afternoon of the next day, Sharif believed that even miniscule traces of the massacre had vanished. Chief Ganem had the infamous wall resurfaced and fresh soil placed in the compound. Only one matter remained. Eliza MacKay.

Sharif went to the hospital where the staff knew him well. "Nurse, do you have the pills I requested?"

"Yes, Captain. These are very potent. One should do the job. There are a couple more, just in case. Quick, too."

Chapter 13

CIA agent Frank Hutchinson glanced at the inscription at the CIA headquarters entrance. 'The truth shall set you free.' *And it sure as hell will get you killed, too.*

Frank was a knock-off Middle Eastern man. Fluent in Arabic language and Islam, he could disappear into Muslim civilian population without causing the slightest ripple.

He preferred the 'in your face' type of investigation rather than the usual covert methods of observing from a distance. Frank, aged fifty-three, turning thirty, believed in living in the moment. He had the energy and liver to party hard. He was average in height and build, except for the look of amusement in his brown eyes.

Enroute to his boss's office, he continued through the maze of offices and hallways. A week ago, his boss, Zalman Liba, in the Near Eastern and South Asian Analysis office had presented him with a detailed report concerning the missing fifteen American travelers in RIPT.

The FBI and CIA investigated known suspicious groups. The investigations had taken up valuable time. The evidence trail vanished at Samarra's airport and at the crime scene of the murdered police escorts. Frank and his covert forensic team could see no other option than to continue the search openly on the RIPT's soil.

Agent Hutchinson's confidence stemmed from his innate ability to read body language. Facial expressions revealed more than his victim's dialogue. And what his prey didn't voluntarily say, well, sometimes he thought his job was just too easy.

Frank listened to his last minute orders from his boss.

"President Najeeb appears genuinely anxious to receive assistance in finding our Americans. Your orders are to liaise with the government, observe, interrogate, and do what you do best – be a royal pain until you find our people. If they're dead, get the killers."

"I'll find them, Zalman. Just going to get the latest from our technicians and head to the airport."

Until three days ago there had been no new leads. Then, Frank got lucky. A smile lit up the agent's eyes as he spoke to his boss. "We've got proof. Reserve a cell for Sharif and his men. I'll execute Sharif myself." Frank stretched an inch taller, beaming with satisfaction.

"Just make sure the proof will fly in court. If not, well, someone better pay. You have two days."

Frank's airline tickets, still warm from the printer, outlined his transportation via a commercial flight to Cairo. From there, Frank and another pilot would fly one of the CIA's private jets to the City of Samarra, hopefully in time for an eight a.m. meeting. Frank glanced at the dog hairs on the sleeve of his casual fall jacket. No time to change. In fact, he had roughly two hours to get to the Langley Airport.

His briefcase contained the case files detailing the schedule of each of the American Habitat volunteers, their photos, fingerprints, passport data, home addresses, driver's license numbers, and personal habits.

Frank headed to his next stop - the CIA's Satellite Surveillance – Middle East Division. Personnel who accumulated spy data had their own policy – 'STFU!' The hand written sign was taped to their door. Their work required intense concentration and they viewed conversation as cause for justifiable homicide.

Once Frank produced his clearance on the AHD case, the American Habitat Disappearance, they took him to a viewing room. Frank asked Matlock for an update of activities in Samarra since the day the Americans were declared missing. "Have you seen anything worth noting at Sharif's station?"

Matlock nodded. "Looks like they're getting ready for company. Cleaned the execution wall, fresh soil."

"Not surprised. Anything peculiar about Sharif's activities? What's your impression of the man? Is he capable of mass murder?"

Matlock grimaced. "Followed him for fifteen hours in total. Strikes me as a man with secrets. Looks over his shoulder, doesn't talk much, spends a lot of time at the federal building, probably meeting with the police chief. I wouldn't want him as an enemy."

"Is that so. Why?"

"Tough on prisoners. Often abusive. Strikes me as frustrated. And, I suspect there's trouble at his station."

"Explain."

"There's friction between him and his station partner, Captain Khizar. Arguments in the compound."

"Anything out of the ordinary?"

"Maybe. Recently acquired a female cop. Looks like she does grunt work for the station. Haven't been able to get a look at her. Always behaving like she doesn't want to be seen. Just know she's female by the way she walks."

"Probably nothing. Good work, Matlock." He trotted to the office managing covert communications and cornered his buddy, Muhammad. "What's the latest on Captain Sharif, buddy?"

Muhammad grinned and took off his headpiece. "Ah, yes, the cop that walks the grey zone between the Allah and Satan."

"He's dirty?"

"No, not exactly. Locals suspect he is not opposed to using torture. He's careful with his conversations. Seldom uses his cellphone. Word on the street is he's interrogating gang leaders about the missing Americans. Looking for the driver who drove the Americans' bus."

Frank scratched at his five o-clock shadow. "Interesting. Anything else, Mud? I need an advantage over the man. What does he want, badly?"

Mud smiled. "He's trying to get his family out of the country. Unfortunately, there seems to be a problem getting his family's passports renewed."

Ω

Sharif's inspected his compound, now cleaner than it ever had been. He checked his watch. Twenty minutes after eight p.m. He reviewed the protocol for receiving dignitaries. He knew it by heart but the reading kept his mind off Miss MacKay.

Most of his squad had already been deployed to their routine patrol duties. Sergeant Abdul-Muqtadir and another officer waited for their orders in the officers' lounge.

"Sergeant, have you loaded MacKay's luggage and the massacre files into my SUV?"

"Yes, except for her backpack. Won't let us near it."

He handed a slip of paper to the Sergeant. "I'm taking MacKay to this location. Meet me there."

Sharif headed to his apartment, but halted in the hallway. He tapped his chest, checking for the small pill bottle in his coat breast pocket. The little blue capsules rattled. *Like a rattler*, he thought, *callous killing snake*. His posture stiffened.

Eliza waited on the sofa, browsing through one of his architecture magazines. The spare cot remained with fresh linen. Only *her* things had been removed. He reasoned that if he had cleaned every square inch, it would look suspicious. Besides, no one was looking for Miss MacKay. If anyone asked about the cot, his kids used it on overnight visits. He called out to her, "Miss MacKay, it's time to leave."

She got up. "Any hint on what is happening next, captain?"

He had told her about the CIA investigation and that she had to be moved temporarily. "Get your trauma kit and follow me to my SUV."

She wore the police uniform. Her flak jacket had been returned to the storage room. Eliza put on her dark blue down coat, tucked her hair up inside a knit skull cap, and proceeded down the stairs, her trauma backpack swinging across her back. He grabbed a thick file folder from his office and herded her to his SUV.

As Sharif drove through the dark city streets, she attempted small talk. "Going to be a cold night," she said, straining to see out her side window. "Where's the moon?"

Sharif busied himself with obtaining updates from the squad sergeants on patrol and airport security. So far, he had managed to block out Eliza's voice.

"Wow, look at the stars, captain. That's the advantage of having minimal streetlights on during the night."

He couldn't help but look up at the sky. He winced with the stars' burning glare. Guilt made him avoid turning toward her until thoughts of cowardice dared the move. Mistake. Again, her face lit up when outside the compound but he noted the tension around her eyes. He switched his view to his mirrors. Her gaze in his direction made him feel small, exposed – a chunk of ice cast upon the hot sand.

"Have you ever seen the aurora borealis?"

Sharif made no indication he heard her.

"Sharif to dispatch. I'll be out of service until you're notified otherwise. Notify me if the airport calls about any change in the Americans' flight schedule. Sharif out."

Eliza continued undeterred. "Do you know that some ancestors believed that the Northern Lights were the energies of the souls of the departed? When the fires blazed in the skies, people were to behave solemnly, and children were admonished to quiet down and be respectful of the sky fires. It was believed that whoever disrespected the fires incurred bad fortune, which could result in sickness, even death."

He noted a momentary trembling in the passenger seat. A rush of sweat stung his brow and chilled his body. Made him shiver.

Eliza fiddled with her knit cap, stretching it down over her ears. "And others believed the lights were caused by a magical fox sweeping his tail across the snow spraying it up into the sky. Isn't that beautiful? A magical fox." Eliza chuckled nervously. The pitch of her voice had risen half an octave. "I like this one the best. The Lapps had a belief that if you whistled under the Northern Lights, you could summon them closer, and they could whisk you away with them. Let me give it a try. If you don't mind, that is."

They were stopped at traffic lights. Sharif picked up a clipboard and pretended to study his itinerary for the night. *God, why can't she just shut up?*

Eliza whistled a soft tune, a lullaby that her sons liked. She went on for a minute but Sharif remained tuned in to his two-way radio.

"Nope, I guess it doesn't work. Had to try, just in case," she said with a sigh.

Sharif flipped on his FM radio. *Perhaps that'll shut her up. Damn!* With every passing minute Sharif suffered the pain of something being ripped from his chest. His deep regret nagged. He had to massage his chest.

She groaned. "Okay, I've done something wrong. You're always quiet when you're ticked with me. Just spit it out, Sharif. Maybe, for starters, explain where we are going?"

Sharif gripped the steering wheel. "MacKay, people are coming to find fault with my government. If the CIA discovers the truth, I'll be arrested on suspicion of complicity with the killers, probably shot by the end of the week. I'm in no mood for your chatter." For the next twenty minutes they rode in silence. Sharif battled a mental storm while Eliza hunkered down into her coat, her hands stuffed into the pockets. Sharif glanced at her once while doing a right-hand turn shoulder check. No longer watching the goings on around her, she appeared to be wrestling with her situation. He sensed her nervousness, anticipating trouble.

Finally, he reached his destination and parked in the shadows at the rear of a quality hotel. His family had frequented the lodging during trips to and from Rumi. Thankfully, the management and staff knew him and his family well so they agreed to his request two days ago to the alterations to the door of the eighth floor family room. It could be opened from the hallway, but not from within the room.

He spotted his sergeant standing beside his police sedan and nodded to him. Muqtadir walked up and met Sharif behind the SUV. "Be ready for a fight, Omar," whispered Sharif. "She's not going to like this at all."

"Better than the alternative, Hashim. Does she know we're supposed to have her buried in the desert?"

"Only that the mayor intends to eliminate her." Sharif placed a hand on Muqtadir's shoulder. "My friend, you realize the mayor will put a price on our heads for disloyalty. You can walk away and resume your patrol like you've had no part of this. I'd understand. You have a family who need you."

"So do you. Besides, I'm like you. Got a soft spot for orphans and widows. The Koran's message is very clear about protecting them. And, apparently, she's both. Let's get this done so I can get back to my squad."

Sharif picked up his file folder and motioned for her to get out. "Get your backpack and follow the sergeant." He glanced at his watch and turned to Muqtadir. "I've got to be at the airport in an hour. Means I have to leave here in twenty minutes." Sharif whistled to the sergeant's officer. "Bring her luggage and my folder."

As they approached the rear entrance, Sharif grabbed Eliza's arm. "No talking, MacKay." She cringed, perhaps from his menacing growl, or the look of a predator in his eyes, or due to his painful grip. He felt her body stiffen and heard her gasp. Waiting for the elevator doors to open, he noted her silence, and distance. He knew whatever ground he had made in obtaining her alliance, had crumbled and become unstable.

Though the eighth floor hallway was free of rubbish and grime, cigarette smoke assaulted the senses. The lights sparingly illuminated the faded gold carpet. Barren of décor and color, the walls reflected the emptiness Sharif felt.

Sharif tried to usher her quickly to the room on the eighth floor before anyone saw her. She seemed to be deliberately trying to slow the pace. He had the impression that she was watching a disturbing image. She held her mouth open, fear written in her eyes. *She knows, but how.* He put his hand across her back, encouraging her to focus on his urging her forward.

"You're going to be safe, miss. Keep moving," he said, hoping to comfort her. The sound of his sergeant's footsteps behind him was reassuring. Any trouble Eliza attempted would be brief.

"Can't breathe," she muttered, more to herself than the men. A look of panic in her eyes, then gasping. She looked wildly about. "I need air. Window. Outside, now!"

In one swift move, the sergeant picked up Eliza. In spite of her frantic wrestling, he held her firmly and trotted to room 84. Sharif used his card key to enter the room and flicked on the ceiling light. Muqtadir carried Eliza to the window and set her down. He opened it just enough that she could feel the breeze on her face. She collapsed to her knees, gasping. Her fingers clawed at the window frame until she became dizzy and collapsed.

"Hashim, she's not going to survive this. She'll go insane."

"Let's get her on the bed. See if she's coherent."

As they lifted her up, Eliza swatted at them. "Don't touch me. I can stand on my own." She stood, wobbling and reaching for the wall. "Where's the bathroom?" She flung off her cap and curled her fingers into a tight fist.

Sharif pointed to the other side of the beds and gave her plenty of room to get by him. "Don't lock the door, miss."

She glared at him then stumbled quickly to the bathroom door. She slammed it shut. The sound of a click followed.

"Sounds like she's coherent, Omar." A look of exasperation on Sharif's face amused the sergeant.

The room could accommodate a family. It had two king-size beds, a pullout sofa, TV and radio, a desk and chair, and a standard bathroom with a tub. A half-open window facing the back parking lot invited the cool night air and traffic noise.

Again simplicity and function ruled. The bed quilts and pillows were a dull blue grey, a neutral accessory to the faded gold carpet.

Sharif placed his folder in the closet and put MacKay's suitcase and backpack on the bed. "You might as well go, Omar. Thanks for getting her in here so quick. And -." Sharif paused, searching for the words that would convey his deep gratitude for Omar's friendship.

"Hey, I owe you, Hashim. For the rest of my life, I'll be watching your back like you watched mine last year. You could have been killed when you ran up between me and those assassins. Got to keep you healthy. If some asshole takes you out, I'll be put in your captain's chair." Muqtadir shivered. "No fun at all."

The men went into the hallway. "Try to check on her tomorrow, Omar. Bring some food."

"Got court tomorrow. How come she's so ticked?"

"I wouldn't tell her about the plans. Hates being left in the dark about her future. And, she hates being confined. Big problem with claustrophobia."

"Good luck with the VIPs."

Sharif returned to the room, ensuring the door was left ajar. "Miss MacKay, come out."

After a lengthy pause, she said, "I'm done with you, Sharif. You're locking me up in this damn, stinking, hotel room. You know I can't handle this. So just get out and leave me alone." Her voice trembled. "You and your damned secrets. You don't trust me and that hurts. Really - bloody - hurts - a lot."

Sharif squatted down and leaned against the bathroom door. He was used to being told he was an asshole and a lot worse. Eliza's hurt stung. "Don't take it personally, MacKay. I've never been able to trust." A memory flashed. Being sent away from his home like he was unworthy, when he had adored his parents and they returned the love with betrayal. "Probably never will. But I know you can do this. You must."

"You have no idea how terrifying this is. It's not because I don't like small spaces. It's because of the accident. I was pinned in my car seat. I saw my boys dying in the fire." He heard her voice trembling, groaning like a tortured animal. "Any time I feel trapped, I go through that torture again. You can't do this to me, captain. Please."

"Listen to me, Eliza. Are you listening?"

"I'm not friggin' deaf."

"Pray, Eliza. When you feel overwhelmed by those terrible things, talk to Allah. Allah, the Most Kind, the Most Compassionate, will hear you and comfort you. I promise you, dear Eliza. Will you pray? Like you did by the river. Remember?"

For a while, he thought she had ignored his pleas. Then he heard her blow her nose. Soon, the door opened and he had to jump up to keep from falling back. She stood before him, her eyes red and swollen, her face full of misery. He stepped back to let her slip past him. Instead, she stepped closer.

"Captain, do you have sisters?"

"Yes, but much older than me. Why?"

Eliza hesitated, avoided looking at Sharif. Finally she looked into his eyes and asked, "I know you're not supposed to touch me, but for just a little while, could you pretend that I'm your sister? And hold me?" Her chin quivered. "I really need a friend to hold me."

Tentatively, Sharif reached for her hands and held them tenderly. In response, Eliza tried to move into an embrace. He stiffened and put their clasped hands between them, keeping his distance. His heart pounded. He felt enveloped by a warm glow. And fear of surrendering to his desire for her. "My dear Miss MacKay, though it would please me to offer you comfort, I could never see you as my sister. Do you understand?"

She let go of his hands and took a deep breath. "I'm sorry. I should not have asked." She walked to the open window. Gazing at the night sky, she flicked loose tendrils of her hair behind her ears. "I am grateful, captain. I realize you're taking a hell of a risk."

Her shoulders inched back and chin lifted, she was again the tough and courageous woman he had come to admire. And yet, the vulnerability still seeped through the façade.

She turned toward him and presented a smile. "You needn't worry. I won't cause you more trouble. You've got enough on your plate. I'm fine. Go. I'll see you when I see you."

He took the bottle of pills from his pocket. "These are sleeping pills that a doctor gave to me for you. Said they are strong, so don't take more than one for the night." He set them on the night stand. "Tomorrow, Sergeant Muqtadir will come by with some food if he can."

"He shouldn't trouble himself. I carry emergency rations in my trauma backpack."

He checked his watch. "I'm going to be late if I don't leave right now. The hotel staff won't come into this room and, as you have guessed, you cannot open the door from the inside. Is there anything else you need, er, to know?"

"No. Good luck, sir."

Sharif stepped out of the room and closed the door. He had hoped she would remain sane enough to deliver a severe punch to his gut. It hurt already.

Chapter 14

Captain Sharif arrived at the airport well in advance. He and an army commander confirmed the locations of the military positions along the route to the downtown Sheraton Hotel scheduled to receive the foreigners.

Sharif and Police Chief Ganem greeted the American team - Mr. Hudson, the president's foreign affairs security aid; a Habitat rep, and three forensic technicians assigned to assist the CIA agent.

Hudson turned to Chief Ganem. "CIA Agent Frank Hutchinson will arrive tomorrow. I've been told he's a bit of a character. An exceptional CIA agent. He has promised that within two days this mystery will be solved. For all I know he could have arrived days ago."

Sharif secretly winced. Perhaps the CIA agent had been observing him for days. He resisted the impulse to glance in the direction of his boss.

Sharif breathed a sigh of relief to see the carts of luggage arrive. He cleared his throat and advised the visitors of the transportation to their hotel.

In the morning, the first order of business at the federal building began with a closed-door meeting between the Americans, consulate reps, President Najeeb, and Internal Affairs Minister Rasheed.

Sharif waited outside in the hall with Aamir and Ganem. His superiors spoke quietly and maintained an air of superiority. The CIA's forensic team appeared to be focused on their mobile devices. So far, Sharif hadn't seen or heard of the CIA agent's arrival.

He reviewed his investigation reports halfheartedly. They'd been appropriately doctored. He drifted away to the fountain. Checked his cell phone for missed calls, checked the battery. As the court house was located near the federal building, he listened for the heavy footsteps of his sergeant. In Sharif's world, no news meant bad news.

The door to the chambers opened. The Internal Affairs Minister summoned Aamir, Ganem, Sharif, Mr. Hudson, the CIA forensic team, and the American Habitat rep into the conference room. Windows facing east lined the entire length of a wall. At the far end of the room were refreshments. A large oak table had seating for all attendees, plus the missing CIA agent.

Sharif's army boots propelled him forward into the room. He halted at the sight of his country's esteemed leader, President Najeeb. He removed his hat and placed his documents on the table beside Chief Ganem.

Minister Rasheed instructed Sharif to deliver his investigation report and to provide his interpretation of those details. Sharif needed to swallow the glass of water in front of him. He didn't dare lift the glass. His hands trembled. Feared his voice would betray his guilt. He turned to Minister Rasheed.

Sharif focused on telling the facts, at least up to reporting the Americans had vanished after the unauthorized stop at a gas station. "It is believed my police officers were killed at the gas station while the Americans were busy inside. The military surveillance has not found any trace of the Americans or their property in our country at large. Within Samarra, 'street' people are faithful in alerting me to anything out of the ordinary. Even they are afraid, minister. It appears they dare not speak about the missing Americans."

Captain Sharif had gained enough confidence to grasp the glass of water and drink without spilling it. "Chief Ganem and I have met daily to discuss investigation tactics. Initially we had anticipated a terrorist group would claim responsibility for a possible attack on the Americans, demand ransom or prisoner exchange." Sharif nodded to the minister.

Minister Rasheed returned the nod. "Have you an opinion if the American Habitat people are alive or dead?"

Sharif took a deep breath and exhaled. Drawn to face the Americans, he hoped they didn't notice the sweat on his brow. Their expression of anguish bled away his resolve to comply with the cover-up. He shifted his gaze toward a blank wall. He heard the harsh clicking of the chief's pen, not so different from the sound of a gun being cocked.

"Sir, given the length of time without any contact from the criminals, I believe the Americans are dead." Sudden gasps and moans seared through the grave atmosphere.

Sharif could not offer false hope. These people needed to know as much truth as he dared to reveal. He turned to the Americans and spoke in English first, then repeated his statement in Arabic. "I'm truly sorry, but as we move forward in this investigation, we need to adjust our strategy in looking for their remains."

The room became heavy with sorrow. The Habitat rep sagged in his chair. The minister suggested a brief recess of the proceedings.

"No," cried Mr. Hudson. "This has been hard to hear, but not unexpected. We need to find out what the hell happened. What bastard did this? And why!"

President Najeeb had remained solemn and attentive during the discussion. He stood and buttoned his dark blue business suit. With a nod to his Internal Affairs minister he faced his guests. "Minister Rasheed and I, as well as my entire cabinet are shocked by this terrible act of terrorism." His voice came from deep in his chest. "There are organized dissenters who oppose my government. One or more may have orchestrated the attack in order to cause world governments to reject RIPT's membership in the UN. The intent may also be to cause lack of confidence with world trade agreements. It's unfortunate that we could not locate evidence of a rebel group's location in advance."

President Najeeb walked to a window and for a moment held his back to the group. His form appeared dark against the bright light. He turned and directed his gaze at each person in the room. "You cannot know how much this has distressed me personally. I have failed to protect and to maintain order within my great country. I had believed this civil unrest, this despicable hostility, was behind us."

President Najeeb returned to his chair. "Until we have determined the fate of the American Habitat people, we will continue to work day and night to resolve this to the satisfaction of the United States of America. The American investigators have our full cooperation. Whatever you deem necessary to aid in this investigation, you have but to ask and it will be done."

Suddenly a casually dressed man burst into the room. Sharif reached for his handgun and maneuvered toward the intruder. As he flipped off the safety and cocked his weapon, the intruder turned toward Sharif.

"Sharif, right? Captain Sharif?" He slouched a bit and his feet shuffled as he strode toward Sharif, unaffected by the weapon raised in his general direction. "Pleased to meet you, sir. I'm Agent Hutchinson, but just call me Frank." He thrust out his right hand and waited for Sharif to stand down.

Sharif saw beyond the casual veneer. He noted a shadow behind the agent's eyes. Trapped in Frank's hand grip, Sharif felt naked, like a specimen in Frank's microscope – measured and judged in seconds. Sharif secured his gun back into the holster.

Chapter 15

After introductions, the agent turned to Sharif. "Are you done here? Got a lot of ground to cover in two days." Frank paused, switching to a concerned expression. "You look awful, Sharif. Up all day and night, I suppose, looking for our Americans. Dusting off the furniture." Frank winked. "Not to worry. I won't wear out my welcome."

Sharif looked over Agent Hutchinson's head of bushy dark brown hair, windblown and sitting on his collar. He inspected the man's brown jacket and blue jeans, coated with dust and animal hair. Brushing dust from the agent's shoulder, he smiled and spoke in Arabic, "Came over the desert, Frank? Where'd you park your camel?"

Agent Frank grinned. "Yep, we'll get along fine." He turned to the audience. "Gentlemen," he said, bowing his head, "I'll have answers for you tomorrow afternoon."

He turned back to Sharif. "Let's go, Sharif."

Sharif turned to Minister Rasheed. "Do you require anything further, |Minister?"

Minister Rasheed frowned. "What are your plans, Mr. Hutchinson?"

"Ah, minister, that depends what I find at the captain's station."

Mayor Aamir quickly stepped into Frank's path. "Agent Hutchinson, why the interest in Captain Sharif's station?"

The agent shrugged. "Just procedure, sir. You see, the police officers assigned as the Habitat's escorts were assigned by Captain Sharif. In my book, that's page one."

At Sharif's police station, Frank spoke to the forensic team. "Mr. Sanchez, you and the rest are to interview everyone employed at this station, office staff and police personnel. You know what I'm looking for. Document your findings, all details. I'll meet you back at the hotel for dinner at seven."

Frank turned to Sharif. "Don't worry about my men. Just keeping them busy, out of my hair." Frank casually looked over Sharif's office and adjacent rooms. "What's upstairs?"

"This used to be headquarters fifteen years ago. Upstairs are vacant offices and my apartment."

Frank's eyebrows shot up. "Your apartment?"

"Yes, my family live in Rumi, west of the mountain range." Sharif smiled. "But I suspect you already know that. I stay here to save money and work extra hours."

Frank slapped his chest. "Ah, Sharif, I know all about the hardships of living apart from the wife and kids. Rough, I know. 'Cept your wife, er, ex-wife, lives in England. Right?"

Sharif just nodded. "My apartment is the last door on the right. Be sure to wipe your feet before you enter. My maid just cleaned up."

"Maid?" Frank winced. "Oh, I fell for that one. One for you, Sharif."

While Frank snooped around upstairs, Sharif waited in his office. His gut twisted, wondering if Eliza was still alive. He had an intense need to call Omar – impossible while under the scrutiny of the agent. After twenty minutes Frank came to Sharif's office carrying a small bag that appeared empty. He held the bag up so that Sharif could see its contents.

A long gold strand of hair caught the light and shimmered.

"Found this on your couch. Who does this belong to, Sharif?" Frank bounced his bushy eyebrows and grinned. "Looks nice."

Sharif hesitated. "Checking out my love life, Frank?"

Frank sat down. "Know for a fact you don't have a love life. Single devout Muslim men do not have a love life, especially you." Frank shook the bag. "Who?"

"Why are you playing with hair, Frank? What does that have to do with looking for your Americans?"

"Because it's out of the ordinary. Whose is it?"

"It must have hitched a ride on my uniform."

"Who? And don't give me that girlfriend bullshit."

"Could be my mother's. Sometimes she cleans my apartment. Want to check out my computer files?"

"No thanks. You've already dumped your hard drive. Your mother has yellow hair?

"Grey, actually but parts appear more yellow. You hacked into my computer? When?"

"Does it matter when?" He studied the strand of hair. "Your momma is seventy-two next month. Now, with the silky look of this strand, I'd say this belongs to a much younger woman. Course this'll undergo evaluation for DNA 'n' such. Unless, of course, you might remember who this belongs to." Agent Hutchinson cocked his head.

"Probably belongs to a woman I helped." Sharif shifted in his chair. "Why were you interested in my computer files?"

Agent Hutchinson pulled out a marker pen and wrote 'Exhibit A' on the bag. "I'll say good day to Blondie, for now." He leaned forward. "Surely you know we've been watching, listening, gathering clues on the whereabouts of our Habitat folks." Frank tucked the bag into his jacket pocket. "Regarding your computer. Actually, Sharif, you weren't on my radar until three days ago."

Sharif could not resist the agent's carrot. "Why three days ago?"

"Intel put you in the spotlight. Tell me everything you know." The agent leaned forward. "And I want the details. Shoot."

Sharif did his hat flip and reported the facts, the official facts starting at the time the airport told him the American's flight had been delayed.

The agent nodded. "You're certain the bus didn't enter Samarra?"

Sharif shook his head. "Frank. I doubt the killers would have risked it. Our police patrols might have spotted the convoy, pulled them over as none were scheduled to pass through Samarra that night. It would've ended up in a battle."

In truth, he knew he would have been contacted before the police squads would have interfered. As it was, another captain had alerted him, but too late. "My theory is that they were picked up by another air transport and taken out of RIPT. Every billionaire in RIPT has his own private airport."

Sharif knew he was being studied, assessed by a highly trained interrogator. No doubt he had reached the top of Frank's list of suspects. "The first place I'd look is Egypt."

"Keep going." Frank waved his hand in a circular motion.

Sharif squirmed, knowing the bull ring was in his nose and being yanked. "Two weeks ago, one of my informants was approached by someone. No words were spoken. The stranger handed him a huge amount of money and a note instructing him to keep the police busy for a while. Indicated a major hit was planned. Said the note hinted at an Egyptian origin."

Frank spread his arms wide and smiled. "Now we're getting somewhere.

Frank stood and waved for Sharif to follow. "Outside, Sharif."

Agent Hutchinson proceeded out into the compound and headed to the execution wall.

Sharif kept pace and held his tongue. The CIA agent stood in the center of the compound.

"I'm told this is where criminals are executed," he said pointing to the wall.

"Correct."

"Messy business. I see you've cleaned up."

"I understand most Americans are a bit queasy about capital punishment. Figured we should clean up. Are you hungry, Frank? There's a great spot for spaghetti and meatballs just down the road."

Hutchinson groaned and started to counter Sharif's insult. Sharif was already heading to his SUV.

Sharif took Agent Hutchinson to a small sidewalk café near the park. As they ate, the agent chatted, asking Sharif about his home life, if he had plans to travel. Sharif responded with vague answers, suspicious of the agent's motives.

Gulping down the last of his coffee, Frank announced he would carry on without Sharif for the remainder of the afternoon. As Frank headed onto the sidewalk, he abruptly turned back. "Oh, we'll be driving out to the work site tomorrow. You know, where the Habitat volunteers were supposed to go.

Sharif stood and nodded. "Fine. What time?"

"Seven." Frank headed back to the sidewalk. He took two steps and turned around. "One more thing, Sharif. When do I get to meet Blondie?"

"She's busy."

The agent returned to stand in front of Sharif. "When you start telling me the fucking truth, I'll stop seeing you standing up against my wall. I have no problem executing anyone who had anything to do with the disappearance of fifteen Americans. Including liars! Is that clear?" Hutchinson paused as if to ensure Sharif felt the full fury of his meaning.

As the agent merged seamlessly with the pedestrians heading into the park, Sharif waited. He couldn't detect anything unusual, but had the distinct feeling of being watched. Sharif fought off the urge to return to the hotel to check on Eliza. Certain that Frank or his cyberspace team spied on him, it would be a mistake.

To do nothing would drive him insane thinking about Eliza. But the agent would use any action Sharif did take as the evidence that he was a liar and killer. He had only one escape.

Chapter 16

Frustrated, Sharif tossed his phone to his SUV's passenger seat. *This has got to end. I've got to get access to a computer that doesn't broadcast input to the whole damn world.* He headed to the Guardian Mosque. Recalling that Eliza worked for her city's ambulance service, Sharif searched the Internet, scrolling through the Edmonton, Alberta's Emergency Medical Department websites and reports. A report dating back to the time of Jasper's Mile of Hell paid dividends in vital information. Reading through the pages, Sharif learned that two men in particular had been diligent in taking care of her home, visiting her in the hospital, and acting on her behalf with a lawyer.

On impulse, he weighed the risk of committing treason. Absolutely forbidden. He made the call.

Once he had the phone number of the ambulance service, he dialed it and tried to get his heart rate down with a few deep breaths. He was entering an uncharted mine field. Every word, the tone of his voice, even his facial expression had to be perfect.

"Emergency Medical Service Department. Is this an emergency?"

Sharif relaxed his shoulders and emphasized his English accent. "No, not exactly. May I speak to the supervisor on duty?"

"One moment, please, sir."

After one minute, Sharif heard a few clicks and road noise. The sound of a two-way radio blared. "Hello, Sierra Two here."

Sharif realized he had called during the service's night shift. "Hello." Sharif chose a fake name. "My name is Adrian MacKay. To whom am I speaking?"

"This is Superintendent 124. We don't give out names. Is your call regarding an emergency?"

"No emergency. Not exactly. I'm looking for one of your staff. His name is Mike Tanasiuk. Is he there?"

"You're in luck. Mike is working an extra shift tonight. I'll get him to call you back."

First snag. Sharif couldn't give a phone number for a call back. Revealing too much information put him too close to grounds for treason – a death sentence. "Can't call back here. Can you patch me through to his unit?"

"You sound like you know about mobile units. You a paramedic?"

"No. I'm a police officer. Scotland."

"You don't sound Scottish. More English with a weird accent." The man chuckled.

"Educated in London. You say I can talk directly with Mike?"

"Stand by."

Another minute, and more clicks, he heard laughing in the background. "Hello, Mike here. Who's calling, please?"

His sweaty palms became glued to the phone receiver. "Adrian MacKay, here. I'm looking for someone. A mutual friend, I think. You know Eliza Ramsay?"

"Christ, how do you know her?"

Sharif created a fictitious scenario in seconds. "Don't actually know her. Just got a call from her a few weeks ago saying she wanted to meet. Said I could be related to her ancestor, a Colin MacKay, I think. She did say her married name had been Elizabeth Ramsay."

Sharif paused a moment. He didn't want to sound too eager. "Just out of curiosity I did a little research. Found out about the accident. Too bad she lost everyone. I guess that's why she was looking for a relative."

"We hoped she'd find someone."

Mike's cautious responses frustrated Sharif. "Well, we agreed to meet at the Edinburgh airport but she never showed. I waited for a phone call from her for a week. Perhaps you know how I might get in touch with her?"

"You sure you want to? She's a handful. Beauty and brains come with a downside, you know, eh."

Sharif chuckled to go along with the ruse. "All the MacKays are warriors. She have a boyfriend?" *Why did I ask that?*

"No. A few were interested but as soon as she told them about the accident, they dropped her. Couldn't handle the PTSD."

"PTSD? Oh yes, she mentioned a bit about that. Said that she has trouble dealing with traumatic children, or something like that."

"Ya. Post-traumatic stress disorder. She's a lot better now but still goes off once in a while."

"What do you mean, off, exactly?"

Mike hesitated. "I'd rather not say. She's a friend. I care about her. She doesn't like disrespect. Her privacy had been trodden on pretty bad for a couple of years after the accident."

Sharif dug in. He wanted Mike to initiate a search for Eliza. "She might be in trouble, Mike. She sounded so eager to meet. Then nothing. Not a phone call. Nothing. She sounded like the kind of person who'd call to cancel. Could this fallout thing have something to do with her disappearance?"

Mike groaned. "I really shouldn't say, but you sound genuinely concerned about Eliza. Just a minute. Got to shut my door."

When Mike returned, his voice took on an ominous tone. "Adrian, this is how things are with Eliza. After the accident she was in a terrible mental state. Attempted suicide three times. Would have died if Don or I hadn't checked on her every day. Between us and her psychiatrist, we kept her out of a mental institution. After two years, it looked like she was on the mend. Except for the triggers."

"Triggers? You mean the things that cause her to have flashbacks?"

"Yes, several triggers. Some we can identify; others are still a mystery. She can now handle scenes of vehicle wrecks with a little coaching. Fire used to be huge, even just a lighter. Still can't handle emergencies with children. Confined in a small space is another one."

Sharif gasped and stiffened. "What happens?"

"She loses touch with reality. She screams, or just mutters on and on. Or she'll just walk for days. We've had to go looking for her and try to get her mind back on track."

Sharif's worries escalated. He hoped Eliza slept through the night and day. "Mike, I'm more worried than ever. If she's in trouble there, her life could be at risk. They might just lock her up. Given what you've told me, I think I should notify the authorities."

"If she's just keeping to herself, like she often does, she'd kill us. If she's in trouble, we would've heard by now. She's not a vagrant. Far from it. Don and I made sure her ID documents were comprehensive. Her cell phone has our numbers. Emergency contact, medical info. You know she has only one kidney? Lost the right kidney in the accident. Has to be careful with drug dosages."

Sharif winced. "If you've got her cell number, how about dialing it? Just in case."

"If that will ease your mind. She might answer and tell us to go to hell."

"I'll risk it. After all, she's the one who was looking for me."

"Hang on, Adrian."

As Mike dialed on another phone, Sharif asked, "Is she really that hard to get along with?"

"No, not actually. She'd do anything for her friends. Very loyal, passionate about her family. But if you piss her off with disrespect or take her for granted, better get the hell out of her range of fire."

Sharif could hear a ringing tone over Mike's receiver.

"Her cell is ringing." Then a message cut in: "The party you are attempting to contact is out of service range or has the device turned off." Sharif tried to remember what he'd done with her cell. *Most likely tossed into the incinerator.*

"Hmm, that's odd," said Mike. "She has an international SIM card and never turns her phone off. It's an old habit. She made sure her boys could call her anytime."

Sharif's confidence grew. He had achieved a measure of success. "It would seem that the phone has been either stolen, or damaged. Would she contact you if she was in trouble?"

"Not necessarily. She's extremely independent. Thinks she's capable of handling trouble with all her self-defense training and …."

Sharif cut in. "Unless she's having, what you called, a mental breakdown." He hoped Mike's concern would escalate to initiate a search. "I'll call you back in another day or two to see if you've been able to contact her. Good luck."

Sharif sat back and assessed what he had achieved. If all went well, someone would commence an investigation leading the Canadian government to make inquiries. Hopefully, all those steps would take only a few days, a week at most. *Canada has a reputation for not making sudden moves, which was unfortunate in this case.*

His solar plexus ached. Time was a luxury Eliza could not afford.

En route to his station, Sharif stopped at the park where he and Eliza had walked. He stepped out of his vehicle and took off his blazer. His body moved slowly, tightly wound up by lies and dishonor. At first, he began to fold his coat and lay it on the passenger seat. His self-loathing erupted. *Bastard.* He flung it to the

passenger seat. *I'm in league with filthy, fucking street rats.* His flak
jacket whizzed through the air as he ripped it off his chest and flung
it past the steering wheel. *Fucking, blood sucking morons.* He threw
his handgun into a secure compartment between the seats and
slammed it shut. *I'm a fucking coward. Yes, sir. No sir. Fuck.* His
handgun harness, hat, shirt, boots, socks flew off and landed
somewhere behind the front seats. "Bloody coward!" he shouted
over and over again.

He stood in the parking lot wearing only a black t-shirt and
trousers. Sharif's skin glowed with perspiration.

He struggled to hold back wave after wave of emotion. He
ran hard. His body vibrated. Grunts from the exertion and more
expletives barely served to vent his festering anger. Daggers dug into
his heart. "I deserve eternity in hell!" He ignored the path's grit
biting into the soles of his bare feet. His muscles burned.

The setting sun winked between the trees along the path. The
celestial orb mocked him - perfection in the sky shining down on
earth's flawed creature. Am I lost, he wondered? His thoughts of
self-incrimination flowed with the same intensity as the river's blind
struggle to run from its source, taking the path of least resistance and
consuming whatever lay in front of it.

When his legs began to tremble with fatigue, he trotted to the
river's edge. He shivered as he pulled off his sweat-soaked t-shirt.
Blood oozed from cuts on the soles of his feet. He stood at the rocky
shore, bent over trying to catch his breath. "Serves you right,
asshole!" he shouted his self-reprimand. As he became calmer, the
soothing sounds of the water's flow penetrated his defenses.

He sat on a boulder and held his head in his hands. Tremors
from deep within his core flooded past the gates. Long-held
disappointments and heartache emerged. His belief that he could not
be loved smacked him. It cleaved a wedge to his soul.

Surrender does not come easy to a man of deep pride and
heavy responsibilities. In the moment of deepest regrets and visceral
fears, he shuddered as the hands of Allah rested lightly on his
shoulders urging him to give up his last defense. He thought he
heard, "Let it go. Let it go now, Sharif."

Sharif froze. Tears welled, and then forced their way through his fingers held over his eyes. The dam broke.

An hour later, Sharif walked back to his vehicle. From several yards away, moonlight revealed a man waiting near his SUV. *Damn, the police chief is spying on me.* However, in another few steps he noted the shape lacked Ganem's prowling animal gait. Finally he recognized the CIA Agent, Frank Hutchinson.

"Hey there, Sharif," the agent shouted. "Hoped you'd get back soon. It's damn cold out here."

Captain Sharif strode up to his vehicle. "Get inside," he said, as he hit the remote button. *Perhaps Frank had witnessed the break down.* His pride tumbled. The agent jumped into the passenger seat.

Sharif dressed and jumped in behind the steering wheel. "Been waiting long?" His voice sounded monotone.

"Not long." Frank eyed Sharif for a moment. "You look like shit."

Sharif turned on the ignition and flicked on the heater. "Been better."

The agent nodded. "Been there, done that, got the fucking straight jacket," Agent Hutchinson said, smacking Sharif's shoulder.

Sharif shifted in his seat, at a loss for words. Without turning towards the agent, Sharif asked, "Frank, you've seen the movies where a man is tied up to a bomb. If he sneezes, twitches, so much as sweats, the bomb goes off. No matter what he does, boom!"

"Yep, love 'em."

Sharif turned to Frank. "How does he get out?"

"Good guys don't always win." Frank shrugged. "Except they always get the girl."

Both men laughed. "Where to, Frank?"

Sharif delivered Agent Hutchinson to his downtown hotel and returned to his station. He lay naked on top of his bed and drifted into sleep. Minutes later he woke, panic-stricken, feeling the walls of a coffin, trapped under six feet of soil. He bolted up, gasping for air.

Chapter 17

Early the next day, Sharif and Agent Hutchinson headed out of town for the three-hour drive to the Habitat's designated work site. The forensic team followed. About an hour past the city limits, they reached a county border security station manned by army personnel.

While waiting for the guards, Sharif idly tapped his fingers on the open window frame. The morning breeze drifted into the SUV's interior and played with the agent's documents lying on the back seat. Hutchinson turned and grabbed them. Sharif watched as the agent turned to a particular handwritten report.

"Ah," said the agent, stabbing the page with his finger. "This is where it first became apparent there could be trouble. It was from this location you received word that the Habitat bus had not arrived. Correct?"

Sharif nodded. "Yes. The officer called me via our shared two-way radio frequency, and asked if the Habitat bus had been detained at the airport. I told him that the bus should've arrived." That much had been the truth. He mentally reviewed the report his boss had fabricated. "By my calculations the bus was twenty minutes late. I made a few calls to our military base and road patrol. No one had seen the bus. That's when I returned to my station and called the police chief."

Boots scuffing along the pavement caught Sharif's attention. Sharif waved a hello to the military officer.

"Oh, it's you, Captain Sharif." The army corporal nodded back with a smile. "What brings you into my turf, sir? Taking the scenic route to your station?" The private chuckled.

Sharif smiled and faked a blow to the private's chin. "Show some respect." He nodded to his passenger. "This is Frank Hutchinson, CIA. His team is in the vehicle behind us. We're heading up to the construction site where the American Habitat people were supposed to work."

"Ah, yes. You're clear to proceed, sir."

As Sharif drove past the raised barrier, the CIA agent spoke. "Just a second, Sharif. Pull up just ahead. I'm getting a twinge in the back of my neck." Frank's forensic team pulled up behind Sharif's SUV.

"Need an aspirin, Frank?" Sharif parked a few yards ahead. "Or is it your GPS microchip?" Sharif smiled. "Maybe your boss is keeping track of you."

Frank held up his hand. "Let me think a minute here." The agent gazed at the surrounding landscape. To his left, about a hundred miles away, a long mountain range rose into the clear blue sky. Snow capped the higher elevations. Forests tumbled down to the highway. Ahead, the two lane highway cut through the terrain. On his right a wide river fought for a path toward Samarra. As the land swept down and away from the mountains, fields of fruit trees grew abundantly in a verdant valley.

Frank spread his road map open against the dash. "Sharif, when the bus left the airport here," he said, pointing to the location on the map, "there were three directions the driver could have taken the passengers. Either turned off ten miles back to go over the mountain pass here," he said, pointing to the jagged dotted line on the map, "or come by this check point, or into Samarra. Right?"

Certain the agent had a detailed mental image of the terrain, he stuck to the truth and described paths not included on the map. "Not exactly. There's a couple of secondary roads that take off from this road here." Sharif pointed at a place a few miles back. "It's not shown on the map, but a four-wheel drive can make it back into these mountains. A bus wouldn't. And another here," he said, pointing to the airport, "a goat trail from the airport heading south."

"Uh huh. Well, it's not likely they headed south after having arrived at the gas station. And they didn't come here. And you don't believe they came into the city. Right?" Agent Hutchinson raised his eyebrows.

"Right, but if you're thinking the driver took a bus over the mountain pass in the dead of night, it would have been suicidal. It's a very long, tortuous path, almost a three-hour drive to the summit road. And that's if there have been no rock slides. On the other side is my hometown, Rumi, populated with people who notice strangers."

Frank rolled up the map. He muttered, "Thank God, dead people talk." He smacked Sharif's shoulder with the map. "Today, we find the bodies. Let's take that trail back into the mountains. What's back there?"

"Mostly just caves. Criminals sometimes hide out back in there. Bus can't go there." Sharif mentally cursed the chief. It had been twenty days since the massacre. Ganem had refused to reveal the location where the bodies had been buried. He hoped they were a hundred miles out in the dirt and scrub brush east of Samarra. "I wouldn't recommend going back there without some backup."

"Sooner the better, Sharif."

Sharif made a bold attempt to discourage the agent. "Frank, if I'd thought there was any logic to the Americans being abducted into this back country, I'd have looked. There's nothing there but rodents and a lot of trash. No terrorist would go up there. It's a dead end. They'd be trapped."

The agent grinned. "How long to get backup?"

Within half an hour, the army pulled up with three armed vehicles and a squadron of soldiers. The convoy picked up the trail and headed into the recesses of the earth's spine, sometimes hugging a ridge, or maneuvering around boulders. As the sun rose, so did the heat. The dusty trail, flanked by evergreens, betrayed their passage into forbidden territory. The trucks growled as they were driven to higher elevations. Sharif noticed the signs of occasional human presence: discarded food wrappers, gas cans, water bottles and a tire.

For an hour they motored on, occasionally stopping with the agent's command to inspect signs that hinted of violence - a large knife, a lone shoe and a bloody shirt. At a point where the trail widened, Frank ordered a thorough inspection.

The forensic team and military escorts split into small groups and were told to search for evidence of anything out of the ordinary. Some began to hike up a rocky trail. Others walked back along the trail.

Sharif stepped to the side of the road and readied his MP5. The cliff dropped several hundred feet. With Frank behind him, he called out, "Still got that niggling feeling in your neck, Frank?"

Frank appeared to be engrossed in the ground, like a hound searching for whiff blood.

Sharif sighed. He grabbed his bottle of water from his SUV. As he drank he noted a dot in the sky. It circled, silently, coming closer with each pass. He looked back at Frank, still inspecting twigs of scrub brush, and the scattering of stones.

The heat radiated off the boulders. A cool breeze teased, then vanished. Scattered evergreens offered patches of shade. Sharif looked for the circling bird. It had come closer as if to inspect the possibility of food scurrying among shrubs. Its wingspan cast a sweeping shadow across the trail below.

He gasped as he identified the bird to be a carrion crow. Then he saw the flies. Hundreds darted about and landed on his face. A gust of wind made him gag. He covered his nose as the smell of decay filled his nostrils - human bodies swelling with putrid gas and turning black.

"Over here," someone hollered.

Sharif fought off his shock and ran with the soldiers back along the trail. Agent Hutchinson darted to the front shouting for everyone to not touch or move anything. He scrambled along the short path that ran ninety degrees to the road. Several yards behind evergreen trees, a steep bank revealed a low wide opening.

A soldier stood pointing to the inside of the cave. "I think this is what you're looking for. Several remains. Smells real bad in there."

Frank ran to the cave's open mouth and asked for a flashlight. An army private knelt down at the entrance and passed him a heavy-duty lantern. The light illuminated a mass of decomposing corpses. They had been haphazardly piled on top of each other. Their bloody clothing revealed the cause of their demise. The missing Americans lay in a cold cave, ready to reveal the savagery of the massacre. In mute terror, they cried for justice.

Sharif scanned the grisly scene as the flashlight lit up the cave. On his left, he noted something odd amid the bones and blood stained clothes. He gasped.

Frank nodded. "Horrible, isn't it? I've never gotten used to mass murders."

Sharif swung back toward Frank, nodded and retreated. He swallowed the remains of his water and wiped his mouth with the back of his trembling hand. *Damn Ganem. Couldn't be bothered to burn the tubing.* He jumped when a hand grabbed his arm.

Frank didn't hide his rage. "Get an army transport vehicle, captain." He turned to his forensic team. "Pull out the remains and do a cursory exam." Soon all twenty-one remains lay in the hot sun.

"Sharif, look." The agent pointed to the bodies of the killers, still clothed in their police uniforms. Their bodies had been at the bottom of the pile on the cold stone surface, and showed less signs of decomposition. "I believe those six men are the killers. Not much to go on, but could you identify any of these constables?"

Sharif stared at the six black and bloated bodies. He gripped his weapon hard until his hands might have bled. "They're not with our police service. Somehow they got our uniforms. Easy enough to do." He gritted his teeth, his hands shook - with rage. *Bastards.*

Sharif shifted into his professional skin. Some bones had been shattered. Skulls had gaping holes. "Indications are that they were shot from the rear, probably running away from the killers."

Frank sat on his heels beside Sharif. "They weren't shot at this location. Some bullets are in the cave. Fell to the floor as the bodies decomposed. Not one bullet or casing is outside the cave."

Frank stood up and waved his arms wide. "Who killed the killers?"

Sharif ignored the question. "We need to ID the killers." Sharif stood and kept his eyes averted from Frank's. "That may give a clue to who shot them."

"There are no documents on them. Perhaps their DNA will ID them, but that's gonna take time. And if they're not in the database…." Frank threw up his hands as if in total frustration. "Perhaps the leaders executed their own men to eliminate witnesses."

"That makes sense." Sharif's relief was short lived. The agent jumped over to a victim attached to some tubing.

And look at this." He picked up the bag still containing fluids. "A bunch of medical stuff. Looks like someone had intravenous fluids for something. This makes no sense at all. What do you make of it?"

Sharif hid his shock by removing his hat to swat at the flies. He glanced at the bones, checking for more of Eliza's gold hair. *Damn, how the hell do I get him off this?* "Frank, this is bizarre." He stepped out of the way of a soldier carrying a loaded stretcher to the truck. The move took him farther away from the agent's view.

Frank turned on his heels, following Sharif. For a few minutes Frank shuffled his feet, muttered to himself, gesturing with his hands in a pantomime of his thoughts. He slapped his chest. "This victim was being treated for injuries. The only way that could've happened is if these killers were killed before the medic arrived." Frank approached Sharif. "That rules out the theory the leaders killed their own men."

Maneuvered into a corner, Sharif swung around to face the torment. A soldier brushed by him. His foot slid off a boulder. He lashed out. "Hey, watch it." Sharif inhaled to reclaim his composure.

Frank's piercing gaze dared him to continue with the lies. *He knows more than he's saying. But what, and how?*

"Sharif, here's what might have happened. The Habitat people were taken to a site. They were killed, except for one. The killers were attacked and killed, perhaps by rival terrorists. At some point, someone with advanced medical knowledge was allowed to provide first aid to one of the Americans. The American died. The bodies of the Habitat people and the first killers were then delivered here." Frank kicked at stones. "Just one problem. Who is the medic? And where the hell is he?"

Sharif nodded, resisted blinking. He walked up to Frank. "Am I a suspect?"

"You know the routine. Everyone's guilty. And you're looking pretty guilty right now."

"Frank, if you were responsible for the safety of visitors to your home and they all died, how guilty would you feel?"

"Did you kill these people, Sharif?"

Sharif's nerves hit bottom. He threw his hands up. "Sure, Frank. I killed them, dragged their fucking bodies up here. Then lied to my superiors. How about motive? Check my bank account. You'll see there's two hundred American dollars. I wanted more for the hit, but the price for this kind of job sucks." He pulled out his smartphone, uploaded his bank account and tossed the phone to Frank.

Frank handed the phone back and glowered at Sharif. "Got a good lawyer, captain?"

Frank barked orders about placing each body in a body bag and carefully loading all twenty-one corpses into the truck. "Take it real slow to the airport. I don't want evidence lost postmortem. Understood?" Frank used a red marker to mark the body bag containing the corpse that had had medical treatment.

Captain Sharif stood beside the agent. "At least, the families can bury their loved ones. There's no more wondering what happened. Do you have everything you want out of the cave?"

The agent nodded. "Let's get the hell out of here."

On the way back to the city, the agent and Sharif rode in silence. Sharif asked the agent if he needed anything – a coffee, pit stop, speak with anyone else, if the temperature in his SUV was comfortable. The agent responded to all his queries with a clipped "No." Sharif delivered the agent back to the federal building. They met with the Internal Affairs Minister and asked that he pull in the other key players immediately.

The minister's staff set up second floor conference room. The floor-to-ceiling windows let in the rays of the sun, flirting with the rain clouds on the eastern horizon. Within twenty minutes all the guests had arrived. They turned down the offer of coffee and food. Sharif saw the fear in their eyes, and wondered if they could stomach the news about to be delivered.

Sharif and Agent Hutchinson sat across the table from Mayor Aamir and Chief Ganem. The room fell into a hush as Internal Affairs Minister Rasheed initiated the meeting. He bowed to the CIA agent. "Please proceed," he said with a distinct ominous tone in his voice.

"Sir," the CIA agent nodded to Rasheed, "Captain Sharif and I found the bodies of our Americans." Gasps and murmurs filled the room. "In fact, the killers were placed in the same cave with the fifteen Habitat people. President Najeeb has approved transporting all bodies back to CIA's lab."

The mayor's head's jerked as if someone had punched him in his jaw. Sharif watched him from the corner of his eye.

Agent Hutchinson went on to describe the day's events, and then wrapped up his summary. "I am returning to Washington to analyze the data I've collected. With permission, Minister, Captain Sharif and I will continue to collaborate on further investigation efforts to determine who orchestrated the massacre."

A Habitat rep spoke. "Do you have any clue who is responsible or why our people were killed?"

"At this time I have only theory. I will not say more until I have verifiable proof. Any further details of my findings will remain confidential. At the conclusion of my investigation, all information will be revealed. We will apprehend those responsible."

The minister rose from his chair. The Islamic robes of his heritage flowed gracefully with his unhurried movements. The attendees turned their attention to the senior government official and waited for his response. He appeared unaffected by the sting of the news. "Gentlemen," he said, with his arms spread slightly apart, his hands open, "I have prayed to Allah. Prayed for nations coming together with one goal in mind. To cultivate a world neighborhood, an atmosphere of respect. To be a people who see how much we are the same, instead of how we are different."

The CIA agent was momentarily silent. "Our business here is concluded for the time being." His eyes were cold as he stared at Sharif. "Gentlemen, the eagle never sleeps."

Captain Sharif was eager to leave the airport once he was satisfied the Americans were safely headed to their departure gates. The CIA agent handed his business card to Sharif and advised him to call 'anytime, anytime at all for any reason'.

Captain Sharif shook the agent's hand and asked, "Did you expect to find the killers?"

The agent picked up his bags and turned to head toward the revolving door. He looked back. "Mostly hoped to find someone worth trusting, Sharif." He produced an agent's smile, without warmth. "Don't lose my card," he said, passing through the door. "Just in case you decide to tell me what you know." Frank disappeared into the airport's security area, and Sharif sprinted back to his SUV.

Eliza had been trapped in the room for two nights and almost two days. He wondered if she had gone insane, if she even survived. Arriving at the front desk, he inquired if there had been any problems. He was relieved that nothing had been reported. Instead of taking the slow elevator, he raced up the stairs. His hands shook, making it difficult to insert the key card

Chapter 18

Finally, the security card slipped into the slot. Laughter from within the room startled Sharif. He glanced at the room number on the door. The locking mechanism released. He hesitated, listening for clues as to the identity of the people within the room. His shoulders tensed, and his grip on his handgun tightened. Then, with the loud roar of a man's voice, he recognized Sergeant Omar Abdul-Muqtadir.

He pushed the door open and stepped into the room. The laughter stopped. The hulking frame of the sergeant spun toward him. "Sharif, how nice of you to drop by. You could've knocked. But no harm." The big man snickered. "Yes, come on in. Have a seat." Omar motioned toward the bed, and then stepped back. "God, what is that putrid smell?"

Though his uniform had been contaminated with odorous body fluids of rotting flesh, Sharif's nose had long since disregarded the smell. He scanned the room and discovered Eliza standing beside Omar's wife.

Eliza wore her lilac skirt and blouse. Her lovely face glowed. Golden tendrils of her hair rested loosely on her shoulders. She could have been Al-Lat, the ancient Arabian Moon Goddess. Warmth flooded his chest, made him gasp.

He held her in his mind, noting that her initial response to his arrival appeared to be filled with relief, maybe more. But in a flash the pleasant expression vanished. Bitterness destroyed the softness in her eyes. She folded her arms across her chest and turned away from him. His disappointment surged. Another battle loomed.

Sharif acknowledged Omar Abdul-Muqtadir's wife and asked, "Have you been keeping Miss MacKay company all day?"

"Yes, Captain Sharif," she said, putting on her head scarf. "I hope you don't mind. We've been having such fun."

Sharif eyed Muqtadir and frowned. He turned back to her and nodded. "More concerned that my sergeant has placed in his dear wife in danger."

Omar's wife came forward. Toughness pushed through her usual soft demeanor. "He's right, Captain. You cannot treat her so carelessly again." She waggled her finger at him. "In the future, ask for help." She picked up a duffel bag. "This is for you."

Overwhelmed by a kaleidoscope of conflicting emotions, he shuffled his feet as if hoping to regain his balance. Relief gave way to frustration. Anger struggled for supremacy but cratered under the weight of guilt. Wave after wave, the emotional tsunami ravaged his thoughts and spirit. His military posture degraded to sagging shoulders. He lifted his hat off his head and slapped it back down again. For two seconds he managed to make eye contact with Omar Muqtadir's wife, then retreated to look over her head to his sergeant. "What's in the bag?"

Muqtadir gathered up his gun, coat and guided his wife toward the door. "You're off for the next two days. Chief Ganem approved the days off. Knows you're in some hotel. Didn't tell him where. I've packed a change of clothes for you." Muqtadir glared at Sharif. "Stay here. Get some rest so you can think rationally." He turned toward Eliza. "You make sure he doesn't leave. Just like we discussed." The sergeant walked up to Sharif and punched his shoulder, hard. "You show your face at the station, I'll kick your ass till you can't sit. Is that clear?"

Sharif massaged his shoulder. "You're insubordinate."

The angry sergeant headed for the door. "Yep, and I look forward to discussing this in front of a hearing committee. Momma, are you ready?"

Mrs. Abdul Muqtadir gave a quick hug to Eliza, and passed through the doorway. "I'll meet you at the elevator, Omar. I have something to say to Captain Sharif."

He followed the diminutive woman to the hallway as her husband headed to the elevator. "Is there a problem?" Sharif softened his stance.

She hesitated, appearing uncomfortable. "Shut the door," she whispered.

Sharif glanced back into the room. Eliza was gazing out the window. "I'll just be a minute. In the meantime, you may consider giving me an opportunity to reassure you this won't happen again."

Eliza turned toward him. Her eyes narrowed. "You don't have a snowball's chance in hell, Sharif!"

So relieved to see her alive and well, he dodged her venom. He shut the door and turned back to Omar's wife.

"I saw how you looked at her," she murmured. "You're in love with Miss MacKay."

Sharif mentally rewound the video of when he had entered the room. "Nonsense. I was only relieved that she hadn't been discovered, or had gone mad."

"You can't fool a woman in these matters." Mrs. Abdul Muqtadir was thoughtful for a moment. "She's a good woman. I like her. And she's strong. But I sense she's been wounded. She covers up her frailty so people won't abandon her. She needs you, but not for protection."

Sharif knew of Mrs. Abdul's gift as a seer, a guarded secret. Sharif sighed. "I'm sorry. I don't understand."

The woman whispered. "You'll have to figure that out for yourself. But be careful. You could easily destroy her. Good day, Captain."

Chapter 19

Sharif mentally filed the prophecy under 'interesting but not practical' and returned to the room. Eliza stood at the open window. Car horns punctuated the soft hum of the streets below. A breeze lifted wisps of her hair. She grabbed an errant silky strand and tucked it behind her ear. Her rigid back betrayed her anger, barely contained.

"Alright, let's have it out."

She swung around. "Just like that. No apology? How dare you! How dare you lock me up so that I can't even escape if there's a fire? Suppose those killers found me! How dare you put my life at risk?" Her fury escalated.

Sharif tried to sidestep her. He slipped between her and the bed, heading for the open window. If they were going to have a row, he didn't want witnesses. Before he could get past her, she caught his foot in midair with her foot, grabbed his shoulders and pushed. He tumbled backwards onto the bed.

In a flash, Eliza straddled his hips and grabbed his shoulders, pinning him down onto the bed. "The one thing I want to hear from you, Sharif, is an apology. A sincere apology."

"Better do what the lady says, Sharif."

Startled by the sudden intrusion, Sharif easily threw Eliza off, sending her tumbling to the floor. He reached for his gun and found nothing but the bed's fabric. In another quick move, he reached for the gun holstered in his chest harness and sprang to his feet.

Shit, no flak jacket. "Stay down, Eliza," he hollered. Sharif flashed his weapon toward the dark doorway. His finger squeezed the trigger, just a hair before firing the bullet.

Frank Hutchinson stepped into the entrance. He glanced at Sharif and walked up to Eliza. "Blondie, I presume." Frank reached out his hand to help her stand. "No need for alarm, miss. I see Sharif is very protective of you."

Eliza ignored the outstretched hand and stood. "You are who?"

Sharif muscled his way between Frank and Eliza. "Frank, you just stepped over the line." Sharif rammed his gun back into the holster. "Why are you here?" Sharif struggled to rein in his frustration. Even so, his fists curled into balls of steel.

"Unfinished business, Sharif. Really needed to see who owned that strand of hair. Figured you might be anxious to see her. It seemed odd that you allowed me every access, except to her," he said, nodding toward Eliza. "Why?"

Sharif had a second to create a diversion and hoped Eliza would catch on to the charade. If he failed, he'd be in a CIA holding cell by nightfall. And his family? He'd never see them again.

"Frank Hutchinson, meet Miss Eliza MacKay. Eliza, my dear, meet CIA Agent, Frank Hutchinson." *Will she catch on to my show of affection -- as if we are lovers?*

Frank shook her hand, then tenderly grasped her fingers. "A pleasure to meet you, Eliza. I should regret the rude entrance. However, rudeness or expediency is a job requirement." He smiled provocatively, tilting his head close to her face. His eyes lingered over her curves. "Sharif, you have excellent taste."

Sharif, shocked at the agent's overt attention to Eliza's form, shouted, "Frank, -."

Eliza's right hand shot up, silencing his attack. Her chin lifted an inch as did the corners of her mouth. "Mr. Hutchinson, it is nice to be appreciated, especially for what matters." Her voice became terse. As the agent attempted to retrieve his hand, she grabbed his thumb, easily twisting it just enough to cause discomfort. "Things like respect and honor. Perhaps they're in your job requirement as well, sir." She released him but remained uncomfortably close as if daring him to touch her.

He nodded. "Obviously, I've misjudged you. My apologies, Miss MacKay."

Sharif put his arm around Eliza's shoulders and pulled her away from Frank. He tenderly placed a kiss on her temple. "My dear, I was in no mood to be of good company these past two days. I'll make it up to you," he said kissing her forehead. He fabricated a look of regret. *Will she play along?* He attempted to convey 'play along' with his eyes.

She roughly wriggled free of Sharif's embrace. "Couldn't even bother to phone, could you?"

Relief showered his tense muscles with warmth. *Maybe she clued in.* Sharif found an opened bottle of water on a side table. "Go ahead, sweetheart. Tell Frank how I neglect you." He forced down a couple of swallows of water and wiped the excess dripping down his chin. He casually scanned the room for his secret documents.

"You'd rather play cop all day long? Fine!" She went to her suitcase and flung it onto the bed. "I've had enough." She stormed into the bathroom to gather up her toiletries.

Damn. She's figured out this could be her way to escape.

Frank pulled out a pair of gloves from his pants pocket and put them on. Glancing at Sharif, he said, "For comparison." Methodically, Frank captured a few hairs from her brush and carefully placed them in an evidence baggie.

Sharif swallowed more water to hide his distress. The perspiration on his brow had nothing to do with the late afternoon heat.

"What the hell are you doing?" Eliza appeared dumbfounded, staring at Frank's careful handling of her hair sample.

Frank ignored her and opened her suitcase. He rummaged through her work clothes. "No pretty dresses for a romantic rendezvous, Miss MacKay?" He began to pull up a neatly folded t-shirt. The Habitat For Humanity logo on the shoulder - almost fully visible. Sharif gasped and coughed as if choking on the water.

Eliza smacked the agent's hands away. "You stay out of my things, Frank. I came here to study the archeology, and maybe have a tasty Middle Eastern dinner," she said, glaring at Sharif. "Don't need fancy clothes," she said, slamming her luggage shut and zipping it closed.

Frank moved to stand between the door and Eliza. "I see you wear a wedding band. You're married?"

"Widow." She looked at Sharif who appeared engrossed in the view out the window. "Hashim, what's going on here?"

Sharif turned around and shrugged. "He's investigating the murder of several Americans. My government has given him approval to look for the killer. We need to cooperate and answer his questions."

Eliza marched up to Frank. "You think I'm a killer?"

"No. However, because of your connection with Sharif, you are a person of interest. Where are you going?"

"To the airport. I'll decide where to fly once I get there. Home, or Dubai, or wherever suits me. After this fiasco, I could use a holiday in my Hawaiian condo," she said placing her suitcase and purse near the door. "Hashim, if can you spare the time, please drive me to the airport?" She pulled her backpack out of the closet.

Sharif swallowed the last drop of saliva. *If Frank decides to open the backpack and discovers she's a paramedic....* He wanted to lunge toward it. *Divert, divert.* He pulled out his handgun and checked the clip. "Frank, stop harassing Eliza."

When Eliza threw her parka onto the bed, stitching on one shoulder caught Frank's eye. "Looks like some rats have chewed on your coat?"

"Maybe. It's just for camping." She retreated to stand beside Sharif. "Well, Hashim. You ready?"

Frank fingered the stitching. "Hmm, looks like a burn. Recent. Edges are stiff instead of frayed. Interesting." He looked back at Eliza and smiled. "I'd swear they look like bullet holes."

Sharif froze. He flinched at the sound of his cell phone ringing. "Hello," his voice was a mere whisper. He cleared his throat and said, "Captain Sharif."

"Hashim, there's trouble," said his father. "Our passport renewal has been denied."

Sharif concealed his shock. "That's odd. Any explanation why?" He managed a casual tone.

"Everything was done right, Hashim. I was called to the office today. They are refusing to renew our passports. No explanation. I don't understand, son."

"Don't worry, papa. I'll take care of it. Goodbye." Sharif tossed the phone onto the bed.

"Your family's passport renewal application has been denied. Right?" Frank appeared pleased, as if another piece to the puzzle lined up.

Sharif's impulse was to ask how the agent knew, but he realized Frank was probably holding back as much information as he was. Like the proverbial straw breaking the camel's back, this final turn of events made him flex his shoulders, and attempt to muster up his resolve to withstand the pressure. He wasn't a gambler, but his English mates would have told him to fold, cash in his chips, and head for the exit.

Sharif never folded, never retreated. *But I can get Eliza out of the country today.*

He turned to her. In a moment of desperation, he wrapped his arms around her waist and pulled her close. "Go home, Eliza." He placed his forehead against hers. "I'm sorry, my dear, for everything." Abruptly he pulled away and looked at Frank.

"Do you mind escorting Miss MacKay to the airport and giving her a seat on your jet?"

Eliza gasped. "But, -."

"I can get her to Cairo. But I'm not done with you, Sharif." Frank tossed the coat aside. He instantly morphed into a model CIA agent – brutally cold, mechanical. He moved swiftly, confident. He spoke to Sharif, his minion. "Sharif, I'm done waiting for you to man up. The Habitat volunteers were murdered in your compound. I know it. You know it."

Sharif wrestled with his impulse to deny the accusation. He knew how to disengage from being drawn into an emotional tirade. "And you believe that because ..." He sounded eerily calm, matching the agent's glacial demeanor, as if both could freeze a glass of water by simply looking upon it.

"One of the victims made a phone call from within your compound. We tracked the signal from her cell phone. The day after the massacre you ordered twenty-four body bags. Fifteen for the Americans, six for the killers, and three for the dead cops." Frank stood toe to toe with Sharif, inflicting him with an accusatory glare.

"Circumstantial, coincidental." Sharif held firm, restraining his rancor. To show his internal storm would be tantamount to admitting guilt.

"Perhaps. Now you're hoping to escape, get yourself and your family out of RIPT. You killed those people, my people, you bastard. If you run, I'll hunt you down and kill you."

Sharif smiled. "Take a number, Frank, and get in line."

Frank shrugged and turned away. "If I can prove you're lying to me, Sharif. I'll take your fucking head. In two weeks, I'll have the evidence to put you against *my* wall." He picked up Eliza's suitcase and marched to the door. "Let's go, MacKay."

Eliza wrapped her arms across her chest, her eyes darting from Sharif to Frank and back to Sharif, obviously wrestling with a decision. One choice could whisk her away from the threat of another 'termination' attempt. The other lived in the grip of a nightmare. She stepped toward her jailer. "Hashim, I -."

Sharif gave her a look, a mere flash of affection in his eyes. "Call me when you can, let me know you're safe." He wrapped his arms around her shoulders and held her against his chest. "Go home." He trembled when her body relaxed into his.

Her arms pulled him even closer. "Hashim, your family needs you and …."

"Shh, this is your chance," he whispered into her hair. In the next breath, he pushed away. "Go!"

Eliza turned back to Frank. "I'm staying, Frank. Do you really think I'd care about this man if he was a killer?" Her eyes narrowed. "You've spent a lot of time with Captain Sharif. How can you not know he's a good man? Got his priorities a bit off, but I suspect he's a better man than you."

Frank's jaw muscles flexed. "Fine." He opened the door, but stopped and turned around. "Of course, there's another possibility. Sharif, if you're an accomplice to a cover-up, you're still going down with them." He reached into his coat pocket and pulled out a cell phone. "Just in case you decide to do what's right, here's my cell phone. More secure than yours. Any time you get the balls to tell the truth, hit the number one button." Frank tossed the phone to Sharif and left.

Sharif stood barely breathing, staring at Eliza. "You could be on your way home."

Eliza opened her suitcase and began to unpack. "Mayor Aamir would kill you, perhaps your children, too. I can't have another family's death on my hands." She sounded tired, her shoulders sagged.

"No. The mayor ordered your execution. He expects you're dead by now." He closed her suitcase and headed for the door. "Eliza, get moving. We'll catch up with Frank. He can get you past airport security, directly onto his jet. Move!"

"No. Every day I'd wonder what happened to you. The not knowing would destroy me." She squared her shoulders with Sharif. "I'm not leaving this country until I know you'll be safe."

Sharif stared at her as if her body glowed, his eyes wide with wonder. A smile flickered on his face. He caressed her cheek. "You're going to drive me crazy, Eliza."

Eliza grinned. "Being crazy's not so bad."

Sharif tucked the CIA's phone into his shirt pocket. "Gather your stuff, Eliza. I've got to see Chief Ganem."

Eliza positioned herself between Sharif and the door. "Omar told you to stay here. For the next two days."

Sharif frowned. "Sergeant Abdul-Muqtadir and you conspired against me?"

"Him and his wife. Anyway, he said we're not supposed to leave here." She stepped up, blocking his reach to his MP5.

"Miss MacKay!" He put gentle pressure on her shoulders. "I'm exhausted. Just do as I say. Ganem needs to know -."

"Like Omar said, you've been given two days off. Now sit down."

Sharif's attempt to head to the door and sidestep Eliza again suffered the effect of her foot. Two hands pushing on his shoulders sent him careening down onto the bed behind him.

"Damn you, Eliza." In one fluid movement he stood again with his MP5 in both hands. "Don't you ever do that again!"

Eliza faced him. She grabbed the MP5. It was the first time she had placed her hands on his weapon. "Let it go, Sharif."

He blinked and stared at her. "What?"

"Let it go, please. Just let it go."

Sharif's mind flashed back to the previous evening. The hands on his shoulders, the voice. The message to 'let it go' he recalled hearing. He released his grip on the gun as if it had become hot. He watched as Eliza set the weapon against the far wall. It had always been an extension of his arm, a vital part of his body and survival. Removed from its weight, his sense of purpose and role as a cop took a back seat to exhaustion. Her hands guided him to sit on the foot of the bed. She knelt down and untied his bootlaces. The intimacy caught him off guard.

"Miss MacKay, this is not proper."

"Just medicinal, captain. Strictly medicinal."

Sharif mumbled his objections, a feeble resistance as she pulled his foot out of his boot. He looked at the top of her golden head. Her hands were firm, and yet the soothing effect of being cared for abolished attempts to regain control. He knew he should be pulling away, telling her to stop.

"Whew! Omar was right. You do need to wash." She looked up at him and grinned. "You might as well take advantage of some warm water in the shower." She continued to remove the other boot.

He noted the shadows of her long eyelashes on the delicate skin below her eyes. "Miss MacKay, I didn't pay for more nights. We have to go," he said with lack of commitment. "I can't afford another night." At the moment, the financial cost paled in comparison to the worst of his worries. He pictured Allah's displeasure, plunging his soul down to hell's gate.

She tossed the boots to a far corner and looked up at him. "It's all paid for. Three more nights, plus room service. Omar and I took care of it. If you wish, I'll take another room so you can have privacy – since you don't trust me."

Sharif winced. "What do you mean? Of course I trust you."

"If you trusted me, you would have talked to me about your plans." She stood up and went to the next bed and sat down. "You left me in the dark, and I'm not talking about being locked up. No, you think I wouldn't listen to you, or care about your family's safety. That's mega disappointing." She lay down, pulled a blanket over her and turned her back to him.

He sighed from both exhaustion and her verbal assault. It struck him harder than if he had fallen out the window and tumbled down the eight stories. "The bodies, the Americans. Frank found them in a cave. We pulled them out. They're heading home now."

"He suspects you're connected to their deaths."

Sharif headed to the bathroom. "At least he doesn't know about you. The real you." He turned around. "How did you know to play the role of, you know …."

She turned back to face him. "You kissed me. You'd never do that unless you were trying to mislead the agent."

Sharif struggled for words that would express his gratitude - more than just 'thanks'. Her sacrifice deserved so much more. But anything more would drift into territory he must deny himself. "The chief will be relieved to know the cover-up is safe. At least, I'll let him think nothing's changed." Sharif continued into the bathroom.

When he stepped out of the shower, he discovered his clothes had been removed from the bathroom. "Miss MacKay," he called out. "Where the hell are my clothes?"

Chapter 20

"I've sent them for cleaning. The duffel bag has a change of clothes for you. It's on the toilet," she hollered from the other side of the bathroom door.

His anger reached the upper limits of livid. Sharif wrapped a towel around his waist and stomped out of the bathroom. "How dare you? And what were you thinking, coming into the bathroom while - - I mean, you know the rules, miss!"

Eliza sat on the far bed in her lotus position. Her eyes became wide with surprise. Her mouth dropped open for a moment. "Wow! Nice legs, captain."

Sharif scurried back into the bathroom. In the duffel bag, Omar had provided him with a black golf shirt, khaki pants and his long thobe. He also found a pair of his sandals, and underwear.

Sharif stepped out of the bathroom in his long thobe in preparation for evening prayers. Evidence of his power over her now lay only in his height and physical strength. He doubted his gender had any influence.

Before he had an opportunity to assert his dominance, the call to prayer began. He dashed out of the room, and returned fifteen minutes later.

Eliza had set up a table and chairs between the beds. "I ordered a light supper. It should be here in a few minutes." She paused, as if waiting for his complaint or approval. As if on cue, the meal arrived. They ate in silence – too tired to risk more verbal confrontation. Eliza appeared content to quietly enjoy her meal.

Once the tray was removed to the hallway, Eliza motioned to the end of the first bed. "Sit down, captain."

Grateful she referred to him by his rank, Sharif's apprehension faded. Without giving any thought to her instructions, he sat down. To his surprise, she pulled up a chair and sat facing him. A squeeze bottle lay in her lap.

"Give me your foot, captain." She leaned down and lifted his bare left foot onto her knees.

He started to resist.

"Strictly medicinal, captain."

Eliza squeezed a dab of gel onto his foot. He caught the fragrance of mint as her fingers spread the slippery solution from his toes to his ankle. Her firm strokes encouraged the release of tension in his foot. She worked on each toe, flexing and extending each joint.

He resisted the urge to submit to the massage's relaxing effect. The rare comfort soothed his aching body, and more. And yet, he needed to appear unaffected. "You're trained in this art?"

"I know things."

"Yes, a paramedic. But this is …."

She interrupted. "Not just a paramedic. I have certain abilities. As a seer, I pay attention to my intuition."

He tried to process her statement. "So, I guess you don't hate me. For locking you up, leaving you to handle your claustrophobia alone, and everything."

Eliza stopped her ministrations. Her eyes met his. "Omar explained a few things about the stress you've been under. You haven't had any time off for over a month. Probably because of me." She returned to the massaging. "Working that hard can make anyone stupid, temporarily I hope. Consider yourself on probation." She glanced up and smiled.

He smiled. "That's kind of you."

"You'd be more comfortable if you'd lie down. Shimmy up to the pillow and lie down. Make yourself comfortable."

"Eliza, I mean, Miss MacKay, this is not …."

"Suit yourself," she said, as if it didn't matter to her.

Reluctantly Sharif did as she suggested. He grabbed the pillow and pushed it under his head. He should be watching, guarding, or something appropriate to a police captain and a devout Muslim man. As her hands worked their magic on his foot, his thoughts floated into oblivion. By the time her hands moved to his leg's calf, all thoughts of resistance deserted him. He restrained a deep moan as his foot was wrapped in a warm towel. Then the other foot received her attention. His attempts to remain conscious dissolved.

Four hours later he woke. Curled up in a fetal position, a warm blanket around his body, the luxury of feeling cared for was intoxicating. Deep shadows in the corners of the room spoke of the night's arrival. A soft light from the bathroom filtered into the room. The grey curtains at the open window fluttered lazily. A pleasant hum from the slow moving vehicles and murmurs of pedestrians tempted him to close his eyes - if not for the form of Eliza lying in the next bed. Her breath had the rhythm of sleep, deep and dreamless.

Sharif sat up. A covered snack plate waited on the table. Fruit, cheeses, olives and a spicy sauce arranged on his favorite bread woke his appetite. Quietly he ate, watchful for movement by Eliza. She lay on her side, her hair loose. He found himself gazing at her bare shoulder and admonished himself for wondering if she slept naked.

If there was ever an enigma he couldn't manage objectively, Eliza was it. He had become fond of her, cared for her as if she had become his sister. In the moments when he thought about her leaving, a stabbing jolt struck his midsection. Like the arrival of a puppy, the longer it remained, the more it became a member of the family. And Eliza had become the puppy that was going to be difficult to give up.

Quietly, he left the room to join the hotel guests in the designated room for midnight prayer. Content with his pleas for Allah's forgiveness, he returned to the room and lay down. Sharif thought about the evening when she had asked him to hold her. Just before sleep engulfed his exhausted body, he wondered what it would be like to hold her. *Better than anything I've ever experienced in my life.*

Sharif woke to the sound of thumps and grunts. He bolted upright in his bed. Momentarily dazed by the unfamiliar surroundings it took several seconds for his mind to comprehend the source of the disturbance. Someone was working themselves into a balanced and controlled position he recognized as the yoga 'downward dog'. "Oh, it's just you, Eliza!"

He gasped with relief and flopped back down on his bed. "Does yoga have to be so noisy?" His complaint fell on deaf ears. He sat up again. She wore lose white cotton pants. The purple tank top kept all her charms secure and hidden. The taut muscles in her arms and shoulders reaffirmed she had unusual strength for a woman.

She stood, arms held high then lowered gracefully, extended at shoulder height. Shoulders lowered and relaxed. In a fluid movement she knelt on the floor, extended one leg behind and flexed it. Her back arched until her foot touched the back of her head. In Sharif's mind, the moves resembled a ballet.

"Do you mind if I watch?" *I shouldn't*, he thought. "It looks, ah, difficult."

"Most men can't do the moves." Her voice sounded strained from the effort to maintain the pose. "Joints lack the range of motion," she groaned, then switched positions to the other leg. "Want to try?"

Sharif watched a bead of sweat trickle down from her throat and disappear beneath her top. "I'll pass, thanks. Like you said, too inflexible." He grinned. Sharif noted the slight quiver of her lips as she squashed a grin.

She continued with a few slow moves. "If you want to use the bathroom, this would be a good time. I'll meditate for an hour."

She maneuvered into her lotus. "There's some juice and toast and cheese for your breakfast."

Sharif completed his morning routine, trimmed his short beard and showered. Dressed in his casual khaki pants, black golf shirt and sandals, he attended the sunrise prayer, then returned to find Eliza napping. Now comfortable with Eliza's presence, he lay down on his bed and drifted off to sleep. Several hours later he woke to the discomfort of the midafternoon sun's heat. It had invaded the hotel room through the open window. The grey curtains fluttered as the warm breeze skipped over the windowsill.

Eliza stood by the window gazing toward the street below. She wore her lilac skirt and blouse. A tortoiseshell hair clip imprisoned her hair. He noted a blue mood had descended upon her. "Everything alright, Miss MacKay?"

She jumped and spun around. "Oh, sorry. Did the street sounds wake you? It was getting awfully hot in here."

"No. It's time for mid-day prayer. Wait here while I'm downstairs."

Eliza shrugged. "Uh huh," she muttered. She turned back to view the outside activities.

Sharif walked up to her. "I know this is very difficult for you. You like being outside, keeping busy."

Eliza shrugged. "Put in a good word for me, if you feel it's appropriate."

"I always do, Eliza." Sharif slipped past the doorway, hesitating as he realized he'd left his monster gun in the room. He couldn't remember the last time he'd gone anywhere without its reassuring weight attached to him.

After prayers in the hotel's lobby, Sharif enjoyed casual conversation with the men. For a change, they viewed him as simply a devoted Muslim, rather than a cop taking time out for prayer. He overheard whispers about the American investigation team. People were nervous. He paid little attention to their embellishment of the facts.

A couple of hours had passed when he decided to return to his room. On his way to the elevators he bought a sports magazine for Eliza and a newspaper for himself. In the room he handed the magazine to Eliza. "For you," he said casually. "Realized after I bought it that you may not care for sports."

"Nice try, captain. It wouldn't matter. I can't read Arabic. At least not well enough."

Sharif appeared dumbfounded. "How could you learn Arabic without studying the writing?"

Eliza flipped through the pages of the magazine illustrating soccer heroes. "I rented part of my home to an Arabic family. The parents had five children. I taught them English and I learned Arabic, mostly from the kids as the parents were busy at jobs."

"That explains why your pronunciation is a bit off."

"I guess if my words were not perfect, the kids didn't correct me. I shudder at what people here must think when I'm speaking."

"Probably think same as me -- impressed that you make the effort." He tensed upon hearing a knock on the door.

"Room service."

Sharif cautiously opened the door and allowed the man delivering the tray of food to enter.

He sat back as Eliza filled his plate with the bread and meat sauce, cheese and fruit.

"Enough?" she asked.

He smiled. "Plenty, thank you, Canadian."

"What are the names of your children?"

Sharif relaxed. "My son, Mustafa, is seven and daughter Farah is six. Good kids. Smart too." He hesitated. "We don't talk much. And it's getting worse. My son is always talking about his mother. I wish ....."

"Sharif, it's important that you support his love for his mother. If he talks about her, ask him how she is, what fun things she's doing. Don't put him in a position of having to choose between

153

you and his mother. He'll be so happy and relieved to know you respect his feelings. Does that make sense?"

Sharif sat down on the bed across from Eliza. "You were a great mom, I guess."

Eliza paled. "I can't go there, please." She handed the hotel's phone to Sharif. "Call them."

"Now?"

"Right now."

Sharif grimaced. "They're going to want promises. Things I can't give them."

"They mostly want to hear your voice."

Sharif breathed a sigh of resignation and dialed his daughter's cell phone.

Farah answered on the second ring. "Hi Farah. How are you?"

"Papa, is that you?" Sharif heard her yell to her grandparents. "Papa's on the phone. Papa, where are you? Are you on your way home?"

Her tiny voice caught Sharif unaware, and his defenses cratered. "Not yet, Farah. I'm still in Samarra. I was thinking about you and thought I'd call. How was school today?"

"Oh pretty good. My best friend and I got top marks in our arithmetic test."

"Wonderful. You studied."

Eliza grimaced. "No, no," she whispered. "That's what her teacher would say, not her loving father. Perhaps you could say you are very proud of her? Try again."

"I mean, I'm very proud of you, Farah. You and I are alike. Arithmetic was my favorite subject." He glanced back at Eliza. She gave him a thumbs up. "How is grandpa?"

"Grandpa wouldn't play with me yesterday. Maybe he's sick. You comin' home, papa?"

"Soon. Your grandpa is fine, Farah. Perhaps he's just tired. Is Mustafa there?"

"No. He's at his friend's place tonight. Just me and Grandma. Grandpa is in the orchard."

That was a telling remark. Whenever his dad was upset, he walked in the orchard. "Okay, I'll talk to Mustafa tomorrow."

"I love you." The declaration didn't come from his daughter.

Sharif's eyes shot up to Eliza's. Her voice had been like silk, breathless. Her eyes shone. Unbidden, his hand rose to her face and caressed the soft cheek.

Eliza inhaled, then blinked. "Tell her." Eliza pointed to the phone. "Tell Farah you love her."

"Farah," he said looking into Eliza's eyes, "I love you."

Sharif hung up the phone and gazed into Eliza's eyes. "Eliza," he tried to begin, then watched as she got up and slipped away, retreating to the window.

"You did very well, captain."

He hesitated, standing as if unsure of the direction he should move. He went to do his hat flip but nothing was there.

Never in his life did he believe anyone could love him. As a child he'd been sent away from the family home feeling like he had been an inconvenience, unwanted, unloved. That belief continued while living with his sister in England. His wife made it clear the arranged marriage was based on his prospect of being a successful engineer.

He moved to stand beside her. "Eliza, do you realize I've never heard those words before? No one has ever said to me, 'I love you.' Not ever."

Her gaze focused on the street below. "I simply thought Farah needed to hear you say how much you cared. That's all." She wrapped her arms around her waist, clutching the fabric of her clothes.

Sharif moved between her and the window. "That's all? You're sure? That's not what I heard." He searched her face for a hint of affection.

Chapter 21

Eliza looked squarely into Sharif's face. "Perhaps, sometimes, I think of you as a brother." She turned away, twisting her gold wedding band back and forth as if attempting to remove it. "You needn't worry. I won't compromise your morals. William's infidelity broke my heart. I'd rather die a lonely, old woman than be subjected to another man's lies." She turned her back to him and straightened the bed covers, tucking the sheets snug under the mattress.

Sharif silently cursed. *You're a stupid asshole. Like she would have any interest in another man who failed to keep his wife happy.* He shoved his shoulders back. His ego thrashed his disappointment into submission. A painful emptiness remained lodged in his chest. Seeing his MP5 leaning against the wall in the corner, he resisted the temptation to crawl back to its hard edged security. *Just another crutch.*

He didn't know what to say. The longer the silence went on, the more it felt heavy, laden with an unease that had not existed between them before. "My apologies, Miss MacKay. I didn't mean to suggest -."

"I do care about you and your family." She stopped fussing with putting the room in order. She appeared worried as she moved toward him. "But I do feel guilty that my presence has caused you great amount of trouble. Just being in this hotel room with you is enough to send you to purgatory for half of eternity." She blushed and turned away.

Sharif gently turned her around to face him. "Let me be one hundred percent clear, Miss MacKay. Though I find you attractive, you are incapable of causing me to step outside of my moral boundaries. While I'm with you, it's only as a police officer." He said it as if he believed it.

Eliza nodded and produced a faint smile. "Yes, I know." She patted his shoulder. "I may seem ungrateful, stubborn. But I'm aware of the risk you've taken to keep me safe."

A slight tremble in her body coaxed him to lower his defenses. Her face softened, glowed pastel rose. She uttered a small gasp. Her eyes shone. Watching her pupils dilate, his cop resolve began to yield, slip and slide out of his reach. The moment bordered on erotic. It claimed him, body and soul.

Hashim stepped back from Eliza. "I've got some thinking to do." He headed for the door. "I'll be back late."

Sharif walked for miles. Upon finding some shade in a park, he sat and watched happy people strolling together. It saddened him knowing that he could never have that.

With the arrival of midnight curfew, Sharif returned to the hotel. After prayer, he entered his room quietly and sat on his bed. Eliza slept curled up like a cat in its round bed, snuggled under the covers.

He remembered his promise to call the Edmonton paramedic tomorrow. He had no idea how that fish would fry but he refused to risk Eliza's life with Frank Hutchinson and the CIA. Their focus rested on finding the guilty, not in rescue. Sharif believed the CIA considered loss of innocent life in the course of tracking down the guilty simply a matter of expected and acceptable fallout. He wondered how close Frank was to springing his trap.

He noted his uniform hanging on a hook. The hotel staff had removed all trace of the previous offending odor. He scanned the room for his weapons. His MP5, still leaning against the far wall, waited for him. His handgun and the rest of his police paraphernalia were out of sight and, at the moment, he didn't really care where.

He undressed down to his boxers and eased into his bed. For a short while, he listened to the soft sounds of Eliza's breathing. He remembered the words, 'Let it go,' and he fell asleep.

The next morning Sharif dressed in his black golf shirt and khaki pants. Eliza wore her Habitat clothes, loose-fitting cream colored pants and shirt. Omar called to advise Sharif that his SUV had been returned, and was parked in the rear. When it came time for lunch, Sharif suggested they pick up some food and travel to the outskirts of the city. He hoped this peace offering would rebuild Eliza's trust in him.

"Yahoo!" She did a strange kind of happy dance and headed for the door with her backpack.

Sharif grinned watching her odd behavior. "So is this a Canadian thing, or do you have gum stuck to your shoes?"

Chapter 22

They picked up grilled turkey Reuben sandwiches, iced tea and water and headed to an area several miles south of the city. Stunted evergreens and shrub brush dotted the length of a wide stream. Grasses sprouted in the grit, revived by the fall rains. Several miles to the south lay a gravelly desert extending to the foot of a mountain range. Rocks and dust of the ancient land mass lay sullen. Though the wind teased at the troughs and rough hillsides, the land appeared devoid of spirit.

But that wasn't how Sharif saw it.

No one knew he came here after a shooting. Though Sharif killed ruthless men, he suffered some guilt by the fact that he saw both sides. He killed violent men who led lives of desperation and hatred - either by design or defeat. Perhaps suffered insanity. Poverty, loss of a sense of self-worth, weak of mind and spirit, they fell and were swept away in a spray of gunfire.

Here in the quiet of the desert, he prayed for the mercy of Allah on the souls of the deceased.

Sharif prepared for Zuhr, the mid-day prayer while Eliza set up a picnic spot in the shade near the stream. He felt his shoulders relax as calm washed over him. He retrieved his prayer rug from his vehicle and set it down so he could face the holy city of Mecca. Dipping his hands into the stream he began the sacred ritual of cleaning before prayer.

"Keep an eye out for strangers, Miss MacKay. People seldom come here, so if you spot someone, they're probably not friendly."

Eliza scanned the horizon, scattered with brush and scree. In every direction, the land rose several feet. "Wonderful," she said mockingly. "I won't see them until they're really close. Better keep a few rocks handy."

Not amused with her comment, Sharif presented her with a scowl. "I will be close. In fifteen minutes, I'll be back." He began to walk away when he realized she was collecting several fist sized rocks. He rubbed the back of his neck. "Okay, point taken. I don't suppose you know how to handle a gun?"

Eliza chuckled. "You remind me of my brother David Cropley -- David Bruce but I called him David the Brute. He thought he knew everything. Big guy. When we were teenagers he was impossible. We fought every day. One day he said I needed to get an education on guns and practice shooting. 'Every farm kid does,' he told me. Told him I hated guns and would have nothing to do with them." She glanced at Sharif, focused on the horizon. "Are you listening?"

"Uh huh. Is there an ending to this fascinating monologue?"

Eliza rolled her eyes. "Just like David. Quick with the wit. Anyway, he nagged and nagged until one day I gave in to target practice. He got his rifle and took me out to the 'shooting range' which was in our raspberry patch. The target was the usual circles on a paper nailed to a tree half a mile away."

"That far?"

"Oh, you are listening. Well, not that far. Fifty yards, maybe."

Sharif laughed. "More like thirty yards, at the most for a beginner." He waggled his finger at her. "Don't exaggerate or I won't listen."

"I'm not fudging the truth. I'm just not good with distances. Anyway, he handed over his rifle and started telling me how it worked and how to hold it. I got bored. I put it to my shoulder and while he was jabbering on about lining up the sights, I squeezed the trigger." Eliza snickered. "Caught him off guard. Saw him flinch. Was he mad!"

Captain Sharif had a smirk on his face. "Missed by a mile, didn't you? You should've been listening."

"Ha! Typical male response. David figured I missed, too. He walked to the target and came back. 'Lucky shot,' he muttered. So I asked, 'Where did I hit it?'"

"He puffed himself up like some frustrated rooster, and eventually said I got the bull's eye. 'Try again,' he ordered."

"And again he ranted on and on about wind, gravity, distance -- and again I aimed and fired."

"Missed, didn't you?"

"Nope. Never did miss the target. Ever."

"I'll keep that in mind if I'm looking down the barrel of a gun in your hands."

She smiled. "Wise man."

"Okay, let's see if you've gotten rusty over the last fifty years." Sharif grinned and dodged her punch. He removed the magazine from his sidearm, racked the slide. "Here," he said, handing the weapon to her, "show me you know how to load and unload this."

To his surprise, Eliza expertly loaded and unloaded the gun. "Your brother taught you this?"

"No," she said, handing the weapon back to him. "Weapons class in our paramedic program. Had to be familiar with guns and the types of injuries inflicted." She crossed her arms. "Now I suppose you want a demonstration?"

"Come with me." Sharif quickly looked through items in the back of his SUV. He found a paper plate intended for their picnic. "Shooting a stationary object is one thing. Shooting a killer running toward you is totally different." He found a spot to cross the stream and set the plate hanging from the branch of a tree. It swung in the breeze.

He returned to her, not sure if his stomach's flip-flops were excitement in the challenge of teaching her, or premonition she

F. Stone

might suffer for it. "That," he said, pointing to the white object bouncing in the distance, "is thirty feet away. I want you to put at least three bullets through it." He stepped back. "Now!" he barked.

Eliza raised the weapon, aimed, hesitated for a full two seconds – and fired. She continued to pull the trigger until there was nearly nothing left of the plate. Her hands shook as she released the magazine, racked the slide to eject the bullet in the chamber, and handed the weapon back to Sharif. She grinned. "Would you like to go and confirm if I hit it three times, sir?"

A slowly evolving grin cancelled all hope of appearing stern. "Tell me, Miss MacKay, is there anything you can't do?"

"I'm a lousy cook. Have trouble keeping track of my finances. And worst of all, I have no sense of direction. Put me in a shopping mall and I'll be lost in ten seconds. Those are the top three."

Sharif chuckled, but it morphed into a belly laugh. The happy sounds spread, capturing Eliza until she lost all control, and laughed, too.

A gate had opened. They both knew it, and understood that the other knew it. For a moment, Sharif longed to step through that passageway, and yet also feared it. Then the moment was gone.

"Keep watch, Miss MacKay," he said, reloading the gun and handing it back to her. "Wait here."

After Sharif's performed the ablutions again, and the mid-day prayers, they ate their lunch in companionable silence. Sharif relaxed, content they were both safe. He caught her eyes. "What do you think?"

Eliza raised her eyebrows, "You mean about this place?"

"Uh huh."

She smiled. "A person can hear themselves think here. But, at the same time, I'd rather just sit and not think. Disappear into the landscape, be one with it. Sorry if I'm being too mystical," she chuckled.

163

"I know what you're saying and you say it so much better than I could."

"You come here often?"

"Some. Wondered if you'd like it. Let's go for a drive."

He headed to the driver's door. "Get in. Let's have some fun."

Eliza halted at the open passenger door. She stared at Sharif getting in the driver's seat, her eyes turning bright with the possibility of excitement. A hint of a smile grew on her face. "Fun? Did you say 'fun'?"

Once Eliza fastened her seatbelt, Sharif slammed the gearshift into drive and hit the accelerator hard. The vehicle bolted and skidded sideways as he sped along the barely visible track in the desert. He heard her yelp as he jerked the steering wheel right to left. He welcomed the exhilaration to throw caution to the wind and push his masculine energy into the red zone. In one grand push in a straightaway, he hit the brake hard as he yanked the steering wheel to the left. The vehicle lurched in a tail spin, shooting up dust and rock.

A blood-curdling scream pierced through his amusement. Eliza's scream of terror went on and on. Sharif slammed on the brakes and looked at Eliza. Her eyes were wide open as she screamed. He grabbed her and shook her violently but the screaming went on. He got out and raced to the passenger door, pulled it open and dragged her out. Her eyes were still fixed on some point in the distance calling the names of her children. *Her kids. She's seeing the death of her kids all over again.* Sharif groaned with deep regret.

He pulled her down to the ground and wrapped his arms around her. As he spoke, her screaming subsided. "I'm sorry. So sorry, Eliza. What do you see, Eliza? Tell me what you see?"

Her body trembled. "Noah, Noah. No, no." She moaned as if in agony. "Nathan. Please no!"

"Eliza look! You're in the desert. It's hot and dry." He shook her shoulders and made her fingers scoop up the grit. "See. We're in the desert just outside Samarra. You're fine. We're all fine."

Her screaming stopped. She looked about frantically, as if trying to make sense of what she saw.

"I'll get you some water. Wait here." He retrieved a bottle of water and returned to her. "Here, drink."

Eliza stood in front of Sharif like a wild animal not knowing which way to turn. Her hands and arms could not settle on a position for more than a second.

Sharif coaxed her to drink the water and led her back to the stream. He dabbed a portion of his shirttail into the stream and wiped her face. "Okay?" He searched her eyes for signs of being focused.

"I'm sorry for making such a scene. I know you were just being playful." She collapsed to the ground and covered her face with her hands.

Sharif shrugged his shoulders and sat down beside her. "Some wounds take a long time to heal."

He gave her time to collect her thoughts.

"I've struggled to fix this. Nothing works."

"Some parts of your mind remember, Eliza. Those parts want you to put those memories to rest. But you have to make peace with them first, don't you think?"

She gazed at him for a moment. "You and my psychiatrist should get together. So far, we haven't made much progress."

"Uh huh. Now let's try again. This time, I'm putting you in the driver's seat."

Eliza backed away. "No thanks. You drive. You can even drive like a crazy man if you want. I can handle it if I have some warning."

Sharif thought Eliza would welcome a chance to take control. Then it dawned on him. She'd been driving when the accident occurred. "When's the last time you drove?"

She swallowed hard and turned away.

Chapter 23

Sharif grabbed her arm and led her to the driver's side of his SUV.

"Get in." She struggled but couldn't escape his grip. "Eliza, I need you to be able to drive." He grabbed her around her waist and then shoved her onto the driver's seat. "Move over a bit." He placed his hip beside hers. "Start the vehicle."

She tried to push him off the seat. "You're a goddamn bully."

"We can sit here all day and night or …."

Eliza reached for the keys in the ignition and turned on the engine.

Sharif felt her body tremble. "No harm can come to you out here. Look," he said, waving his left hand toward the empty expanse ahead. "Other than rocks and grass, maybe a stray camel …."

Eliza glowered at him.

He waved off her rebellion. "Now put it in drive. Don't take too long to decide. If we run out of petrol it's a long walk to Samarra." He grinned at her. "If you like, I'll help you steer, but you're going to have to put your foot on the brake to shift into drive. Then it'll be up to you to step on the accelerator."

"I bloody well know how to drive. I just don't want to." She glared at him. He returned the stare. She looked away first, then slapped her left hand on top of Sharif's gripping the steering wheel. She glanced down at the floor to see the brake pedal and applied pressure to it with her foot. Her right hand reached for the gear shift handle. She pulled it back, moving it from park to neutral. The vehicle moved slightly. She gasped and shifted back into park.

"I think I'm going to throw up."

Sharif shifted away from her. "Just give me fair warning. Try again." And again she attempted to stay in drive. And every time the vehicle shuddered to life, she retreated and hit the brake, sometimes with both feet.

Eliza shook her head. "I should be able to do this," she muttered. Again she grabbed the gear shift handle and eased it into drive. In another moment she took her foot off the brake. The vehicle rolled forward. Her left hand clutched Sharif's on the steering wheel. Her right hand still rested on the gear shift handle. She pushed it back to park. Again and again, she failed.

"I'm sorry. I need a drink of water, please."

"Sure. I'll grab it from the back seat. You stay put!" He stepped out and when he had the bottle of water, he returned to perch his right hip beside Eliza and hang on to her headrest with his right hand. As Eliza reached for the bottle, he threw it several yards ahead of the SUV. "Now, if you want that water, drive to it."

She frowned. "That's mean."

"Yep. Now how are you going to get that drink?" Sharif's foot tapped on the running board. "Ten more seconds, and I take my left hand away. You'll have to control the steering wheel alone."

"That's not fair. You know I can't …."

"One."

"I need water." Her voice sounded hoarse.

"Two."

"Let me out of here, you bully." Eliza tried to muscle her way past Sharif.

"Four."

Her eyes widened. "Four?" she gasped.

"Five."

167

"Okay, please just let me have one drink, then I'll ...."

"Seven."

"Where'd you learn to count?" she shouted.

"Nine. Should've known you couldn't do it. Women shouldn't be allowed to drive anyway."

Eliza stared venomously into his face. "What did you say?"

"You heard me. Women shouldn't be allowed in the driver's seat. Haven't got the brains or the skill," he muttered, with his left hand swatting away a fly.

"God damn you!" Eliza slammed the gear into drive and hit the gas pedal. The vehicle lurched forward and stopped.

"Oh my god, look out. A woman is driving!" he said sarcastically. He went to put his left hand back on the steering wheel for her to hold onto.

"Shut up, asshole!" She slapped his left hand away and placed both of hers on the steering wheel. She again placed her foot on the gas. This time she kept the vehicle moving forward, jerking from slow to fast. She managed the steering wheel alone, making over-corrections.

Sharif had to hang on tight as the vehicle bounced and veered erratically. "Careful. Don't drive over the bottle."

Finally, she drove up alongside the bottle. He retrieved it, had a couple of good swallows. He made sure she saw the water dripping from his mouth, then walked to the passenger side and got in. She lunged for the water bottle just as he threw it again.

"What the hell are you doing?" she shrieked. "I didn't even see where it went."

"Well you had better find it before it all leaks out. Drive. And hurry up. I'm still thirsty."

She glared at him. "You'll pay for this, I swear."

Sharif sneered. "And you call yourself a paramedic. A paramedic that can't drive! Do all your patients die waiting to get to the hospital?"

"Bastard!" Eliza slammed the gear into drive and sped forward. It took another six minutes to find the water bottle. By the time she drove up beside it, she appeared to have forgotten about being scared. When the bottle was in sight, she roared up to it, making sure it was on the driver's side. She slammed on the brakes, jumped out and managed to get it before Sharif.

As she twisted the cap off the bottle, she noticed the SUV rolling forward.

"Eliza, you didn't put it in park. Get in and stop it! Hurry up!"

Eliza hesitated for a brief moment. The vehicle picked up speed, about fifty feet ahead. She sprinted and reached the back bumper. The rough ground rose to the left and caused the driver's side to veer off to the right. She had to run hard to reach the driver's side and grab the grip in the door frame. She swung onto the driver's seat, hit the brake and pushed the gear shift into park. "Wow," she said, panting, and waiting for Sharif to catch up to her.

"Well done, MacKay." He buckled up his seat belt. "Now how about some fun?" His dark eyebrows waggled.

For the remainder of the afternoon Eliza and Sharif took turns at the wheel, speeding, gliding, spinning. The desert's afternoon heat soared as all their cares fell from their shoulders, old wounds and fears gone. By evening, both they and the SUV were covered in dust and desert grit. They forgot about the massacre, forgot about him being a cop, and forgot about wanting to return home.

Sharif convinced Eliza to drive back to their hotel. She put up a small resistance but by the time they reached the hotel, she had regained much of her confidence in dealing with traffic.

Eliza parked and sat back. She closed her eyes and took a deep breath. She covered her face with her hands and wiped tears from her eyes. "Hashim," she said softly while her eyes were still closed, "do you have any idea that you've performed a miracle this afternoon?" She turned to him. "People who care about me, others who are professionals, failed to do what you did."

Sharif smiled. "Just not as inflexible as me, I suppose. Chances are I could get rid of all your triggers."

She turned to him. "How can I thank you?"

Sharif looked into her lovely eyes, shining with tears. "You just did," he said as he jumped out of the SUV.

"Wait," said Eliza. "There's something that I've been wondering about." She took a couple of hesitant breaths and looked down at her hands. "Captain, you've been good to me. More than one would expect, given that I'm your prisoner. And not all that cooperative at times. I'm grateful, but -."

"But what? First, I see you as someone under my protection. Not a prisoner. Certainly, not a criminal. Second, when I was a kid, I lived with six older sisters. Two were old enough to be my mother. If I didn't treat them with respect, I paid for it." Sharif smiled. "Third, I like you. Let's get our stuff and check out."

Eliza showered and changed into a fresh police uniform. They checked out and headed back to Sharif's station. He announced, "I'm going to stop at the Guardian Mosque. I want to introduce you to imam Bashir."

As they approached the Guardian Mosque, her eyes followed the contours of the ancient building. The bright evening lighting embraced the pillars and contours of the dome. "It's beautiful. I've never been in one so grand."

He looked her over to ensure she was properly dressed. "Let's go. Bashir is not pleased about our living arrangements, but I've assured him this is only temporary and necessary for your safety."

They entered the large courtyard about four blocks wide and deep. Eliza examined the detailed carvings on the four minarets. The next prayer wouldn't be called for another hour, so they were alone except for a few people enjoying a leisurely stroll among the benches and flower beds. The mosque's striking arches and open, breezy spaces made Eliza stop and stare. Sharif pointed out the blue and gold glazed tile, and the walls displaying foliage motifs, Arabic inscriptions, and arabesque design work. At the center of the courtyard an ornately carved fountain greeted the faithful.

"There's no water running in the fountain."

"It hasn't been working for many years. In fact, this mosque is years overdue for an overhaul. Our imam has consulted with me about the engineering required to restore it."

The sound of glass breaking echoed toward them. Eliza jumped. "What was that?"

Sharif pointed out broken tiles along the walls and columns. "The tiles are falling off. We can enter the interior over there." Sharif pointed to a doorway that had the ceiling reinforced. "All other entrances are blocked. It's not safe to go near the walls."

"It looked so beautiful from a block away. But up close, I see scaffolding and supports against the walls. Why has it not been maintained?"

Sharif shrugged. He urged her to follow further toward the interior. "No money. Fewer people are attending and supporting the imam's requests for funds. If something isn't done soon, our government will declare it unsafe and tear it down. Our imam has been struggling for years to gain government aid."

The interior of the mosque contrasted with the elaborate architecture in the courtyard and exterior. Simplicity. Only the huge marble columns spoke of the outer grandeur. The massive empty space encouraged quiet contemplation and focus on prayer. Along the walls of the prayer hall, bookshelves held copies of the Qur'an, other religious reading material, and individual prayer rugs.

Sharif led Eliza down a hallway and a flight of stairs. In the lower floor he walked up to a closed door and knocked.

The door opened to reveal a thin older man. His greying short beard and hair accentuated his soft blue eyes. For a split second, the man frowned and appeared shocked to see Sharif. The man quickly shifted his reaction and greeted Sharif with a broad smile and embraced him.

"Come in Hashim. Come in. Oh, and you brought a guest. How wonderful. Come. Sit."

"Imam Bashir, this is the lady I've told you about, Miss Eliza MacKay." Sharif turned to Eliza. "Miss MacKay, this is imam Bashir, my most beloved mentor."

Eliza made a slight bow, clutching her fingertips in case the imam was opposed to shaking hands with a woman. She smiled. "Very pleased to meet you, sir."

"Please call me Bashir, Miss MacKay." He sat behind his desk and turned to Sharif. "Now, Hashim, how has your investigation into the massacre been going?"

Sharif had entrusted the imam with the cover-up and the CIA's involvement. "Not good. Right now my main concern is Miss MacKay. If I am killed there is no one to protect her. I'm hoping you might either offer her refuge or relocate her among people who can."

Eliza's eyes popped. "Oh, no, Hashim, er, captain. No, you must not ask this of him. Enough people are in danger."

Bashir held his hand up. "Calm yourself, miss. Hashim would not ask if it was not acceptable or possible. Now, would you, dear lady, please tell me about your situation?"

Eliza glanced back at Sharif and winced at the sight of his scowl, a 'keep quiet' command.

The imam waved his hand and said agreeably, "Don't look at him, miss. I'm glad you are here, for now I might get the whole truth. Not the Sharif abridged version."

"Imam Bashir, it's Captain Sharif and his family that need help. The mayor ...."

"Eliza, that's enough. You ....."

"Quiet, Sharif. Don't interrupt the lady. Go on, miss."

"Captain Sharif's family is at risk. That frightens me more than anything else. The government office has refused to renew their passports. Unless Captain Sharif can get his family to safety, I'm afraid there will never be justice for the massacre."

The imam spread his arms wide. "Ah, finally. Thank you Miss MacKay." He stood and appeared to be mentally reviewing the facts and pondering alternatives. "First, Miss MacKay, do not fret over my safety. I have survived battles that were vile." He turned to Sharif. "Yes, of course, Miss MacKay will receive my protection."

Bashir moved to Sharif's side. He placed his hand on Sharif's shoulder. "Let's focus on what you need today. Prayer will clear your mind. Go upstairs and take advantage of the quiet. Evening prayers begin in one hour. I need to make some phone calls." Bashir ushered them to his door, and offered them the traditional blessing of peace and mercy, "*Wa alaikum assalam wa rahmatu Allah wa barakatuh.*".May the peace, mercy, and blessings of Allah be with you.

Sharif thanked the imam. "*Shukraan*, imam Bashir."

Sharif led Eliza to the prayer hall. They removed their shoes and Sharif surrendered his weapons to a man at the entrance. The wood-paneled walls of the huge room, called a musalla, were devoid of ornaments, statues, or paintings. The pristine hardwood floor reflected light entering from the skylight above. The sanctuary felt alive with warmth and peace, freely offering the devoted the bliss of prayer and quiet contemplation.

Sharif motioned for Eliza to walk with him to the center of the floor, beneath the massive dome. Feeling reverence for the sanctuary, Eliza repositioned her blue scarf. Though Sharif spoke in hushed tones, his voice skipped around the room, then was absorbed into its centuries' old wood. The sanctuary received him. "In a few minutes, this room will be full of men. The women go up to the balcony."

"Can I stay with you?" she whispered.

"You can remain at the back until prayers are over," he murmured and pointed to a nearby wall. Stay within my visual range. I need to perform ablution. I'll be back in ten minutes." He headed to the side room equipped with water basins.

Ω

In Mayor Aamir's office, Ganem failed to rein in his fear. Aamir sat in his chair, his gaze upon the police chief hard as a rock.

"Where is Sharif?"

Ganem shrugged. "Days off. Staying at a hotel. He'll resume his shift tonight."

Aamir stood and slowly walked to the front of his desk. "Has he followed my orders?"

Ganem stepped back. He hadn't heard from Sharif but Sergeant Abdul-Muqtadir reported that no execution had been committed. He had said that the reputation of the police chief's office had been protected. Furthermore, he verified that the CIA were not looking for Eliza, and therefore it was not worth the risk of murder.

"Mayor Aamir, thanks to Captain's Sharif's ingenuity, we didn't have to commit murder. In a few days the CIA will hunt elsewhere for the terrorists. Soon we can put this business behind us." Ganem hoped his boss would agree.

Aamir took a deep breath through his nose. He nodded. "But we still have to deal with that woman," he said, frowning. "Tell Sharif to report to me this evening." He returned to sit behind his desk. "Bring him to me personally. Understood?"

"Yes, sir."

"You, Sharif and I are going to wrap up this business tonight. Be back in my office at seven."

Ω

After prayers, Sharif decided to make his follow up call to Tanasiuk, the paramedic in Edmonton. The imam ushered him to a spare office. Sharif dialed direct to the Edmonton Emergency Medical Services. "This is Adrian MacKay calling. Can I please speak to Mr. Tanasiuk?"

"Ah, Mr. MacKay. There's a message here for you. You're to call RCMP, K Division. Here's the number."

Sharif copied the number. He sat for a moment preparing himself for making the call to the Royal Canadian Mounted Police. Eliza's life depended on this one call. His life. His family. Perhaps the future of his country. He had to focus on one thing - giving just enough of the right information. It occurred to him that he might have to drop the persona of Adrian MacKay. He had to be credible.

"K Division." The male voice sounded automated.

"I have a message from Mike Tanasiuk of the Edmonton Emergency Medical Services to call this number regarding Elizabeth MacKay Ramsay."

Silence. "This is regarding the MacKay file?"

"Yes, sir." *So far, so good. Let them do the fishing.*

"One moment please." Silence.

Sharif waited. Four minutes crawled on by. He expected they would be listening for background conversation or sounds, or tracking his call. Finally, another voice responded.

"What is your name, please?"

"My name is irrelevant."

"Hmm. I see. Let's cut to the chase. You gave a fictitious name to Mr. Tanasiuk. You gave him a phony story about your relationship with MacKay. You're uncooperative. All I know with certainty is that this call is coming from Middle East. What do you want?"

Sharif swallowed. "I don't want anything. Eliza MacKay, however, needs your help."

"I see. Can I speak to her?"

His heart pounded. "No."

"Has she committed a crime?"

"No. She witnessed a crime."

"I see. Her life is at risk?"

Sharif had a death grip on the phone. "And others."

Silence. "Yours?"

Sharif hated to admit he feared for his life. He hesitated. "I'm risking being arrested for treason. Rescue would need to be careful, low key. My family will suffer consequences if my betrayal becomes known. Is that clear?"

"What I know of Mrs. Elizabeth Ramsay, otherwise locally known as Eliza MacKay, is that she has suffered mental instability and periodically goes AWOL. No one has reported her missing. I'm sorry, but she's not a case we would act upon. Good day, sir."

Sharif nearly threw the phone to the far side of the room. After regaining his composure, he admitted the effort had been a bloody waste of his time. *I'll handle this without them. Better without foreign involvement.*

Sharif returned to the mosque's entrance, collected his handgun, and found Eliza among the hundred faithful men and women. She was chatting with a group of young children and their mothers. He caught her attention. With his brief, almost imperceptible nod of his head, she broke off her conversation and caught up with him at the entrance.

"Everything okay, Sharif? You look a bit agitated."

"I'm late for my shift." By habit, he studied the gathering of people in the courtyard as he led her down the bank of wide steps. "Hopefully, everything is going to be back to normal." He breathed a sigh of relief. The moment of calm evaporated as he remembered that Frank Hutchinson was probably studying every detail of the items he had bagged, including Eliza's strand of hair. The IV bag and tubing. Sharif felt for the CIA phone the agent had given him and remembered he had left it in his SUV. His MP5 was also in his vehicle. Panic made him catch his breath. *I've been careless.*

Eliza grabbed his arm. "Sharif, something's wrong." Her hands were cold.

He glanced in her direction. "Later. We've got to get to my truck. Hurry." He ignored her pallor and fearful eyes.

"No, captain. We're in danger. I feel it."

"We're on sacred ground. Don't be foolish." He trotted down the last bank of stairs. "Keep up, Eliza."

"No, no, no," she cried out. Again he turned to her. She stood several feet behind him. She appeared dazed, unaware of people moving around her.

He sprinted back to her and shook her shoulders. "Trigger?"

Startled, she looked in his eyes. "No. But I see trouble. Terrible trouble," she whispered. Her body shivered as if she lay naked in freezing water.

As Sharif turned to view the movement of hundreds of people leaving the mosque, he spotted six heavily armed men moving toward them They were spaced in a wide arc, blocking any chance for escape. "Oh God," he groaned. "Eliza, get back into the mosque. Hurry." He roughly turned her around and pushed her back through the crowd.

He looked through the mosque's entrance and spotted imam Bashir. The man he had trusted with his secrets turned and strode back inside. Eliza followed the imam and disappeared past the throngs of people.

Chapter 24

CIA agent Frank Hutchinson had a stranglehold on his cellphone pressed hard against his ear. "You lost him? How could you lose him?" He glanced at his watch – eight in the evening in Sharif's world. "I know it's dark there but our satellite can spot him for a while longer. How long ago did you lose him?"

"He was seen entering Guardian Mosque two hours ago, sir. He's never in there more than an hour. We had switched to scan the cave zone, and routine surveillance. He hasn't returned to his vehicle."

"I'll be there in fifteen. Mobilize! Fucking find him!" In sixteen minutes he blasted through the CIA's Washington office doors of his boss, Zalman Liba. "Well?"

"Steady, Frank. We're backtracking through clips of people at the mosque."

"He's probably a dead man by now."

Frank and Liba headed to the surveillance room. Several large monitors displayed segments of Samarra's streets. Other personnel wore headsets, focused on calls to operatives.

Frank nudged Matlock. "What happened to the tracking device I placed on Sharif's MP5 shoulder strap?"

"In his SUV parked near Guardian Mosque. And your cellphone is there. His vehicle hasn't moved since he arrived at that location."

"How much time do we have until our satellite is out of range?"

Matlock checked the time. "Forty-five minutes, Frank."

Frank turned to Liba. "Who do we have on the ground there? Anyone close?"

"Closest team is in Israel. Few men scattered closer. They've been put on alert and are moving toward Samarra. Should be there in two hours."

Frank glanced up at the videos displaying a grid of streets, moving second by second from the city's center to the outer perimeter. "Shit," he muttered. "Listen, what was Sharif doing when he entered the mosque?"

"He was with that woman, MacKay. They appeared relaxed, just preparing for early evening prayers. Several hundred people entered soon after he arrived."

Frank turned to his office manager. "Check the communication file. Get me Sergeant Abdul-Muqtadir's phone number and Sharif's station office. The sergeant's the only man there I halfway trust.

Within five minutes, Frank had Abdul-Muqtadir on the phone. "Sergeant, where is that blasted Sharif?" Frank paced, barely containing his panic.

Sergeant Muqtadir hesitated for a moment. "Who is this?"

"CIA, Frank Hutchinson. Where is Sharif?"

"Late for his shift, as a matter of fact. Why?"

"We know his vehicle hasn't moved from the mosque's parking lot. Is there an underground tunnel to the Federal Building? Would he have met with the police chief?"

"Hang on, Frank. I'll make some phone calls. Don't hang up."

Frank listened to the sergeant's calls placed to the hotel Sharif had stayed at, then to Police Chief Ganem's office.

"Hello, Frank. The hotel desk clerk said Sharif mentioned he was working tonight. He might have decided to meet with Ganem.

But Ganem's not answering his phone. Either he's left for the day, or -."

"Omar, in a worst case scenario, if Sharif was abducted and killed, where would he be taken?" He heard the sergeant groan.

"East. Assassinations have occurred, and that's where the bodies are usually found buried. Nothing out there but dirt and maybe a stray camel."

"Where would he be held until then?"

"He could be in the cells in the sub-basement of the Federal Building. There is a secured garage and underground exit. That exit appears above ground three blocks to the east."

"Who, Omar? Who wants Sharif dead?"

"About a hundred badass criminals, and the mayor."

"Understood. Get Sharif's vehicle and call me back on the CIA cell phone so we can maintain a private communication link. Got that?"

Frank's surveillance team zeroed in on the area that included the mosque and the Federal Building. "Keep an eye on all major trunks that lead east out of the city. Perhaps a few vehicles travelling together. Probably unmarked."

The big city's heavy traffic challenged his staff. Again and again, they zoomed down on a possible convoy. The room became silent as the satellite technicians focused on their screens. Frank watched and listened to the clicking of keyboards and the muttering of the men.

"Hey, look at this," hollered Matlock. "Shit, they're really moving, heading east. See," he said, chuckling like a boy catching his first frog. He gave the coordinates to the others. Instantly six pairs of eyes glued on to the image of an SUV and two sedans travelling five miles beyond the city's eastern border.

"We've got 'em," Frank said, ramming his fist into his other hand. He grabbed his cell phone with Abdul-Muqtadir waiting on the line, and gave the coordinates. "You and your squad head out there."

The convoy drove for another twenty minutes, pulled off the highway, drove half a mile through rough terrain, and parked near a dry riverbed. They stopped behind a line of thick brush.

Liba nudged Frank and pulled him away from listeners. "You think the sergeant can stop this?"

"Not sure. If Sharif's killed, we need to keep the sergeant alive. Bettin' he knows everything Sharif does." They returned to watch as Sharif was yanked out of the van. Sharif had been handcuffed. Frank gaped at the video. "Look, there's Police Chief Ganem. Shit, I figured him for a weasel, but this?" Frank spread his arms wide and looked at his boss. "Someone else is pushing Ganem into murder, Zollie." Three armed men shoved Sharif forward near two deep open pits. The headlights from the vehicles traced the men's movements.

Frank alerted the sergeant to the events at the site. "Ganem and three men have Sharif in handcuffs. How far away are you?"

"Another fifteen minutes. I'll call Ganem's cell phone again. Maybe he'll answer it this time."

"Tell him we're watching. If he kills Sharif, I'll have his ass cooked for my dogs tonight."

"Frank, are you good at lip reading in Arabic?" asked Petrie.

Frank narrowed his eyes. "Pretty dark there. I might get the gist of what they're saying." The video winked, then brightened as the men positioned Sharif near one of the pits. He glanced at his watch. Eight minutes until the satellite is out of range.

Frank stood back for a moment. *Where is MacKay?*

Sharif fought hard. He snarled what appeared to be venomous threats at Ganem and the gunmen. Kicked in the gut, he stumbled but sprang to his feet again. Frank noted Sharif's trembling legs.

Frank watched Ganem's mouth. "He's telling one of the men to shoot Sharif. By the look on the chief's face, he's not enjoying this. Telling Sharif he's sorry but there's nothing he can do.

Sergeant Abdul-Muqtadir shouted on his phone, "Ganem's not answering."

"Omar, I saw Ganem checking his phone. Keep trying." Frank winced. "Those bastards are pounding their fists into Sharif like a punching bag. Got him on the ground and kicking. How far away are you now?"

"Five minutes."

Frank could see Sharif was nearly spent, barely able shield his body or stand.

Ganem appeared to be shouting, "Just get it done."

One of the men cocked his gun and strode up to Sharif.

"Goddamn, Omar, we're too late," shouted Frank.

Frank heard a mournful cry from the sergeant.

"What the fuck? Omar listen, the gunman just killed Ganem. Do you hear me? Ganem's dead. The gunmen just shot Ganem and tossed him into the pit. Holy fuck, they've shoved Sharif into the other pit. They're shoveling the dirt into the pit over him. I can see him trying to get out."

The image went blank.

"Omar, get there fast. We've lost the satellite." Frank tossed the phone across a desk and onto an office chair. "Hang on Sharif, the cavalry is coming."

Frank waited another agonizing fifteen minutes gazing into a blank monitor. Finally he heard the sergeant's voice coming from his phone. "Omar, what the hell is happening there?"

"We've got him, Frank. Bad shape." Omar's voice sounded strained and breathless. "Killers took off. My men are in pursuit. Right now, I've got to get Sharif to the hospital fast."

"Good job, sergeant."

Abdul-Muqtadir hollered, "Frank, where's Eliza?"

Frank's gut clenched. For a moment his mind reeled back to the pretty woman in Sharif's hotel room.

"If she was with Sharif when he was taken, I think you know the answer to that, Omar. She's dead. Frank out."

Frank headed to the forensic lab and greeted his team. "Have you looked at the strand of hair, Betsy?"

His best technician, Betsy, nodded. "We identified most of the DNA and found a match."

"In our database?"

"Not in our database. I found a strand of hair with the same DNA on the remains of the woman who received medical aid. And, all over the intravenous bag. Medic probably held the bag in her mouth."

"Her? You mean to say that the person who had given first aid is the same person who had been in Sharif's apartment? And the woman in Sharif's hotel room?"

"Same. Yes, sir."

"Son – of – a - bitch." Frank eyes bulged. "Well, fuck me." His arms stretched out wide, then slapped down on top of his head. "The same woman. That sneaky, lying bastard." He leaned on the technician's table. "Have you checked on her ID? I was told her name is Eliza MacKay. What do you have on her?"

The technician gave Frank a thorough report describing Eliza's youth on up to her three suicide attempts up to last year. "She's not stable, Frank. We think she's capable of anything. People with PTSD range from mildly odd to a danger to themselves and others."

Frank walked aimlessly around the room, his arms and hands in a pantomime of his thoughts. Finally, he turned back to the technician. "She's not a killer, Betsy. But she is in trouble. She's a witness." Frank stood still. "Holy shit. Sharif is trying to keep her alive." He smacked his chest. He turned to Betsy. "I offered to take her to Cairo. Sharif encouraged her. But if she left, - holy shit. He would be executed for treason, and that's why she wouldn't leave. It's because of the death of her family. She would rather die than put another family at risk." Frank headed for the exit. "I've got to get back there."

Frank strode into his boss's office and stood while he reported the news. "Zalman, we need to get MacKay and Sharif's family out of RIPT. We'll never get Sharif's cooperation until his family is out of danger." Frank sat down. "I know how the massacre went down. Sharif tried to stop the killing but got to his compound too late. Found one survivor, MacKay, who then tried to save the life of one woman. I'm not sure who is controlling Sharif. Someone is threatening him to keep his mouth shut."

Frank leaned forward. "Both of them are bound to have a price on their head. MacKay won't be around much longer."

Zalman nodded. "Good job, Frank. We're light-years ahead of where we were yesterday. Problem is, we still don't know if anyone in RIPT can be trusted, from Captain Sharif to President Najeeb. Given that Captain Sharif has continued to lie and hide the facts smacks of complicity with the killers."

"Loyalty to family and country in the Middle East is akin to a blood oath. Few of us can relate to the depth of their obsession to honor family ancestors and tribal bonds. I understand Sharif. I've seen him in agony being torn between his faith and morals on one hand, and obedience to his superiors and his country's honor on the other hand. He's in a no-win situation."

Zalman banged his fist on his desk. "Do you see a sign on my door that reads 'Search and Rescue?' You give that bastard too much credit, Frank. He's a goddamn liar. I'll authorize nothing to save his ass." Zalman stood up. "Our priority is to find who is responsible for the death of our people. Getting involved in the rescue of Sharif's family or MacKay would be good press, but none of them can point to the organization we're looking for. Focus on the root, Frank. Once we know who is responsible for the death of our people, and there's time and manpower, then we can initiate a rescue mission."

"MacKay is a witness. We need to get her out."

"Unfortunately, she is of no use to us. I want to nail the terrorists who organized the massacre. That's all."

Ω

Sergeant Abdul-Muqtadir's men had chased after the three killers while he grabbed Sharif and hauled him out of the grave. Sharif was covered with dirt and grit, bleeding, unable to stand, and struggled to breathe. Once Sharif was placed in the back seat of his sedan, he roared off to Samarra General Hospital.

Once Omar Abdul-Muqtadir was allowed to enter Sharif's room, he saw his friend closer to death than ever before. He'd been intubated and was attached to tubes and monitors. Sharif's face was unrecognizable. Eyes swollen shut, nose battered, lips cut. Dried blood covered most of his face and hair.

The doctor stepped up beside the sergeant. "Captain Sharif probably will not respond for several hours."

"How bad is he?"

"Three cracked ribs, concussion, and facial trauma. Mostly soft tissue damage. He's likely going to survive so long as we don't find internal bleeding. But his family should be here. What happened to him?"

"I received an anonymous tip that he had been attacked." For the time being, he had to keep Ganem's murder a secret. "I'll let his parents in Rumi know. Not likely they can get here until tomorrow. You know his father hasn't been able to drive far since his second stroke."

"Yes, Sharif and I had discussed his father's recovery months ago. It's your call, Omar. Will you be here for the night?"

"One of my men will remain at the door. For his protection," Abdul-Muqtadir said, nodding to Sharif. He swallowed and hitched his shoulders. "If he gets worse, tell my officer. I'll get back as soon as I can. I've got to chase down a missing prisoner." He raced back to his sedan and spoke to his team positioned at the Guardian Mosque. "Have you found her?"

"We've got Miss MacKay, sir. Unharmed. Wants to know about Captain Sharif. Is he's going to make it."

Sergeant Abdul-Muqtadir figured the best place to put MacKay was with the captain. The officer guarding the door might as well keep an eye on MacKay, too. "Bring her to the hospital and put her in Sharif's room."

He held his phone for a moment, rehearsing his message to Mayor Aamir. First, he called Ganem's home. He needed to make it look like he knew nothing, that he was only following protocol when an officer is hit. He left a message at Ganem's house that Sharif was in the hospital. He carried on with his night patrol duties for an hour, then called Aamir.

"Mayor Aamir, sorry to call you at this late hour. I've been trying to contact Chief Ganem to notify him that Captain Sharif has been severely injured and is in the hospital. As I've been unable to speak to Chief Ganem, I'm forwarding the information to you, sir."

Aamir responded in his usual dismissive tone when speaking to subordinates. "Not surprised. Sharif has plenty of enemies. Surprised he's lasted this long. As far as Ganem, he's probably on one of his late nights chasing women. Call me when I'm in my office." The call terminated.

Sergeant Omar Abdul-Muqtadir ground his teeth as he tossed his phone onto the passenger seat. "I'll get you one of these days, Aamir."

Ω

Eliza hovered beside Sharif's bed in the trauma ward. She alternated checking his tubing and holding his hand. His battered wrists made him wince when she lifted his hand. If someone bumped his bed, his body trembled. Dirt remained embedded in his hair. His breathing came in gasps, and his head jerked as if he remained locked in a continuous replay of the torture.

She gently stroked his forehead. "Hashim, you're safe," she whispered near his ear. "You're safe. Omar found you. You're in the hospital. You're going to be fine. No permanent damage." He became calmer. "Omar has one of his officers at the door." When his grip on her fingers relaxed, she let out the breath she had been holding. He had heard her. "I'm fine. Imam Bashir took care of me. He and so many others wouldn't let those armed men near me."

It had surprised Eliza. "The imam told some of the men that I was a friend of Captain Sharif. The word spread. In seconds, we were surrounded by your friends. They had no weapons but made the attackers leave." She again stroked his forehead. "You have so many friends, Hashim."

She had to take a breath and calm down. "You just need to rest." Her voice had begun to tremble. "The doctor said you can go home when you wake up, tomorrow maybe. You're safe, Hashim."

She felt his body slip into a restful sleep. Her eyes filled with tears. She had come so close to losing him. The thought jarred her. Her hand massaged her chest over her heart. *How can this be? When did I become so deeply in love with him? I cannot bear the thought of losing him. And yet, I must.*

She sniffed and shook her head. You're getting way ahead of yourself, stupid woman. What makes you think he'd want you? He even said that he's only a police officer when we are together. So there. He's made that clear.

The thought made her sadder. I can never tell him how much he means to me. He's got enough on his plate. Focus on staying alive.

The next afternoon, Aamir strode up to Sharif's bedside. He stared at Eliza for some time. He had never seen her before. "Miss MacKay, I presume. What are you doing here?"

Her heart kicked up its pace. She straightened her back and squared her shoulders with the man who wanted her dead. "I was placed here by Captain Sharif's men. The officer outside the doors was placed there for the captain's security, and mine." She held onto his eyes, daring him to pursue his intimidation. "As you can see, Captain Sharif is recovering. Sergeant Abdul-Muqtadir gave him an update just a few minutes ago."

Sharif opened his eyes and coughed when he tried to speak. The breathing tube had been removed but it had made his throat sore. Sharif couldn't yet see through his swollen eyes. "Eliza."

Eliza placed a hand on his shoulder. "Captain, Mayor Aamir has come to see you."

"Mayor Aamir. My condolences for the loss of your friend, Chief Ganem." Sharif's voice, though hoarse, clearly spoke of his scorn. The effort to sit up taxed all his strength. He collapsed with as much dignity as possible.

Aamir feigned surprise. "What do you know about Ganem's disappearance?"

Sharif was still trying to regain his breath so Eliza answered. "Mayor Aamir, Sergeant Abdul-Muqtadir was alerted by the CIA that chief Ganem had taken captain Sharif prisoner out past the city's eastern border. Three men tortured Sharif and murdered Ganem. Ganem was buried. They attempted to bury Captain Sharif alive until the sergeant and his men arrived."

Aamir slapped his chest and looked as if struck with a horrific image. "Ganem dead? Where are those men?"

Sharif snickered, but winced and placed his hands over his ribs. He took a few short breaths. "My sergeant reported those men have not revealed who hired them. For their safety, their whereabouts are secret. You understand, I'm sure." Sharif tried to smile in spite of his swollen face.

Aamir stood silent. The façade disappeared. In its place Aamir showed his true colors – a picture of ice and steel. He slowly brought his attention back to Eliza. He smiled. "Never mind." He marched to the door, but stopped and slowly turned around. "Captain, has that CIA agent discovered any new evidence?"

"He knows we're a bunch of liars."

Eliza didn't know whether to feel relief at the sight of Aamir shrinking, or fear that he might now take drastic measures to correct his mistake. The man quickly regained his composure. He stood like a superior, but one who'd lost a little of his arrogance.

As long as Sharif's family remained in Aamir's crosshairs, Sharif had no leverage. But now Sharif had won a slight advantage. With Ganem's killers in Sharif's grasp, the mayor had less of a stranglehold on him.

When she was sure the mayor was gone, Eliza released her need to appear strong. Her body trembled. "Sharif, now he's going to be more determined to kill you. He has to."

"Not for a while. Not so soon after Ganem's murder." He shook his head. "He knows he's fairly safe even if those killers talk." He winced with the effort to speak. "I'd need a lot more evidence to arrest him. He's too smart to risk ..." Sharif closed his eyes. Exhausted, he fell asleep.

The next afternoon, Abdul-Muqtadir carried Sharif up to his apartment and laid him on his bed. Sharif pulled a blanket over his head and told them to get out.

Sergeant Abdul-Muqtadir turned to Eliza. "Is this going to be a problem for you? I mean helping him with whatever he needs?"

"This is my work, Omar. I'm a health care professional."

He nodded. "I met with Mayor Aamir. He's initiated a search for the chief's body. Making it look pretty authentic. Sergeant Muntazar is keeping the killers locked up at the airport. Just a warning, Miss Eliza. If you so much as see Aamir's shadow, get Sharif up."

Sharif's recovery progressed slowly. For two days he barely moved. He relented to let Eliza help him walk to the bathroom. In the next two days, Eliza noted his mood drop further. He sat at his kitchen table, uninterested in food or conversation. Worried the torture he suffered was taking its toll on him mentally, she asked Omar on the fifth day to get his white van and help her get Sharif into the passenger seat. Ever the pleasant and willing friend, Abdul-Muqtadir ignored Sharif's protests, and had the grumbling man buckled in.

She drove the route to the trail beside the river. Sharif brightened marginally. Before she had a chance to help him out of the van and treat him like an invalid, he shuffled in his sandals down the path. He glanced back at her, his eyes narrowed. "Coming?" His irritation with being forced out of his dark apartment wavered.

He was a sight. The sergeant had helped him dress in some old clothes, faded black and baggy. He stood like an old man and walked as if he suffered from arthritis in every joint. The bruises on his face, swollen black eyes, and the stitch in his lower lip echoed the fact he'd been in a battle for his life.

Eliza went to the rear of the van, retrieved a blanket and his daughter's pillow teddy bear. "You need some sunshine, captain. We won't go far. And the second you want to return to the apartment, I'll drive you back, on one condition."

The Sharif scowl appeared. Eliza smiled, relieved that a portion of the tough Sharif had surfaced.

"What condition, miss?"

"We stay for a minimum of half an hour. Tomorrow, we'll increase that to one hour."

"Bossy woman. You're lucky I have no energy to argue. Where are we going?"

"Over there. A nice grassy spot under those trees." She pointed to a quiet area away from the trail and out of view of people passing by. He lay down on the blanket, tucked the pillow under his head and turned his back to Eliza. He slept for three hours. The next day he slept for one, then suggested they sit by the river.

The peaceful river, lazily susurrating, vanquished fears and stress. Once he was seated on a boulder, Eliza asked, "Would you like to be alone, captain?"

He shook his head. "No." He glanced at her. "And, no, I don't want to talk about it."

Where have I heard that before? She recognized the defiance. Several times she had told her psychiatrist where to put his invitation for her to 'talk about it.'

She kept busy looking for small flat stones and returned to him. Standing near the river bank, she tossed a stone, trying halfheartedly to get it to skip across the water's surface. It skipped once.

She adjusted her technique, but failed to get more than one skip.

"You're doing it all wrong," Sharif shouted. "You've got to hold it lightly on the edge."

"Like this?" she said holding it toward him.

"No," he frowned. "I thought you had done skipping before." He got up and threaded his way to her. "This way," he said, demonstrating how to hold the stone, then flung it across the water's surface. It skipped five times. He braced his healing ribs and moaned.

"Wow. Whose lights got punched out that time?"

Sharif studied her for a moment. "Pretty cleaver, aren't you."

She presented him with a winning smile. "Just celebrating our anniversary. Do you realize we met one month ago and, in spite of Aamir, we are having a wonderful day?"

"Just one month?" He frowned. "Feels more like –"

Eliza cocked her eyes and raised her eyebrows.

Sharif cleared his throat and looked down at his feet. He shrugged and looked back at her. Gradually a smile erased the signs of his inner battle scars. "Feels like I've known you all my life, Miss MacKay." He headed back to the walking path. "I suppose I could buy you another jar of blueberry jam."

"Perfect. And what shall I get you?" she asked navigating around a boulder.

"How about cleaning up my SUV?"

"I'll do that anyways. Something special?" She tugged on his shirt to get him to stop.

He turned around. While still out of sight of prying eyes, Eliza wrapped her arms around his shoulders and gently hugged him. She nestled her face against his neck and whispered, "You're the most amazing friend I've ever known. Thank you for everything, Hashim."

Perhaps he simply forgot to resist or push her away. He took a step back and nodded when she released him. "Let's go," he said.

As they walked back to his van, Eliza decided she might be able to give Sharif more leverage against his enemies. "I'd like to go to a bank and set up an account. While I'm there you could get a safety deposit box for your documents." He agreed. They returned to his station, collected his secret documents, her backpack, and headed to his bank.

They each wore the black police uniform and flak jacket. Sharif frowned at her as she used her black hat to fan her face. She gave him a pretty smile and placed it back on her head. They requested a safety deposit box – one big enough for the fingerprint documents and photographs.

Once the items were stowed, Sharif sat down while Eliza went to the teller's window. "I need to open an account, a large account - 560,000 in local currency," whispered Eliza. "The equivalent of one hundred and fifty thousand US dollars. I will need to connect with my bank in Dubai." The teller mumbled something and disappeared down a hallway.

In another two minutes, the teller returned with a man in a business suit. He directed Sharif and Eliza to follow him to his office. Eliza showed him her passport and her bank card for an account in the Dubai National Bank. "If necessary, you can contact my Dubai lawyer for verification."

"I see," he said, studying her passport. The manager advised her he would need to make some phone calls to verify her claims.

While they waited for the manager to return, Sharif asked, "Why do you have a lawyer and an account in Dubai?"

She looked down at her hands resting on her lap. "Long story. Not ready to talk about it."

The manager returned. "I've been advised your request to transfer funds from Dubai is well within limits given your balance in the Dubai bank. I will have my secretary complete the documents. It will take just a few minutes. Once you've signed the documents, I will issue you a bank card. Will you need some cash today?"

"Sir, Captain Sharif will also have access to this account. Full signing authority and he can deposit and withdraw as he wishes."

The account's manager studied Sharif as if waiting to receive a response from him. When Sharif appeared just as surprised, he said, "Can you wait or will you be coming back this afternoon?"

Eliza glanced at Sharif, then smiled at the manager. "We'll sign them now, please."

Sharif's mouth dropped. With his signature, he had become financially affluent, twice more than he'd earn in five years.

"Are you absolutely sure, Eliza?"

Eliza turned to the manager. "Would you give us a few minutes of privacy, please?"

When the manager left, Eliza sat back and grinned at Sharif. "Yes, I am sure. For good reason, too."

He frowned. "I don't mean to sound ungrateful, but in this country, this kind of thing is looked upon with suspicion. Like bribery, or -."

Eliza took his hand and gently squeezed it with both of hers. "I understand. You and I need to admit we're in a losing battle unless the playing field gets leveled. Money can be a great equalizer."

She got up out of her chair and walked to the window, frosted to ensure privacy. "There are no strings, Hashim. You can use this money however you wish. If you decide to withdraw the entire amount and disappear, you do not need to say anything about it to me. It will not leave me destitute."

Sharif stood and raked his hand through his hair. "But, why?"

Her eyes became glassy, tears settling into her lower lid. Eliza turned away, took a deep breath, and began. "As you know, four years ago my family was destroyed. The company responsible for their deaths was eager to make restitution." Eliza took another deep breath. "They admitted total responsibility and ensured I was financially compensated for the loss of my parents, brothers, my husband and sons."

She stopped again, visibly trembling. She had a mixture of rage and devastation in her eyes, flashing back and forth.

"Compensation!" Her voice barely registered. She grabbed some tissues from the desk, wiped her eyes and blew her nose. "I'm sorry. Sometimes I can talk about this and not fall into pieces. Not today, I guess."

"I'm guessing they gave you a lot of money."

Eliza nodded. "So much that, in fact, I'm not allowed to discuss the balance with anyone. When the agreement was signed, the money went straight to my lawyer, then to my financial advisor. I've never looked at that account, never touched it. For a long time I wondered how I could get rid of it. Then it occurred to me that it could be used to help another family. Like you and your family."

"Whew! I don't want it either, Eliza. I'd be gaining on your loss."

"At least sign the document. You don't have to use it but it's there if you need it. Perhaps it could help get the passports approved for your family. Think about it."

"Save a family to make up for losing one."

Eliza smiled. "Exactly."

"And it won't leave you penniless?"

"No. There's a lot more where that came from. And William had a substantial life insurance policy. I'm well taken care of financially."

Once they received their bank cards and some cash, they headed back to the station. Before arriving at the station, Sharif pulled over to a side street. "From now on you wear a flak jacket and helmet constantly. Agreed?" His eyes narrowed to make sure she took him seriously.

In the early afternoon on the following day, Sharif dressed in his uniform. He found Eliza working in the washing room building. She had brought a cup of coffee and a sandwich to eat while doing some laundry. "I'm heading out. You need anything?"

She noted the swelling and bruises on his face. A twinge of sympathetic pain made her wince as he braced his left side. "We'll need some food but that can wait for a couple of days. You're going to meet with the mayor?"

"Why do you ask?" He brushed away a crumb sitting on her upper lip.

"The only time you get ready for work early is when you're heading to the federal building." She returned to sorting clothes for the next washing load.

"Just the routine captains' meeting with Mayor Aamir and Captain Khizar. You know he is now the interim police chief." He headed for the door. "Make sure you fold my shirts carefully, Miss MacKay."

She heard the smile attached to his words. The spot where he had touched her lip remained warm. It was a most personal act for a Muslim man. It touched her deeply. *I'm going to miss him.* She sighed and pulled out clothes from the dryer and set them on a table. Selecting one of his uniform shirts, she tenderly laid it flat, arms wide. A vision flashed in her mind. Arms holding her, his face close to hers. *Stop it. Just bloody stop it.*

For the next three weeks Sharif and Abdul-Muqtadir focused on getting the police chief's three assassins convicted for the murder of Chief Ganem. Busy with collecting evidence, completing reams of reports, and meetings with the prosecutor, Sharif had no time for Eliza.

The court's verdict offered no mercy. Execution. Sharif and Abdul-Muqtadir stood shoulder to shoulder as the three prisoners stood against his wall. The rifles of Abdul-Muqtadir's squad fired. Again the wall and the soil bore the signs of a storm full of hate and need for vengeance.

Frank Hutchinson had been conspicuously silent. Tension grew in the station. Khizar's men rebelled against Sharif's strict leadership. Frustrated and stressed, Sharif's temper flared. Eliza gave him space. *This silence between us is unbearable. I see him every day, but I miss the man who makes fun of my size ten shoes, claims the coffee I make will poison him, and sees me, knows me like no other man has.* She paced. Meditated. *Oh Allah, Most Benevolent and Compassionate, help him, please.*

Eliza felt a slow boil would soon upset their frail peace. It happened on the way to the market. Eliza clung to the vehicle's shoulder harness. Sharif's dark mood was translated into his aggressive driving, erratic lane changes, and muttering curses at the traffic. Her temper flared.

"Why don't you meet with President Najeeb? Tell him the truth."

"Quiet. You stay out of my business, Miss MacKay."

"Now that you have proof Aamir killed Ganem, you could end this damn cover-up. You have to do this. I can't stay shut up forever. If you don't tell Najeeb, I will."

He glared at her. "I don't have sufficient proof. Ganem's killers refused to talk. You'll just keep quiet and do as I say. I know what's best for you. Is that clear?"

Eliza jerked toward Sharif. "You're just as guilty as that monster in the mayor's chair. What do you think will happen when everyone believes you created the cover-up along with Aamir? Najeeb will throw your ass in prison. The only way you can wash yourself of this cover-up is to confess to Najeeb."

Sharif stopped at a red traffic light. He gripped the steering wheel as if to keep his hands from strangling her. "Who do you think put Aamir in the mayor's chair?" He turned to her. His mouth was curled with hatred. "President Najeeb selected Aamir himself." The light turned green and Sharif punched the accelerator pedal. "For the last time, you just keep out of it," he shouted over the roar of his SUV's engine.

"I swear, Captain Sharif, I can't take much more of this. I can't just sit by while you and Aamir hope everyone is going to forget that fifteen people died. If you don't do something, and soon, I'll -."

"You'll what!" Sharif yanked his SUV to the side and slammed on his brakes.

Eliza had to grab the dash to keep from being thrown against the windshield. "I don't know. Something. I can't take this waiting anymore."

Sharif shook his head, then resumed driving. "Do you give Tanasiuk this much trouble?"

Eliza gasped. "What? What did you say?"

"Tanasiuk, do you give him this much trouble?"

"What do you know about Tanasiuk?" Eliza's eyes were wide with fear.

"I called him. Figured it was time your friends started looking for you."

Horrified, she shot back, "You got my friend involved in this?"

"It seemed the best way to get people to notice you're missing. Didn't tell him who I am or where you are, yet."

Eliza stared at him for a moment. "Sharif, how could you talk to him without talking to me first? If you wanted to get the word out, I could've given you names of people in the police force. Not my friends. You've just put my friend's life at risk. He has a wife and family." Her voice escalated. "Damn it. He's likely to do something crazy." Eliza put her hands over her face. "Oh my god. This is so typical of you, Sharif." She punched his shoulder hard. "You just charge ahead as if no one else has a say. Damn you!"

He stopped at the intersection's red traffic light. Eliza unbuckled her seatbelt and jumped out of the SUV with her backpack. Quickly mixing in with the crowd using the crosswalk, she ran to the sidewalk. Without a backward glance she trotted past a few buildings and found herself at a park.

Now you've done it, she chastised herself. *You don't know where the hell you are and people are beginning to stare.* She walked across the park to the next street and looked for the street signs. They were written in Arabic which she couldn't read. She hailed a taxi and jumped in. "Take me to a moderate hotel, please. Clean and reputable."

"That would be the Peace, miss. Only twenty minutes away."

Tomorrow, she thought, *was going to be living on her terms. Maybe I'll rent a car.* She paid her fare as the driver dropped her off at the Peace Hotel's front doors.

From the clean parking lot and maintained entrance, she guessed the hotel might rate three stars at the very least. Upon entering through the gleaming double glass doors and noticing the elegant ceiling lights, polished white tile floor and happy potted ferns, the rating went up to three and a half. The rating shot up to four with the warm welcome from the desk clerk and staff eager to greet her. *Ah, friendly faces at last.*

Ω

Half way down the block a vehicle pulled to the side of the road. The driver watched as Eliza entered the hotel. "Bitch!" he cursed. "Now to set up the bait for Sharif!"

Chapter 25

Captain Sharif 's temper bordered on livid. *Why didn't I grab her the second she had opened the passenger door?* When she had run out into the crowd he had hesitated too long, figuring she'd run to the sidewalk, perhaps realize her mistake and return to him. Instead she had disappeared among the throngs of people rushing home from work. Drivers were honking their horns, annoyed at being blocked by his SUV still parked in the middle of the intersection.

He jumped back into his vehicle and slammed it into gear. As it lurched forward he smashed his fist onto the steering wheel. *God help me if I get my hands on her again! Stubborn woman. You'd think she'd know better than to go running about alone in this city. Any woman with half a brain wouldn't go anywhere alone. Especially one that looked like her.*

Sharif parked and got out, sprinting in the direction he last saw her. He hoped to spot her moving swiftly, zigzagging through the crowd. He scanned the area. Eliza had disappeared like a phantom. *Where the hell are you?*

Sharif checked his watch. His shift began in a half hour. Sharif returned to his station.

$$\Omega$$

Eliza chatted with the hotel's desk clerk for a few minutes. She needed to develop a rapport with the man, in case she needed a new ally. Grudgingly she also told him that if she needed help, he should call Captain Sharif at the central precinct.

He looked surprised. "You know our famous captain?"

"Only recently," she said. "I'm working with him and the police chief on a medical program. Do you know how to contact him if it's urgent?"

"Yes, miss. Here is the key to your room on the third floor. The elevators are to your right. If you are interested, there is a café down the block open for evening meals. I wouldn't recommend you go there alone but I'd be happy to pick up something for you when my relief returns."

"You are very kind, sir. Here is some cash for the meal. I'll leave it up to you to pick out some food. Will this be enough money?"

The clerk appeared very pleased. "Absolutely, more than enough."

"Keep the change. Just knock on my door when you are able to bring it." The clerk nodded and Eliza breathed a sigh of relief. She had finally gotten a smidgen of control over her life.

She found the room compact and tidy. She opened the window and saw the street below. The rush hour traffic had slowed. She spotted a couple of cars arriving at the hotel. There were several cars in the parking lot, a sign the hotel had a good reputation. She checked out the bathroom. Again she looked forward to having a long shower with warm water. She threw her hat onto the bed.

Eliza couldn't relax. She returned to the window to watch for the clerk bringing the food back. In another hour she saw him head down the sidewalk toward the café. The setting sun created long cool shadows and a peaceful aura. She checked her watch. *Nearly seven p.m. Captain Sharif will be busy getting his officers debriefed on their assigned missions for the evening.* She pulled out the cellphone that Sharif had allowed her to keep, for emergencies. *In all fairness, I should phone him. Let him know I'm fine.* Her anger still burned. *No - let him stew for a few more minutes.* She tossed the phone back onto the bed.

A couple of vehicles roared up to the hotel's front entrance. The driver from one vehicle jumped into the passenger seat of the other. She noticed the clerk with her food pass by the vehicles and walk into the front entrance. Finally, some food.

She turned her attention back to the two vehicles. One drove toward the rear of the hotel. The other remained parked. The driver below got out of his vehicle. The hair on the back of her neck prickled. Her gut twisted and shivers travelled up her spine. She recognized Khizar.

Her intuition screamed, "Get out!"

Chapter 26

Swift as a gazelle running for its life, she grabbed her backpack and ran to the elevators at the end of the hallway.

She looked at the elevator's direction sign. *Too late. It's coming up. They're on the elevator. Go back? No. Find the stairs.* Eliza dashed left around the corner. A few yards ahead were the exit sign and stairs.

The elevator door opened. Male voices. "Boss says to keep her alive. Bugger!"

She gasped. *Maybe they're in the stairway, too.* She heard a maid vacuuming in a room across from the stairs. She slipped into the open room and hid behind the door. The maid gasped, on the verge of screaming.

Eliza pressed her hands together in prayer form, held them against her heart, and bowed to the woman. The maid stood still. Eliza put a finger to her lips indicating to the maid to say nothing. The maid's mouth hung open for a moment. Then she heard the men's voices. Again, she held her hands as if in prayer. The maid resumed her vacuuming.

Listening at the open door, Eliza heard the knocking on the door to her room. A man called out, "Miss, I have your dinner."

He waited a moment and knocked again. Becoming impatient he called out, "Your dinner, miss. Open the door."

Eliza trembled in her hiding spot, clinging to her backpack. She took a few deep breaths and tried to calm her racing mind. The maid stopped vacuuming. She heard another man with an unsteady gait walk down the hallway toward her room's door. "You haven't got her yet?"

Khizar!

"Shoot out the lock!" he ordered. After a gun blast, someone kicked the door open. Eliza had maybe three seconds while the men stepped into her room. She whipped around her door, ran across the hallway to the exit door, quietly opened the exit door and ensured it closed softly behind her. Eliza flew down the stairs and into the lobby. She didn't dare run out into the street. *Khizar will have guards posted out there.*

She ran up to the frightened desk clerk. "Those men, they are not my friends. I need to hide," she whispered, trying to catch her breath.

"I'm sorry, miss. They said …."

"I need to hide now!" Her eyes narrowed.

The clerk motioned for her to come behind his desk. When he pointed to a three foot high cupboard under the reception desk, Eliza gasped. "I'll suffocate. No, I can't." Already she could barely breathe enough to speak. She shook her head and pulled at the collar of her shirt. "Please, something else."

"Hurry, or we'll all be killed. Get in." The clerk pulled the sliding door more fully open. When he heard the elevator ping and the doors begin to open, he grabbed her arm and shoved her roughly inside the cramped space. The sound of footsteps made him bolt upright. With his shoe, he quietly and gently closed the door - until it jammed in its sliding track. He didn't dare look down to see how much of the opening exposed the woman.

The clerk pounded the keyboard as if to hide his trembling hands. He turned his back to the men rushing into the lobby. Papers flew out of his hands. Cursing at his clumsiness, the frightened man picked them up and shoved them into a wastebasket. Finally, he could check the open cupboard door. Her boot was barely inside. He tossed the waste basket onto her boot and then give her foot a kick. The door refused to release. "Damn door," he grumbled, and kicked the cupboard.

Forbidden

She jammed her left shoulder against the far wall. Claustrophobia's claw gripped her throat. *Breathe,* she repeated over and over again. *I'm okay. Just focus. Air in, air out.*

The muffled sound of feet scrambling into the lobby made Eliza flinch. She held her breath, focusing on voices, footsteps.

"Did that woman come through here?"

Almost as if rehearsed, the clerk motioned to the front doors saying, "A woman ran outside a minute ago. Is there a problem?"

The men ran out to the front parking lot. They separated and started to search the grounds. All except one.

Khizar approached the clerk. He plunged his sidearm into the shoulder harness. His grim expression and hunched posture rivaled that of a lion pursuing its next meal.

"Captain Khizar, do I need to sound the alarm to evacuate my guests?"

"No. What do you know about that woman?"

"Only that she looked terrified when she ran out. I know nothing about her except her name. Her passport said she's Canadian. Is she a spy or terrorist?"

"She must be apprehended. It's a matter of national security. Anyone found giving her aid will suffer dire consequences. Understood?"

The clerk nodded and returned to his reception desk duties. Eliza didn't hear the captain leave and the clerk gave no indication she could escape. Nausea exacerbated her efforts to breathe quietly. Her heart pounded like a tribal war drum. Sweat streamed down her chest. She swallowed the last of her saliva. She desperately needed to bolt out through the six-inch opening. She squeezed her eyes shut. *Calm down. Think. Go to that place my psychiatrist talked about. Somewhere I know is safe.*

It had been years since she felt safe. The triggers followed her, day and night. But then, while eavesdropping on Sharif's prayers, a transformation had begun. She recalled his words, the sound of his voice. The reverence. The total submission to Allah's love and forgiveness. As she recalled Sharif's supplication, she was mesmerized by the softness of his voice, the assured commitment to placing his life in Allah's omnipotent wisdom. The memory carried her away from the torment of the present. She was offered a gift. For a moment, Eliza was seated beside Sharif, feeling his magnificent energy, his unwavering protection. The sound began as if music had begun to flow into words. Sharif's prayer.

Allah is the Greatest! Praise and glory be to You, O Allah. Blessed be Your Name, exalted be Your Majesty and Glory. There is no god but You. I seek Allah's shelter from Satan, the condemned. In the Name of Allah, the Most Compassionate, the Most Merciful. Praise be to Allah, Lord of the Universe, the Most Compassionate, the Most Merciful! Master of the Day for Judgment! You alone do we worship and You alone do we call on for help.

Eliza had finally found her safe place where nothing could diminish her courage.

After fifteen minutes she heard the men come back, out of breath.

"Can't see any sign of her, captain."

Silence.

Eliza heard the sound of footsteps coming toward the reception desk. Pacing. She heard the clerk walk away. Other footsteps were coming around the reception desk, going into the room behind the desk. Doors and cupboards were opened and slammed shut. Footsteps approached her cupboard. Someone tried to open it but found that it had jammed and quickly gave up.

"I'm sorry, captain. That cupboard always sticks. Shall I try to open it for you?"

"No!"

"Excuse me, sir. I need to do some business in my office. Do you need me for anything?"

"Go!" The captain remained standing near the cupboard.

Eliza heard the clerk walk away to a nearby room. Will he remember to call Sharif? Would he even dare?

The clerk returned to the reception desk. Soon the lobby became quiet again. At nightfall, an hour later, he drew the lobby's window curtains closed and allowed her to come out from the cupboard.

"I'll call a taxi for you, miss. You better go far from here, perhaps to the Hilton downtown. Yes?"

Eliza nodded. "Thank you so much, sir. You are a hero." Her muscles ached, stiff from being confined for well over an hour. She hesitantly looked between the curtains. Vehicle headlights and tail lights blazed through the intersections. She jumped when the front doors flew open. Hotel guests chatted happily as they had returned from a day of shopping. They must have seen the fear in her face. The men quickly herded their women to the elevator.

She realized that she had left her hat and phone in the room but she didn't dare go back to get it. "I'm sorry to be so much trouble," she said softly to her hero. "I need something to cover my head. Do you have a suggestion?"

He thought for a minute. "I'll ask my wife. She usually has an extra scarf here." A few minutes later the maid who had helped her appeared with a scarf. She put it on Eliza. "Good luck, my dear," she said.

The clerk smiled at Eliza. "We know that captain. He's trouble. Sharif knows him too. No good!"

"Were you able to call Captain Sharif?"

"I called but the dispatcher was unable to contact him. I left a message for him to call here."

Eliza slumped into a chair. *This is my own fault, running off like a fool. I'll have to fix this myself. Captain Sharif has more important duties to attend to.* She paid for the scarf. "I cannot express my gratitude enough. I'm very sorry for the trouble."

"Just stay safe, miss. Your taxi should be here soon. Relax while I get you a cup of coffee."

The desk clerk and his wife left Eliza alone. She looked out the lobby doors to see traffic with their bright headlights flash through the dark streets. Finally, she saw the taxi pull up. Relieved that she could soon be safe at the luxury hotel, she sprinted out to the doors and got into the taxi's back seat.

Just as she closed the taxi door, the clerk rushed toward the lobby doors. She couldn't hear him say, "Miss, not that taxi. Don't get into that taxi." The taxi sped off into the night.

Ω

Sharif struggled to inhale. In a city of over three million people, many who were poor and desperate, survival for a woman alone in the dark streets depended upon the mercy of those around her.

Finally, when the night had descended upon his compound, Sharif gave up the hope that Eliza would swallow her pride and call. Infuriated with her disrespect, he tossed his coffee cup into the sink. It shattered. "Damn woman," he cursed out loud. "More trouble than she's worth!" He regretted the thought even as it slipped past his lips.

He threw on his combat gear and rushed out to his SUV. Sergeant Abdul-Muqtadir and his elite squad had been impatiently waiting to begin their patrol. Sharif gave the nod. The constables trotted to their six half-ton trucks, specially equipped to go over or through anything. The sergeant flicked on the emergency lights of his sedan and gave the siren a whoot, whoot, wail.

Sharif jumped into his SUV and motioned to his men. "Move out." He didn't get fifteen feet toward the gate when Captain Khizar's SUV pulled into the compound. *That's odd*, he thought. *What's Khizar's vehicle doing here? And that's not Khizar at the wheel.* He strode over to the driver. "Where is Captain Khizar?"

The constable stood rigid beside the SUV's open door. "He's still handling his underground operations. Some of his moles are busy apprehending a criminal. Didn't want to use his SUV in hell's row. Told me to drive his vehicle back here."

He scanned the constable, noting the skinned knuckles. "Why didn't you return with your partner hours ago?"

"Captain needed an extra pair of hands."

"Yes, I can see that." Sharif stared into the constable's eyes. "Where is Captain Khizar? Exactly."

"At the Peace. Told me to give you this."

The constable reached over to the vehicle's passenger side and picked up two items. He held up Eliza's cap and cellphone. Sharif snatched the items. "Where were these found?"

"Peace Hotel, sir."

"The owner of these items is Miss MacKay. Was she there?"

"Don't know for sure. Not that I saw, sir. Captain Khizar and his moles were looking for a woman. Didn't give a name other than, er, Sharif's bitch." The constable avoided eye contact. "The captain's words, sir. Exactly."

Sharif clenched his jaw shut to refrain from an unprofessional retort. "Was she apprehended?"

"Sir, I was on the periphery mostly. I heard gunshots. Heard a woman had been shot. And, no, I don't know who. Apparently the woman ran off. They were searching for her when I left."

Sharif struggled to maintain his composure. A knife plunged into his belly. For a moment, Sharif's mind froze on the sight of Eliza's body, bloody and dead.

The constable continued. "Khizar called me in to help subdue a prisoner. He gave me those items."

Captain Sharif eyes narrowed. "If you've been involved in any shady activities, I'll have you in my interrogation room tomorrow."

The constable shrunk. "Just following orders, sir."

"Dismissed," barked Sharif.

Sharif brought the hat and phone back to his vehicle and called his men over. Sergeant Abdul-Muqtadir noticed it first. "Captain, that's Eliza hat, isn't it?"

"It is. That constable said a woman had been shot at the Peace. Khizar and his moles were on scene."

Sharif looked more closely at the brim and noticed a strand of gold hair. Turning the hat towards his SUV's headlights his gut clenched at the sight of the dark red smear. *Blood.* "Shit!"

"She's in trouble, captain," exclaimed the sergeant.

Another spoke up. "Probably dead by now."

"Probably," Sharif said, straining to be heard. The knife went in deeper and twisted. Sharif repeatedly smacked the cap against his other hand.

Another constable spoke up. "I don't think so, sergeant. If he killed Miss MacKay, he'd have delivered her body personally."

"This smells like a setup, captain." The sergeant shook his head. "Why's he at the Peace anyway?"

"Sounded like he's working with the mole unit, Omar."

Sharif grabbed his cell phone and called dispatch. "Have there been any responses to the Peace Hotel area?"

"No, sir. Quiet in that area as usual."

"I'm concerned about Captain Khizar. See if you can contact him. Call me back on my cell phone."

A minute later a dispatcher called Sharif. "Sir, Captain Khizar is not responding to our calls. He did book out of service hours ago. Oh, one more thing. One of the dispatchers did get a phone call from the Peace a half hour ago. The caller didn't indicate any trouble but he did ask for you. You were off duty so they left the message with Captain Khizar. Khizar said he'd call you."

"Damn!" he muttered. "Dispatch, I received a report about shots at the Peace. Are there any available units to slide by the Peace? Give a visual check?"

"No, sir. All units are on calls."

"Fine. Sharif out." Sharif groaned. He considered calling the captain of the Peace Hotel district but that would involve more people with Eliza's political situation – and take valuable time.

Sergeant Omar Abdul-Muqtadir nodded to Sharif. "Ready when you are captain. It'll take us fifteen minutes, tops."

Sharif gave the nod. "Listen up. Code Delta Force, blue response. Absolute radio silence en route. Cellphones on buzz or vibrate. Full combat gear. We may be up against dirty moles." They had encountered Khizar's moles many times - a ruthless bunch of underground cops.

"We'll take four corners at the Peace. Move out!"

Procedure dictated that he should advise dispatch on his whereabouts and activity. "Dispatch, this is Captain Sharif. My squad and I will be unavailable until further notice. Sharif out."

The team jumped into their vehicles, switched on their sirens, red and blue flashing lights, and virtually flew toward the Peace Hotel. Within five blocks of the Peace, they shut off all vehicle lights and sirens. Like hawks, silent and swift, they closed in on their target from different directions.

The hotel's 'No Vacancy' sign lit up the front parking area. The team set up a perimeter, blocking traffic from entering or leaving the parking lot. Dressed in the black uniform, helmet and flak jacket, each man became invisible in the hotel's shadows. They moved forward at precise intervals, leapfrogging toward the front and rear doors.

A scream came from within the hotel. Each man held his breath in order to hear more acutely. Another cry of terror, laced with pain, pierced through the darkness. Sharif waved them forward, signaling caution at the same time. Sharif at the front door, Omar at the rear.

Sharif carefully approached the front door and peered into the lobby. It appeared normal until he saw a splatter of blood in front of the reception desk on the polished white tile floor. Sharif pulled out his cellphone and called dispatch. "Dispatch," he said, in a low voice, "send an ambulance to these coordinates." He gave the location of an intersection two blocks north of the hotel. "Tell them to park there until I clear them to move in." The dispatcher acknowledged.

Delta Force entered the hotel. They darted forward through the doors, spreading wide into the small lobby, hallways and staircase. Sharif placed an officer at each exit, elevators and stairs. He nodded to three officers. "Keep everyone out."

The men kept low and moved with speed but without a sound. A short distance down a hallway, to the left of the reception desk, muffled sounds indicated fists being pounded into flesh.

"What do you know about that woman?" a man growled.

"Please, we don't know anything. Oh, please -"

"Liar!" The beating continued. "Why did you hide her from Captain Khizar?"

A woman sobbed, begging for mercy.

Sharif expected to find guards posted in a hallway but none were there. Clearly, the moles were confident they could conduct the interrogation undisturbed.

Two officers and his sergeant followed Sharif down the hallway. They strained to hear sounds, anything like the shuffling of feet, a gun being cocked, the slightest tremor in the spaces ahead and behind. He waved his men forward toward the next door, their guns ready.

Swiftly, like a cat, each man trotted toward the source of the sounds. They froze at a door that had blood smears on the frame. Instantly, the men pressed themselves against the wall and waited for Sharif to give the next order.

Sharif knew the moles worked in pairs. He gathered his men a few yards beyond the door. "Got to be careful. Sounds like there are two civilians in there. Can't rush in." He nodded to a constable. "Create a disturbance down the hall. I want one of the men to come out to check for trouble. Omar, you grab whoever comes out but don't alert the man inside that we've grabbed his partner."

The sergeant grinned. "No problem."

Two men moved back to the reception desk and started ringing the desk's bell. After a couple of seconds they started pounding the desk and yelling, "Let's have some service here! Come on, we need a room." They continued to raise a fuss and get louder, banging on the walls.

Sharif and the sergeant waited around a corner. They heard some grumbling from inside the room. A man armed with a handgun stepped out. Just as he shut the door, Muqtadir lunged at him.

Ω

Eliza directed the driver to take her to the Hilton. She sat in the taxi's back seat watching for familiar landmarks. Street lights barely illuminated the signs. Out her side window she could see the bright downtown section, the high-rise hotels lighting up the night sky. Her nervousness rose to a new level when she noticed the driver didn't turn onto a main street. She asked him why.

He ignored her and activated the security window between the front and back seats.

Eliza hugged her backpack to her chest and tried to recall the city's road map. This area had not been a section of the city she committed to memory. The streets showed their age and became narrower. Garbage lay scattered in the gutters. She unfastened her seatbelt and sat forward.

She pounded on the glass and shouted, "Driver, where are you taking me?"

The driver accelerated.

"Stop this car, stop right now!" She slammed her fist against the shatterproof security window.

The driver yanked the vehicle in a couple of sharp turns, turning down alleys and across another dark street. She froze in disbelief. How can this be happening again?!

With every passing second, she was heading rapidly beyond Sharif's reach. The relief she had felt at the hotel disappeared like a stone tossed into a pond. She looked closer at the cab's interior.

There was no meter clicking away the miles and cost. The ripped cloth bench seat exposed the foam padding. She gasped at the sight of a dark stain in the center of the back cushion. If fear had an odor, its pungent stench permeated every surface inside the cab.

If the driver arrives at his destination, god only knows what they have planned. I have to get out. Get out now. Eliza covertly felt for the door handle and gave it a tug. Nothing gave way. *Trapped. Oh my god!*

She struggled to calm her racing mind. *Breathe, breathe. You know how to get out of this. Breathe, damn it.* She mentally flipped through her self-defense training manual.

Eliza heard the driver mumbling into his radio's microphone. She looked into the rearview mirror to read his facial expression. The dashboard lights illuminated the man's face. Loathing flashed back at her reflection in the mirror.

He had successfully intimidated her enough to make her flinch and divert her eyes toward the windshield. She noted the windshield had damage. A large bull's-eye, center and low. *Perhaps bullets had nearly penetrated the glass.*

She searched through her backpack for a metal tool that could break the tempered glass in the rear passenger window. The heavy metal laryngoscope handle was shaped like a flashlight. It could work if the hard metal protrusion pierced the tempered surface.

Grasping it in her left hand, she inched closer to the right side window. A few seconds later a car veered in the taxi's path making the driver hit the brakes. Her best chance for escape had arrived.

In that instance, Eliza struck the handle into the window with all her fear behind it. The glass exploded into tiny bits. She thrust her backpack through the opening and plunged head first after it. Her shoulder hit the pavement hard.

Thanks to an insensitive martial arts instructor, she knew how to fall. Curled into a fetal position, she rolled, protecting her head. In one quick move she got up, shook off the pain, grabbed the backpack, and dashed for the sidewalk and a dark alley.

The driver slammed on the brakes, spinning 180 degrees. Shouting obscenities, he ran after her. The driver grabbed her shoulder just as she reached the alley. His hands snatched her backpack and flung it aside. He growled through clenched teeth. "Stupid bitch, you'll pay for this!"

Built tough like a featherweight boxer, the driver had superior strength. He pounced on her like a wolf trapping a cornered rabbit. He dodged her attempt to knee his groin. "You try that shit on me and you'll die slow. Real slow!"

He caught a handful of her hair, jerked her off balance, and threw her face-down onto the asphalt. Like a pro fighter, he had her incapacitated in seconds and sat straddled across her hips.

Eliza could hear the sound of metal jangling in his hands. Handcuffs! His one hand tried to hold both of hers while the other fumbled with the handcuffs. Any attempt to reach, kick, twist failed.

Desperate for any advantage, Eliza suddenly remembered her instructor's 'last ditch' advice. Play dead.

While in the throes of fighting him, she gasped, and went completely limp. The risk? Enormous. She gave him free rein to do whatever he wanted. The gamble paid off. The man dropped the handcuffs and flipped her over. He shook her violently. Eliza let her head wobble. Finally, he released his grip on her.

In a flash, she thrust her fist into his throat. He clutched his throat and gasped for air. His struggle to breathe gave her the advantage of getting out from under his weight.

She whirled around to face him.

"You're gonna be sorry, bitch." His voice sounded horse, larynx badly bruised. He reached to a scabbard attached to his thigh. Swift as lightning, he grabbed a knife and sliced it through the air. An eight-inch blade caught the beam of the taxi's headlights. It glowed with deadly brilliance. He waved it back and forth. "I'll cut you slow."

Chapter 27

Sergeant Omar Abdul-Muqtadir grabbed the mole from behind, slapped his hand across the man's mouth, and pressed a large knife against his throat. "Not one sound! Not a whimper," whispered Abdul-Muqtadir. The man's eyes bulged with terror as blood flowed from a gash. He nodded.

Sharif burst into the room. A man standing over a bloody and bruised man swung toward Sharif. He reached for the pistol in his belt holster. Sharif fired a shot just to the right of the man's head. Shards of cements cut his neck. Sharif shouted, "Dead or alive, you choose." He smiled maliciously.

The mole hesitated, released his grip on his weapon, and finally raised his hands. A sneer traveled across his dark, thin face.

"Assume the position. I'm sure I don't have to instruct you on that."

The mole turned around and placed his hands on the wall. Sharif kicked the man's feet further back and apart. "Don't move," he ordered as he put his gun into its holster. Pushing the man's head into the wall, he pulled the mole's weapon from its holster. He glanced at the couple tied in chairs. The sight of their battered and bleeding faces outraged him. "An ambulance will be here shortly."

He turned back to the mole. "You piece of filth," he muttered as he cuffed the man's hands. "You're under arrest for assault and battery. More charges are pending the condition of a missing woman."

"Sharif, I presume." The man chuckled. "Khizar was right. Said you'd come after the b…."

215

With lightning speed, Sharif spun the man around. He grabbed the mole's throat and shoved him back against the wall. Blood spurted out from the back of the mole's head.

"Where is Khizar?"

Dazed, the mole struggled to remain standing. He winced when he noticed Sharif's fist aimed at his nose. "I know nothing. I just follow orders. Said to make this bastard pay for lying to him," he grumbled and nodded toward the desk clerk.

Sharif untied the man and his wife. They shivered and tumbled into sobs.

He placed a comforting hand on the clerk's shoulder. "Listen. What happened to Miss MacKay?"

The clerk straightened up for a moment. "Oh, captain, you must go after her. She's in grave danger. She got into a car she thought was a taxi." The man grabbed Sharif's flak jacket. "But it wasn't. It was a ruse to capture her."

Sharif led the couple to sit behind the reception desk and suggested they call the manager.

Sharif laid the prisoners out on the cold tile floor. "Listen up. I have one question and I'll be reasonable only once. Where is Miss MacKay?"

"Go ask Khizar. We're just his muscle, Sharif."

Sharif stepped up to the two prisoners. "I'm sure you both know about water boarding."

The first mole grimaced. "Ya. And it's forbidden."

"True. But I'm in a hurry. Sergeant, I need a board, a cloth, and a large pitcher of water."

Abdul-Muqtadir said, "With pleasure, sir."

Sharif's men tied the mole's head to a board and placed a thin cloth over his face. Sharif poured water down onto the cloth. It took a mere fifteen seconds for the confession from the drowning man.

A garbled shout vibrated throughout the lobby. "Hell's Gate," he blurted out, coughing.

"Exactly where?"

The mole quickly gave up the address. If Sharif and his men drove like wild men, they could be there in six minutes. "I'll have you up against my wall tomorrow if she dies."

Sharif nodded to two of his men. "You two take this garbage to my cells. Sergeant Muqtadir, you and your men follow me."

Ω

The taxi driver held his knife within an inch of Eliza's face. His face glowed with a menacing stare.

Eliza stumbled on the uneven ground. Her heart pounded against her ribs. *Look for a way to escape.* Her eyes darted about. Another five yards and she'd be trapped against a fence blocking the alley's rear access.

He tossed his knife back and forth between his right and left hands. Her attacker appeared confident, *perhaps over-confident*, she thought.

She had never used her Tae Kwon Do training outside sparring competitions. It was forbidden – except in dire circumstances. Eliza had to face a black hole. Her life revolved around her gifts as a healer, not a killer. If she killed him, could she ever wash his blood off? It sickened her.

"You're nothing but white trash. I'm gonna fuck your corpse," he said, clutching his crotch.

Her survival instincts surfaced with lethal force. Her posture shifted. She became the predator.

The man slashed at her mid-section. She felt the tip of the blade snag on the button of her black shirt. The button flew.

She resumed the position that provided balance and strength. *I can do this.* She moved in.

"Bitch!" He spat a wad of saliva at her. The tobacco-stained slobber hit her neck and dribbled down under her collar.

She ignored his taunts and stench. *Focus meant survival.*

She visualized her next move. *Bring one leg back. Make it look like I'm stepping away from him. Make the first kick fast and hard. Don't just injure the asshole.* She recalled her instructor's warning. *A wounded animal's rage reinforces its strength.*

He gripped the knife handle as if to impale her belly with the blade. When he leaned forward and swung his arm back to gain momentum, Eliza made her move. She took a deep breath. Her body flew up and twisted around in fluid motion. Her leg shot up for a hook kick. Her leg muscles, from her hip to her foot, seized power. She stiffened her foot and ankle, making it rock hard. Her firm leather work boot provided extra impact.

She heard, and felt, the blow to his temple - the slap of her boot's leather against his head, the crunch of the hard sole as it tore into his skull. His head rocked to the side, twisting toward his right shoulder. Blood splattered onto the pavement from the gash along the left side of his head.

A hardened street fighter, the man staggered down to one knee but recovered quickly. She had used speed instead of killing power in the attack. A mistake, perhaps. Eliza had but a second to reverse her direction away from being cornered. She managed to get near the street before he lunged at her, his hatred and power piqued by the pain. She took a breath.

He had strength. She had only flexibility and quick maneuvering. If he cut her, badly, it would be a short fight. Eliza knew her next move had to be final.

She ramped up her fury and snarled at the man. "You prick!" A flash of light from his blade high in the air warned of an imminent slice to her throat. He stepped closer. She eyed his midsection. She kicked her boot into his gut as if aiming for his spine. The knife fell. He doubled over. In a continuous move, her boot shot up to his nose. As she smashed his nasal bones into his brain, the man dropped to the ground.

She stood, crouched on the spot, hands and feet braced for another volley. She panted, her muscles trembling with adrenalin. Her heart raced. The silence struck her. The stillness. The taxi driver was dead. She had killed. She looked about to see if anyone had witnessed the assault. The vacant street lay quiet.

Static got her attention. "Tiger, where the hell are you?" someone hollered on the taxi's two-way radio.

"Shit," she muttered. She ran back to the cab and shut off the radio. The keys dangled in the ignition. She could drive away, but she might be more easily tracked, and trapped.

She checked the front compartments for a map. In the driver door's side compartment, Eliza saw a pistol. Her trembling hand reached for the weapon. Her fingers felt clumsy around the barrel of the gun. Finally, she seized it with both hands, and tucked it under her belt in the small of her back.

She heard the sound of other vehicles approaching, screeching tires and roar of engines powered to the max. She bolted upright. About ten blocks away, the bouncing headlights revealed at least two vehicles racing in her direction.

Find cover. Run!

Across the street she saw a small used car lot. Ahead, a gas station's sign indicated it was closed for the night. She'd be too visible in the outdoor areas of both places. Across from the gas station on her side of the street, a vacant parking lot also offered no sanctuary. Further down loomed a large dark two-storey building – perhaps a department store.

She retreated to her backpack in the alley. The dead man's blood flowed across the sidewalk and down into the gutter. Deliberately, she stepped into the crimson stream.

Vehicles were racing toward her, five blocks away. Eliza ran in the direction of the approaching vehicles, staying tight against the dark buildings.

As the vehicles neared, she had run already two blocks down from the taxi. By now, the blood on her shoes no longer left tracks on the sidewalk. As the vehicles passed by, Eliza hunkered down into an alcove of a shop's doorway. It appeared to be a pawn shop full of a mishmash of trinkets, knives, jewelry. She held her breath, trying to be thinner than the paper sign in the window.

A breeze lifted her blonde hair. *Oh my god, this will give me away.* She tucked her hair down inside her shirt and lifted its collar high. She shivered with fear, watching as the two vehicles roared up to the taxi.

While they focused on the taxi, Eliza darted out onto the sidewalk again and quietly trotted to the end of the street and turned left.

Down the side street she flew for another two blocks. Turning left again at the next intersection, she doubled back toward the department store's block. Running softly for several yards, then she stopped to listen. Again and again she looked back to see if her con had failed.

She heard yelling, someone barking orders. More vehicles arrived, their tires screeching to a halt.

She began to doubt that hiding inside a building was a wise choice. Her confidence evaporated. *Could get trapped.* She felt the urgency to just keep running. Her spine tingled, sensing trouble closing in. *Find a place to hide. Got to find a place to hide. Any place. Run! Don't run. They'll spot movement. Don't breathe so hard. They'll hear that.*

Eliza dashed to the next street. The department store should be close. Without street lights, street signs and landmarks became nearly invisible. She almost sailed without her feet touching the ground for the next two blocks. Then the crash. She tumbled straight into a row of empty metal garbage cans behind the store. *Damn! Perhaps they're too far away to spot the direction of the sound.*

At the rear of the store, her hands guided her in the darkness, looking for a door. She traced the wall of the building. *A door.* It opened. She slipped inside. As she took time to calm down, her eyes adjusted to the darkness.

There were aisles with shelving, empty display cabinets, racks for hanging clothes, and cashier counters. But there was no stock. The store appeared to be abandoned. Making not a whisper of sound, she followed an aisle. Eliza hoped to find another door in case she needed a fast exit.

The headlights from the vehicles parked a block away stole through the windows of the store. She saw five vehicles and at least six armed men scurrying about. Some appeared to be using their cell phones. Others disappeared beyond the street. Many appeared to be running in the direction of her bloody trail.

One in particular walked calmly in his uneven gait. He turned in different directions like an animal sniffing the air for scent of its prey. He pointed his MP5 suddenly in her direction. *Damn, it's Captain Khizar.* He talked on his cellphone for a moment, then stuffed it back into his inside pocket. She watched as he turned toward the store and studied it for a while. She froze as he approached the front door.

When Captain Khizar arrived at the door, he ordered one of men, "Get to the rear entrance. Watch for anyone in the alley or trying to escape from this building."

The front door groaned as Khizar pushed it open. The bottom dragged against the cement floor. *Shit, shit, shit.* Gulping air and her heart racing, she fought the urge to panic and run. In the last second, she spotted a sliding door to a waist-high cabinet. She slid the cabinet door open and silently climbed in just as Khizar slammed the front door shut.

A light bounced around the room like a firefly hovering from one corner to another. She heard his shuffling footsteps approaching. The light became brighter and wavered as Khizar moved forward. The rear door opened. The sound of footsteps echoed as if dozens of men entered the room. Eliza held her breath. Khizar called to the man.

"Keep watch outside. If she comes out the rear door, kill her."

"Yes sir."

The gun in the small of her back pressed painfully on her spine. She tried to shift slightly. The movement caused her boot to knock against the cupboard wall. The sound echoed. Footsteps trotted toward her. A beam of light fell on her. He had set his flashlight on the cabinet. Eliza gasped. She hadn't realized the cupboard functioned as a display cabinet. If he looked down, he'd see her through the glass top. *Don't move. Oh god, Oh god!*

"I know you're in here, MacKay."

Breathe, just breathe. Get the gun. No, too risky to move. Leg cramps tortured her. His footsteps circled the cupboard.

Silence. Shuffling, then no sound. She lost track of Khizar.

Her mind raced, chasing chaotic strategies. The walls of the cabinet closed in. She held her breath but her lungs screamed for more air. Sweat flowed down between her breasts. *Sharif, where the hell are you?* She squeezed her eyes closed as tears threatened to crush her tough exterior.

Her chin quivered. She took a deep breath. *Focus, damn you. She gritted her teeth.*

Bang, clunk! Her eyes darted up to the sound above. The captain's rifle lay a mere foot from the top of her head. His finger still held the trigger.

Dust fell onto her face and stung her eyes. She blinked repeatedly. *Don't move. Shadow movement will tip him off.* Each eyeball screamed for relief. Tears ran down her cheeks.

"I've got no time for this shit." With a grunt of frustration, he hurried away.

Breathe. Just breathe. She cupped her eyes and wiped away tears. *Damn dust.* Her dad called her Dusty. She earned the name on the farm. Grain dust, hay dust, road dust in her hair and clothes. Always with her dad on the tractor, in the barns, or herding the steers down a dirt road, she didn't mind the aching muscles at the end of the day. Her dad was her hero since the day he revealed the secret.

At seven years old, she had come home from school and declared she was too good for sitting in a class all day. The truth was that she had been bullied for a while. When she rolled up her sleeves her dad noticed the bruises.

"You're going to finish your education, Dusty. You're smart."

Eliza broke down into sobs. "No, daddy. They're mean. Call me names and stuff."

He lifted her up onto the back of his half ton truck. "Now you listen to me. I've seen you get those steers to move out of your way. You weren't afraid. Fear makes people weak. Weak and stupid." He smiled. "If you start feeling afraid, imagine God's love as a bright beam of light over your heart, right here." He placed his finger on her chest over her heart. "Never be afraid, Dusty. You can get through anything when you're not afraid."

He had helped her off the truck and grinned. "Now, we'll see about some self-defense programs."

She heard the sounds of approaching vehicles, coming fast and braking hard.

Khizar ran to the rear exit door and shouted to his men. "Get up on the roof. Cut Sharif and his men down." The sudden rat-tat sound of automatic gunfire made Eliza flinch.

The captain ran to the store's front windows. "Look out, Runner," he hollered though his man couldn't hear him. Gun fire became louder. "Damn you, Sharif, you're going to pay." He ran to the rear exit door.

She stepped out of the cupboard door with her backpack and scurried to the front windows. Sharif's men darted about in battle, crouched low and moving swiftly from building to building. They executed their leapfrog formation until they arrived across the street. She checked her gun and headed to the front door.

She spotted Sharif almost a block away. He crouched near the side of the gas station building, straining to see through the windows. Suddenly he fired. Two men had jumped out from an alley and attacked him. More gunfire came from nearby the store's alley.

Sharif leapt for cover too late. His body twisted violently and fell. His men raced to cover him.

Eliza ran out to the middle of the street, staring at his body, waiting for him to get up.

"Watch out," shouted Khizar. "She's got a gun."

She wheeled around to face Khizar. He aimed his sidearm in her direction. She froze as though suddenly encased in ice. Eliza expected a spray of bullets to cut through her flesh.

"She killed Sharif," Khizar hollered to Sharif's men.

She looked down at the gun in her hand. Looking back at Khizar, she shook her head, "No, Captain Khizar. I didn't."

One of Sharif's men hovered over his fallen captain. Another stood at Sharif's feet, facing Khizar. Another stood several feet away to her left and shifted his AK to his shoulder strap. His helmet made it difficult to see his eyes but she felt, more than saw, his body brace for a fight. He started to trot toward her.

Khizar stood thirty yards away from her. More of Sharif's men appeared on the fringes of her peripheral vision. Sergeant Abdul-Muqtadir's hulking frame came into view on Khizar's right side.

"Omar, I didn't, I wouldn't. Please, Omar, I didn't fire this gun." She held her weapon in her open palm away from her body. "You can see for yourself."

The sergeant hollered to her, "Miss MacKay, there's no way out of this. You're under arrest. Surrender your weapon." He appeared mean and ready to take revenge. "Now, MacKay!" The sound of weapons being cocked rang in her ears.

She backed away a few steps. The men would rather believe Khizar than her. They appeared tense, glancing at each other as if telepathically planning an attack. Eliza wondered, would a cop kill another cop? Probably not. Khizar would not allow her to live. That was certain.

She looked back at Sharif's inert body. *Sharif, dead.* Her imminent death paled in comparison to the loss of Sharif. She swallowed. *My stupidity, my selfishness destroyed Sharif. How can I live with this guilt? Again.* It was impossible to inhale. She heard sounds of voices, Omar shouting at her.

Still aware of the pistol in her hand, Eliza fell into self-preservation. She racked the slide and staggered back further. Her finger inched around the gun's trigger. Her left hand braced her right hand.

Chapter 28

Khizar's menacing face came into view.

He killed Sharif. Bastard!

The next moment slowed into milliseconds, each spaced as one would observe successive still photographs.

She saw Khizar's twisted face, eyes narrowed and lips curled.

Khizar shouted, "She's not going to ruin Aamir in a courtroom."

Sergeant Abdul-Muqtadir shouted, "Khizar, stop."

Time moved slower still. Eliza lifted her weapon until Khizar's sneer appeared in the sight line of her gun. *Don't breathe.*

Khizar's teeth clenched as he squeezed the trigger.

Crack of thunder. Again, and again

Her dying prayer, *Sharif, please forgive me.*

Thunder from somewhere near. *Omar, please, no.*

She squeezed the trigger. Gun jerked hard. Wrist seized with pain. Smell of gunfire residue stung her nostrils.

In her mind she saw the bullets hurtling toward her. Eliza braced for the bullets tearing into her flesh.

Dark blur. Black and heavy. Grunting, twisting. Falling down hard. Pain.

F. Stone

Pain told Eliza she had survived. The back of her skull had hit the pavement hard. Dazed, she looked up into the starlit sky. She felt almost giddy. The adrenalin flooded her mind. The moment felt surreal, a dream.

Gradually the scrambling sounds of heavy boots brought her back to the present. A constable lay beside her, struggling to regain his breath as though his wind had been knocked out of him. He'd been hit several times in his flak jacket as he rushed between Khizar's bullets and her. He sat up, repositioned his helmet, and looked over at her. "You okay, miss?"

She blinked in disbelief. He had risked his life for her. The words 'thank you' paled in comparison to his courage. Her thoughts slipped into neutral, unable to comprehend his loyalty to duty. "Thank you, sir."

Sergeant Omar Abdul-Muqtadir inspected the body of Captain Khizar. "Great shot, Lizzy. Got him right between the eyes." he said, grinning at her.

Trembling, she knelt on the pavement. Gingerly she felt the back of her head. Blood oozed onto her fingers.

Abdul-Muqtadir picked up Khizar's gun. "Course, I got him first right through the temple," he boasted. "Damn dirty cop."

"Omar, I thought you ..."

"Ya, I know. Sorry to scare you but I wanted Khizar to think we were siding with him. Hoped he'd stand down and let us arrest you." Abdul-Muqtadir helped her stand up. "You okay?" he asked.

Tears filled her eyes. "I think, maybe." She looked about, still trembling like a leaf. "Sharif?"

"Alive." Abdul-Muqtadir set about ordering the men.

Like an apparition in the night, he stood a half block away from her. A halo of light cast from vehicle headlights surrounded his head and shoulders.

He straightened and walked slowly in her direction clutching his MP5 in his left hand. She took a few steps toward him. The cool night air made her shiver. *From the dampness of her clothes*, she thought. But then, she knew that wasn't true.

Sharif stood ten feet in front of her. She straightened, calling in reserves to put forward a class act of being tough and in control. Crossing her arms, she kept a firm grip on her gun.

Sharif looked her over. Relief became evident as his shoulders relaxed. He stepped forward and held out his hand, "Give me the gun."

His voice lacked the usual tenacity and demanding tone. His body spoke of a man who knew he had just escaped his grave – shuddering, attempting surreptitiously to catch his breath as if in pain.

He braced his left arm close to his side. Ragged holes in his flak jacket revealed how much the death angel hungered for him. Blood flowed from his left arm and hand, along the barrel of his gun, and dripped onto the pavement.

She hid her worry and casually stated, "You need medical attention."

"You're a mess," he said, looking over her disheveled hair and the untucked, dirty shirt gaping open at her waist.

She inched her shoulders back and lifted her chin. "Been busy." She tucked a strand of tangled hair behind her ear. Her bruised arms ached and blood trickled down the back of her neck. Street grime crunched in her teeth. She moistened her lips and tried to wipe off the dirt with her sleeve.

Sharif moved forward once more. "Fun's over. Now hand over that piece, please!"

She grinned. "You worried I might shoot you? I did have some pretty nasty thoughts about you over the past couple of hours."

"Miss MacKay, this evening I violated several operation protocols and risked the lives of my men to save your damn impetuous butt. Again!"

Omar Abdul-Muqtadir roared up with Sharif's SUV. "Three dead moles, plus Khizar and a taxi driver. Not sure what happened to him. No bullet wounds. Face destroyed." Abdul-Muqtadir turned to Eliza. "Would you know what, or who, killed him?"

She hesitated. "He had a knife, Omar. He, he swore he'd kill me."

Both Abdul-Muqtadir and Sharif stood with their mouths open. "Are you saying you took him out?" asked Sharif.

"I know Tae Kwon Do." Her eyes darted from one man to the other. "I had no choice."

Abdul-Muqtadir grunted. "I'd like to meet this Tae Kwon Do." He turned back to Sharif. "Picked up all evidence. Heading to the hospital morgue. Meet you there?"

Sharif smiled at his sergeant and nodded. "Good job, Omar."

Abdul-Muqtadir turned to Eliza. "You can take care of this casualty?" he said jerking his head toward his boss.

"Where's my backpack?"

"In the back of the SUV. Anything else, captain?"

"On your way to the morgue, double check the Peace. Make sure it's secure and our men are back on patrol. Oh, and one more thing. Give me Khizar's cellphone. I want to see his call records."

The sergeant handed over the cellphone. He sped away in his sedan, leaving Sharif and Eliza standing alone in the street. The smell of gunfire residue and blood hung over them like a menacing demon. Cold air nipped at their faces.

Sharif stood in the light of his SUV's open passenger door. Eliza noted that the loss of blood showed in the pallor of his face. He turned away from her momentarily to place his weapon against the side of his vehicle. He moved closer until his boots touched hers. "Hand over that weapon."

Sharif's gruff voice had no effect on her. He gazed into her eyes. "Eliza," he whispered, "Don't ever run from me again!" Relief, maybe something more, had evicted the anger from his eyes.

"Uh huh. You harness that bad temper and I'll stand on my head for you."

A crooked smile slowly eased across his face. "It's a deal. But look who's calling the kettle black. Your fuse is pretty short. Got you in big trouble today."

Eliza hesitated. The truth stung. Her rash actions had put both of them in danger. "You're right. But, I've been scared for so long, especially at night when you're away. I just needed to get away from all this. It was really stupid, I know. I am sorry."

She gazed into his eyes, so warm and soft. At the moment she didn't care about tomorrow, or if they stood in the middle of a war zone. Sharif was alive.

Suddenly, Sharif wrapped his right arm around her waist. When he grabbed onto her gun with his left, he didn't let her go. The embrace must have muddled his Muslim mind. He relaxed into her warmth, his eyes drawn to her lips.

Eliza surrendered to the velvet eyes. "I missed you," she said softly.

Light as a butterfly on rose petals, his lips touched hers. It felt as though the kiss was intended to be a simple light touch, a son kissing his mother hello. He hesitated.

Eliza felt his passion erupt like a tsunami wave. He held her body against his, possessing all her curves. His lips imprisoned hers, played feverishly, released and seized again and again. She felt his body tremble with desire.

Her body capitulated under his burning ardor. Yielding to his passion, Eliza wrapped her arms around his shoulders. Fingers locked into his hair. She released her pent-up lustful emotions and kissed him back, yearning for that intoxicating climax. Her affections became tempestuous; more than his injured arm could bear.

"Argh!" he cried out and released her.

Eliza reached out to him, to his injured arm. "I'm so sorry, Hashim. I shouldn't have …."

He stepped away from her. "No. My fault." He took a deep breath and leaned against his SUV. "Can't say I'm sorry, though."

He gave her a knowing grin and tossed her gun into the back of his SUV.

"Please let me look at your wound. You're losing a lot of blood."

"Never mind. I'll get the ER doc to stitch me up." When he tried to lift his MP5 with his wounded arm he cried out in pain.

"I'm looking at the wound whether you like it or not. Sit!"

He put up a feeble resistance. "You don't give orders here, miss." He staggered and headed for the driver's side.

Eliza blocked him. "You bloody well sit on the passenger side or Mr. Tae Kwan Do and I will kick your butt."

Sharif chuckled and put up his right hand in surrender. "MacKay, I am at your mercy."

Eliza prepared to give him a shot of Demerol. His eyes opened wide as she approached him with the needle. "You're not going to pass out on me are you, dragon man?"

Sharif gritted his teeth. "Just get it done."

Within a few seconds, the pain was dull enough she could pull off his coat and shirt. "Looks like the bullet grazed your bicep. You'll need some repair work. I'm going to put on a pressure bandage."

She worked within his intimate space, her loose hair tickling his chest. Sharif stiffened. "You're being very familiar, miss. This is quite …"

"Yes, I know. Forbidden. You just kissed me, remember? Sit still!" She wrapped his coat around his shoulders. "Stay warm." She realized the tone of her voice was brisk. The kiss had befuddled her brain. Part of her wanted to maintain the relationship as it had been. Business, friendly business. Another part yearned for more of his kisses. Her ability to converse took a back seat to her heart's desperate struggle to let go of what had been forbidden in her world –giving her heart to another man.

In another five minutes Sharif briefly nodded off. He murmured, "You're one in a million, Eliza. I think you're almost worth the trouble." The painkiller had numbed more than his pain. "What's this dragon man thing?"

"I like dragons." She closed her trauma kit and put it on the back seat. Sharif slouched in his seat. When she had wrapped the seat belt around Sharif, avoiding those dark eyes, she shut his door and headed for the driver's side.

"You know what else?" He perked up as she got into the driver's seat. "You kissed me back." He wavered in his seat, then sat back contentedly, dizzy on the narcotic and low blood volume.

"Strictly hormones, Sharif. Now give me directions to the hospital."

Sharif flicked on the emergency lights for her. "Proceed through the red lights." He paused and grinned. "You do know how to do that, right?"

Eliza glared at him for the insult. She drove through the intersection and picked up speed.

At the hospital, Eliza waited as Sharif received surgical repair to his wound. With his arm in a sling they headed to the nurse's triage desk and into a room used by security. Two security officers watched monitors, scanning the parking lot and various locations in the hospital. Sharif moved into a small lounge area used by police.

"Have a seat while I make some calls." He pulled out Khizar's cellphone and studied the calls he'd made and received that evening. One number belonged to the mayor's home. Several others were to and from one source.

Chapter 29

He glanced at Eliza. No hat, hair tangled, blood stained shirt, and a button missing. She looked pale and worn-out. He felt drawn to her, wanted to hold her.

The moment before he had kissed her, his entire being had felt flooded with desire. He had felt invincible at having survived, euphoric in seeing Eliza - *alive*. He awoke to passions locked in a cold vault. The rush captivated and ruled out police protocol and Islam's Sharia Law. *I kissed her. I should feel regret, shame.* He focused on her scuffed boots, smudged with blood.

He wondered if she could handle the emotional baggage that results from having killed. A compassionate person like her might suffer from overwhelming guilt. "You okay?"

She sat down on a white plastic chair facing the open doorway near the triage desk. "Looks like a busy night. What time is it?"

"A bit after one." He stepped up closer and leaned down to her ear. "Are you okay?"

"Hungry. Cold. I'd give a fortune for a long, warm shower right now."

"No. what I mean is do you need to hash over -."

"What I did to the cab driver and Khizar?" She swallowed and visibly shivered. "Right now I'm just so relieved it's over. Maybe if I hadn't worked as a paramedic and hadn't seen people die, I'd be a mess right now." She reached for his hands and held them. "Later, when I have time to feel remorse, I'll send my forgiveness to them, maybe hope they are guided to the Light, to Allah." She caressed his knuckles with her thumbs and then let go of his hands.

Sharif breathed a sigh of relief. *She'd forgive them? Pray for them? Is she really that strong, blessed with such deep wisdom?* He went to the coffee counter and poured her a cup of hot brew. He stirred in sugar and milk, and sat down beside her. "This will have to do for now."

Eliza reached for the cup. "I'm so grateful." She wrapped her fingers around the cup and gazed into his face.

"That you're still alive?"

She hitched a shoulder. "Yes," she said, taking a sip of the coffee, then looking back at him with unrestrained affection in her eyes, "and that you are."

Sharif smiled. "Me, too. This isn't over, Eliza. I've got to make a few phone calls. I want you to just sit quiet no matter what you hear. Agreed?"

She nodded. "Put your arm back in the sling, please."

"Later." Sharif prepared his iPhone to record the conversation. He used Khizar's phone and dialed the number he'd called last. He listened to the ringing, three times. He checked his watch. Nearly one-thirty.

"Well?" An unfamiliar voice sounded irritated. "Sharif and the woman dead?"

Sharif assumed the voice and personality of Khizar. Sharif's voice was deep but not as deep as Khizar's gravelly tone. He shifted his larynx. "Like to see for yourself? They're in the University Hospital's morgue."

"No. That's your job."

Damn, thought Sharif. He'd hoped to bait the man into showing up at the morgue. "You sure? Sharif's bitch is something else. Laid out naked on the table waiting for you. Still warm." He glanced over at Eliza. He caught her disgust as she turned her back to him.

"She's all yours, Khizar. Did you find any of the Sharif's CIA records?"

Bingo! Sharif put his ruse into fast forward. "Couple of things. A notebook, pretty much all in code, and a special cellphone. Not issued by the service or available in this country. I suspect it's from the CIA. You do know that the CIA are identifying the killers."

"Uh huh. How much do they know?" The man sounded more alert. A lot more alert.

"Just that the locals were told to create trouble, draw the cops away from Sharif's compound."

"Do they know about Aamir's British connection?"

Sharif hesitated, nearly losing the beat. "Not so far. Should I expect to hear from the Brits?"

"You and Aamir need to return to daily routine. I'll take out the rest. The Brit's unit is setting up to close off loose ends."

Eliza got up and walked out to the triage desk.

Sharif continued to bait his fish for a meeting. "Sharif had loyalty of a lot of cops. When they find out he's dead, there's going to be revenge, stir up trouble. We should get together to discuss strategy."

"Fuck," the man muttered.

At that moment, Sharif heard the hospital paging system call out, "Paging Captain Khizar, Captain Khizar report to the triage desk."

"Sounds like you're being paged." The man sounded more relaxed. "I'm returning to Cairo to meet with Omega. I'll stop by the mayor's home on my way to the airport to hand over payment. If you discover anything more about Sharif's work with the CIA report only to Aamir. Understood? I'll be back in a few weeks." The man hung up.

Sharif ran his fingers through his hair. Who the devil is he? And who is Omega? There was only one chance to find out.

Eliza strolled back into the security office. "How was that?"

"Brilliant. It worked. I now know the mayor is a front line player." He handed Khizar's cellphone to Eliza. "Put this where no one will find it, like where your passport had been."

When she had it secured in her backpack, they headed to his SUV. "Do you mind driving? My arm is screaming."

"Put your arm back into that sling," she said, jumping into the driver's seat. As she headed out of the parking lot she gave him a list. "You need to drink plenty of fluids, keep your arm elevated, don't use it for anything, not even ...." She looked at him fiddling with his smart phone. "Who are you calling?"

"My family. Just in case the media gets wind of this and report that I'm dead." He looked at his watch. "Almost two o'clock. They'll be sleeping. It'll be a shock."

"If they're anything like you -."

"I know, I know. They deserve a son who doesn't cause such misfortune in their lives."

"No. I meant they're probably as stubborn, I mean, tenacious."

Sharif ignored the jibe and the compliment. His parents' phone rang six times before his father answered.

"Is that you, Hashim?"

"Who else would be rude enough to wake you up at two in the morning, papa? Are you awake now? You've got to listen carefully."

"Alright, what's wrong?"

"You might hear a report saying that I was killed last night. Someone tried, but I'm fine."

"Why would ...."

"Just listen, papa. Just be careful. Watch out for strangers."

"So long as you're okay."

Sharif shrugged his shoulders. "Yes, except for a scratch. You must not let the kids phone anyone. Very important. No communication with anyone. I'll call you tomorrow night about seven. Bye papa."

Sharif put away his cell and glanced at Eliza. She had a smirk on her face.

"How many stitches did you get in that scratch?"

"Eighteen. Hurts like a bugger!"

He speed-dialed his sergeant's cell number. "Omar, Khizar had taken on a contract to kill Eliza and me. I just called the hitman pretending to be Khizar. He's heading to the airport but stopping at the mayor's house. I need your plainclothes team to find out how the mayor is involved. I want the hit man tagged. Photos, passport, audio, everything until his plane leaves."

"Got three in plainclothes tonight. They'll be pleased for a new assignment."

Sharif breathed a sigh of relief. "Omar, does the name Omega mean anything to you?"

"Other than it's often used to describe the last, the end, or the ultimate."

"Get those officers on the move. Sharif out."

At his office, Sharif grabbed a coffee and tried to calm his nerves while he dialed Agent Hutchinson's cell phone and left a text message. 'Mayor Aamir & hit man hired Khizar to kill me. Khizar now dead. Man heading to airport, destination Cairo. Standby for more info. Sharif.'

At four, the sergeant and his underground team stood in the conference room while their captain leaned against the front edge of a table. They eyed the blood-stained bandage on his left arm. "That's a pretty nasty wound, captain."

"Could've been worse. Still have my arm. Show me what you collected."

They inserted two camera memory discs into the room's computer and downloaded data from their iPods. "Got some good stuff, captain. Listened in on the conversation between the mayor and the hit man. Mayor called him 'Black Ice'." The men snickered. "Won't last long here," joked the lead officer.

Sharif became surly. Weakened from loss of blood, his sense of humor paled. "I don't have time. Give me the highlights and a couple of photos for the CIA agent."

The man's posture straightened. "Yes, sir. Got several photos of Black Ice in the mayor's home. Ice told Aamir he'd get paid only after he made a positive visual ID that you're dead. Ice made some threats that the 'Office' is not happy with the delay. Sounded like the mayor was to have eliminated you during the massacre. We followed Ice to the airport."

"What's the name on his passport?"

"Sergeant Muntazar said the passport looks authentic enough to pass inspection. Name reads Peter Phillips IV. Brit, lives in London, England, 66 years old. Five eleven, solid build, dark brown greying hair, collar-length. Striking features – piercing golden-brown eyes and prominent nose. Walks with an air of superiority. Very little eye contact except when questioned by security. Wore gloves. Hands appeared stiff."

Sharif shuffled to his chair and sat down to view the surveillance photos. He took his time studying the face of Black Ice. "He's definitely heading to Cairo?"

The officer checked his hand-written notes. "Flying in a private jet owned by a numbered firm in Cairo. The aircraft is a Challenger CL604 MMA. He's scheduled to arrive in Cairo at seven forty-five - in another three hours."

"Excellent work."

He dialed Agent Hutchinson's phone and downloaded the data from the computer and turned back to his men. "Did they talk about when Khizar got the contract?"

"No. Sir, do you know anything about Global Islamic Council? Ice mentioned it a couple of times," said the undercover cop.

"They're rumored to be connected with Egypt's Brotherhood." Sharif's gut flipped. *The massacre? Maybe.*

His thoughts raced on, scanning his memory for what he could remember about the GIC but it remained sketchy. As the men left the station, Sharif motioned for his sergeant to follow him into his office. He glanced at his watch. Four-thirty. "You call Aamir. Tell him that Khizar was killed and that I'm dead, too. Test him, see what reaction you get. I'll call Agent Hutchinson."

When the agent answered, all Sharif heard was casual chatter in the background. He waited for a couple more minutes, eavesdropping on Frank's soup order and rant about a mix-up at some airport. It sounded like he was having a late lunch in Washington.

Frank snorted. "Damn mindless stickmen." Then Frank burst into a laugh. "Got them in the end." The sound of people laughing and getting out of chairs indicated the conversation might be over.

Sharif groaned. "Hello," he hollered in case the agent had forgotten about the call. "Frank, I haven't got time!"

"Steady, Sharif. Interesting data you sent. Is this legit or are you still playing me for a fool?"

"Anyone who thinks you're a fool better run for cover. No pun intended."

"You sound a bit testy. Looks like you've been busy."

"I've been up for nearly forty-eight hours searching for Eliza who decided to run off into Hell's Gate. I'm low on sleep, food, blood and patience. What do you know about Black Ice?"

"Brit blue blood. Name's Peter Phillips. Claims to be related to the British royal family. Disinherited when a scandal proved he'd acquired his wealth via nefarious means. Surprised he came after you. No offense, but his victims are usually higher up in the food chain."

"Perhaps you should show me more respect, Frank. Looks like he has connections with an organization called GIC."

"If GIC is behind the massacre, RIPT is in trouble. We need to keep the rumor alive that you're dead. If we're lucky, Aamir will do something that will implicate his involvement with this contract. We need something more than his discussion with Ice."

"Fine. I'll head to Rumi. Take Eliza."

"Okay. You realize that as soon as Ice knows you're still alive, he'll come back for you. Not under contract. Just pure vengeance."

"Business as usual, Frank. No different than any other day here. Frank, who or what is Omega?"

"Omega? Shit. Only know Omega is something or someone connected to GIC. No images, no communication. Just rantings of a dying agent. Why?"

"Black Ice said he was going to report to Omega."

"Uh huh. I doubt it. That bastard's got an enormous ego. Only GIC's inner sanctum seems to have access to Omega. We've never been able to get close. All we hear is that this Omega claims to be the second coming of God's prophet. Even heard he's gifted, got some kind of super power. Naturally, all madmen have those delusions, but -."

"But what? Where's his army?"

"Doesn't need an army. After all, every Muslim, Christian, Hindu, maybe even the Jews, cannot turn away from the lure of meeting the next Jesus, the next Muhammad, the next ...."

"You're serious. I've never heard of such heresy."

"This is our theory. The secrecy, the mysticism, the appearance of total benevolence. It's the latest addiction. Save the sinners, offer unconditional love, absolute forgiveness; promise of wealth and eternal life with Allah. Tell me Sharif, what would you give up, what would you do in order to touch the hand of a prophet?"

"Humpf. I'd need a lot of proof."

"Really? Churches are empty. Mosques are quiet. People are despairing for the sight of God's emissary. Through the destruction of RIPT, which could be viewed as God's will due to the relaxation of Sharia Law, Omega might begin to exert control – not by force, but under the guise of saving the world."

"And you, or whoever, believes Armageddon would follow?"

"If you recall your history lessons, every time there was a major shift in a population's allegiance to a new religion, the result has always been war, poverty, disease, famine. It happened between the Christians and the pagans, and the Crusades. And since Muhammad began his following, thousands have been murdered among Shia and Sunni in the dispute over leadership. We're still killing and competing for God's love." Frank paused, as if to collect his emotions. "RIPT's imminent demise could be the catalyst that ignites Omega's launch."

"You've got to get hold of Ice, Frank."

"My men in Cairo will get him. I'll let you know what we discover. Oh, and Sharif?"

Sharif thought the agent was going to thank him for getting the data. Or say that he was relieved that he survived the attack. Maybe, even tell him he was off the list of suspects and forgiven for the lies. "Yes, Frank?"

"You found MacKay?"

"Yes, she's fine."

"You've been lying about Miss MacKay and a whole lot of other details. My boss is looking forward to putting you away, maybe permanently. Anyway, give Eliza a kiss for me."

"Frank." Sharif clenched his jaw and took a deep breath. "If I don't make it, will you get Eliza out? Take care of her?"

"We both know if you don't make it, she'll go down with you. Adios amigo."

Ω

Mayor Aamir banged on the locked morgue's door. After ten minutes a thin man in a lab coat opened it. Aamir marched through the doorway into the dim light of the morgue. He stopped abruptly, causing his bodyguard to bump into him. Aamir hated the smell of embalming liquids. He gagged and whisked out a cloth from his pants pocket and placed it over his nose.

To the right of the entrance large refrigerated drawers lined both sides of a dimly lit hallway. Aamir glanced at the embalming room beyond the hallway. A bright light illuminated a naked body on a steel table. Even from several feet away he could see the scalp had been pulled down over the face and the abdominal cavity organs lay in a container on the floor.

The embalmer smiled sheepishly. "Sorry. Was taking a break and fell asleep." The thin man rubbed his eyes. Stepping aside, he switched on bright lights. "Do you have a body for me?"

The mayor grimaced. "No. I'm Mayor Aamir. I was informed Captain Sharif and Captain Khizar were killed. Show me the bodies." Aamir's eyes narrowed. "You do have Sharif's body. Correct?"

The thin man motioned for the mayor to follow. "Don't have Sharif but Khizar is here." If the mayor looked more closely at the attendant, he might recognize the police uniform pants and shoes. Captain Sharif had taken the precaution to misdirect the mayor.

"Why isn't Sharif's body here? All cops killed are brought here. Where is he?"

"The Medical Examiner approved of moving the body to Rumi. His family insisted. That's all I know about that." The thin man opened a drawer and unzipped the body bag to reveal Khizar's remains. "Here is Khizar."

Blood and torn tissue disfigured the man's face. "Our visual inspection revealed two wounds from two different firearms. Shots all to the face." The thin man stepped back and crossed his arms.

The mayor stood gazing at Khizar's body. His shoulders sagged as he gazed at the naked body from head to toe. Suddenly, the mayor gasped. "Where are Khizar's personal effects?"

"There was nothing on him. No wallet, no firearms, nothing."

242

"No cell phone?"

"No, sir."

Aamir gritted his teeth. "Damn!"

Aamir swung toward his bodyguard and motioned to the door. "We're going to Sharif's station. I've got to find that cell phone."

Ω

"Omar, the agent says I need to stay dead a while longer. No one can know I survived, including Aamir. Can you do a quick doctoring on the vehicle video that recorded the assault in Hell's Row? Proof that Eliza and I were killed."

The sergeant nodded. "That's easy enough if you don't want high quality. Just a second, my phone's ringing." In the next minute, the sergeant hollered to Sharif. "Get out of here. Aamir is on his way from the morgue."

Sharif ran up the stairs taking two steps at a time. He pulled a sleepy Eliza off the couch. "Eliza, wake up. We've got to get out of here." He threw her coat over her shoulders. "Get in the van. Hurry."

They nearly tumbled down the stairs. As they ran into the storage building, the call to the six o'clock morning prayer sounded above the clamor of the massive overhead door opening.

"Quick, get in. Don't slam the door," urged Sharif.

Eliza giggled. "I haven't played hide and seek since I was a kid. Do we count to a hundred?" She jumped into the front passenger seat.

Sharif glared at her. "Not amusing, miss." He softly closed his driver's side door.

"I'm sorry. I'm so tired I just don't care anymore." She let her head fall back against the side window. "Or hurt anymore."

He heard a commotion outside the building. "Aamir has arrived. It's too late to drive out." Sharif squeezed through the front bucket seats. "He's not going to look for me here." He lowered the seat backs and retrieved a blanket. "Come back here, Eliza. Get some sleep."

"It's time for prayer. Aren't you - ?"

"Allah forgives." He guided her through the seats and down onto the small makeshift bed. By the time he pulled out Farah's teddy pillow and placed it under her head, she was asleep.

He hesitated for barely a heartbeat. Then he collapsed down beside her, holding her close, and fell asleep.

Ω

Mayor Aamir arrived at Sharif's nearly deserted station and bolted into the evidence room. Not finding the cell phone, he barged into Sharif's office and confronted Sergeant Abdul-Muqtadir. "Report," he shouted. "What happened to Khizar? Where's Sharif's body?"

Omar gave a summary of the events, as best as he could remember given his state of mind. His most trusted leader and friend was dead. He gave a stellar performance. Anger laced with rage, sorrow, and despair. "See for yourself, mayor. The vehicle videos recorded everything."

The mayor hit the 'play' button, watched as Khizar murdered Captain Sharif. Moments later he saw the battle between Khizar and MacKay. Both went down. Pleased his mission succeeded, he shrugged off the fact the video skipped over scenes.

"Are you aware Sharif's body is not at the morgue?"

"You must be mistaken. I delivered his body there myself. Unless the family requested it be delivered to Rumi. The medical examiner should not have released it."

Aamir's cell phone purred in his coat. He checked the call display and ran back to his vehicle. "Yes," he barked.

"Is the problem finally eliminated, Aamir?" Her voice sounded cold, menacing.

"Yes, I have just witnessed a recording of his death." There was no need to explain further. The least said the better, when dealing with the GIC liaison. He had met her a few times. He fanaticized having her. She'd enjoy rough sex. Maybe not, but that didn't matter so much as the erotic pleasure of fucking Sharif's ex-wife.

"Finally," she groaned. "The abduction will be less troublesome."

Ω

A little after seven, Sharif called his sergeant. Abdul-Muqtadir verified the station was quiet. He'd sent all the cops out so Sharif and Eliza could return unnoticed.

As his sergeant was heading off duty, Sharif pulled him aside. "Eliza and I are going to Rumi. It's the best way to stay out of sight."

Sharif and Eliza prepared for the trip. "I'll make arrangements with a friend of mine while you pack. Just a change of clothes for both of us and some food."

Sharif knew a pilot, Thaeer, who owned a Lear jet, a C-21A. It was fast and could carry up to eight passengers. There was no better pilot in all of the Middle East. Thaeer had followed his hero, Buzz Aldrin, the pilot of the first moon landing, like nothing else in the world existed. Since then, Hashim called him Buzz.

His call was answered by a sleepy and irritated man. "This better be damn important."

"Assalam alaikum, Buzz."

"Oh it's you. Who are you chasing, Sharif?"

"I know you're semi-retired, but do you still have the Phoenix?"

"Am I going to get killed if I answer yes?"

Sharif played along. "Buzz, you cut me to the marrow." His voice echoed his disappointment. "I'll be at your airport in an hour."

"Bring a thermos of strong coffee, something sweet, and I'll take you to the moon. Got to register a flight plan and list of passengers. Who is coming along?"

Sharif thought for a moment. "Make up a name for a husband and wife. Report what you have to but don't get friendly with anyone at your airport about this trip."

"Getting better by the minute. Your girlfriend pretty?"

"Ugly as sin. But she is sweet. How much?"

"A hundred million."

"Thief. Be ready in an hour."

Eliza crammed in a change of clothes and her coat into her small suitcase and added the advanced medical supplies to the backpack. She packed some snack food and quickly made a thermos of coffee. In another hour, they arrived at the small private airport, Thaeer Flight School.

Buzz appeared pleased. Either it was the free breakfast that put the smile on his face, or the sight of Eliza's pretty face. He grinned and shuffled his feet like a shy school boy. "Why is she dressed in a police uniform?"

"Secret mission, Buzz. In fact, you never saw her or me. Understood?"

"Same old stuff, Sharif. Welcome aboard," he hollered as the jet's engines nearly drowned out his voice.

They trotted up the steps and sat down as Buzz closed the door. Buzz grabbed the thermos of coffee from Sharif, and made a brief introduction to his co-pilot. The young man appeared just days out of flight training school, wide-eyed with enthusiasm and eager to get the takeoff checklist completed.

"ETA in Rumi, Buzz?"

"Relax. I'll get you there in an hour forty, barring hitting the mountains. Touch down at ten-fifteen. Buckle up."

Ω

Dr. Sharif's right hand gripped his car's steering wheel. Never before had the children behaved so badly. His wife sat quietly in the passenger seat gazing into the distance. She could tune them out in a blink of an eye. Though their high energy amused the elderly couple, the children could push Dr. Sharif's buttons if he felt fatigued. Right now, Dr. Sharif felt more than simply tired. Worry weighed heavily on his mind.

Just a scratch, Hashim had said. Likely had a huge laceration across his throat, if I know my son's habit of shading the facts. Dr. Sharif's medical knowledge worked on his imagination.

Pounding on the back of his driver's seat reminded Dr. Sharif that his granddaughter, Farah, was on the verge of a meltdown. For a six-year old she could kick hard enough to cause damage to his immaculate seats. She was giving his seat a thorough beating.

Dr. Sharif stopped driving alongside his orchard of orange trees. "Stay put!" he ordered his grandchildren, and turned to his wife. "My dear, I'll be just a couple of minutes." He jumped out and strode up to one of his trees. Pulling out a small pocket knife, he cut off a thin branch and returned to his car. He opened the door to the back seat and pulled out Farah by her wrist. "Stand there," he ordered, pointing toward the back wheel. She danced and whirled as though she hadn't heard.

He waved the switch in front of her with his left hand. Since the day of his first stroke, his right arm had lost much of its strength. As a physician, he was now limited to office calls. As a guardian of his grandchildren, hugs were limited to one-armed embraces.

He gave one searing smack of the switch to his left hand. Farah jolted still. "There," growled Dr. Sharif again, pointing to the rear tire. Farah stepped quickly to stand in front of the wheel. "Miss Sharif, for shame," he scolded shaking his finger at her. "I have taken you and Mustafa out for a nice breakfast and now you misbehave so badly. What are the rules about riding in my car?" He raised the switch high.

Farah demonstrated more shock than fear. Grandpa had never struck her. "Supposed to be quiet. Not touch stuff. Don't spill my drink." She checked her fingers, opening one for each rule, but was stuck on the pinky. "One, two, three, and, and …."

Dr. Sharif again flung the end of the switch against his open palm. He scowled at the diminutive and delicate frame in front of him. *So beautiful, like her mother,* he thought. *And stubborn, like her papa.* "And?" He brought the switch closer to her.

Farah's eyes widened. She gasped. "Oh, I remember. No kicking or hitting."

Dr. Sharif stood tall near his most loved grandchild. He loved Mustafa but the boy had become more sullen and resentful since being abandoned by his mother. Nothing seemed to lift the boy's mood or alter his constant need to talk with his mother. With Farah, all she wanted was to be with her papa. Even though she didn't see enough of Papa, her happy soul filled Dr. Sharif's days with joy.

She peeked up through the long dark eyelashes, and grinned. He looked down his nose at her. "And how do you atone for misbehaving, Miss Sharif?"

She puckered her mouth into a pout. "I'm sorry," she murmured, looking down at her feet and digging the toe of her sandal into the grit.

"Oh, I must be getting deaf. Did you say something, Farah?"

Farah grimaced and put her hands on her hips. The defiant child spoke up, nearly shouting, "I said I'm sorry, grandpapa."

Dr. Sharif scowled. "Such disrespect. How would you like to walk back home?" Again he flicked the switch hard against his open hand.

Mustafa whined. "Farah, if you don't smarten up, I'll …."

"Quiet, Mustafa," said Grandmamma. "It's none of your business. Tell me how your mother is. I see she sent a text message to you this morning."

Mustafa frowned. "You read my mail?"

"No, my dear boy. But I do keep track of who you talk to. Is your mother still not feeling well?"

"She's not sick or anything. Been busy, lots of stress, I guess. Said her father was away and she missed his help in the office. That's all. Mostly."

By then, Dr. Sharif and Farah had worked out their differences. Dr. Sharif drove up the driveway to his rural home. He waited for a moment and watched the east-facing windows.

A shadow moved into the kitchen. A man's form was cautiously walking from room to room. "Trouble," he said and shifted into reverse.

"Papa," screamed Farah. "Papa's home." Farah opened her door and ran toward her home's front door. "Papa, papa."

Dr. Sharif yelled to Farah. "That's not your papa, Farah. Stop. Stop right now!" he hollered as he raced after her.

Chapter 30

Buzz adjusted his speed and configured the Phoenix to climb. The mountain loomed another one hundred fifty miles in the distance. Snow in the higher elevations glistened in the sun among the jagged peaks.

"Better have a seat, Sharif. Going to get rough. Buckle up your friend, too." Buzz turned to check on Miss MacKay. "Shit, what is she doing?"

She stood at the tail section in the aisle, wobbling with the aircraft's movement on the wind currents. Her bare back faced the men. She appeared to be looking for something in her backpack.

Sharif lunged to stand behind her back, blocking the pilot's view of the semi-naked woman.

"What are you doing?" he growled. "This is not permitted."

"I spilled hot coffee on my shirt. It burned like crazy. Just give me two minutes to change into a clean shirt." Eliza shrugged him off. "Turn around."

"You're indecent." Sharif knew he should tear his eyes away, and turn around. The shape of her back, the soft shoulders, and her curves reminded him of the undulating terrain of the Sahara. The waistband of her pants rested low on her hips. Fighting his body's traitorous desires, Sharif growled, "Get into the bathroom."

"Too damn small." Eliza snatched a black lace camisole from her backpack and held it against her chest. "Go back to Buzz. I'll be properly dressed in two minutes." The plane lurched to the right. Eliza lost her balance and placed her feet farther apart.

Sharif grabbed her around the waist and pulled her back snug against his chest. He whispered into her ear. "Eliza, when are you going to stop tormenting me?" He half-hoped she didn't hear his confession above the roar of the twin engines.

"Do you want me to shut off who I am?"

He felt her body tense as if preparing to fight him off, then melt into his wall of muscle and bone.

The intimacy threw him into panic. In the span of one breath, he felt the old inclination to shun the pleasure, even to feel repulsed by the bliss. *Allah forbids.* But his drive to be honorable refused to allow the lie. He could no longer deny that Eliza, the impetuous and insane woman who had the audacity to expose his humanity, had become very dear to him.

"No, never," he said, placing a brief kiss on the corner of her mouth. Though he had met her just seven weeks ago, he knew her as if they had spent a lifetime together. He knew the cadence of her voice, the swing of her stride, and the nuances of her moods. He marveled at the light that shimmered in her hair and lived in her eyes. He knew the capricious scent of her body, and could spy on her thoughts through the tilt of her head and curve of her mouth. He found it mystifying at the depth to which he understood this woman, like no other. Wanted her, like no other.

The warmth of her body spread like a warm breeze into his. Numbed by isolation and practiced sacrifice, fragments of his passion flared out of control. Hashim Sharif moaned. He couldn't tell where his body ended and hers began. The dim light of the aircraft cabin sighed over her shoulders. If not for the lace camisole concealing her most alluring charms, his lust would have ruled his actions.

Over the years, the words "I love you" had become mute, lost under the weight of perceived duty and disconnection with his emotions. He was Captain Sharif, the noble Muslim warrior. He was not Hashim Sharif, the good man, worthy of Eliza MacKay.

Soft and warm, her hands covered his. Sharif shivered with need - to declare to man and Allah, Eliza was his. A violent shake of the aircraft shattered his lustful intentions. Sharif straightened, and

251

wrestled his inner cop back into control. Love was for people not running for their lives.

She buttoned up a fresh shirt, turned to face him and flipped up her hair under the police cap. "There, no harm done."

He lifted his cap and slapped it back down. "Around my family, we'll have to maintain physical distance. No unnecessary conversation."

"You're the boss." She smiled and patted his chest. "Anything you want, it shall be done."

For the next hour Sharif and Eliza rested, fitfully sleeping, half relieved to be away from the terror in Samarra, and yet anxious about finding a resolution to the Sharif family's safety. Sharif bolted upright in his seat when Buzz shook him awake.

"There's trouble in Rumi, Sharif," Buzz hollered. "Captain Khattab and his men are set up to meet you on the tarmac."

Chapter 31

"My children, they're gone. Please help us," the woman screamed into the phone. "They took our children." It took a few seconds before Captain Khattab recognized the voice of Mrs. Sharif, wife of the local physician and friend, Dr. Sharif. She wailed and screamed again. "They're gone."

An ambulance and two police units arrived at the Sharif rural residence. Mrs. Sharif, crying hysterically, ran to them. Dr. Sharif was lying dazed and bleeding near his vehicle parked at their driveway's entrance.

Captain Khattab arrived as the ambulance rushed Dr. Sharif to the hospital. The intensity of his bright blue eyes had the power to make a liar think twice. Even so, his wide smile was warm and framed by a trimmed brown beard.

He firmly guided the distraught woman to his SUV.

"Mrs. Sharif, you must calm down. I need you to tell me exactly what happened."

The elderly woman trembled as her hands gestured with her report. "We had gone out for breakfast." She succumbed to more fits of fear and despair.

"Yes, Mrs. Sharif, and then what happened?"

"We drove back into our driveway, my husband slowed down and stopped. He saw someone in our house, a stranger. But Farah thought it was her papa and jumped out of the car. Mustafa followed her. They were so excited. Hashim hasn't been home for over two months." Mrs. Sharif took a deep breath.

"Yes, Mrs. Sharif. What happened then?"

"Three men ran from the house. Two grabbed my grandchildren while the third fought with my husband. Oh, in the name of Allah, the most merciful, Captain Khattab, please, you must find my children."

Khattab felt momentarily stunned. Violent crime in the rural area around the city of Rumi had been non-existent for the past ten years. Abduction of children - unthinkable. "Did you recognize them? What did they look like?"

"They were completely covered. Even wore gloves, sunglasses." She thought for a moment. "They were well dressed, their clothes like businessmen." She looked at Khattab with a look of shock. "Mustafa has a cellphone with him. Perhaps we should try to call him."

"Not yet. I hope he's got it concealed. Perhaps he'll try to call us when it's safe. What is your son's phone number?"

Khattab tried to call Hashim Sharif but the call failed to connect.

"Damn." He called his sergeant. "Block all exists from Rumi, including the airport. Send a team to the airport. Ensure there are no take-offs or landings without special security check. Set up security around Rumi's perimeter." Patrols were sent to block the two roads leading out of Rumi. The Rumi Mountain Pass was notified to check all vehicles. He turned back to Mrs. Sharif. "They have Farah and Mustafa, but they'll not get them out of Rumi." He instructed an officer to thoroughly examine the residence for clues and hazards, and then he turned back to Mrs. Sharif. "I need to figure out the motive for the attack. Usually ransom. I'll take you to the hospital to stay with Dr. Sharif."

On his way back to police headquarters, Khattab received an urgent call.

"We got a situation, sir," said Khattab's sergeant. "A private jet landed two hours ago. It was required to go through the routine customs and agri-inspection. Parked inside the hangar. The pilot and his three travelers are back and demanding to be allowed to leave. Threatening the hangar staff. Security is requesting backup."

"Shit. Get all available units to the airport."

By the time Khattab and his men arrived, the travelers had left, disappeared back into the city.

"Rumi Airport tower to Captain Khattab."

"Khattab here."

"A jet is approaching It's Buzz from Samarra. He's bringing Captain Sharif."

Just the man I need. "Let Buzz land, but no one else."

Captain Khattab and four of his officers waited on the tarmac just as the Phoenix's wheels touched the landing strip. Buzz taxied to one of the six gates at the terminal. He met Sharif bounding out of the aircraft and offered his hand. "Glad you're here, captain. There's bad news."

"My family? Let's have it." Sharif braced for a shock. His eyes bore into Khattab.

"Your family was attacked an hour and half ago. Someone has kidnapped your kids. Your parents witnessed it. Your father tried to fight them off. He's at Rumi Hospital, nothing too serious."

"What about my kids, Khattab? Where are they? Is there evidence they were injured?" His body posed like an animal ready to attack.

Khattab led Sharif to his SUV. "There's no evidence to indicate they have been hurt. The attack took place at your home. Very quick. Professional. I've had all exit routes blocked. So long as we got that done in time, your kids are still in Rumi. I believe the culprits just tried to fly them out. When we refused to give them access to their aircraft, they bolted."

"Good job, Khattab."

"Your mother saw everything but didn't see their faces. She's in a pretty bad state. Do you know why your children have been kidnapped? Would it be ransom?"

"No, it's definitely not ransom. I don't have all the facts but I've been threatened. Told if I didn't keep my mouth shut, my family would pay." Sharif continued to give Khattab the backstory.

Khattab shook his head. "No shit. This is getting double bad. He looked back to Buzz. "Buzz, good to see you. Come along, in case we need your help." Khattab glanced at Eliza. "Who?" he asked nodding toward her.

Sharif motioned for Eliza to come forward. "Captain Khattab, this is Miss MacKay. She witnessed the massacre I tried to stop. She's under my protection until I can get her out of RIPT. Can't do that until my family is safe."

Eliza nodded to Khattab. He noted the stress in her face. You look worried, miss. "Do you know the Sharif children?"

"No. But I'm all too familiar with the loss of one's children. There's nothing more devastating." She jumped into the SUV and sat beside Buzz. Hugging her backpack, she turned to Buzz. "Welcome to my world, Buzz."

Khattab drove them to the hangar to inspect the impounded jet. They walked around the beautiful sleek aircraft. "Our records show this aircraft arrived from Cairo. My staff is checking on the pilot's and travelers' customs records. We'll get prints, swab it down thoroughly for DNA."

Buzz whistled. "That's one fine jet. Only the elite fly a plane like that. That's a multi-million US dollar Challenger CL804 MMZ. Equipped with fire power for defense. You've got powerful enemies, Sharif."

Khattab nodded to Sharif's pilot. "Buzz, I'd like you to work with my squad on this aircraft. See if the instruments tell us anything about who owns this aircraft, where it has been." Buzz agreed.

Khattab turned to leave. "We've got two kids to find. Let's go, Sharif."

Khattab, Sharif and MacKay first stopped at Rumi Hospital. Khattab and Eliza waited in the hallway while Sharif had a brief meeting with his parents.

When Mrs. Sharif spotted her son, she cried out, "Hashim, my dear son, praise to Allah the Most Powerful, you are here. We are safe now." She clung to him and cried out, "Mustafa and Farah, they are gone." She continued to describe each detail amid sobs.

Sharif took her by the hand and sat her down beside his father's bed. He nodded to his father. The elderly parent gingerly reached for his bandaged head. His hand wavered and his eyes had a glazed look. Sharif held his father's hand. "Rest, papa. Captain Khattab and I will find the children. I promise. Before dark, I will bring them back home." He checked his watch. Almost eleven. He had about five hours to make good on his promise - find his children and get them back alive.

When they arrived at Khattab's police headquarters, Khattab updated Sharif and Eliza on his team's latest findings. "We know the kidnappers planned on grabbing the kids, and flying them out. Things went south when their jet had to go through an extensive inspection. We've checked your parents' home. Nothing. My staff are working on the ID we have at the airport customs with Samarra's intel records. That'll take time. Media have broadcast the kidnapping. Warned people to be on the lookout for your kids. How much time do you think we have before these assholes get desperate?"

Sharif did his hat flip. "We'll have to assume they have unlimited resources. They might bribe border guards. Worst case scenario, if they feel trapped, they'll kill my kids and dump them to save their own hides. Any idea where they could be hiding?"

"Dozens of places. Rural most likely. Lots of greenhouses and farms abandoned this time of year. Harvest season is over so the farmers work in Rumi during the winter."

"What about GPS? Can you track my son's cellphone?"

"Nothing so far. His phone has probably been destroyed."

"I'd be surprised if they'd find my son's. He's got ways of hiding his stuff. I found his cellphone in his shoe once." He thought for a moment. He knew someone else who was skilled at clandestine maneuvers. "Khattab, there's someone who might be of use to us.

I'm working with a CIA agent on a case in Samarra. Agent Hutchinson. Any objections?"

"I'm not opposed to any help. We've got to get your children found quickly. The longer the delay, the less likely they'll be found alive."

Sharif gritted his teeth. He was painfully aware of the risk to his family. Hearing it from a police officer stung deeper. As he dialed Frank's number on his CIA cellphone, and considering it would be evening in Frank's world, he hoped for an immediate response. There was none. He left a message. "I'll try again later."

Eliza approached the men. "Do you have something that belongs to the children? I'd like to see if I can connect with them. Get a sense of where they're at."

Sharif rolled his eyes. "That's a waste of time, MacKay."

"At this point, I'll try anything." Khattab handed a blue coat to Eliza. "Mustafa left this in Dr. Sharif's car."

She placed it close to her face, inhaled the remains of Mustafa's scent, and closed her eyes. She stood still for several beats of her heart, eyes staring blankly into space. For some time, Sharif couldn't detect signs of her breathing. She appeared momentarily suspended from the space beside him.

Finally, she folded the coat neatly. "Mustafa is fine. He's seems only annoyed, like something he treasures was taken away. I sense he's beside his sister. She's frightened and whimpers."

Sharif looked at the captain and shrugged. He appeared embarrassed with Eliza's proclamation. "Nonsense. Another woman's delusions …."

"At this point, Sharif, I'm willing to stretch my beliefs. Miss MacKay, are there any other clues?"

Eliza hesitated. Again she appeared to drift mentally to an altered state. "They're cold. Not moving, as if they're trapped or afraid to move." She shivered and paused. "The children – it feels like they're being bounced around, like in a vehicle travelling over a rough road. Can't tell where."

"I'm sorry, Khattab. This is a waste of your time."

"I'll keep it in my back pocket, captain. Let's take a look at our terrain map." Khattab traced the path of the roads leading out of Rumi. "Let's see. Rough roads," he muttered, and pointed to his map. "Here," he said, stabbing the map, "the mountain road to the pass gets pretty rough going through the higher elevations."

Eliza looked over the shoulder of the men. "Maybe. It felt more like a level road, maybe even just a trail."

Sharif sighed. He turned to Eliza and pasted a smile on his face. "See that comfortable chair over there?" He pointed to a grey plastic chair in the hallway. "Wait there until I call you." He leaned forward into her space, daring her to confront him.

Eliza shifted her nose higher and headed to the chair. "I'm almost never wrong."

Khattab followed her for a few steps. "You do this for a living? Take money?"

"I sometimes do this for people, and I never take money."

"You're accurate?"

Eliza looked slightly embarrassed. "I do this when I have a difficult medical case. No one is aware that I'm probing psychically into the person's body. But those situations are different from lost dogs."

"Lost dogs?" asked both Sharif and Khattab.

"Uh huh. Challenging when the animal is being pursued. I don't get a clear impression of their location."

Khattab motioned for Eliza to return to the map. "If you look at the map, is it possible you'll get, I don't know, some vibe that says where we should start looking?"

Eliza glanced at Sharif. The tightness of his lips and shoulders clearly indicated his patience hung by a thin thread. "Captain," she said, "at least let me try to narrow down the search area. Better than just blasting down every road."

He roughly waved her forward. "Just hurry."

She gazed at the four by six foot topographical map. Major roads radiated like a spider's web from the core of Rumi to the rural zones. They all ended abruptly at the base of the mountains and lakes, except for two – one leading to the pass, and another that traversed the valley's length of about three hundred and fifty miles.

"I'm drawn to this area, captain." She pointed to a twisting road that followed the base of the mountains to the east. "And, out here." Eliza's hand hovered over an area far from Rumi.

Sharif frowned. "There's no road out there. And it's at least two hundred miles outside the city limits. Miles off the grid."

Captain Khattab gently placed his hands on Eliza's shoulders. "Excuse me, miss. I need to look closer."

Eliza stepped aside and turned to Sharif. "We'll find them, captain. They are not harmed."

Sharif's patience fell. "Not harmed?" he shouted. "My kids have been forcefully taken from their home and terrorized. They're probably physically traumatized and …."

"Try to stay calm, Hashim," coached Khattab. "The location Miss MacKay has pointed out is interesting." When Khattab ran his index finger from the first location along the road into Rumi, it passed in front of the Rumi airport. He again stabbed the map with his finger. "You see this location? It's about twenty miles from town. There are some old shacks out there. Abandoned a few years ago."

He moved his focus to the second location. "And this location," he struck the map with his fist, "is out in the middle of nowhere, and no way to get there. There is an old road that becomes a trail, just like she described, though I don't know why anyone would head out there. No place to hide."

Sharif appeared puzzled. He frowned and splayed his arms wide. "So we're going to run out there in the hopes that -."

"I don't run anymore, Sharif. Too old."

Khattab called out to his sergeant. "Get the beast fired up. Notify Alpha team. Meet in my boardroom in fifteen minutes."

Sharif and Eliza watched as a flurry of activity surrounded them. In the boardroom, they listened to Khattab's detailed report delivered concisely and calmly. Collectively, a team of six men developed several contingency plans.

The strategy took Sharif by surprise. He'd never employed collaboration. By fear or out of respect, his men followed. After five years, they knew him well enough to anticipate his next move, his methods. It worked well enough. But here, he saw each man contribute, build a strategy and consensus. Within ten minutes, they had fire in their bellies, ready to charge into the task as one fierce unit.

As Alpha team trotted out, Sharif heard a continuous, deep growl. The building shivered. When he heard the whine, he recognized the earmark of a chopper. But this sounded like no chopper he'd heard before.

Khattab beamed with pride. "Ah, love that sound. That's the EC225 super high capacity SAR chopper. Integrated sensors, inertia reference system, FLIR and radar systems for all-weather capability – the works. Less than one meter hover accuracy, fully automatic changeover to hover and automatic fly-away. We have room for six and up to three stretchers, and a range of 1,100 km, endurance of five and a half hours."

Khattab poked his thumb up. "All muscle. She's used mostly for rescuing idiots off the mountains. I assume both of you are coming along."

Sharif frowned at Eliza. "I suppose, if I told you to stay here, I'd be wasting my breath."

"Don't even think it, captain." She picked up her backpack. "Your children may need medical care. And -."

"Fine," he said, with a hint of relief in his voice. Sharif and Eliza each put on a helmet and flak jacket. He readied his weapons and ammunition. "We're set."

Khattab notified the airport tower of their imminent search and rescue operation. He nodded at Sharif and Eliza. "Let's go."

Khattab, two officers, Eliza and Sharif sprinted to the back of the station and out the exit door. In the middle of a large asphalt pad a fire engine-red-and-gold helicopter sat like a cat ready to pounce. The ground trembled as the engines warmed up. The blades sliced through the sunlit sky, catching the light from the chopper's blue and red beacons.

Grit stung their faces and wind whipped their hair. Khattab shouted into Eliza's ear, "Have you been on a chopper before?"

She nodded. "Lots. I do medivacs."

They scrambled aboard and buckled up. Eliza held her backpack on her knees as Khattab handed headsets to her and Sharif as the chopper rose high above Rumi.

"We'll head out to the mountain road first. If no one is there, we'll continue on north to the trail."

"How long to the dead end road?" asked Sharif.

"This isn't a speed bird, Captain. Built for power climbs and tough rescues. But we'll be there in thirty-five minutes, give or take, well ahead of the ground response team. Then to the remote site."

Sharif leaned against the side window, scanning the ground below. As they headed out of the city, the squawk of the chopper's two-way radio confirmed the response crews were well on their way. The airport tower acknowledged them and advised that no other aircraft was in the vicinity. The sky was theirs alone.

Half an hour later, Khattab spotted abandoned property and instructed the pilot to circle the area, getting lower to the ground with each pass over the battered buildings. "Put her down and leave when we get out," he instructed his pilot. "No one seems to be around but we better be ready for a fight." He looked at Eliza. "You stay here with the pilot."

Sharif grimaced. "Good luck, Khattab. She's not good at following orders."

Eliza glared at him, then turned back to Khattab. "Call if anyone needs medical attention."

"It's a deal." The chopper landed several yards away from the buildings, the four men jumped out, and lifted off.

Sharif listened. Other than Rescue One's faraway drone, and the hush of long grasses swaying in the breeze, silence dominated the expanse among the ramshackle wood shacks. Deserted years ago, the buildings proclaimed their sullen mood. The men closed in on a building that could have been a storage shed. A battered wood door hung partly open. Two windows conveyed a vacant stare.

The men dashed to the ground, expecting to receive gunfire. Khattab hollered, "Rumi Police. Surrender your weapons and come out."

No sound, nothing. The breeze nudged the open door a few inches further. "Rumi police. Surrender your weapons and come out now." His voice roared into the gloom.

Sharif gripped his assault rifle, ready to cut down anyone firing a weapon. Finally, Khattab gave the signal to enter the building. His officer led the assault, first by tossing in a dark object to draw fire from the hidden enemy. They heard the object tumble across the floor. The sound echoed throughout an empty-sounding space.

Hashim's pulse raced. His adrenalin reached a fever pitch, coating his skin with sweat. He shouted, "Mustafa, Farah, can you hear me?"

Silence.

The officer switched on his bright flashlight and charged through the door with his handgun ready to fire. Khattab and Sharif, hunched low, followed in rapid succession. Their footsteps pounded across the wood floor. The building shuddered. The officer's light danced about the walls. The dust on the wooden floor hadn't been disturbed for years.

The police officers proceeded to the next building. Again Khattab shouted a warning: "Rumi police. Drop your weapons and come out." Again his demands were met with silence. The officer struck the door with his boot. It caved in. He shone his light into the room. "Look, captain. Footsteps." They followed the trail cautiously to a kitchen and two more empty rooms.

"Just as I thought," growled Sharif. "This was a fool's errand. No one is here."

Khattab's radio alerted him. "Go ahead."

"Khattab, go to secure channel."

"That's the pilot. Trouble." Khattab switched a dial on his two-way radio. "Khattab here."

"Sir, the airport has reported another aircraft appearing on his radar. Still a long way off. Maybe from Samarra. Heading toward the second coordinates. They're not responding to the air traffic controller's call."

"We better move out right away. Pick us up near the buildings."

In five minutes, the beast was heading for the second location.

The pilot updated the men on the arrival of another aircraft. "Airport says it must be a chopper. Too slow for a fixed wing. The pilot is still not responding to the controller's calls."

"What is the aircraft's latest heading?"

The pilot frowned. "A bit erratic, like the pilot doesn't have a specific destination. Or could be a student. Common to have student pilots practice flying over here."

"If Miss MacKay was right, we should spot a vehicle moving fast." Khattab turned to Sharif. "I think you owe the lady an apology."

He frowned and glanced at her. She smiled sweetly back.

A thermos of coffee was passed around to the men and Eliza. The officers continued to discuss tactics until they were within twenty minutes of the coordinates. Everyone knew his job. In another minute the pilot exclaimed, "Dead ahead, Khattab."

The pilot pointed toward his left. "Look. Sedan. Really moving."

The airport controller called. "Sir, that chopper is heading in your area, flying low, about sixty miles directly north of your location."

"Ten-four. Keep us updated." The men readied their assault rifles and packed extra ammo. Khattab focused on the car. "Okay, let's see if they're friendly. Fly down to the driver's side but maintain a hundred yards' distance. If you hear me say 'Gun' get up and out of range."

The pilot zeroed in on the driver's side and flew alongside. He slowed down to maintain speed with the racing car. The vehicle bounced and swerved with every rut and hole.

A hand gun appeared through the rear side window.

"Gun!" Khattab hollered. As the pilot turned on Rescue One's climbing power, Khattab called his response team. "Alpha team. We're under fire." He repeated the message.

"We've got your coordinates from the tower. ETA forty-five minutes."

"Okay, about a mile ahead, we'll try to make the driver veer off up there. Just up on the top of that hill," Khattab pointed towards a rise in the landscape. "He might get stuck in loose ground or a hole. First, look for the kids. If we don't see them, they're in the trunk. Second, Sharif, you and I are going take out the wheels. Third, once we're hovering a foot off the ground, we'll jump out. Fourth," he said, giving one of his two officers a nudge, "you two take out the driver and front passenger. Sharif and I will go after the rear passengers." He grasped his pilot's shoulder, "Once we're out, keep Rescue One out of range. If necessary, disappear until backup arrives." Khattab and Sharif opened their side doors and shouldered their rifles. Sharif glanced at Eliza. "You stay put," he shouted.

She gave him a 'thumbs up' salute.

It took ten seconds for the chopper to descend to near the ground and face the approaching car. The pilot hovered there for a second, then charged ahead. The driver attempted to challenge the chopper. At the last second, the sight of the blades whipping close to the ground discouraged further heroism.

The driver swerved off the road into the loose ground. The car's front left tire shredded as bullets pummeled the wheel. The wheels spun and kicked up rock and grit. The vehicle kicked sideways, almost trapped in the loose soil.

Two passengers fired at Rescue One while the driver struggled to get his car back onto the road. The pilot anticipated their attack, lifted up, and swung toward the rear of the car. Bullets struck the skids and Rescue One's frame. Sparks flew as the four men jumped out of the chopper. Rescue One growled and climbed high.

Sharif and Khattab's officer ran to the driver's side of the car. The officer fired his weapon toward the driver, now hunkered down but twisting at the wheel. The car shifted sideways. Sharif scrambled to avoid being trapped under the tires.

He ducked low and glanced through the rear side window for signs of his children. Not there. A rear gunman fired his weapon toward Sharif. He fired back, taking aim at the rear passenger's head. His MP5 bucked and kicked hard. The passenger fell lifeless down behind the front seats.

He heard Khattab's gun in an exchange of gunfire with the other rear passenger. Sharif jumped onto the trunk and dashed up onto the roof just as the rear window shattered. Bullets licked at his pant legs, tearing the material and biting into his shin. His adrenalin surged, masking pain, silencing his fear. He hollered, "Mustafa, Farah!"

From the corner of his eye Sharif saw Khattab's officer fall. Sharif fired rapid shots toward the driver. Frustrated in not getting a clear shot at the man, he jumped down.

Khattab continued firing at the passenger until a spray of blood gushed from the passenger side windows. The car continued to swerve and buck as the driver attempted to get back onto the hard packed trail. Finally Khattab's officer got close enough to aim at the driver. He pulled the trigger, once, then again. The car stopped suddenly. The driver flung his door open and stumbled out. Wounded, he struggled to stand, his hands up in surrender.

Sharif kept the driver in his sights. Khattab nodded to Sharif and noted the blood on his lower leg. "You okay?"

"Just a scratch." The driver's hands had shifted. "Twitch, and I'll kill you. Where are my children?"

The driver shrugged. Sharif fired his gun at the driver's feet. He flinched and stepped back.

Again Sharif called for his children. "Mustafa. Farah."

A muffled sound came from the car's trunk. It momentarily distracted Sharif. The driver took the moment to pull a knife from its sheath tucked between his shoulder blades.

Sharif sensed the movement. "Bastard." Sharif fired. The bullet struck the driver in the split-second before he released the knife, and his aim went awry. The blade merely nicked Sharif's ear. The driver collapsed to his knees, then fell back, lifeless.

"Quick," Sharif ordered. "Get the keys. My kids are in the trunk." Blood trickled down his neck and beneath his shirt collar.

Khattab grabbed the keys from the ignition and used the remote button to unlock the trunk. Up popped Sharif's son and daughter. "Papa, papa. Oh, papa," they cried.

Sharif pulled them out as if they were merely small bags of groceries. He wrapped his arms around them, then quickly ran his hands over their bodies. "Are you okay? Are you hurt?"

"Khattab," called the officer, "Rescue One has the other chopper on visual. About two miles."

"Ten-four. How is your partner?"

"He's got a couple hits in his leg. Can't walk."

"Let's get out of here, fast. Rescue One is landing over there," he said, pointing toward the west. Khattab and the officer lifted the injured man and dragged him to the chopper. Sharif carried his children in a frantic dash toward the landing site.

Sharif heard the sound high in the sky. "There," he said, pointing to a dot in the distant sky.

Khattab swore. "Shit, hurry."

Rescue One swooped down and hovered just a dozen yards from the runners. They scrambled into the chopper. The children clung to their father as the bird climbed fast and high. The body of the chopper vibrated as it used its full power.

Sharif secured his children into seats in the rear section while Eliza tended to the injured officer. "Stay here with Miss MacKay," he shouted to them, wrapping blankets around both children. "We're going to be fine. Understand?"

They nodded, tears running down their cheeks. Mustafa brought his mouth close to his father's ear. "They took my cellphone, papa."

Sharif caressed his son's head. "We'll get another. You okay, Farah?"

Farah nodded, chin quivering, fighting to be brave. He kissed her small hands. "I'm so proud of both of you. You must stay here with this lady."

Sharif jumped back to his seat and got his gun ready. He put on his radio headset. "Khattab, what is the plan?"

"That's mostly up to our pilot. Their chopper has lots of fire power. We've got to stay out of their line of fire. I've never had to bring down a chopper before, but our pilot has military experience."

The pilot joined the conversation. "I've got to stay above that chopper. If he raises his nose to fire at us, he'll lose speed and fall back. We don't have a chance to outrun him. Guts and muscle power is all I've got." They got a closer look at the chopper as it approached. "Hang on."

Khattab hung on to a hand-hold as Rescue One climbed higher. "Take it easy. They're not going to destroy us," he hollered to the pilot via his headset. "I'm certain they want to take the kids and won't chance on doing anything that will kill them."

The pilot shook his head. "They may be willing to risk killing the kids. Maybe they know Captain Sharif is on board and want him dead more than getting his kids." The pilot resumed his maneuvers to avoid being in range of the chopper. "Look out. Here he comes. I'm going to get on top of him."

Sharif looked startled. "You're going to do what?"

Suddenly Rescue One swung up and around, almost laying on its side, as the pilot maneuvered to be behind, then above, the other chopper. Sharif heard his children scream. He looked back. "Hang on tight."

The attack chopper quickly responded to Rescue One's challenge and dipped down, picking up speed. The chopper then raced ahead of Rescue One and climbed. In seconds it flew ahead and swung around. Flashes of light sprang from the attack chopper's nose.

Rescue One dove as bullets struck its body. A few penetrated the body but failed to cause injury to anyone or to damage the chopper's vital systems. Sharif lost his headset as he dashed toward his children. He lost his balance, but as he tumbled, he shouted, "Eliza, get down, now!" Once he found something solid to hang on to, he placed his body around his children like a shield. "Stay down, stay down!" he hollered in their ears.

Sweat glistened on the pilot's forehead. "I'm going to play the lame duck." He adjusted controls. Instantly Rescue One fell. It rocked and whirled in a circle. "Get ready for attack!" he roared, his face contorted with alarm. "Here they come."

Sharif hung on as Rescue One plummeted toward the ground. He hadn't heard the pilot's scheme and believed their chopper had been fatally disabled. The rotors still whirled but the engines had lost their growl. He gasped in horror with the feeling of a freefall out of the sky. The side window revealed the ground rising up faster and faster with each second. The cry of the wind whipping by the door frame made him shudder. He inhaled deeply several times and braced for a painful impact. *My children, oh my God, my children will die.* His mind became dizzy with erratic thoughts.

"Papa, papa," cried Farah.

The fall felt like an endless descent into death's embrace. Sharif hung on, his body a barrier between his children and the imminent deadly impact.

The attack chopper pursued Rescue One as it fell. Its guns, constantly aimed at Rescue One, remained silent. Nearer the ground, the attack chopper flew on ahead. Once Rescue One was out of visual range, its pilot revved the engines back to full power. Fifty feet from the ground, the rotors caught the wind to break the fall. As he brought Rescue One's tail up, the skids kissed the grasses of the field.

Eliza put her arms around the children and held them snug against her chest. "They'll be okay, Sharif. Go."

Sharif exhaled through pursed lips. His muscles twitched with fatigue. "Stay right there," he hollered to his children, as he returned to his seat.

Rescue One's pilot swung the bird up hard but just enough to sneak up behind the attack chopper, now only thirty feet from the ground. Its pilot appeared to have intentions of landing.

Rescue One's pilot positioned his chopper to ride just yards above the attack chopper, and slightly ahead with a nose-down angle. For a moment the two choppers flew forward in tandem. The attack chopper didn't dare move ahead of Rescue One. The wash from Rescue One's blades could cause the attack helicopter to be pushed to the ground. The attack chopper was too close to the ground to lift its nose to fire. And, it was at risk of falling due to formation of a vortex ring.

Any move the attack helicopter made, Rescue One hovered directly above. The pilot motioned to Khattab. "See if your guns can do some damage."

Sharif and Khattab slid their doors back and shot at the chopper below. The wind tore Sharif's headset off. His short hair felt like it was being pulled by its roots. Wind burned his face. He was shaken by the deafening growl and whine, the fumes of gas and oil, and the sight of the ground speeding by directly below his feet.

Most of their bullets were thwarted by the rotor's rapid rotation. Sharif's MP5's throaty bark continued until finally oil spewed from the attack chopper. The attack chopper hit the ground hard, shearing off the rotor blades. They hurtled hundreds of feet before being embedded into the ground.

The men reloaded their weapons. Khattab motioned for Sharif and the officer to jump off as soon as Rescue One landed. In seconds, all three rushed toward the downed attack chopper. Rescue One leaped out of gunfire range.

The chopper, still in its death throes, refused to surrender – rear rotor still turning, whine and groan from the main rotor's engine. The body continued to convulse and growl as savagely as a wounded wild animal.

By the time Khattab and his men arrived within fifty feet of the chopper, five men had tumbled out. Bloody and bruised, they ran and stumbled. Inside the cockpit, the pilot appeared either too dazed to move, or was dead.

"Rumi police. Surrender or I shoot to kill!" hollered Khattab.

The men, dressed in only casual clothes, fired at Khattab. Their aim suffered from their disorientation. Sharif and Khattab returned fire. The killers dashed for cover.

Sharif held his fire. Khattab hollered again, "Surrender your weapons now. Surrender!"

They fired back with vengeance. Their aim had improved.

Khattab's body twisted and tumbled. He lay motionless. The officer beside him went down, wounded. Sharif retaliated. His gun sprayed bullets in a wide range. In seconds, three gunmen lay dead; two others dove back behind their chopper for cover.

Sharif looked back to Khattab and hollered, "Khattab, answer me. Khattab."

Khattab rolled over, gasping for air. He gave Sharif a nod. "Wind knocked out of me. That's all, mostly." He got up slowly, watching for the killer's movements. "Let's finish this," he snarled.

271

They headed for the attack chopper. Sharif had lost sight of the men who hid behind the chopper. Upon hearing a high-pitched whistle and a snap, he stopped and crouched down. His gut roared a warning. A small fire licked its way up and around the belly of the chopper.

"Run. It's gonna blow!" hollered Sharif.

Sharif and Khattab ran, grabbed the wounded officer and dragged him until they were thrown down by the force of the blast. The two gunmen behind the chopper had no chance to get far enough away. In the next second another explosion hurtled more shards of fiery shrapnel. The chopper's frame became a molten mass of steel and glass.

Khattab counted six dead men from the chopper, three from the car. His officer had several hits to his flak jacket and a wound to his thigh. Semi-conscious from blood loss, he moaned with pain. Khattab radioed his response team. "Two officers down. Flying back to Rumi hospital. Take control of the scene and report your findings. Over."

"ETA six, seven minutes, sir. We saw a fireball. Glad to hear from you. Did you find the children?"

"Affirmative. Alive and shaken, but no harm. Sorry you missed the action. Process both scenes. Make sure all nine bodies are properly packaged and delivered to the morgue. Khattab out."

Sharif comforted his children, Eliza cared for the officers in Rescue One as they flew back to Rumi. The chopper landed at the hospital's helipad where emergency medical teams waited. Once the wounded officers were off-loaded, Khattab instructed Sharif to return to the police station once the doctors had checked his wounds, and to bring his father.

Sharif had a chokehold on his children's hands as he and Eliza walked to his father's bed in the emergency department. The patriarch was dressed and talking with other patients - his head bandage askew.

Sharif marveled at his father's stature. In spite of his eighty years of toil and his two strokes, he remained unbroken. His close-cropped dark brown hair and short beard should have been grey long ago. The skin of his face and hands were leathery from tending to his orchard. He wore a brown jacket that swallowed his thin shoulders. His cotton off-white shirt and faded black pants bore rips and blood stains, evidence of his struggle with the kidnappers.

Relief washed over Sharif the instant he saw his father's broad smile. His mother, weeping with joy, reached for her grandchildren.

"Mama, papa," he said, extending his arm toward Eliza, "this is Miss Eliza MacKay. She's a paramedic from Canada." He wasn't ready to admit that without her, they may have never found his children. "She kept two wounded Rumi police officers alive during this rescue."

The elderly couple took a moment away from their grandchildren to nod and smile.

Eliza produced a gracious smile. "I'm so pleased to meet Captain Sharif's family." She stepped forward. "I'll ask a doctor to check your wounds, captain."

Sharif hadn't noticed the condition of his clothes – or his body. Overwhelmed with relief, only now did he realize his lower leg burned as the uniform material pulled on the blood caked over his wounds. He smoothed his hair back and felt the sting of a gash in his ear. Now that his adrenalin had faded, his muscles threatened defeat.

"Yes, son. Let's get you registered." Sharif submitted to his father's assistance but turned to face Eliza. "After I'm done in emergency, Papa and I need to meet with Khattab at his station. Please take mama and my kids to the cafeteria, Eliza. Wait for me there."

Sharif spoke in a hushed voice to his father. "There are things you need to know, papa."

"I don't understand, Hashim. You, me, the children. Why has our family become a target?"

Sharif whispered his response, revealing the highlights of the massacre, the cover-up, the truth about Eliza, and the mayor's threat.

"It's been almost two months since the massacre. I promised Aamir to protect the cover-up." He squeezed his father's arm. "But there's someone who wants us eliminated."

The elder's eyes conveyed his shock. His father straightened his back. "Wounds, first. Khattab, second. Then we take care of your business." As he rose to greet a nurse, a tray of food appeared beside him.

"I figured you two might be hungry." Eliza smiled at the two men. "Dr. Sharif, I assume you like your coffee like your son, just black. But there's cream and sugar, just in case. Sandwiches look pretty fresh and the muffins are yummy." She handed the tray to Sharif. "Everyone else is hungry, too, so I'd better get back to them. Later." She gave Sharif a brief smile and then hurried out of the examining room.

Dr. Sharif raised an eyebrow. "Just how well does Miss MacKay know your preferences?"

Even though practiced in keeping his emotions in check, and concealing his thoughts, Hashim Sharif feared his father could read his mind. He pictured the sister who raised him, thirty years older than him and now morbidly obese. "Like a sister, papa. That's all. We'll eat this while the doctor is fixing my cuts."

When Sharif and his father arrived at the Rumi police station, Khattab led them to the evidence collection room. Two officers were cataloguing documents and photos.

"Fingerprints, ID from the vehicle and chopper, and cellphone records haven't given us any leads, so far. I'm hoping the two of you can be more forthcoming than all this," Khattab said. "It's going to take days, maybe weeks, to find what's real and what's fake." Khattab headed down a hallway. "Come. There's something interesting for you to see."

He led them to his office and shut his door. On his desk lay a leather briefcase. "This briefcase was in the car's trunk where your kids were put." Khattab opened it and swiveled it toward Sharif.

Sharif stepped forward. Immediately he spotted the black booklets. "Passports?"

F. Stone

"Fake, but first class job. As you can see, we've already dusted for fingerprints. Take a look." Khattab picked up the four passports. He opened each one, quickly flashing the photos of Sharif's parents and children. "Dr. Sharif, they were also going to abduct you and your wife. I think they decided to leave without you since they'd have a hard time explaining your wounds at security check points." Khattab frowned as he looked over the old man's bruises. "I guess they were figuring you had no courage. Do you have any idea why you were attacked?"

"No. I have no enemies."

Sharif barely heard his father's response. He felt momentarily stunned. He swallowed and looked back at Khattab. "They were going to take my kids out of RIPT? I thought the mayor might just -."

"Sharif, this," Khattab said, waving the passports, "and the executive jet, and the attack chopper are way beyond Mayor Aamir's doing. He hasn't got that much clout or money."

"There's another possibility." Sharif told Khattab about the hitman. "My undercover officers heard the hitman mention that GIC needed proof I was dead. The CIA and I believe he's connected to the organization that planned the massacre."

"GIC? Frankly I don't see them involved with something so minor as a police captain and his family." Khattab rubbed his face, and groaned. "Sharif, the bits you know about the massacre could cause trouble for RIPT, but not GIC. Why do you think GIC is behind the kidnapping attempt?"

"The only connection is that Mayor Aamir was involved in the contract, and he's been threatening me to keep my mouth shut about the massacre. Said I'd lose my family." Sharif clenched his fists. "Damn!" he shouted. "My family. They're alone in the hospital cafeteria."

Khattab stormed out of his office and called someone. "Get two officers over to the hospital cafeteria. Don't make a scene but bring Sharif's family here. And get someone over to the airport. Find Buzz and ask him if he can fly the jet out of RIPT." He returned to his office, his face on fire with adrenalin. "Sharif, I'm going to turn

275

these passports over to you. You and your family are getting out of RIPT tonight, by midnight. I'll have police protection documents written up and approved. I need a destination."

Khattab slowed down but the stern expression on his face made it very clear there was no room for discussion. "Sharif, you and your family are a target. Rumi is a small city. I need you and your family out of Rumi. If GIC is behind the attack, they'll come back harder and with more fire power. We don't have the kind of resources to fight them."

Sharif gripped the passports. Never before had he surrendered his ethics. "Understood."

"Cop to cop, brother to brother. As of right now, these documents have gone missing." Khattab hitched his shoulders and splayed his hands wide. "It happens,"

An officer stepped in and told Khattab that Buzz had agreed to fly the jet.

"So, where are you taking your family?"

"Not me. I can't leave. There's a CIA agent who has got a satellite on my ass. He believes I'm part of the cover-up. If I try to run, I wouldn't last a day. Besides, I feel responsible for the death of the Americans. I need to get evidence on who hired the killers."

Sharif stood up and slapped his hat onto his head. "I need to go home and get my parents' medication, a change of clothes."

"Dr. Sharif, get me a list of what they absolutely need. Captain, you'll need transportation back to Samarra. Once your family is gone, my pilot will fly you and MacKay back in Buzz's plane."

"Fine. Papa and I need to talk about where they can hide."

"Good. And be quick. I'll need a couple of hours to make arrangements at the destination airport and with the local police. Your family will be under police protection for a couple of days. Most I can afford on short notice. Oh, one more thing. We found your son's cellphone on one of the deceased in the sedan." He tossed it to Sharif. "That should make the boy happy." Khattab extended his right hand." It is we who show the effort. It is Allah who grants the success."

Ω

Waiting in the cafeteria, Eliza hoped Mrs. Sharif might give her the benefit of the doubt. Her police uniform, soiled with blood and dirt, didn't impress the lady at all. Attempts at conversation were met with polite indifference and attention to the children.

She cleaned up in the bathroom the best she could using wet paper towels. By now, her backpack was a mess. Sterile bandaging packages and medication was mixed in with clothes and toiletries. She reorganized everything and found her deodorant, toothbrush and toothpaste. The comb had vanished, perhaps having fallen out inside the chopper while tending to her patients. Freshened and ready to give Mrs. Sharif another try, she tucked her hair under the cap and returned to the table.

The children had shed their trauma as quickly as if it was a cold, wet blanket.

"It's okay, Miss Eliza," came the tender voice of Farah. "You look scared. Here's my teddy bear. He always makes me feel better."

Eliza knelt down and tentatively reached for the much loved teddy bear. It had seen better days. Its worn, brown fabric had been repaired and patched, eyes replaced with two pretty blue buttons, and one arm dangled like it had suffered too many tug-of-wars.

Farah proudly handed the bear to Eliza. "His name is Peekaboo." The child giggled. "Silly, isn't it?"

"Wow. Oh, he is lovely, Farah." Eliza squeezed the bear for a moment. "You are right. I think Peekaboo is magical. I feel better already. Thank you, Farah." She handed Peekaboo back to Farah. "Can I give you a hug?"

"Sure, if you want."

Eliza wrapped her arms around the child's shoulders. Light-headed, she pushed back memories. Most fell back into her vault. All except one. The last time she hugged Noah, four endless years ago,

277

she felt the same cherished heart flutter within the child's chest. Before she uttered her son's name, the grandmother tugged on Farah's hand and pulled her away.

Chapter 32

Eliza breathed a sigh of relief when she arrived at Rumi's police station. Mrs. Sharif proved to be quick and agile as she herded her grandchildren into the staff lounge. Sharif and his father cheered at the arrival of Mustafa and Farah. Sharif swept his son up onto his lap while Farah was scooped up by her grandfather. The happy reunion made her want to join in. She watched Sharif stroke his son's head and hold him close to his chest. The boy wrapped his arms around his father's neck and whimpered. Sharif patted his son's back but focused on a discussion with his father.

Sharif's mother served coffee and juice to her family. They sat in a closed circle around a table while Eliza stood on the periphery. A pang of longing swept through her chest.

"I have some money, Papa. That is, Miss MacKay and I have an account that -."

"You and this woman have a joint account?" The elder's eyes narrowed.

"Just business, papa." Sharif nodded to Eliza. "You agree? We give papa money to travel and live on for a while?"

She moved closer to the table. "Yes, definitely, whatever they need." She noted the grim expression on Dr. Sharif's face. *Perhaps it's just his pride that's been bruised.* "I owe you my life, captain. There's something else you might consider." Eliza dug into her backpack and pulled out a key. "A few months ago I discovered my husband had a house in Dubai. It's been vacant for four years. I was going to sell it once my work here was finished. The house is a thirty-six hundred square foot bungalow. Plenty big enough for all of you. What do you think?"

"It belonged to your husband?" asked Sharif.

"Yes, apparently William bought it a year before his death." She crossed her arms, hands fisted. "He used it to entertain his harem."

Sharif frowned. "Harem?"

"Yes. William was a gifted surgeon, a brilliant scientist. Lousy husband and father." Her voice trailed off to little more than a whisper.

Sharif's father stood up and gruffly motioned for his son to follow.

Alarmed by the men's surly demeanor, Eliza moved to the room's doorway. Their voices carried from the exit door

"What exactly is your relationship with this woman?" growled Dr. Sharif.

"Papa, are you accusing me of having a sinful relationship? You know me better than that. And, she has been very respectful of my authority and my faith."

"She is pretty, my son. Pretty woman not of our faith have different morals. They prey upon lonely men. You cannot be blamed for, ah, such things. Yes, she is a widow and orphan. The Koran is very clear on taking care of them. But she is not destitute."

"Why are you afraid of her, papa?"

"Hashim, she will corrupt you. You must get rid of her. Promise me, Hashim. Promise you will get rid of her."

Eliza's knees threatened collapse. Her mind froze, fixed on the raspy voice of Sharif's father. And the following silence.

Time for the sunset prayer, Maghrib, was announced by the melodic sound of the muezzin's call. After ablutions, the family headed to the station's public park across the street. Eliza remained in the station's parking lot. The Sharif family had made it crystal clear. Her presence irritated them, and they wanted Hashim to terminate their alliance.

She understood and harbored no malice toward the family for their unkindness. They were vulnerable to an unknown enemy. It was natural to close ranks and be suspicious. Watching Sharif as he guided his children to the park, she smiled at seeing his softer side. His cop personae surrendered to reveal a patient and gentle man. More than ever, she wanted to remain with this complicated man. Now, she knew that was impossible.

Being with Sharif's family and fearing for their safety awakened her wretched past. Haunting memories, stored pain edged forward. She felt the weight of sadness threatening the walls she had built.

What did he tell me? 'Some parts of your mind remember. Those parts want you to put those memories to rest. But you have to make peace with them first.'

He's right. Until I face those ugly parts of me, I'm more like an automaton than flesh and blood.

Ω

Sharif's thoughts spun out of control. *How can I do this? What can I tell her? Should I say anything? Perhaps - .*

"Silence, son. You're thinking so loud it hurts my ears. Quiet your mind. Enter the sacred space with peace in your heart."

As the people moved forward, he stood, grounded to the pathway's entrance, wondering why Eliza had not arrived. She enjoyed the hypnotic sound of the prayers, or so she had said.

Someone nudged him to move aside. Ahead, his father waited for him, his wise and kind eyes watching Sharif. He motioned for Sharif to stand beside him. Sharif's feet felt heavy. For a moment it struck him that he did not belong there. *Not worthy. My inappropriate thoughts, holding a near naked woman.*

Two things gave Hashim Sharif the courage to protect the citizen, to do things most people dare not think about - his love for

281

his family and for Islam. Both seemed to be at odds with what he valued, opposed to what he thought was right. A headache crept up the back of his neck and settled across his forehead.

The warmth of someone's hand enveloped his. It startled Sharif. He saw his father begin to wrap his arms around his shoulders, embrace him to his chest. His senses became acute - the roughness of his father's beard, the smell of soap from his hands, the warmth of his arms, the beat of his heart. The words his father whispered shook him.

"Let it go, my son. Let it go."

His father released him. Lovingly, he cradled his son's face in his hands. "Come. We'll let go of today's violence together." The strength of his father's hand lifted him. Together the two men prayed, then sat in silence until the small gathering departed.

Dr. Sharif turned to his son and again held his hand. "When you were very young, our house was full of noise. Your sisters were much older and louder than you. You were the one in the corner quietly studying your lessons. When I look back I can see how you got lost in the midst of the chaos of my ambition to be an excellent doctor and owner of a fine orchard."

"I never felt lost, papa." The bitterness he'd collected for so many years dissolved.

"Don't interrupt. There was much civil unrest. For your safety we sent you to live with your oldest sister in England. Thinking she would provide a nurturing home, I passed over my responsibility to her. It was a mistake." Tears filled his eyes. "I've made too many mistakes. But today, I'm going to fix at least one." Still clinging to his son's hand, he said softly, "I love you, Hashim. It doesn't matter what you do, I will always love you." He lifted his son's hand and placed it over his heart. "There are no words, even Rumi's poetry cannot express how much I love you. You are a good man of great courage and yet not so arrogant that you do not see the sparrow fall. You reach to save its tender wings. I could not be more proud of you."

Tears began to well in Sharif's eyes. "I've been angry with you and mama. Since you sent me to England, I believed you thought of me as unworthy to live with you. All my life, I've feared rejection." Hashim Sharif rubbed the tears from his eyes. He smiled back at his father. "Now I see you were speaking the truth, that you only wanted me to be safe."

"My son, I ask you to not make the mistake I made. Your children need you," he said, poking his son's chest. "Every day they need you, their father, their papa. Come with us to Dubai. Together, we can find a place more suitable. Not a harem house, my son."

"Papa, some innocent people died in my compound. They and their families deserve justice be served. If I leave, that may never happen. Or the wrong people may suffer. I must find who sent the killers."

Dr. Sharif groaned. "That could take months. Or years."

Ω

Eliza had watched the small pious group until the prayers began. She had listened to the voices, in unison reassuring Allah their heartfelt devotion. She walked away, not aware that someone noticed she had left the group.

Spurred on by memories of her dead family, she began to run. The last of the sun's rays on her tear-filled eyes blinded her. She felt the scream before she heard it erupt from her chest. A tree in front of her burst into a wall of fire. A gust of wind pushed her down, throwing her into the inferno's path. Guilt fed the fire. Flames towered over her as she felt the regret of convincing the family to take one more trip, guilt in having survived. The heat seared into her bones.

Eliza knew she had to find the courage enter the storm. Trembling, she faced the inferno, feared the scorching pain. With each tenuous step, she gasped to discover the flames had no power over her. Then she saw them. Nathan and Noah behind the blaze. They were smiling, playfully nudging and pushing each other. As she neared, their image softened and blurred.

She heard Nathan declare, "We are fine, mom,"

"Yep, fine mom," echoed Noah with a giggle.

Nathan waved and smiled. "You're the best mom, ever."

Before they vanished, Noah spread his arms wide. "Ever."

And then, the tree reappeared before her. She glanced around, wondering if she had made a spectacle of herself. Everyone seemed to be in small groups, still absorbed in the sunset prayers or focused on a book, perhaps the Koran.

She spotted a nearby bench and sat down. For several minutes she felt disoriented and overwhelmed with a kaleidoscope of emotions. It felt like a swarm of fireflies suddenly released from a cage, aglow with bliss. Every knot that had trapped her in PTSD had given way.

She felt a twinge of fear. She was no longer Eliza, the survivor. Maybe no longer the Eliza who escaped the massacre. *Who am I?* Then aloud, she whispered, "Who am I?"

"Who do you think you are?" The voice sounded amused.

Though surprised by his presence, Eliza welcomed Sharif's company. She moved aside and patted the seat beside her, inviting him to sit with her. "Captain, you wouldn't believe what just happened." She turned to him, wondering if she should try to explain the vision. She felt calm in his gaze, his eyes perhaps seeing more of her than she knew of herself, "I feel like I just woke up from a nightmare." She shook her head as if to indicate the subject was beyond explanation. "Where's your family?"

"Back at the station. Khattab saw you head this way. You shouldn't have left without me. "Again," he smiled and nudged her shoulder with his.

"Sorry. I needed time alone. To think."

"I apologize for my family's rudeness, Eliza. I am most grateful for --" he stumbled over his thoughts, "for everything. Papa is, um, overly protective of his family." He frowned. "Always has been."

"They've just been through a terrible crisis. I understand them. But there is something I need to know."

"Uh huh." His gaze never left her face. His nod urged her to continue.

"How or when are you planning to get rid of me?" A slight tremor betrayed her.

"You were eavesdropping. Very bad, Miss MacKay." Sharif shook his finger as if to chastise her disrespect, but then couldn't restrain a chuckle. "I would have done the same thing in your shoes."

"Well?"

"At the very least, I'm going to send you back to Canada. As soon as we get back to Samarra, you are -."

"Oh, no you're not. I won't go until I know you are out of harm's way. Besides, I may need to put more money into that account. And, if I'm gone, the mayor will panic. He's crazy, insane, Hashim. We know he's connected to the massacre - damn you're not listening."

Sharif had taken out his police cellphone, hit a few buttons, and appeared to be waiting for someone to answer. He seemed oblivious to her rant, waiting for someone to answer his call.

"Omar, answer the phone." Sharif stood up and turned to Eliza. "And, yes, I'll put you on the plane myself. Handcuffed, if necessary!" Sharif lifted his hat and slapped it back down on his head, hard. "Omar, where the hell are you?" he muttered into the phone, after the voicemail message ended. "Look, if you get this message before sunrise, I need ammo for both my weapons. And a fresh uniform. I'll meet up with you at …" Sharif froze, then suddenly slapped the phone closed. "What if?" he whispered. He stared into Eliza's eyes. "What if he can't answer?" Sharif dialed a number he knew well – Omar's home phone. His grip on his phone would have strangled a cobra. "Not in service? What is going on?" he growled.

Sharif sat down and quickly dialed another number. "If they've got him, Eliza -. Damn, they'll use him to get to me."

Eliza noted Sharif's hands trembling. His voice vibrated as if his heart pounded in his throat. "Sergeant Omar Abdul-Muqtadir is no ordinary cop," she said with authority. "He might have -."

"Hello, Captain Akyol. This is Sharif." Sharif frowned as he listened. "Just listen Akyol. I need to contact Sergeant Abdul-Muqtadir. He's not answering his cellphone. And his land line is not in service. What is -" Sharif rubbed his hand on his knee, leaving sweat marks. "Ah, yes, I'm still alive but you must not mention I called you. Omar should be on duty. Where is he?"

Sharif stood and paced as he listened to Akyol. "Are you sure? Not like him to get involved with the mayor's business." More listening. "Yes, I know Khizar was killed but -." Sharif switched the phone to his other ear. "Fine. Thank you." He closed his phone and sighed. "Akyol says Omar was last seen with the mayor this morning. Akyol is going to check on Omar's home."

Sharif gritted his teeth and clenched his fists. "If he dies because of me,…" He turned to the darkening horizon and fell to his knees. He covered his eyes with both hands but tears oozed between his fingers.

She knelt beside him. "You'll survive, Hashim. And, you'll know that, most of all, this crap is beyond your control. "

He shook his head. "No!" he roared as he bounded up. "No, I've been running. Like a damn coward, running." His mouth became twisted with his rising self-loathing. His rammed his fist into a tree's trunk. "Protecting everyone, the mayor, the police chief, my country's honor. Just like papa." He turned to Eliza standing by his side. His eyes wide as if startled, seeing something miraculous for the first time, he said, "Just like papa." He shook his head.

"My dear Miss MacKay, when we get back to Samarra, I'm going to do what I should have done the night you arrived." He spoke with unreserved finality.

Eliza shivered at the menacing look on Sharif's face. "Which was?"

F. Stone

"I should have put you on a plane home before Aamir had time to put you on a "No Fly" list. And made sure the United States knew of the massacre. Tomorrow, I'm setting the record straight."

"You mean expose the cover-up?" Eliza lowered her voice and glanced around her. "Tell the CIA? That's like friggin' treason." She gasped. "You'll be executed. Right? You said the minister can't be trusted. That he and the mayor -."

Sharif fumbled for his CIA phone in his pants' pocket and hit auto call. In seconds, the agent answered. "Frank, you got anyone in Samarra? My sergeant may be in trouble."

"I can be there in about three hours. You'll both live longer if you keep your distance from each other. No contact of any kind. Understood?"

"That's not how it works in my world, Frank. I'll be back in Samarra tomorrow. Meet me – I don't know. Where?"

"Sharif, as long as you have my cell phone, I'll find you. But, listen to me, Sharif. Don't go near Aamir. We're tracking his activities and communication. The last we saw your sergeant, he was entering the Federal Building. Probably doing your job as acting captain and -."

Sharif disconnected the call. He stood up and motioned for her to follow. "What does your psyche say about our future, Eliza?"

"I haven't a friggin' clue."

Back at the staff lounge, Eliza handed Sharif the house key for the place in Dubai, and a card. "This business card has my lawyer's phone number. I'll call the lawyer's office and leave a voice message. I'll ask him to pick up your family at the airport and take them to the house." Sharif and Eliza gave instructions to his family and finalized the arrangements.

By eleven in the evening, Sharif watched his family's jet fade into the night sky.

When he caught up to Khattab and Eliza near Buzz's jet, his son's cellphone rang. The display indicated the last person in the world he wanted to speak to - Serena.

Ω

Black Ice hated Cairo's insufferable heat. His shower had shed the dust and sweat, but failed to rid him of his regret for letting some half burned out cop take the contract. Pacing in his boxers, he waited for Aamir to confirm he had visual confirmation of Sharif's corpse.

"That lying prick." He opened his suitcase and collected the few clothes he needed to return to Samarra. "Bastards. I'll get rid of Aamir, then Sharif." A sensation of pleasure erupted in his groin. A string of profanities continued to punctuate his visions of revenge. "It'll be a fucking pleasure," he shouted. He checked his watch: *six-fifteen. Time enough to catch my eight-thirty flight, then be in Samarra. By midnight, Khalid's problems will be buried. Surely he'll be grateful enough to let this one screw-up go.* He shivered as if enveloped in England's damp autumn air. Ice knew Khalid well enough to know that, in spite of the man's fanatical religious convictions, he never forgave.

Ice threw his clothes into his suitcase and collected his toiletries. Suddenly, the front door burst open and three armed men plunged into the room. He glanced toward his sidearm, a million miles away on the other side of his bed. He bolted toward the television and grabbed his stiletto knife. Before he could remove it from its sheath, bullets ripped into his hand and arm.

Someone hollered, "Don't kill him. They want him alive."

Ω

When Mustafa's cellphone stopped ringing, Sharif accessed its phone records. He found a text message – from his ex-wife. Sharif nearly dropped the phone as he read the message.

'My dear Mustafa, we will be together very soon. Do not be afraid. Grandpa has sent some very good men to rescue you and bring you and Farah to me. Be very brave, my dear son. Mama.'

F. Stone

"That damn woman." Sharif chucked the phone to Khattab. "My ex-wife, she's behind the attempt to kidnap my kids. She might already know that the men she hired are dead. If I don't answer her call, she'll think her children died along with the kidnappers. If I talk to her, my cover is gone." He turned with a jerk towards Eliza. "She and Aamir hired Ice."

"Is she that desperate to get her children back?" Eliza's hand braced against her chest.

"I'll answer on the next ring," said Khattab. In another minute, Serena called again. "Rumi Police, Captain Khattab speaking. Who is calling?"

"Abdulla Khalid. Why do you have my grandson's phone?"

"I believe you know why, Mr. Khalid. We are investigating an attempt to kidnap Farah and Mustafa Sharif. I've noted an interesting text message your daughter sent to Mustafa Sharif. It appears she knew about the abduction, maybe planned it."

"What? How dare you?" Khattab and Sharif heard the man's pretentious bluster, angered by the insinuation of being party to a crime. "I have no need for such barbarism. We heard their father had been killed. Of course, they needed transportation to return to their mother. Where are my grandchildren now?"

"The children and their grandparents are under police protection. We did receive notice that Captain Sharif had been murdered. It would appear that the Sharif family has been targeted. Until I know who is behind the attack, the family will remain at a secret location."

Khattab heard someone grab the phone from Khalid's hands. Restrained shouting indicated Khalid and a woman fought over the phone.

"This is Serena Khalid. Let me speak to Mustafa. I must speak to my children. I demand you hand that phone over to Mustafa."

"I'm sorry, Miss Khalid, but your children are not here. In fact, they are no longer in Rumi. Our investigation indicates they are in grave danger. It is unfortunate that their father has been murdered."

"That bastard? Useless and penniless laborer. Good riddance. Don't get in my way, Khattab. You cannot keep me from my children." The call ended with the slap of her phone closing.

Khattab handed the phone back to Sharif. "Good luck. Sorry I can't restock your ammo. Not allowed. Some damn policy on district exchange rules."

"No problem, Khattab. Thanks for getting my family out." Khattab waved goodbye as Sharif and Eliza boarded Buzz's jet.

Just as Sharif and Eliza buckled, the CIA phone rang. "Sharif here. You got news about Omar?" He jammed the phone against his ear, making it bleed again.

"Bad news, and bad news," said the agent.

"Dead?"

"Not dead. Under arrest. Both of you are charged with the murder of police chief Ganem. When the mayor couldn't find your body in Samarra or Rumi, the mayor figured he'd been conned. The mayor is waiting for you to surface. You have roughly twenty-four hours to surrender or Sergeant Abdul-Muqtadir will undergo a quick trial and be executed."

"And?"

"He's added treason. Military personnel and police are under orders to shoot if you resist. I doubt you'd survive even if you surrender. Every road and airport is looking out for the two of you. You definitely cannot go back to your station."

"Frank, I'm through listening to people telling me what to do."

"Sharif, you're out of more than just ammo. Friends. No one will dare give you shelter. I can get you and MacKay out of RIPT. Confess to the cover-up and hand over the evidence. Then-."

"Prison. You bastard. You'll see that I'm convicted for the deaths of the Americans. You'll never get GIC or Omega. But you'll satisfy your need for revenge with my execution."

"You'll have a better chance with the CIA than Khalid. Don't try to run. If you run, I'll kill you."

"If you kill me, you've got nothing. No evidence, no cell phone. Sharif out."

Ω

When Eliza and Sharif arrived at Buzz's airport in Samarra, it was still dark. Sharif directed the pilot to let them off at the far end of the runway. They tossed their gear out and tumbled out as the aircraft slowly made the turn heading toward the small terminal. In the pitch black of the tarmac, they edged toward the periphery of the airport. The high fence blocked access to hide in the scrub brush.

"We'll wait here. Once they release the pilot, they'll get bored and shut down. Probably turn off the lights."

Eliza tugged on her down coat's collar. "I hope it's not long. Won't they be suspicious?"

"No. For one thing, he's a cop. And he's going to tell them he was under orders to return Buzz's aircraft. Won't be long till a taxi picks him up. Cold?" He put an arm around her shoulders. "You're shivering."

"I'll be fine when I know how you're going to rescue Omar."

"Not to worry. Aamir's not going to harm Omar while he knows I'm alive. How much ammo you got in that pistol?"

"Last I checked, I have a total of two bullets. You?"

"Zilch. Scared?"

"What's next?"

"You're going to get a room at a fancy hotel. Aamir won't expect us to be guests at the *Argos in Samarra*. Still working on the details. Okay, look. The lights are off. Let's get to my van."

The van appeared to have been untouched. Slowly, they rolled away from the terminal and drove on Samarra's back roads until reaching a quiet street. While waiting until for the curfew to end with the morning prayer, they considered their options.

Sharif let his head drop back against the partition behind his driver's seat. "I've never been here before. I mean without any firepower and backup. Always had backup." He muttered on and closed his eyes.

"What about Omar's squad?"

Sharif shook his head. "I'm not getting anyone else involved. They'd fight to the death to get him out. I need to find a way that doesn't put anyone at risk. They all have families. No, I'll work out a deal with Aamir."

"How? Surely you're not going to surrender."

Sharif sat up and turned to Eliza. "First, I'm going to make sure Agent Hutchinson gets you out. When it's safe, take him to your bank and hand over the documents and Khizar's phone."

Eliza glared at Sharif. "You're going to surrender, aren't you?" Tears began to well in her eyes.

He gazed into her face. "Eliza, there may be no way out for me. Either the CIA or Khalid will -."

"Hashim Sharif, don't you dare give up." Her eyes narrowed. "Khalid must be stopped. You must stop him."

"Time for morning prayer." He pulled out the handi-wipes Eliza carried in her trauma kit. "Perhaps Allah, the most Wise, will direct my path to a greater wisdom." He surreptitiously watched Eliza pull herself together and wipe her face. *She must survive. Above all, she must accept this.* After ablutions, he found a grassy spot, faced the direction of Mecca, and proceeded with his morning devotion.

In fifteen minutes, he was back in the van. Sharif put the van in gear and ventured out into the morning traffic rush. "Miss MacKay, if we're hiding out with the rich, we'd better look like we belong." He pulled over to a mall and parked near an exclusive shop where his ex-wife shopped. Sharif purchased a wool blend Armani suit, dark charcoal, and accessorized it with a crisp white shirt, silk blue tie, shoes, watch – the works. Eliza found a deep-bronze colored dress – Erdem, a modern elegance inspired by Audrey Hepburn - the pinnacle of perfection, fitting snug to her waist, complete with drop waist pleats sure to fit right in with the Breakfast at Tiffany's crowd. She accessorized it well. To hide her working-woman's nails, she wore a pair of short black gloves.

By the time they finished shopping, their bank account had bled out a hair's breadth more than ten thousand American dollars. Their last purchase was a suitcase. At the van, they filled the luggage with their clothes, Eliza's backpack, and Sharif's handgun.

Once they found a place to shower and primp, they dressed in their fine clothes, and took a taxi to the *Argos in Samarra*, a world-class hotel with a reputation for romance and relaxation. By noon Eliza was registering them as Mr. and Mrs. Ramsay. Sharif stood to the side pretending to examine the quality of an ornate wood staircase leading up to the private lounge.

They quietly moved toward the elevators. No one gave them a second glance. Sharif had left his monster rifle hidden in his van. Eliza's pistol was tucked in her Versace black suede Medusa clutch.

In their penthouse's foyer, a cream plush carpet and pale sage-colored walls greeted them. The ambiance offered quiet and calm – a sanctuary. Eliza found the bedroom and collapsed on one of the king size beds. Sharif sat down at the mahogany desk in the office and began dialing a number on his CIA cellphone. "Ready, Eliza?"

"For what?"

"Say hello to Aamir."

Eliza rushed into the room. He wondered if she was about to throw up. Her pale face with the dark circles under her eyes turned deathly grey. "You better sit down, Miss MacKay."

"No, Hashim. Please, no." Her weak voice quivered.

He grasped her arm, eased her down into a black leather club chair, and patted her shoulder.

293

"Captain Sharif speaking. Mayor Aamir, please." He sat down on the arm of the chair. While waiting for his nemesis to respond, Sharif checked out his image in a mirror. "Thanks for the clothes, Miss MacKay. Makes me feel like the engineer I used to be. All those lessons on principles of balance, counter weight, alignment, displacement."

He loosened his tie and flexed his shoulders. "And, the power of water. Do you know that water resources engineering is a discipline that combines hydrology, environmental science, meteorology, geology, conservation, and resource management. No mention of assault rifles." He chuckled. "Building bridges was my gift." He set his phone down on the desk and removed his suit jacket. Hearing the mayor's voice barking, he took his time downing a glass of water.

He checked his watch and whispered to Eliza. "Almost time for Zuhr prayer. You coming with me?"

"I'm not letting you out of my sight, captain."

"Okay, we pray here." He picked up his CIA phone. "Ah, yes, Mayor Aamir. I received a message that you have charged Sergeant Abdul Muqtadir with police chief Ganem's murder. I trust you're open to another alternative? One that is more conducive to you remaining in the mayor's chair?"

Sharif listened momentarily to the mayor's protest, then disconnected the call. Already, he had distanced himself from his enemy's attempt to claim authority. He stepped into the bathroom and completed the ablutions. He placed a clean towel on the sitting room's carpet and began the salah.

When his prayer ended, Sharif softly uttered the words, "O Allah, I ask you to make me do pious deeds, and that which is lawful. Prevent me from doing that which is forbidden. Let me do that which is good." He looked over at Eliza, still seated in her chair, and who appeared to be in deep meditation. "Protect us, have pity on us, admit us to your mercy, and cause us to die without ever having been seduced to evil, by your mercy, O the most merciful."

He took the phone and started to dial Aamir's number.

"Hashim, do you believe I'm going to hell?" Eliza spoke softly.

He liked the sound of her calling him by his first name. In spite of that pleasure, his chest tightened. His ever-deepening affection for her opened up a passage to disappointment. *She is not mine to have. I have nothing to offer but a life of turmoil and lack. Lack of comforts. Lack of stability. I must send her home.* A wave of sorrow made him shudder.

He bent down on one knee in front of her. "You mean, because you're not Muslim?"

"No. What is your judgement?"

"The short answer is, only Allah can judge you. Not me or anyone else." He shifted to sit on the floor and wrap his arms around his knees. "To be clearer, ever since Shia Islam and Sunni Islam united, the emphasis has been to honor the Koran as religious doctrine and apply the word of Allah to the culture of modern times. I am Muslim, period. I pray because I wish to, not because the Koran says I will go to hell if I disobey the word of Allah. I find peace, even strength from the times I spend with Allah."

He stood up and began to resume his call to Aamir. "Frankly, Miss MacKay, if Allah sends you to hell, there's not a whisker of chance for me." He paused when Aamir came on the line. "Aamir, here's the deal. You release Sergeant Abdul-Muqtadir and I'll hand over Khizar's cellphone." Sharif listened for a few seconds. "No, *you* listen. We'll make the exchange inside the Guardian Mosque. Leave your gorillas outside. I will be alone and not armed. You have two hours. Be at the mosque at three-fifteen. Sharif out."

He made his next and last call. "Sergeant Muntazar, Sharif here. Do you have time to leave the airport for a few hours? I need your help in getting my sergeant out of prison."

Sharif paced. "No, just stand by at the Guardian Mosque and wait for Omar to arrive with the mayor. I'm trading some evidence for Omar's release. Then you will get him out of there."

Sharif shook his head. "The less you know the better. Meet me at the fountain at quarter to three. Sharif out."

He took Eliza's elbow and led her to an elegant loveseat. He recognized the design his ex-wife loved - Constantine collection with intricate wood trims accentuating the base, rolled arms and carved feet. Deep brown leather cushions felt soft and supple. The pillows upholstered in a mixture of gold and brown fabric exuded opulence.

"Sit down, Miss MacKay. Once Agent Frank gets here - ..."

"How does he know where we are?"

"His CIA phone tracks us. In case I'm incapacitated, he can still find you. He should be here in about two hours." Sharif gave her his most fierce scowl. "I have enough to handle without trying to keep you alive. I don't need the distraction. You go home." He tried to swallow and take a deep breath to slow the thumping of his heart. It raced on.

Part of him hated treating her so callously. His logical side applauded. "I won't be here when he arrives. Do not give Frank any trouble." He sat down on a sofa and turned to look out the wall of window. The distant Guardian Mosque's massive dome glowed in the afternoon sun. *Will I die there? Better than in the mayor's graveyard.*

"Fine. As you wish, captain." Her voice sounded distant and frail.

Sharif twisted back to face her. Her sudden acquiescence shocked him. "What? No argument?"

She stood, hesitated for a moment as if to get her balance, then marched to the bedroom. With each step, she walked with greater determination. Her shoulders first, then her arms. "I better get my things in order." Her voice became strong, assertive. "I feel a bit guilty leaving just when you're facing off with Aamir." She grabbed her backpack out of the suitcase. Her dirty uniform got a quick fold and tossed into the luggage.

"Whew, this stuff stinks," she said standing back. "You know the worst part of travelling is arriving home and having to do laundry." She zipped the backpack closed. "I hope Frank doesn't mind if I ask him to stop for a snack. I bet he'd be a fun date. Lots of stories." Her gaiety changed into a groan as she lifted her backpack off the bed. "Why do I overpack? I bet you're thinking typical woman," she snickered as she placed the pack in the foyer. "What time are you leaving?" She smiled and trotted off to the kitchen. "Can't remember last time we, er, I ate? Must be something nice to eat in here."

He checked his watch and followed her. "Thirty minutes." He had suspicions about the authenticity of her bubbly attitude. "Don't forget Frank's motives are pure business." *Surely she doesn't have romantic notions?* "But he might take you out to celebrate. Case almost wrapped up. Probably get promoted."

"Good idea." She looked like she'd just opened a gift. "Why wait?" She walked over to the lounge and opened the bar fridge. "Ah, here we go. A lovely bottle of champagne. Dom Perignon Blanc, one of my favorites." She selected a champagne glass from shelves of crystal. "Obviously, you won't join in, and shouldn't, given that you need to have a clear mind." She popped the cork and laughed as a little of the bubbly rushed over the rim of the bottle. After filling her glass, she raised it in a toast. "To your very good health, sir." After downing a mouthful, she closed her eyes. "Ah, so delicious." She topped up her glass and downed that.

Sharif walked up to her. "You shouldn't, you know. You're exhausted, hungry. Wait until Frank gets here and he can take care of you."

She stabbed him in his chest with her fingers, pushing him out of her way. "I can take care of myself, thank you. No hard feelings, my dear captain. You have been a perfect gentleman and most courageous warrior." She did a wobbly curtsy. "I am eternally in your debt. You'd make an awesome Canadian." Standing by the windows, she swallowed another mouthful. "I can hardly wait to see Mike."

Some friend. Couldn't get the police to launch a rescue. "Miss MacKay, I hoped we could part friends."

"I'll always remember you with fondness." Eliza drank the last drop in her glass and then filled up it again. She set the glass down on the bar and sat on a stool. She held his gaze for a moment.

Are those tears in her eyes, or had the alcohol begun its hold on her?

"Like you said, my business here is done. Your family is safe. You don't need the distraction."

He detected a tremor in her voice.

"I'll be home by tomorrow morning."

Sharif's gut twisted into a painful knot. "What are your plans, I mean after you've settled back into your home?"

She shrugged and dipped her finger into the wine. As she licked her fingertip, he swallowed and braced shoulders against a marble pillar. He needed its cold shock.

"I suppose you'll go back to work, right?"

"Maybe not. I've gotten used to having you around. Feels good to know that someone cares. Maybe there's a man for me, wants me in his life," she winked, "and his bed." She laughed. "I can't believe I said that."

His knees buckled. He rolled down his sleeves and buttoned the cuffs. "I'll get my family relocated as soon as - ."

"No rush. You can stay in Dubai, the harem house," she laughed. "Until you find yourself another wife." She filled her glass of champagne and wandered into the office. "I'll make sure my Dubai lawyer registers you as tenants. No charge. I'll take care of all expenses until you get established. I owe you my life, at least twice over." She disappeared behind a wall of book shelves. "I think you and your family will be very happy there." She reappeared. "But if it's not to your liking, find something that suits you." Down went another mouthful. "Notify the lawyer and he'll get in touch with me. Capiche?"

Sharif felt stunned. He didn't know this Eliza. Distant. Aloof. Drunk. Almost arrogant. "Papa and I will - ."

"Yes, I know. Here's your coat." Eliza helped him slip into the sleeves. She faced him and offered her right hand. "Good luck, captain."

"You too, Miss MacKay, Eliza," he said, shaking her hand. He leaned closer, looked for a hint of affection in her eyes. She pulled her hand free and backed away.

"When you see Omar, please wish him well for me." She turned her back to Sharif and began to walk away.

"If things at the mosque go badly, if Aamir has his way ... may I ask you to take care of my family until papa can take over?" He felt chilled to the bone.

Eliza stood still. She turned, eyes focused his, her mouth open but she seemed unable to speak for a moment. "Of course. I'll make sure they are safe and want for nothing." The tone of her voice emphasized the clarity of her mission. The alcohol's spell had become subservient to her tenacity. She stepped forward and took his hands into hers. "Forgive me for sounding so cavalier. It is hard for me to say goodbye and walk away from you." A tear escaped. Her chin quivered. "But I must respect your wishes. You are a wise man, a good man. I pray Allah keep you safe and strong."

Her voice and eyes conveyed compassion bound in the unwavering strength of a warrior. He felt mute, unable to find the words that would excuse his callous determination to send her away. He looked at her hands, caressing his. Never before had he experienced this uncharted territory, seeing what he wanted deeply, but believing it was wrong, unattainable, resolute that he knew what was best for her.

She kissed his hands and released them. "I may depart this land, my dear Hashim, but part of me will never leave you." She turned away, went into the bedroom, and shut the door.

Sharif's hands trembled as he grasped his sunglasses and put them on. Racing down the hallway he strangled his grief into submission. He punched the elevator button and jumped in, mindless of the flow of humanity. The front reception desk blurred as he trotted out through the entrance doors and jumped into a cab.

He couldn't recall any portion of the forty minute ride to the mosque. The touch of Eliza's hands, her tears replayed in an endless loop. Her parting words, "will never leave you," echoed with every heartbeat. *Why would she say that? Is it possible she meant --? No,*

299

she couldn't. How could she love me? He felt as though he'd just run a marathon. Breathless, sweating, muscles quivering, his mind racing, he wondered if he had missed the signs of her wanting him. *Why would she want me?*

Memories flashed. From the most innocent to the erotically seductive, waves of delight made him gasp. The warmth spread, as if Allah's love moved within his entire being.

He covered his face with his hands, and leaned over his knees. Alone, he crumbled from the pain of loss.

He paid the driver and headed for the mosque's square. As he walked on, he tried to remember who he was the day before Eliza arrived. If he survived this day, he'd have to resurrect the brooding and callous cop. A wave of revulsion settled in his gut.

He climbed the massive stretch of stairs and sat down on a wood bench near the towering archway of the entrance. His shoulders sagged. A bit of lint on his sleeve caught his eye. *At least I can be buried well-dressed.* He wore a morbid smirk. *Thought I could find the killers. Outsmart the CIA. See justice served. How naive.* He kicked off his shoes and cursed. "Damn you."

Anger, like a lacerated artery, soaked into his bones. Instead of its killing poison, it became the antidote to his smothering self-pity. Sharif directed its fire to his mission. As he gathered up his energy reserves, a shadow fell across his face.

"I've been waiting for you."

Chapter 33

Imam Bashir approached Sharif with his usual welcoming embrace. "I've been hearing the most incredible news. Apparently you died two days ago. And here you are, so lifelike." The imam glowed with enthusiasm and rubbed the top of Sharif's head. "Well done, my friend. And look, so well dressed. How are things in Heaven?"

Sharif restrained a sarcastic remark as he followed Bashir through the archway past marble columns.

"I'm in no humor, imam Bashir. And you will not be pleased with me. I have arranged for a prisoner exchange here." Sharif explained his desperate situation. "I don't have the cellphone I promised with me. I'm hoping the mayor will believe I handed the phone over to you. Does he trust you?"

The imam shrugged. "Depends. What can I do for you?"

"You and your staff must keep your distance."

"My men will provide you with a weapon, Hashim."

"I promised the mayor I would be unarmed. Nothing must be done to risk Omar's life."

"Does the mayor have legal grounds to arrest you?"

"No, but I know too much about his involvement in Police Chief Ganem's murder. And his connection with the hit man hired to kill Eliza and me." Sharif shook his head. "I knew the man had a history of being ruthless, but I hoped the rumors were exaggerated." Sharif updated the imam on the attempt to kidnap his children. "

"Hashim, there's much you don't know about Aamir."

Sharif stood dumbfounded as he learned about Aamir's history. "It all makes sense now. No wonder he has hated me."

"He will kill you, Hashim."

Sharif spotted Sergeant Muntazar and motioned for him to join him.

"Where do you want me positioned, captain?"

"Out of sight. No gunfire unless to protect Omar. You're in charge of getting Omar back to his family. Nothing more."

When Muntazar and Bashir had slipped back inside the mosque, Sharif turned to feel the sun's warmth on his face. The hour of the exchange passed. Sharif paced, fearing the worst for his friend. After another hour, he resisted the urge to call Aamir. *Don't push him. Offer the man the trust he doesn't deserve.* He shed his suit coat and rolled up his sleeves. Outside he scanned the courtyard and distant parking lot. Workers and shoppers heading home had begun to fill the streets. A harmonious hum enunciated his separation from their carefree lives.

The late afternoon sun had begun to cast the mosque's shadow across the Federal Government's entrance. Recalling Ganem, a momentary sting of sorrow caught him by surprise. Then he saw them.

Four black SUVs and the mayor's limo drove into the parking lot and proceeded to the courtyard. Eight armed men formed a line at the steps. The sound of their weapons being readied echoed.

Just like an execution in my compound. Sharif raised his arms, showing his palms were empty. Slowly, he turned his back to them to show he had no weapons there. His nerves sent shock waves through his muscles. They twitched and ached. He clenched down on his instinct to run for cover. In rapid succession, he flexed power back into each muscle group. When he heard boots pounding up the stairs, he turned to face the guards.

Two pushed him against a pillar. Sharif winced at their probing and jabs. As far as the public's perception, the guards were apprehending a criminal.

They placed him in handcuffs and signaled the waiting men. They fanned out to cover the entire front exposure. As they checked every angle, Aamir stepped out of his car. By the drape of his suit, Sharif suspected the man was armed.

Sharif's heart rate neared the panic red line. He was reasonably sure the men with him had orders to shoot only after the mayor got what he wanted. He controlled his breathing, making every effort to appear calm and in control. Surveying the perimeter, Sharif noted a silver van half a block away. The driver slowed, made a U-turn and sped on to the street that circled around behind the mosque. The black tinted windows kept the identity of the driver hidden. *Transport for my body, perhaps?* His gut threatened to flip what little he had in his stomach onto the steps. *Breathe, just breathe.*

Aamir scaled the steps and stood twenty yards away from Sharif. The guards doubled their grip on his upper arms. Jabs of pain travelled down his arms to his fingers. Other than the glow of sweat on his brow, he made no protest or sign of distress.

Aamir remained silent as he glanced over Sharif, perhaps not used to seeing him out of uniform. "Captain Sharif," he said with a curled lip. Hate radiated from the man. "Where is your CIA spy now?"

"Not interested in you anymore. He has MacKay." He looked up into the blue sky. "Probably in his jet half way out of RIPT by now." Checking the parking lot for another vehicle, he asked, "Where is Sergeant Abdul-Muqtadir?"

"You'll see him when I see the Khizar's cellphone."

"It's safe with imam Bashir. First remove the handcuffs and send your men off these steps. There will be no violence in this sacred place. Bashir promised he and his men will not interfere. Surely you trust Bashir."

Aamir paused, his eyes unfocused, perhaps recalling a time when he and Bashir were soldiers. The cuffs were removed and the guards retreated.

"Now, Sharif. Hand over the phone."

Sharif turned to the entrance and gave a thumbs-up signal. "Bashir will bring it." *What if I make Aamir remember? It might shake him up enough to hesitate.* "I didn't know you were a hero, Mayor Aamir." He casually took a step forward.

Aamir frowned. "What are you talking about?" He moved toward Sharif a few feet.

"This mosque. Twenty-seven years ago, you were a member of the platoon who saved the Guardian Mosque. You were probably here on this spot pushing the terrorists back. Bashir speaks very highly of your bravery." Sharif noted the look of shock on the man's face. He pressed on. "So many gave up their lives. Their sacrifice is scarcely remembered. We owe the protectors like you our respect. Allah, the most benevolent, saw your courage, Mayor Aamir."

Aamir grimaced as if tasting a bitter memory.

Sharif took a step forward. He had Aamir's attention. "Your friend, Abdul Zydan, died. In his dying breath, he made you and Rasheed promise to find his imprisoned wife and daughters, to end their suffering. It must have been torture to carry out the blood oath, to kill them."

"Shut up. Just shut up." Aamir's eyes narrowed and spit flew from his mouth. "You have no right to speak of this to me."

Sharif knew he was pushing Aamir into forbidden territory. "You could not know the wife was the sister of Khalid, my former father-in-law. Since then, he has made you pay for her death. Like me, you have become a victim of his madness."

Aamir stepped forward. He pulled out his handgun and switched off the safety. "Khalid and I ..." He inhaled and shook his head. "My business with you is done. You are under arrest for the murder of police chief Ganem."

"Mayor Aamir, the CIA knows everything about Khalid and his intent to cause havoc in RIPT. You've been a pawn of Khalid and have failed to carry out his orders to have me killed. His cover-up has been exposed. Surely you know that Khalid doesn't forgive failure."

"You're wrong. Once you're dead, he will release me." His voice wavered.

Sharif moved toward the mayor but stopped when Aamir raised his gun. "Aamir, so many have died. Omar doesn't deserve the consequences of our mistakes. Please, let him go." He moved forward a step. "You can kill me here and now but it won't change the fact that the CIA considers both of us as criminals." A few more steps, fifteen yards - .

Aamir fired his weapon. Birds scattered. Frightened voices and screams peppered the stillness. The grimace of the mayor's face froze.

Sharif stood, unharmed.

The mayor's violent trembling had caused him to miss. Aamir growled. He straightened, pulled his shoulder back. Sharif saw his adversary rein in his emotions. He wouldn't miss a second time.

"At last, I'll be free of you and Khalid." Aamir calmly lifted his gun. Sharif leaped toward the mayor. Twelve yards - ten too many. As Aamir squeezed the trigger, the imam's melodious voice announced the time for prayer. Vibrations of his song flowed, even into the dark recesses of a killer's mind. Aamir paused. It was enough to distract him until Sharif could grasp the weapon and disengage it from his enemy's hand.

"Aamir, the time for war is past," he said as dozens of people approached the base of the steps, unsure if it was safe to proceed to the sanctuary. Sharif waved, reassuring them the conflict was over. He removed the clip and chambered bullet. "Now, release Omar."

"I suggest you comply, Mayor Aamir."

Aamir whirled around. The CIA agent sauntered out from the entrance and stopped.

305

"Frank, what are you doing here?" Sharif stared at the agent in disbelief. "Where's Eliza?"

"Hell if I know. Like I told you, the cellphone will lead me to its location."

Sharif patted his pants' pockets, then grabbed his suit coat. He found the cellphone. In a front pocket "That sneaky, stubborn -." Warmth flooded his chest. *That beautiful, brilliant woman.*

He turned to Aamir. "Release Omar. Now."

"Or, what?"

Sharif spoke in Aamir's ear. "I'll give Khizar's cellphone to the CIA right after I tear you limb from limb. You'll die in dishonor."

Reluctantly, Aamir signaled to his men. They pulled Sergeant Abdul-Muqtadir out from one of the SUVs. Muntazar dashed out from behind the SUV and pulled him away from the steps.

"Good to see you, Sergeant. Now get out of here." Sharif shouted.

Sergeant Abdul-Muqtadir waved, hesitating to get into Muntazar's vehicle. "I suppose you're going to be late again for your shift tonight?"

"I'll call you later." Sharif placed his hand over his heart. No man had a more loved brother. Nothing more needed to be said.

As Muntazar and Abdul-Muqtadir drove away, Sharif turned to the mayor. "I don't have the luxury of exposing your involvement in Ganem's murder. But keep in mind, if I go down, you'll go down harder. The American government will make you pay every day for the rest of your miserable life." He tilted his head in the direction of the agent, out of listening range. "What I know, he knows. He's just waiting for Eliza or me to turn over the hard evidence."

Aamir glanced at the growing crowd. They moved quietly around him and Sharif, taking off their shoes, women covering their hair with scarves. "CIA can't touch me," he sneered. Aamir squared his shoulders with Sharif. "Khalid has both of us in his snake pit, No way out." For a moment, his eyes darted about, as if searching for an enemy in the crowd. Quickly, he descended the stairs to his vehicle and left with his men.

Agent Frank Hutchinson strolled over to stand with Sharif. "I thought you were good as dead for a bit there."

Sharif sat down on the top step. "Were you going to shoot him to save me?"

The agent sat down and shook his head. "I might have, if the imam's men hadn't taken away my weapons. Sorry, but I, ah. -- Truth is, I've never seen anything so reckless, and well, just wondering if you'd like to work for me?"

Sharif laughed. "As you know, I'm not very good at being devious. Not a good liar either, no disrespect intended." He handed the CIA phone back to Frank. "Don't need this anymore. The party is over. I'll contact you in two or three days. You'll get most of what you want." Sharif stood and proceeded down the steps.

"So, do I get Eliza?" asked Hutchinson.

Sharif stopped and grinned at the agent. "Remember the night you told me the good guy doesn't always win, but he always gets the girl?"

Frank nodded.

"I don't think you're that kind of good guy, Frank."

While Sharif waited for the taxi he ordered, he dialed his hotel's room number. It rang several times. He tried his son's cell number. It rang and rang. His heart pounded in his chest. His mind raced over the possibilities why Eliza wouldn't, or couldn't answer the phone. She had a gun. It had two bullets. If she believed he was dead ... would she - .

The forty minute taxi ride felt like an eternity. The hotel elevator tortured him until sweat poured down his back. "Eliza, Eliza, please be okay," he muttered. His room card slipped into the slot. The lock released. Grasping the handle, he struggled to inhale. "Eliza," he called out, "please answer me." He turned the handle and pushed the door open an inch, then five. When he could finally view the foyer, all the vitality that kept him from falling apart vanished. He faltered, crashed into a closet door, and fell to his knees.

The sun's rays, streaming into the sitting room, washed over her form. It cast a halo on her head, made her appear in shadow. She stood facing the door, arms raised and both hands grasping the gun, ready to squeeze the trigger. For a long while, she appeared more like a store mannequin, lifeless, unblinking.

"Ha, Hashim - ," she barely breathed his name. She blinked. Her arms fell to her side. The gun, still clutched in her hand, would fire if she twitched. She shuffled to his side as if in a daze.

"Give me the gun, Miss MacKay," his voice sounded raspy with fatigue. "It's over now."

"Over?" She looked down at him.

"Over." He carefully pried the gun from her hand and ejected the two bullets. "Well, mostly over. Still got Khalid on our tail. But - ."

"Hashim." She half fell, half lowered herself. She lightly touched his shoulders and traced the contours of his arms and chest. "You're not hurt?"

He could read her thoughts as the light returned to her eyes. She had feared someone was phoning to tell her he had been killed. The thought made her throw up. He smelt it on her breath.

In his mind, he told her how much he loved her. He said things he could never speak out loud. Like how the terrible accident that destroyed her family brought her to him. That he was sad he could never be good enough for her. That she had shown him what real courage looked like – without armor or weapons.

He stood, helped her to the bedroom, and settled her into the bed. She was asleep before he turned off the light. For the next two days and nights, they barely ate or spoke.

Chapter 34

One the third morning, Sharif awoke to discover Eliza had moved from her bed to his. The fresh fragrance of her recently washed hair teased him awake. She wore the black silk and lace robe provided by the hotel. Still on top of the bed covers, she had cuddled close to him and appeared deep in sleep. As he rolled away, she murmured discontentedly and wriggled closer, curling around his frame. "Miss MacKay, I suggest you sleep on your bed."

She woke. "Uh oh, I didn't intend to go back to sleep." She blushed. "I was just watching you dreaming. It looked like you were having a nightmare. I thought if I, you know, cuddled you, the dream would stop." She made no effort to shift away from his gaze.

With an unrestrained moan, he turned to her. "My dear Eliza, do you have any idea how much I want to make love to you?" He caressed the curve of her ear lobe.

She frowned. "Is it love or lust, Hashim?"

He jumped off the bed and faced her. "How can you not know how dear you are to me?"

"I've noted the lust," she said, grinning. "Clearly the level of passion in that one kiss at Hell's Gate was an earmark of lust. You're a great kisser." Eliza sat up and tightened the belt of her robe. "You are special, Hashim." Her voice became soft, hesitant. "I owe you a lot. But I've kept my heart in check." She stood and moved closer to him. "You had said that your role was only as my protector, being a police officer."

Sharif stepped back a half step. His eyes darted from her face to the floor, then back to her again. "It has been necessary to keep a respectful distance. To maintain my objectivity." He frowned and shifted his position, massaged the back of his neck, and tried to do his hat flip with no hat. He looked into her eyes, hesitating to say the words, as if the language he needed to speak was foreign. "You can't, I mean, there is no way ..." he winced as if in pain. He shook his head. "Never mind, Miss MacKay. Let's get dressed and go down for breakfast."

The loss of his police officer personae made Sharif jumpy. During breakfast Sharif complained he needed to return to what felt familiar. "Not feeling like a cop." He loosened his tie and tugged at the cuffs of his white shirt. "I miss that gut intuition that keeps me on edge." He wolfed down his plate of toast and eggs. "Target practice, that's what I need."

"We'll need to change into our work clothes. The hotel staff cleaned and repaired them."

"Good. Once we change into our police clothes, we'll pick up my van and make quick stop for ammo at the station." Sharif easily sifted into his cop psyche. Back in control again, in charge of his next move, he felt a rush with the resurgence of his authority. As they drove to their picnic site, he wrestled with his conscience. *What happened to the idea of letting go of the need for the uniform, for my badge?* By the time they arrived, his agitation pushed his mood into a dark place.

Near the stream's gravel bank, he hit the brakes, making the van slide to a stop. "I'm going for a walk." He slammed the van into park and shut it off. "Stay here." He got out and opened the rear passenger door, reached for his flak jacket in the back seat, swung it up over his head and fastened the sides down. He put on his helmet. He moved quickly, decisively. Both his weapons received a cursory once-over.

Sharif grabbed a bottle of water from the center console, then flung it into the back seat. "Where is my phone?" His agitation soared. "What did you do with my phone?" His scowl flashed.

"Which one?" She remained unaffected by his temper.

He gave her a look as if she'd pushed his impatience into the red zone.

Eliza shifted her body, her shoulders squared with his. "Your police phone is in your shirt pocket. Mustafa's phone is in my backpack." She opened the glove compartment and pulled out her cellphone. "Here is mine. You can use it but keep in mind the battery needs charging soon." Eliza hit the 'on' button. It buzzed and beeped as it came to life. Before she could toss it toward Sharif, he'd slammed the door shut.

Grit and gravel crunched under his lunging stride. He looked like a hulking beast, bent with the weight of his equipment and trouble. The sun's rays glanced off his helmet and the barrel of the rifle. Dust rose into a play of the light around his boots as he continued to force down an internal scream that threatened his rigid control.

The murmuring of the stream etched its way into his chaotic thoughts. Its cheerful sound irritated him. He maneuvered further down the boulders, jumping down from one to the other until he stood in the rushing water. The eighteen-foot-wide stream appeared shallow enough to allow crossing.

He took one bold step into the current. The cold water made him cringe as it filled his boots. He fought for his footing on the slick rocks. The frantic water grabbed his raised foot as his other foot slipped off a rock. His body convulsed into a tailspin, sending him flying into the rushing water. His automatic response to break his fall with his outstretched arm saved his head from a full spontaneous baptism. The rest – clothes, face, weapons -- were submerged in the cold water. His helmet had flipped off and disappeared under water.

He jumped up. Once he cleared the water from his face, he saw his police cell phone floating downstream, bouncing in the turbulent water like a tiny raft. "Bugger!" Trying to retrieve the cell, he dashed through the water, still slipping and groping to maintain his balance. Twice more he stumbled, before latching onto the probably now-defunct device. Finally, Sharif simply collapsed to his knees in the midst of the churning water.

He fought the inner voice mocking him. There was nothing amusing about his ruined clothes, boots. It would take hours to make his weapons clean and useable. His hands and knees had bruises and cuts from colliding with the rocks. His butt hurt. He felt like a vehicle wreck – mangled and unrecognizable. *What the hell is wrong with me?* Sharif's panic grew to fever level.

Let it go.

He heard Allah's gentle voice urging him to let it go. He stood and shouted, "How do I let it go?" His body stiffened. He attempted a step toward the far bank and fell again. This time, he remained in the water, laying back on the rocky bed and letting the flow of water wash over him. Only his face remained exposed to the bright sun.

It started with a grunt, then a growl, then a sound that broke free from his mid-section. Then a couple of coughs - a feeble attempt to regain control. The water tickled his ears. The sound of the stream murmured like the voices of children playing.

The sunlight blinded him, coaxing tears to fall from his eyes. It came in a rush. A dam broke from somewhere in his soul. All hell and fury rushed to be released. Sharif swore at the top of his lungs. Fuck! Fuck Aamir and Frank. Double fuck Khalid. The torrent of anguish came from his belly. It pushed through his protective wall, ramming it into small pieces. Sharif growled a battle cry again and again. Within five minutes he felt drained.

The need for control, the desire for acceptance, hope for recognition, he let it all go.

His limbs relaxed, freely floating with the stream's current. He looked up into the cloudless sky. He could almost feel as though he was flying in that intense blue space. Light and carefree. The thought put a smile on his face. And the smile made the rest of his body smile. New energy surged – a soft yet omnipotent energy. It made him chuckle. The sensation in his stomach felt warm in spite of a layer of icy water above.

A small bird circled and landed on a boulder near the shore, just outside Sharif's grasp. It drank, then pooped, and flew off. The irony of it hit Sharif. Tiny bird, small mind, fragile body, yet in harmony within its world. Sharif, intelligent and fierce, but bruised and soaked to the skin. Sharif roared. The more he laughed, the harder he laughed. Finally he had to sit up to catch his breath.

He looked up in the direction he'd parked his van. The silhouette of Eliza stood high on the bank several feet away. Her femininity and beauty echoed in the way she moved. He noted her ease, confidence. She didn't need to prove anything. Lately, she had less of a need to keep her backpack in reach.

She strolled closer, stopped at the top of the bank adjacent to Sharif's wading area and cocked her head. He caught her mischievous grin.

"I thought you might like some water, but ...."

Sharif roared again. His laughter echoed down the length of the stream. He stood. "Alas," he said, bowing somewhat wobbly, "what I need is not water but ...." He gingerly stepped through the rushing water, climbed the bank's mass of boulders, and stood boot to boot with her. The warmth of his smile echoed the love in his heart. Tenderly he caressed her face. Softly he said, "All that I want, or need, is standing right in front of me."

She smiled and playfully punched his chest. "Hmm, maybe you've decided you like me?"

Sharif held her hands, brought his forehead to rest against hers, and closed his eyes. A flood of anger, disappointments, regrets, and grudges flowed into nothingness, like the fire from a dragon's breath vanishes. Instead of the weight of the endless night within, he felt enraptured. It surged forth. Yes, the good man had never been broken or lost. But it took the love of a strong woman to help him discover the truth. He held her hands to his chest.

"My dear lady, I've liked you since the day I found you crawling in the dirt and blood in my compound." A smirk eased its way across Sharif's mouth, and he laughed as he wrapped his arms around her. A shiver shot through him. The love he saw in her eyes took his breath away. It had always been there. Now he could see, feel it. Her sweet gaze captivated him so deeply that he knew, even without the intrusion of words, that her love came from her soul – for him, all of him.

When he could finally speak, it came as a mere whisper. "I love you." His hands touched her face, fingers lightly tracing her temples, her cheeks, her mouth. He lifted her chin up as his lips fell upon hers, just touching.

"Pardon me? Did you say something?" Her lips teased him with feathery kisses to his mouth.

"I said, I love you," he murmured. He trapped her arms within his embrace and showered hot kisses down Eliza's neck.

"I'm sorry, but you're mumbling. What did you say?"

He pulled back a little and noticed the raised eyebrows and inquiring look. Sharif shouted to the sun in the sky, "Eliza MacKay, I love you." He looked back into her eyes. He smiled and kissed her lips. "I always have, I think. I know I will always love you."

"I'm frightened, Hashim. I'm frightened that I will displease you."

He caressed her face. "Impossible. My greatest desire is for you to be happy. I know you're not my possession. You'll always be free to choose your own life, where you live, how you live."

Tears flooded her eyes. "I love you so, Hashim. So much more than I can say. I was so frightened that you would send me away. That was more terrifying than anything else. Anytime I thought I might not see you again, I could barely breathe."

"You'll always be beside me, or in my heart." He held her hands tightly to his chest. "Elizabeth MacKay Ramsay, my dear Eliza, will you do me the honor of becoming my wife?"

"My heart says yes, absolutely yes."

"I hope you know life with me is going to be bumpy. The dragon will not surrender to a typical domestic life."

Eliza wrapped her arms around his shoulders. "The truth is, I like the dragon. I'm a bit worried, though. Your children are not ready for a stepmother to invade their lives. They've been under a lot of stress since their mother left. And, I don't think your dear mother, um, sees me as measuring up to her idea of a good Muslim daughter-in-law. And, we've known each other barely two months. Not enough to -."

"Minor compared to losing you." He kissed her.

"And, I'm not supposed to have any more children."

"I can barely manage the two I have." He kissed her more passionately.

Eliza stepped back.

Sharif straightened his shoulders for a moment. "You're wondering if I'll be another William." He wrapped his arms around her, and buried his face in her hair. "Our bond is sacred, my dear Eliza. There is nothing you can do that will make me turn away from you. I love you, all of you." He released her.

"Eliza, I have secretly thought of you as my wife. I have prayed to Allah, promising to love you and only you for the rest of my life." He turned away, shoulders slumped. "But my dear, as a husband, I should have something to offer you. I have nothing, no property, no security, nothing that a man should bring to a marriage. You already have all you need. You don't even need my protection. How can you want a penniless cop?" He stood tall, shoulders squared with hers. "And, listen, I do not want any of your wealth. I want to live modestly. Is that a problem for you?"

Eliza took his hands, and guided them to wrap around her waist. She looked up into his face. "No problem at all. You, Hashim Sharif, are my home." He didn't pull away. It encouraged her to reveal everything. "Hashim, what you don't know is that you can provide me with many things I dearly need. A family, your family. And you promised to get rid of all my triggers. I'm going to hold you to that." She kissed the underside of his chin. "Only you know how to do that."

She continued to plant feathery kisses from his ear lobe and down to the hollow of his throat. "But you offer something greater than all of that. When I'm with you, I feel more alive than ever before. When you touch me," she gasped at the thought, "I feel your passion. And, when I listen to your prayers, I feel showered with God's love. You have a gift. You are very powerful." Eliza stepped back. "So you see, what you can provide is far more valuable than a house or money."

He pressed his lips onto her forehead. "I do love you. So very much." He took a deep breath, and held her even tighter. "I never spoke those words. Didn't dare." He looked into her eyes. "I thought that if I didn't say the words, 'I love you,' it wouldn't hurt as much when you left."

"Hashim, I'm not leaving you. How soon can I be your wife?" She kissed him without restraint. "I will deny you nothing." Passion erupted, beyond the bounds of mortal power or any moral code.

When Sharif and Eliza returned to their hotel under the cover of night, they showered and packed. "We've been in one place long enough," said Sharif. "After the marriage ceremony at the mosque we should find another place for the night." His voice was soft, hesitant. "Any place in particular you would prefer?"

Eliza had changed into the lilac wrap linen lilac skirt and top she wore the first time Sharif took her to get groceries. Miraculously, her silk, lavender scarf had survived multiple packings. "I must thank Omar for bringing a change of clothes for us."

"More likely, it was his dear wife who had the foresight to know what to bring." Sharif checked his watch. "We have to decide, Eliza. The curfew will start in about two hours."

"I'm thinking, Hashim." She zipped their luggage closed and turned to him. She flashed a grin, her eyes bright as if holding a secret. "I know where. Let's go."

"Where?"

"You'll see. We shouldn't keep imam Bashir, and Sergeant Omar and his wife waiting."

They entered the Guardian Mosque and performed the ablutions. Within the hour, in a simple traditional Islamic ceremony, wearing their best casual clothes, accompanied by their best friends, Hashim and Eliza were declared husband and wife.

Rushing to be off the streets before midnight, Eliza directed Sharif to drive to the park along the river. "Are you suggesting we … in this van … in plain view of -?" Shock overwhelmed him.

"It's the one place where I have no terrifying memories. And you said we are to live modestly."

"Not bloody homeless. Don't you want a comfortable place to be on your wedding night?"

Eliza took his hand from the steering wheel. "All I need is right beside me."

Stopped at a traffic light, Sharif turned his face to her and smiled, which quickly turned into a laugh. "Should I assume that my life with you is going to be one continuous adventure?"

She kissed his hand. "You're going to know how it feels to be loved."

The moon traced the path through the trees along the walking trail. They parked among large trees, concealing the van. As Sharif shut off the van, Eliza looked at her husband's face. A frown had developed and his mouth shifted into his worried look.

"If you are really uncomfortable with this, we can still find a hotel close by, or your apartment."

Hashim chuckled. "Not worried my dear." He eyed her from her head to her feet and back to her eyes. "Just wondering where would you like me to start."

The next morning, Sharif and Eliza first checked into a modest hotel, then waited impatiently for their bank to open its doors. Both wore their casual civilian clothes. They stood at the heavy blast-resistant doors, counting the minutes.

"Two more minutes," whispered Eliza. "You sure we don't need our passports? I'd feel a whole lot better if we had them, just in case we need to make a run for the border. I keep imagining Aamir's shadow trailing us."

"The more I think about it, the more I'm inclined to agree with you." Suddenly the sound of the doors' locking mechanism got Sharif's attention. "Okay, here we go. Ready?"

Eliza nodded. She inhaled deeply and braced for a stressful afternoon.

Sharif and Eliza passed through the security scanning device and spoke with the receptionist. "We don't have an appointment," said Sharif, "but it's very important we speak with the manager. You should tell him Eliza MacKay is here to see him."

Quickly, the bank manager approached the couple. "Ah, Miss MacKay. How can the National Bank of Samarra be of service to you today?"

"I need to update my account records. Hashim is now my husband. We need a special favor." She lowered her voice. "We have urgent business and hope you may be able to maintain secrecy of our presence here."

After a momentary tense silence, Sharif began. "My wife and I are being shadowed by mercenaries. I've made certain no one followed us here so there is no risk to you or your staff. The problem is we need to prepare a confidential report to the president of our country and the Minister of Internal Affairs here. We need access to a private office and a computer that's off the grid. I cannot risk those documents falling into the wrong hands if Eliza and I are captured," he hesitated, "or killed."

The manager stiffened. "I cannot risk the safety of my staff, or the reputation of this bank. What are you hoping to achieve?"

"In the secured boxes we obtained here a few weeks ago are documents concerning the murder of fifteen Americans and three of my police officers. Eliza survived the attack. Certain officials forced me to comply with a cover-up. Now that I have evidence of the truth, our president must receive these documents. First, I need to put them in an orderly report."

"Yes, there was mention in the news that the CIA found their bodies. We have heard nothing of the capture of the killers." The bank manager stood up and gazed out the window. It was clear he needed time to collect himself. He muttered. "So many innocent people died."

Eliza worried they'd caused the man too much distress. "My apologies, sir. We've been too much trouble. Captain Sharif and I will take our documents and find other means of -"

"No, your request is acceptable. Please allow me to assist you. As long as there's no risk to my staff or bank security, I will help. Just be sure to leave my participation out of your files. Agreed?"

Sharif's police documents and photos were retrieved while the manager's secretary set up a laptop in a small office.

Eliza and Sharif went to work. After two hours of intensive sorting through collected evidence, they outlined the sequence of events, list of suspects, and further detailed the subsequent crimes since the massacre.

"Done." He downloaded all the data onto three flash drives – a copy for the minister, one for the CIA agent, and one to keep in the safety deposit box along with the documents and Khizar's phone.

As they drove away from the bank, Sharif's next move was to meet with the Internal Affairs Minister. "I'm not sure I can trust him, but I have no choice. Perhaps he will attend the Guardian Mosque mid-day prayers."

Eliza didn't like the idea of being exposed in a large public gathering, but she acquiesced. It was anyone's guess how desperate Aamir had become. By noon they were at Guardian Mosque in time for Dhuhr prayer.

"Stay behind me, Eliza, directly behind me all the times. Understood?"

Eliza smiled. "I love you, too. I'm ready."

For a second, Sharif's stiff demeanor wavered. "Just please don't die." They removed their shoes and passed through the mosque doors.

The muezzin had begun the plaintive cry for all to turn toward Mecca and again declare Allah as the one true god. The crowd thickened at the entrance as everyone removed their footwear and placed it among the many tired sandals, three-inch spike heels, and Italian leather business shoes on the steps. The faithful proceeded to washing stations to perform the ablution.

The more than two hundred men, women and children organized themselves into rows on the prayer rugs. Most of the women had ascended to the second floor. Eliza joined the few women who remained standing against the wall at the back of the room. Though the men stood, she clearly saw Sharif, his head and shoulders above many of the others.

Eliza surreptitiously checked the faces of the women standing with her. Some wore voluminous robes which cloaked their shape – or maybe concealed a weapon. Her fear seized control of her body. From up above, someone would have a clear shot at Sharif.

The imam appeared at the minbar and the recitation of passages from the Koran began.

The melodious sound of the followers chanting the prayers failed to quench the fire in Eliza's mind. She'd told Sharif she was ready. It was a lie.

The devout began the ritual prostration, proclaiming unwavering obedience to Allah and reaffirming their devotion to the word as written by God's prophet Muhammad. Eliza attempted to follow the routine. She felt hollow and finally reverted to her practice of meditating in her lotus position. Little by little, she silenced the thoughts that tempted her toward hell's gate of terror.

Soon, she felt a hand on her shoulder. Her eyes shot open only to discover Sharif standing in front of her. "Let's go." His voice sounded mechanical.

Sometimes, he was so typically a Middle Eastern man. Reserved and in control of his softer emotions – at least in public. He stood over her like a disapproving parent.

She stood up, restraining the need to reach for him. "Smile for me, please."

He did, but only with his eyes.

People were collected in small groups or were bunched up, trying to make their way through the doors to her far left. A hint of a breeze kissed Eliza's brow and gave relief to the stale air and odor of too many bodies in close proximity to each other.

"A man had been watching me," Sharif said quietly, "but when I approached him, he walked away. We need to be vigilant, my dear." His voice had transformed to that of a loving spouse. "Did Allah speak to you?"

"There was a message. That you are loved," she said softly. "Shall we return to our hotel room or did you spot the minister?"

"He's not here, which means I have to come up with another strategy."

"Okay. Just so I'm clear on what you want to achieve. You want to get a message to the minister asking him to meet with you. Is that right?"

"Yes. But I have to make sure only he receives the message. I don't want the mayor to get wind of my intentions. If he sees me talking to Rasheed, he could panic."

"Sometimes people receive a bouquet of flowers at their office. Everyone is excited to see the beautiful flowers but no one ever reads the card attached to the bouquet."

Sharif's eyebrows shot up. "Brilliant."

"You could write whatever you want on a note, something that would not be understood except by minister Rasheed."

Sharif grinned. "Bloody brilliant," he exclaimed in his British accent.

At a flower shop, Eliza looked for a prepared arrangement that had a masculine feel. She spotted an orchid plant that appeared to be growing out of a simulated weathered log. The plant had several large white blossoms along two long stems. "That one," she said to the clerk. "It looks very happy."

Sharif nodded his approval and handed the card to the clerk. It read:

"Fifteen visitors, plus three brothers, wish to express their gratitude. Please call."

Sharif added his son's cellphone number. He hoped the cryptic message would capture the minister's curiosity – enough that he would personally follow up on the request to call.

He advised the flower shop manager of the importance to deliver the gift directly to Mr. Rasheed, Minister of Internal Affairs. On the order slip he wrote down the address and phone number of the minister. "Instruct the man delivering the plant to keep this card in his pocket until he is with the minister. The delivery man and the plant must go through security screening."

The clerk shrugged as if his instructions were not unusual. "It will be as you have directed."

"How soon will you be making the delivery?"

After a brief conversation with the minister's secretary, the clerk hung up the phone and said, "Mr. Rasheed is in a meeting and cannot be disturbed for the rest of the day. His secretary advised he will be available tomorrow morning from nine o'clock to nine fifteen to receive your gift. We will ensure your gift is delivered at that time."

Chapter 35

Still in his boxer shorts and bleeding, Black Ice focused on the men in the next room. The pain barely registered in comparison to knowing the terror that awaited him. His room's glaring light illuminated the sweat running down his face. His wrists chained up toward the ceiling made breathing a conscious effort.

The men seated in the basement's adjacent interrogation room repeated his name with disgust. Ice remained silent as he gathered up a sliver of dignity. Often they gravely shook their heads, sighed, and pointed with contempt toward their captive.

An eternity later, measured by a shadow on the floor creeping towards him, one of the men approached and spoke. "Mr. Phillips, you have disappointed GIC. Observe the video on the monitor."

He watched as a scene came into focus. He recognized the location - the Guardian Mosque. Sharif was standing with the MacKay woman. For a brief moment the camera, probably hidden in the button of a spy's clothing, captured his look of vigilant soldier. Then the cop turned his back and led the woman away.

"That video was obtained this afternoon. Obviously, Captain Hashim Sharif is alive and apparently free to do as he pleases." The interrogator's voice sounded robotic.

Ice grimaced as he inhaled, and opened his mouth to speak. The GIC man glared at him.

"Furthermore, we have obtained information that you have revealed your association with Omega. Surely, you know that is forbidden." GIC man turned his back and left the room.

323

Footsteps echoed from down the hallway. They were unhurried, bearing the weight of a man, a man of prestige and omnipotent power. Finally, a tall and well-built man entered the room. Khalid.

Khalid wore his fifty-six years well. Immaculately dressed and manicured; dark hair and short beard perfectly trimmed; cologne of the finest fragrance. He exuded a regal deportment. Time waited on him. Space bowed to his pleasure.

Ice rested his gaze on the square jaw. Safer than looking into the vacant and cold blue eyes.

Khalid held out his hand toward one of Ice's captors. An iron rod came to rest on his palm. The distant end was curved in the three inch shape of the omega symbol. It burned with a fiery glow.

If Black Ice had nursed any hope of receiving clemency, it was now shattered. Ice merely mouthed his plea, "Omega. Mercy, I beg."

The torture began.

Chapter 36

Minister Rasheed waited at his highly-polished dark walnut conference table while his unexpected guests settled into their chairs. His secretary had set a carafe of coffee on a side table. She collected pastries, set up the fine bone china coffee cups, and white cloth napkins for the minister's well-dressed visitors.

The royal blue leather office chairs rolled silently on the deep gold carpet. The room and table could accommodate thirty people. He felt proud of the luxury at his fingertips – a clear indication of his success as a leader, and RIPT's prosperity, until recently. Minister Rasheed's days had become an endless stream of meetings with his cabinet leaders. The economy showed signs of crumbling.

The slide had begun suddenly and in synch with the massacre. There had been no outright declaration announcing an embargo of shipments to and from the Republic of Islamic Provinces and Territories. No report of Americans demanding overt retribution. But trade contracts and business agreements with the United States, Europe and China wavered, then, within one week, completely dissolved. Business with other countries followed suit. Daily he received reports from all provinces indicating the fall had begun.

Yesterday, the United Nations Assembly called, politely but firmly demanding the attendance of President Najeeb at an emergency meeting. Rasheed wondered if a Trojan horse had rolled into RIPT's gates.

The cold demeanor of his four guests implied grave trouble. The men had entered his office and demanded a meeting. The brief introductions indicated a lack of trust, and clearly placed Rasheed in an awkward position. "Please help yourselves to the coffee and food."

"No thank you," replied the taller man who called himself Zahid Weir. He spoke Arabic with an Egyptian accent. His dark complexion, fine facial features, and piercing blue eyes indicated a mixed heritage.

Minister Rasheed waited as the men removed their suit jackets and sat down. He knew their organization mainly by reputation. They were regarded as intelligent and effective – and deadly. He saw they all were well-built and quick on their feet. They exuded confidence. Although outwardly polite, Rasheed saw through their disguise. These were fighting men.

When everyone was settled and the secretary had left, the lead visitor said, "Let's begin, Minister."

As the meeting continued, Mr. Rasheed learned the men had an agenda that left him speechless. After two hours of discussion, punctuated with marginal evidence, Zahid said, "It is imperative you cooperate. Sharif and MacKay must, ah, disappear. The attack will be quick and fatal. Your country's reputation will be secure."

Minister Rasheed stood and sighed as he walked to his window. Though rude, he turned his back to Zahid and his men, reaffirming he remained in command. Finally, he returned to his chair but remained standing. "Your plan is fraught with risk to the public. If innocent bystanders are killed -."

Zahid bolted out of his chair. "Rasheed, we are not amateurs."

"Fine. I will agree to your plan."

The next morning, Internal Affairs Minister Rasheed was surprised when a gift arrived. He received the orchid plant along with the mysterious card. For him, the message was clear enough. For the past several weeks, the massacre had been on his mind daily. Fifteen – the number of Americans killed; and three – the number of police officers killed. He had no idea who had sent the gift but he was certainly going to call the number. His call was answered on the first ring.

"Hello, who is calling?" the deep voice demanded.

"This is Minister Rasheed. Your gift has arrived. To whom am I speaking?"

"Is this conversation recorded?"

"Yes, of course."

"I can only say that you know me. I need to speak with you urgently, privately and away from your office."

"Why can you not come to my office?"

"There are government officials who would prefer that I was silenced, permanently. Please call me from a private line to advise when and where to meet." The call ended abruptly.

Chapter 37

That night about eight o'clock, Mustafa's cell phone rang. The digital caller ID was blank. "Hello," said Sharif.

"This is Minister Rasheed. I'm calling from a public phone. I don't expect anyone is recording our conversation or listening. Please, to whom am I speaking?"

"This is Captain Sharif, sir. Have you decided to meet with me?"

"Meet me in imam Bashir's office at the Guardian Mosque in one hour," replied Rasheed. "Unarmed."

The call was disconnected before Sharif could respond. But he did note a hesitation in the minister's response. "I think he's either suspicious, or he's hiding something," he said to Eliza. "He has agreed to meet. By tomorrow," he said playfully nudging her shoulder, "we could be in Dubai."

They sorted items to take with them for the trip. Eliza removed all her medical supplies from her backpack, and packed their casual clothes and Eliza's dress. The cabby's handgun, loaded and the safety on, was positioned for easy access in a side pocket.

"I'll wear my Habitat shirt and jeans," said Eliza. "Are you going to contact Agent Frank?" Eliza asked as she set his suit out for him to wear.

"Rasheed should hear my confession first. Later, I'll hand over the key to our safety deposit box to him. He and President Najeeb can take ownership of the evidence." He picked up his military boots. "Not going to miss these."

A half hour later, Eliza and Sharif waited in their van near the mosque. The mosque's lights lit up the night sky. From a block away, they saw Rasheed's men inspect the area and sweep toward the mosque's entrance. Several went inside while other guards remained posted nearby.

"Be ready for anything, Eliza," Sharif said, still gripping the steering while. He drove up closer to the minister's convoy. "There's the minister's car pulling up close to the entrance. Let's go."

Sharif and Eliza walked towards the mosque's entrance. The guards swung in their direction. Thirty long guns bore down on Sharif and Eliza. They stopped and raised their arms. "I'm Captain Sharif. This is Eliza, my wife," he said nodding towards her. "We are unarmed."

Several guards approached and patted both of them down. An officer said, "My men will follow you into the mosque and down to the imam's office."

In a board room, they stood before the revered minister. Sharif studied the man's eyes. He felt a sudden cold rush. The man had secrets. Like Aamir. Sharif offered his right hand. "Minister Rasheed, thank you for coming. I shall not waste your time."

As the minister shook Sharif's hand, he made an obvious scan of Sharif's body. "It would appear the rumors of your death have been greatly exaggerated. How fortunate for Samarra." His smile quickly faded. "Please introduce me to your companion, Captain Sharif."

"Minister Rasheed, this is Eliza MacKay. She is now my wife. She is the survivor of the massacre."

Eliza smiled and nodded. "It is an honor to meet you, sir."

The minister frowned. "Survivor?" He looked at her as if she was an annoying child, and then turned to imam Bashir. "Thank you, Bashir, for permitting me to use your facility. You should dismiss your security staff now. I will take up no more of your time."

Bashir stood firm and politely nodded. "Even if I should command them to leave, they will not abandon the mosque. Nor will I abandon my friend, Hashim Sharif." Bashir spread his arms wide toward the official and his security staff. "Welcome, everyone. Please, sit."

The minister rubbed his brow and grimaced. Standing at a chair at the head of the table, he motioned for his staff to leave. "Is your investigation complete, captain? Do you know who is -."

A commotion could be heard outside the conference room. The guards stiffened and created a wall between the door and the minister. One of the guards received a call on his two-way radio. He listened to the message through his ear-piece, then turned to the minister. "There's a Frank Hutchinson outside demanding to be allowed in. Says he's a CIA agent."

Sharif looked at Eliza, his face holding a frown. "Guess who's been listening to our conversations?" He turned to the minister. "You've met Agent Hutchinson, sir. He does have a right to this information. I was hoping to discuss this with you first, but since he's here -."

The minister nodded to the security officer. "Let him in."

Frank Hutchinson arrived, somewhat disheveled and annoyed. He briefly greeted the minister, then turned to Sharif. "You owe me," he barked.

Sharif frowned. "I always had the intention to reveal the truth."

Frank turned away and selected a chair beside the minister, who appeared unaffected by the CIA agent's bluster. As they sat down, the tension in the room felt volatile.

Sharif sat down across from Frank, Eliza beside her husband. He handed a flash drive each to the minister and Frank. As they inserted the drive into their devices, Sharif announced he was terminating his role in the investigation. "In fact, I am resigning from my employment in the Samarra Police Force. My family has suffered greatly because of my involvement in the massacre. It is time I made them my first priority."

Silence. Minister Rasheed nodded. "Your years of service have been ... noteworthy. Samarra citizens are grateful. On behalf of

F

President Najeeb, Mayor Aamir and our council, I wish you well, captain." His sentiment sounded authentic.

"Minister Rasheed, Eliza and I have information that has been withheld from you regarding the killing of the fifteen Americans and three police officers. It was withheld as Police Chief Ganem and Mayor Aamir threatened to kill my family if I revealed their cover-up initiative."

"Cover-up?"

"They feared they would be held responsible for the failure to protect the Americans, be sent to prison where they most certainly would not survive. However, I now suspect Mayor Aamir was a key player in the planning of the attack. And, I believe he ordered the murder of Chief Ganem, though I cannot prove it. My report is on these flash drives. I sincerely regret to have cost our government and Agent Hutchison, time; and worst of all, failure to uphold our government's integrity."

"Summarize, Sharif." The minister's reaction to Sharif's report was disturbingly calm. "Who is responsible for the massacre?" Rasheed set his device down. "And who knows what happened here?"

Sharif nodded to Frank. "Frank, you can articulate that answer better than me. You always knew more than I did."

Frank leaned back in his chair. "When my investigation started, I knew the massacre took place in Captain Sharif's police compound. And I knew of the cover-up. As of a week ago, minister, the CIA is watching a man in London, England - Captain Sharif's ex-father-in-law, Kareem Khalid. We believe he planned and funded the execution of the Americans."

Sharif watched the minister's expression. Surprisingly, the man didn't appear shocked to hear Frank's revelation. That worried him.

Frank continued. He revealed a GIC cell in Cairo is involved "All evidence points back to Khalid who we suspect is also known as Omega."

"Omega?" The minister rose from his chair. "Mr. Hutchinson, your report has been enlightening. Thank you. Captain Sharif, I applaud your courage to come forward with this report. I will take the information provided this evening to President Najeeb. We will evaluate what action needs to be taken." He motioned for his security personnel with a nod. "Please let a few of my security staff escort you back to your lodging."

Sharif stood and probed the minister's eyes, hunting for a trace of subterfuge. *Am I being paranoid or what?* "Thank you for the offer. We will be fine on our own."

"Fine," the minister said, shaking Sharif's hand, then the agent's. "I will contact you again via the phone number you provided, captain."

The minister left with his entourage. Frank and Sharif stood, facing each other with a mixture of distrust and admiration. Sharif spoke first. "I am sorry for misleading the CIA." He held out his right hand.

Frank shook Sharif's hand. "You can't be that easily forgiven."

Sharif interrupted. "Your superiors want my hide?"

Frank shrugged. "Something like that. This isn't over. Even if you two get out of Samarra, GIC and Omega will not rest until they have your blood. Goodnight."

Sharif and Eliza chose a different hotel, a modest building but in a familiar area. They lay down on the bed, hope drained to a mere trickle. For the duration of the night, they simply held onto each other.

Late the next morning Sharif received a call on Mustafa's phone.

"Captain, this is Minister Rasheed. As-Salaam-Alaikum."

Sharif wasn't sure if he should breathe a sigh of relief or prepare for bad news. He glanced at Eliza and braced himself for the latter. "Wa Alaikum Salaam, Minister."

"I met with President Najeeb after I left the mosque last night." The minister paused to take a breath. "He was most distressed to receive the news of your report. In fact, he immediately contacted the American president and arranged for a flight to the United States. He should be there soon. Inshallah." The minister paused again. "Captain Sharif, President Najeeb wishes to express his sincere regrets that you and Miss MacKay received such terrible treatment by the chief and mayor. I need to meet with you and your wife this afternoon to discuss your future. Are you willing to meet with me again?"

"Yes, sir. We are eager to get on with our lives. What do you suggest?"

The minister said for Sharif and Eliza to meet him at the market at the city's eastern border. "It's very large and if we all dress casually, we won't be noticed. My men will still be there but incognito. Do you agree?"

Sharif agreed, hesitantly. "GIC or Khalid are likely still looking for me. Anyone near me in public is at risk."

"Understood. We must ensure the mayor does not get wind of our complicity. I will see you and your wife at the orange fruit stand at three o'clock."

The minister hung up his phone. He glanced up at Zahid Weir, standing with his hands on his hips, his eyes - hard, determined.

"He agreed?" asked Zahid Weir.

"Yes. Both of them will be there at three." The minister rose slowly out of his chair. He felt exhausted. But that was nothing compared to his fear. "This is …"

"The only way," barked Zahid.

The minister turned away. "Fine. Get your men in position."

Chapter 38

Sharif and Eliza dressed in their casual clothes. Sharif wore his khaki trousers and black golf shirt and Eliza wore her lilac outfit. Her hair was loose, laying on her shoulders and down her back. They couldn't eat lunch. They couldn't sit still.

"What do we take with us?"

Sharif pulled his hand through his hair. "Probably just our passports, your credit card, some money. Leave your backpack here." He paced. "Can't help but feel like something's wrong. What do you think? You sense anything?"

Eliza wrapped her arms around his waist. "I think we've been running for so long it's going to feel strange to stop." She kissed him softly on the tender hollow at the base of his throat. "I'm thinking about the look on your kids' faces when they see you walk in the front door. Can you imagine how happy they'll be?"

Sharif relaxed a little. "Tell me more," he murmured into her hair.

"I've been thinking we should take everyone on a cruise. Go around the world. That would be a good education for Mustafa and Farah, good for your parents, and we can spend all day in bed if we like."

He kissed her passionately. "Yes, I think I like that idea." He released her for a moment. "Eliza, if there's trouble at the market I want you to promise something. Run away, fast. Don't look back. Just run. Please promise me you'll …."

He couldn't finish. Eliza's lips were on his, smothering him with luscious kisses. "There won't be any trouble and, no, I won't run. Let's go."

The market was crowded with farmers, sellers, buyers and tourists. Tent stalls with awnings lined up, row after row, in a huge parking lot bordered by a school, an arena, and a park. Some of the stalls spilled over into the school's soccer field. The stalls' fronts faced each other but were far enough apart that a vehicle could pass between, usually to load or unload products. Crowds of people ambled lazily down each row. The chatter and laughter reminded Eliza of the fairgrounds at home.

Eliza marveled at the colors she saw down the length of one row, designated for clothing. Beautiful handmade shawls, dresses, scarves, skirts, coats, sweaters of every color and design fluttered in the hot breeze. The heat doubled from the sun reflecting up from the pavement.

She and Sharif strolled to another row. Baking. The delicious aromas tempted them. They had to move on to find the growers' market stalls. Sharif continued to watch for anyone following them. He wasn't used to appearing nonchalant, like a visitor or buyer. He felt naked without his flak jacket. Eliza led him down a row where farmers were selling their vegetables and fruit.

Eliza was excited to find a seller of spices. Sharif had to contain her excitement when he finally spotted the tables of oranges. He glanced around. "Look for the minister, Eliza."

He looked behind him. He saw only the throngs of men and women, some dressed in colorful shirts. "Lot of tourists here today," he said, indicating some with expensive cameras.

"What time is it, Hashim?"

He checked his watch. "Five minutes after three. I don't see any sign of him or his men." He looked ahead, then behind again. A sedan, followed by another, was rolling slowly toward them. "Step aside, Eliza. Some cars are passing by."

Eliza scooted up to the inner table of oranges. Sharif continued to watch for the minister. His heart raced and his gut tightened. As he turned to check on Eliza, he caught sight of the second sedan's back wheels, just a few feet ahead. The back doors were flung open.

Eliza was laughing with the farmer at the orange stall. Two men dressed in suits suddenly appeared at Sharif's side. In spite of their faces hidden by dark sunglasses and heavy beards, he instinctively knew an attack was imminent. He saw a glimpse of white teeth grinding behind curled lips.

Chapter 39

"Eliza, run!" he hollered, and prepared to fight to keep them away from her.

Eliza turned, her eyes still bright with amusement. She froze, her face suddenly ashen, mouth open.

Strong hands clamped down on Sharif's arms and neck. He struggled like a wild man. These men weren't street fighters. They knew how to quickly subdue and restrain a man. The crowd of onlookers scurried away.

He saw a blur of lilac fly through the air. Eliza had jumped up onto the table which then collapsed under her weight. Oranges tumbled onto the ground and scattered around his feet. Another two men grabbed Eliza and pulled her out of Sharif's view.

Using techniques on pressure points, the two men soon had Sharif down on his knees. He gritted his teeth, preparing for a bullet to enter the back of his head.

He heard Eliza scream. "Hashim!" Again and again, her fear fired bolts of anguish into his gut. A gun fired. Eliza's scream suddenly stopped.

Someone in the crowd hollered, "Gun! Get out! Run!" People screamed and dove for cover.

Sharif bounded up, rage searing into his wrenched joints. "You bastards, I'll tear you apart."

In an instant, three men were on top of him, twisting his arms behind his back. He felt handcuffs sting into the skin of his wrists.

"Shove him into the back seat. Quick!" said one of the killers in Arabic.

They rammed the muzzles of their weapons into his throat and gut. "Inside the car. Now!"

Sharif cursed as the men pushed him into the back of the last car. Ahead of his car, a man carried Eliza's limp body and tossed her into the back of the lead car. Blood stained the back of her dress and dripped to the ground. Horrified, he kicked and did as much damage as possible to men sitting on either side. Within seconds he was wrestled into submission in the back seat. A gun appeared in front of his face. The sound of gunfire rang in his ears, the smell of gunpowder filled his nostrils. Then he fell into an empty dark void.

Ω

Minister Rasheed paced inside the hotel room. As ten men rushed into his side of the adjoining room, he asked, "Well, is it done?"

Zahid Weir walked up to the minister. "This evening news will have full coverage, complete with video of the deaths of Captain Sharif and Eliza MacKay. Here's the video for your media outlets." Zahid shoved a camera's memory card into his laptop. "You better sit down, sir. It's rather graphic."

Minister Rasheed gasped as he watched the assault on Eliza MacKay. She had become limp after a shot was fired. Then, within seconds after Sharif was wrestled into the back of the sedan, he saw blood splatter against the back window. The window shattered and the car sped away.

The minister replayed the video of the attack on Captain Sharif. "You've done well." He leaned in close to watch the blood splatter on the back window. "There will be no doubt that Captain Sharif is finally dead."

Suddenly, a scream erupted. Eliza stood in the doorway, transfixed by the image on the laptop, her face filled with horror. She stumbled toward the laptop. One of the ten men grabbed her.

Another man forced her to sit at the table. He grabbed her hands. "Eliza, Hashim is alive. Listen to me, Eliza." He shook her. "Eliza, look at me." He held her face in his hands and forced her to look at him. "Eliza, who do you see?"

Eliza trembled, tears falling down her face. Unable to tear her mind away from the horrific image on the laptop, she fought to move away from him. "Hashim, Hashim," she cried.

"No, Eliza. Look at me," the man shouted, and forced her to look at him. "You know me."

Eliza sprang up out of her chair, pushing the man hard. She glared at the men dressed in suits, still wearing their dark sunglasses. She clenched her teeth. "You killed him, you bastards."

The man made a fist with his right hand and brought it up to Eliza's face. "What is that, Eliza?" he barked at her. "It's a paramedic ring, right? Just like yours."

Eliza gasped and finally looked into the man's face. Tears rolled down her cheeks. "Mike, why are you …." She appeared dazed.

"That's right. Your buddy, Mike." Mike pointed to the laptop. "What you see there was staged to make people believe you and Hashim are dead."

She grabbed onto Mike, a look of desperate hope on her face. "Where is he?"

"Right here, Eliza." Sharif rushed to her side. "I was in the next room having a shower to wash off the fake blood. Are you okay?" He had managed to throw on only his pants when he heard her scream.

Eliza threw herself at Sharif and wrapped her arms around him. "I saw … that is, the blood."

The minister came forward. "My apologies for causing both of you such terrible trauma. It was necessary for the ruse to be convincing. The only thing faked was the blood, and these officers disguised as local killers." Rasheed turned to the men. "Perhaps it's time to remove your beards and sunglasses."

The men grimaced as they removed the well-attached fake beards. Zahid took off his sunglasses and came up to Sharif and Eliza. "Captain Sharif and Eliza, I'm Detective Zahid Weir." He reached into his coat pocket, pulled out his wallet and flipped it open. "Captain Sharif, I'm the one you talked to, when you called claiming that a woman by the name of Eliza MacKay needed help."

Eliza stared at the badge of the Royal Canadian Mounted Police, then gazed at the man's face. She was speechless.

"When we received Captain Sharif's call indicating you needed help, there was some hesitation. Fortunately, your friend, Mike, insisted we look deeper. We snooped more vigorously." The detective grinned. "After some investigating, we prepared to come and get you out of the country. As we gathered more information it was clear that the situation was very complicated. Unfortunately, it required time to ensure we had all the facts and to plan our strategy. We met with Minister Rasheed and the rest is, as they say, history."

Eliza looked back at Detective Zahid's badge. The emblem with the buffalo head was recognized throughout Canada and probably worldwide. The Royal Canadian Mounted Police had a reputation: don't mess with an RCMP officer. "Thank you, Detective."

Detective Zahid held out his right hand to Sharif. "My apologies for roughing you up, sir. You're a tough man. No hard feelings?"

Sharif shook the detective's hand. "No. You and your men might be a bit sore, too." He grinned as he shook the detective's hand. "Thank you, detective." Sharif nodded at each man's face. "Sincerely, I'm truly grateful." He turned to Mike. "Were we both knocked out with a dose of anesthetic?"

Eliza's eyes shot back to Mike. "So that's why I passed out."

Mike chuckled. "I wasn't taking any chances on getting kicked. You were always better at Tae Kwon Do than me. You'll be fine."

Eliza walked up to her friend. "So you're my hero." Eliza glanced back to Sharif. "Do you mind?"

Sharif shrugged. "He's a brother, right?"

Eliza nodded, and then turned back to Mike. Instantly, she had her arms wrapped around him in a bear hug. "Thank you," she murmured, as tears fell. "I love you."

He held her for a moment. "Love you, too."

The minister cleared his throat to get everyone's attention. "We're not done yet. Please, everyone have a seat." As the men and Eliza sat down at the table, he pulled out six passports. "Captain Sharif, the media will receive reports and this video within the hour verifying the death of you and Eliza MacKay. Also, Mike provided us with information on the location of your family in Dubai."

Sharif looked shocked. "How did you ….?"

"Later," said the minister. "I have sent a representative from the Canadian consulate in Dubai to Eliza's residence. Your family will be informed that the news is false and advised to pack. They will be expecting you sometime before morning. I assume, Eliza, you and your husband will be travelling together?"

Eliza smiled and nodded, too overwhelmed to speak.

"Good. Now you both need to understand, you can no longer use your legal names. If GIC, or any of your other numerous enemies get wind you're alive, it would be very bad. My staff has prepared these new passports for all members of your family and Eliza. You, sir, are now Khalil Abd Allah Kylani and, Eliza, you are his wife, Sahar." He blushed. "At the time we made up these passports, we thought it would be a good cover. We didn't know that you had just become Sharif's wife. Of course, in time, you can reverse that and …"

Eliza smiled. "No, that won't be necessary, detective."

Sharif frowned. "What about my friends. Omar, imam Bashir and so many more?"

"I'm afraid they cannot know you're alive. Of course, you can reject this plan. It's up to you."

Sharif turned to Eliza. "What do you think?" He glanced at her passport. "Do you mind being Sahar Kylani?"

She looked deeply into his eyes. "My dear husband, so long as we are together, it does not matter what I'm called."

Sharif turned back to the minister. He stood and offered his right hand to the man who had the courage to take a risk, for his sake, and for that of his family. "I, Khalil Abd Allah Kylani, and my wife, Sahar Kylani, agree to your plan."

The minister stood and accepted Mr. Kylani's hand. "Blessings upon you. Know that our records will show Captain Hashim Sharif died a brave and honorable man, dedicated to the laws of the City of Samarra and devoted to protecting its citizens." The minister turned to the ten men. "I leave it up to you to ensure Mr. and Mrs. Kylani are safely transported to Dubai and then on to their next journey."

Khalil Abdullah Kylani turned to the men. "And just where are you taking my family and me?"

Mike came forward. He had a grin on his face. "We figured all of you could use a cruise. Any objections?"

Ω

The next news report, worldwide, told how Captain Sharif and his wife were maliciously killed at a market. Each TV station showed the video for days, while reporters haunted the police for information on the killers' identity.

The funeral began simply enough. Two closed modest caskets were surrounded by Hashim Sharif's police squad at the mosque. As the mosque filled with members of the police force and military service, citizens filled the mosque's courtyard. It ended as a day of mourning. The city slowed to a stop. Their finest officer, courageous protector, loyal friend, was gone.

EPILOGUE

Several thousand miles away, a family relaxed under the Pacific tropical sun, soothed by the gentle rocking of the cruise ship. Sahar and Khalil stood at the railing of their stateroom suite's veranda. Their children and parents relaxed somewhere, probably at one of the pools.

Sahar teased her husband with feather kisses on his bare chest. "Any ideas what you'd like to do now, my dear?"

Khalil smiled and leaned down to nip at her neck. "I'll give you one guess."

Ω

Minister Rasheed stood in Mayor Aamir's office beside Omar Abdul Muqtadir. Rasheed's trademark calm demeanor wavered. "Get up, Aamir. You and your associates are through with your coup attempt." His voice shook with his contempt for the man he had trusted.

Mayor Aamir sat rigidly, refusing to accept the inevitable. Muqtadir's officers grabbed Aamir's arms and hauled him to his feet. His mouth opened like a fish out of water gasping for air.

As Abdul-Muqtadir read the criminal charges laid against him, Aamir stared wide-eyed at Rasheed. "If I go down, I'll expose you and Najeeb. It's time Khalid knew the full truth. I wasn't alone when I killed Zydan's family."

Rasheed's shoulders sagged. "Najeeb and I confessed to that crime years ago, shortly after the cease fire. The high court and religious leaders know everything. We were pardoned because it was a war time and the dying wish of Zydan to save his family from horrific imprisonment." Rasheed bowed his head. "It was wrong. I have paid the price of that sin every day. I have no peace."

Abdul Muqtadir marched to stand tall in front of his enemy. "Aamir, you are under arrest for the brutal murder of fifteen Americans, Police Chief Ganem, and three police officers. More charges are pending, following further investigation into the deaths of Captain Sharif and Ms. Eliza MacKay Ramsay." He portrayed a mixture of triumph in his posture, sadness in his eyes. When he informed Aamir that a cell in the dreaded C Block of Samarra's prison awaited his presence, his voice betrayed his pleasure.

Aamir's knees gave way. The police officers let him fall to the floor, then roughly pulled him to his feet.

"This is for Sharif," Omar Abdul Muqtadir shouted as he rammed his fist across Aamir's nose. Blood splattered on the prisoner's white shirt and Armani suit.

Minister Rasheed returned to his office. He sighed with relief as he slumped down into his chair. Everything had proceeded as planned. Perfectly. His phone rang.

"Minister," said his secretary, "CIA Agent Frank Hutchinson wants to speak to you. He says he's taken samples of the blood on the pavement where Captain Sharif was killed. He has some questions, sir."

THE END,

or is it?

Dear Reader: My hope is that this story took you to a place you've never been before and that you enjoyed the journey. It would be wonderful if you would check out my blog and other websites and say, "Hello."

Even better, write a review at
Amazon and Goodreads.

Amazon: http://www.amazon.com/Feather-Stone/e/B006AFUTAU/ref=dp_byline_cont_ebooks_1

Goodreads: https://www.goodreads.com/Feather_Stone

Website: http://www.featherstoneauthor.com

Blog: http://www.featherstoneauthor.wordpress.com

Facebook: https://www.facebook.com/FSauthor

Twitter: https://twitter.com/FeatherWrites

Pinterest: https://www.pinterest.com/featherauthor/

The Guardian's Wildchild

By Feather Stone

Published by

Omnific Publishing

2011

Caught in a reckless attempt to stop Dark forces, Sidney Davenport, a young, rule breaking, spirited member of the secret paranormal community of Guardians, finds herself imprisoned on a naval ship and slated for execution. Her struggle with the unfamiliar emotions of fear and anger becomes even more complicated when she can no longer fight her attraction to the very man who has orders to perform her execution.

Captain Sam Waterhouse, a meticulous naval captain who's suspected of treason, teeters on a precipice between Darkness and Light. When he receives an unusual prisoner, a paranormal journey begins to unravel his disciplined life. All the while, humanity is unknowingly at great risk when two Dark forces team up to acquire control of an elusive power.

Sidney and Sam attempt to quiet their powerful feelings for each other, only to discover they can save each other, and in doing so, they might even save the world.

Through stunning imagery, an intricate and adventurous plot, and a strong cast of characters, Feather Stone gives readers a fascinating glimpse into the future-a future that is chilling, yet full of hope.

Purchase locations listed at Simon & Schuster: http://www.simonandschuster.com/books/The-Guardian-s-Wildchild/Feather-Stone/9781936305896

ACKNOWLEDGEMENTS

My decision to write Forbidden didn't come easy. In fact, I fought the inspiration and visions of incredibly courageous and twisted characters, and a plot that required careful planning. I'm a panster, so careful planning is truly not my forte. Most importantly, a tremendous amount of research was required. As I cratered to the overwhelming passion for this story, I gathered an army of support.

Forbidden's resources hero – Imam Mustafa Khattab

When I explained my project to him and what I needed, I could see doubt shadow his kind face. However, before I left his mosque, he had handed to me an armful of reference material, including the Koran. I asked him how long I could borrow these books and videos from his library. He said I could keep them. I was overwhelmed with gratitude. His last advice to me was to choose the middle path. I understood.

Forbidden's consulting hero – Sahar Albakkal:
https://www.facebook.com/salbakkal?pnref=friends.search

Aside from wanting to write the best suspense book possible, I needed to ensure that I had a basic understanding of Islam, and the correct interpretation of the Koran (the middle path). I also needed Arabic names and phrases, customs, and typical cultural behaviors that reflected a modern Muslim man and woman. My search led me to Sahar. She devoted hours each month to review and edit chapters, offered suggestions, and enthusiastically kept me motivated and hopeful that Forbidden was worth the sleepless nights.

Forbidden's Editor Heroes

Leigh Carter, Editor: Forbidden's first and final editor hero was Leigh Carter: https://www.facebook.com/leigh.carter

I was introduced to Leigh Carter by my friend and fellow author, Pauline Holyoak. During the first editing of Forbidden, Leigh provided feedback on plot dynamics and flow. The characters also received her wrath if I had made them step out-of-character. Her superb editing talent included not only polished sentence structure and punctuation, but also provided praise for passages that touched her heart. My gratitude to Leigh goes beyond words. Forbidden's success is because of her dedication to the hours of work over many months.

Gary Nilsen, Book Doctor / Manuscript Critique https://www.facebook.com/gary.: Gary guided me through the difficult task of writing about a region I had neither visited nor experienced the culture. Gary worked several years in Saudi Arabia. He experienced the Islamic culture, customs, language. When I 'fell' upon Gary's blog and LinkedIn site, I knew some divine spirit had nudged me there for the sake of Forbidden. Gary and I worked for months, flavoring Forbidden's setting with the Middle East's exotic and mysterious nuances that few Westerners understand. Thanks to Gary, Forbidden edged further into the heart of a region I see as ancient, and filled with beauty and passion.

Paul McCormack, Weapons Expert Hero: a most interesting and superb expert in the field of weapons played a vital role in Forbidden's final draft. Given that the plot involves several battles, there are a variety of weapons. Paul helped me identify what weapons are most common in the Middle East and what weapons would be used by police, military, and the terrorists. I got a hands-on education – what a thrill to see these high powered guns, up close. For simplicity sake, the author chose to not identify specific weapons in every scene.

BETA READER: Richard Goodship, retired Police Officer/Forensic Investigator. Before retiring Richard worked in the Attorney General's Office, Special Investigations Unit. He is author of 3 novels, The Staff, The Camera Guy and The Ostiary. Richard spent over 22 years in the forensic section (FIS in Canada). Amazon link: http://www.amazon.com/Richard-Goodship/e/B005J5Y494

BETA READER: Marc DiGiacomo is a multi-award winning author of A Small Town Series. Marc is a retired and highly decorated police detective who worked for a small town in the State of New York. During his police career, He has worked with numerous police agencies including the F.B.I., D.E.A., U.S. Secret Service, New York State Police, NYPD, Westchester County District Attorney's Office and many other law enforcement agencies.

Amazon link: http://www.amazon.com/Marc-A.-Digiacomo/e/B009L8F01G

AUTHOR MENTORS: So many other heroes have guided me on this journey. Their encouraging words and professional advice has been a blessing and a safe harbor during days, weeks, of doubt. Years ago when my first novel (The Guardian's Wildchild) was published by Omnific Publishing, I didn't know that I had fallen into the best group of authors in terms of talent and friendship. We call ourselves the Omnific sisters (Nicki Olsen, Jennifer Lane, Nancee Cain, Carol Oates, Susan Kaye Quinn). I owe so much to these amazing women who fearlessly chart their own path in the world of self-publishing and marketing, but also have a level of gusto and guts that's above and beyond. Another group that has kept me from getting eternally stuck in a dark place is the Insecure Writers Support Group, headed by author, Alex J. Cavanaugh http://www.insecurewriterssupportgroup.com/

Authors who inspired, encouraged, and who made me reach for my very best: My instructor, Candas Jane Dorsey; authors Pauline Holyoak, Yolanda Renee, Denise Covey, Joylene Butler, Phoenix Rainez, Roland Clarke and so many more.

The loyalty of friends and family is so cherished. My dear husband, Ralph, and sister-in-law, Peggy Sue Cropley, provided much needed feedback. And neighbors Marge and Ray said they couldn't put the book down, even during Canada Day's fireworks. A colleague with Edmonton's Emergency Medical Services, Nawal Daw-Zinati, helped me understand the complexity of the Arabic language. The list goes on and on.

My gratitude is endless.

GLOSSARY

Republic of Islamic Provinces & Territories (RIPT): Name of country – fictitious:

Samarra, Capital of RIPT: Name of city where massacre took place:

NAME OF ALL CHARACTERS
Primary Characters

Eliza MacKay (Ramsay): Canadian and survivor of massacre in Samarra

Hashim Sharif: Captain of police service in city of Samarra

Secondary Characters

Agent Frank Hutchinson: CIA agent assigned to investigate missing Americans in the Middle East

Captain Khizar: day shift police captain

Chief Ganem: police chief of Samarra

Mayor Aamir: mayor of Samarra

Minister Rasheed: minister of Internal Affairs

Sergeant Omar Abdul-Muqtadir: Hashim Sharif's sergeant and best friend

Supporting Cast

Black Ice: hit man

Sergeant Muntazar: sergeant at airport

Detective Zahid Weir: Royal Canadian Mounted Police

Dr. Sharif: Hashim Sharif's father (physician)

Farah Sharif: Hashim Sharif's daughter

Imam Bashir: imam of Guardian Mosque

Mike Tanasiuk: paramedic friend of Eliza MacKay

Kareem Khalid: Hashim Sharif's ex-father-in-law

Mrs. Sharif: Hashim Sharif's mother

Mustafa Sharif: Hashim Sharif's son

President Najeeb: president of the Republic of Islamic Provinces & Territories (RIPT)

Serena Sharif (Khalid): Hashim Sharif's ex-wife

ABOUT THE AUTHOR

F. Stone (Feather Stone)

aka Judy Cropley Weir

On our cattle ranch, when an animal was in distress or injured, I was put in charge of nursing it back to health. Never mind that I was just a kid and hated the sight of blood, but I had to muster up the courage to apply home remedies. My survival rate was pretty good. It seemed like a foregone conclusion that I would progress to nursing – humans. After one year into nurses training, I bolted. Bed pans and chronic diseases pushed me in different direction; a career of dealing with drug addicts, murder, suicide, fatalities, and biker gangs. In 1983 I graduated with honors as a paramedic and worked in the City of Edmonton's emergency services.

For the next twenty years, I came face to face with scenes most people would rather not think about. I loved it. Having experienced life in the most deadly and gut wrenching events, and work alongside the police and fire services, I gained the fodder for creating intense novels.

My creative DNA shocked me when I was driven to write a dystopian / paranormal / romance novel, The Guardian's Wildchild. After taking several writing courses, I presented the manuscript to Omnific Publishing who published it in 2011. Just when I thought I could get my life back, another story took me prisoner – Forbidden. I couldn't believe there was this kind of story within me and desperate to be told. I resisted. It was futile.

Retired and focused on home life, I'm mom to four pets and one husband. We travel and taste the excitement of other cultures. In between adventures, I've dabbled in water color painting, photography, needle work, gardening – the list goes on. In my next life, I plan to explore the cosmos.

I've learned a few things in my seventy years. Thoughts are powerful. Intention is everything. Passion is the key to success.

Judy and Ralph Weir, a few years ago.

Made in the USA
San Bernardino, CA
29 September 2017